THE BAMBOO STALK

THE BAMBOO STALK

SAUD ALSANOUSI

Translated by Jonathan Wright

دار جـامـعـة حـمـد بـن خـلـيـفـة للنشر
HAMAD BIN KHALIFA UNIVERSITY PRESS

First published in Arabic in 2012 by Arab Scientific Publishers, Inc.

First published in English in 2015 by Bloomsbury Qatar Foundation Publishing.
This paperback edition published in 2016 by

Hamad bin Khalifa University Press
P O Box 5825
Doha, Qatar

www.books.hbkupress.com

Copyright © Saud Alsanousi, 2012
Translation © Jonathan Wright, 2015

All rights reserved.

No part of this publication may be reproduced or transmitted
in any form or by any means, electronic or mechanical,
including photocopying, recording, or any information
storage or retrieval system, without prior permission
in writing from the publishers.

No responsibility for loss caused to any individual or organization
acting on or refraining from action as a result of the material in
this publication can be accepted by HBKU Press or the author.

ISBN: PB: 9789927101793
HB: 9789927101779
TPB: 9789927118036
eBook: 9789927101786
Audio: 9789927118371

2 4 6 8 10 9 7 5 3 1

Typeset by Newgen Knowledge Works (P) Ltd., Chennai, India
Printed and bound in Great Britain by
CPI Group (UK) Ltd., Croydon CR0 4YY

To find out more about our authors and books, visit
www.books.hbkupress.com
for extracts, author interviews, upcoming events,
and to sign up for our newsletter.

Dedicated to crazies who are not like other crazies, crazies who resemble only themselves . . . Mishaal, Turki, Jabir, Abdullah and Mahdi.
To them and only them.

PART 1

Isa . . . Before He Was Born

'There are no tyrants where there are no slaves.'
José Rizal

My name is José. In the Philippines it's pronounced the English way, with an *h* sound at the start. In Arabic, rather like in Spanish, it begins with a *kh* sound. In Portuguese, though it's written the same way, it opens with a *j*, as in Joseph. All these versions are completely different from my name here in Kuwait, where I'm known as Isa.

How did that come about? I didn't chose my name so I wouldn't know. All I know is that the whole world has agreed to disagree about it.

When I was growing up in the Philippines, my mother didn't want to call me by the name my father chose when I was born. Although it's the Arabic equivalent of Jesus and she's a Christian, it's still an Arabic name and *isa* is the Filipino word for the number one. I suppose it would sound funny if people called me a number instead of a name.

My mother called me José after the Philippine national hero José Rizal, who was a doctor and writer in the nineteenth century. Without Rizal the people wouldn't have risen up to throw out the Spanish occupiers, but the uprising had to wait till after he was executed.

José or Isa, whatever. There's no great need to talk about my problem with names or how I acquired them, because my problem isn't really with names but with what lies behind them.

When I was growing up in the Philippines, the neighbours and others who knew me didn't call me by either of my real names. They had never heard of a country called Kuwait, so they just called me 'the Arab'. In fact I don't look anything like an Arab, except that my moustache and beard do grow fast. The image common in the Philippines is that Arabs are hairy, and cruel as well, and the stereotype usually includes a beard of some shape or length.

In Kuwait, on the other hand, the first thing I lost was my nickname 'the Arab', along with my other names and titles, though I later acquired a new nickname: 'the Filipino'.

If only I could have been 'the Filipino' in the Philippines, or 'the Arab' in Kuwait! If only the word 'if' could change things, or if . . . but there's no need to go into that now.

I wasn't the only person in the Philippines born to a Kuwaiti father. Plenty of Filipina women have had children by Kuwaiti men, or other Gulf men, and even other Arabs. The women worked as maids in houses in the Arab world or messed around with tourists from

Arab countries who came seeking pleasure at a price that only someone in dire need would accept. Some people engage in vice to satisfy their natural urges; others, due to poverty, engage in vice to fill their stomachs. In many cases the outcome is fatherless children.

Many young women in the Philippines are treated like paper handkerchiefs. Strange men blow their noses on them, throw them on the ground and walk away. Those handkerchiefs then give rise to creatures whose fathers are unknown. Sometimes we can tell who the fathers are by the appearance of their children, and some of the children have no qualms about admitting they don't know who their fathers are. But I had something that set me apart from those whose fathers were unknown: my father had promised my mother that he would take me back to where I was meant to be, to the country that had produced him and to which he belonged, so that I too could belong, and live as all those who shared his nationality lived, in comfort and peace for the rest of my days.

2

My mother, Josephine, went to work in Kuwait in the mid-1980s, in the home of the woman who would later become my grandmother. She abandoned her education and left her family behind. The family was in desperate straits and her father, her sister who had just become a mother, her brother and his wife and their three children were all pinning their hopes on my mother to provide for them. They wanted a life, not necessarily a decent life, but a life.

'I never imagined I would work as a housemaid,' my mother would say. She was a girl with dreams. She had ambitions to complete her education and get a respectable job. She wasn't at all like the rest of her family. While her sister dreamed about buying shoes or a new dress, my mother dreamed about getting hold of books, either by buying them or borrowing them from one of her classmates at school. 'I read lots of stories, fantasies and ones about real life. I loved Cinderella and Cosette, the heroine of *Les Misérables*, and I ended up a maid like them but, unlike them, my story didn't have a happy ending,' she said.

Circumstances drove my mother to leave her country and family and friends to work abroad.

Although it was hard for a woman of twenty, she had a much better life than her sister, Aida, who was three years older. Aida went out to work early because the family was hungry, their mother was ill and their father was a gambler who wasted his money and ran up debts breeding cocks for fighting. So the parents saw no alternative but to offer their elder daughter, who was seventeen at the time, to an 'agent' who found her work in the local nightclubs and bars and who insisted on his share of the girl's body and earnings at the end of every working day.

'Everything happens for a reason, and for a purpose,' my mother always said, and whenever I looked for a reason for everything that happened, it was always poverty that raised its ugly head.

The further Aida progressed at work, the deeper she sank into the abyss. She started serving in a bar, prey to the eyes and lewd remarks of drunken men, then in a nightclub, where she was jostled by sweaty bodies and groped by stray hands, and then as a dancer in a strip joint, ogled by hungry eyes. So it continued until she reached the highest rank, and the lowest, in the world of night life.

'Will they go to hell?' I asked my mother one day, referring to the prostitutes who came out on the streets as soon as the sun went down, like the crabs that scamper along the sandy beach as soon as the tide goes out. When the sun rises again, the beams of light wash away the sins of the night, and when the tide comes in again it sweeps away the crabs, filling in the holes they have dug in the sand in the water's absence. 'I don't know, but they certainly lead men to hell,' my mother replied without conviction.

For a time young Aida offered her body to anyone who asked, at a price set by her agent. The price for foreign men was higher than the rate that local men with little money were asked to pay. The price varied according to the time and place. There was a price for the hour and a price for the whole night, a price for services provided in the back rooms at the club and another price for services offered in hotel rooms.

Aida become an object, like anything bought or sold at a price. The price was usually a pittance, rarely prohibitive. The price depended on the kind of service she offered. She worked in silence and in sadness, and grew to hate men and their money. What hurts is not that someone comes cheap. What really hurts is that someone should have a price in the first place.

Aida became the family breadwinner. She would come home towards dawn, clutching her little handbag. Her sick mother and her gambler father awaited the contents of the bag with impatience. Sometimes she would come home late and my mother would worry about her elder sister, while the parents saw her lateness as a good omen because it probably meant she had spent the whole night with one of her clients in some hotel. In that case she would fetch a good price, because obviously the man in the hotel would be a foreigner, who would make a larger contribution to the contents of her handbag. Sometimes she would come home with a swollen lip, a bloodied nose or a dark blue bruise on her jaw. Her parents didn't even notice. The only thing that interested them about the brute who had hurt their daughter was the money he tossed at her after sating his lust.

Aida plunged into this world. She drank alcohol and smoked marijuana. To her everything was permissible and nothing in life had any value. She got pregnant several times but her pregnancies didn't last long because she had abortions as soon as she found out. She didn't want the babies and she was under pressure from her parents, who wanted her to keep her wretched job. Then, at the age of twenty-three, she became pregnant with Merla. She kept the pregnancy a secret from everyone except her younger sister, my mother, because she realised it was the only way out of work she had accepted under duress.

Aida didn't tell her parents she was pregnant till it was too late, after she was fired from her job. By then an abortion would have been impossible. She told them she wasn't going back to work. Without her income her mother could no longer afford medical treatment and her health deteriorated. Her father, as ever, was more interested in entering his birds in cockfights.

The family lost one member at the same time as a new member arrived. Just as Merla drew her first breath, my grandmother breathed her last.

Merla looked different. She had the features of a Filipina but she also had a pinkish white complexion, blue eyes and a sharp nose.

By that time my mother was twenty and my grandfather saw her as the perfect alternative source of income for the family, a guarantee of its survival while Aida was out of work bringing up her daughter. Since Pedro, the only son, was always busy looking for work and kept his distance from the affairs of his father and his sisters, the time had come to exploit Josephine.

3

Just as my mother was about to start on the same miserable career as Aida, one of our neighbours came round with a newspaper cutting announcing that an agent in Manila was taking applications from women who wanted to work as domestic servants in the Gulf countries. My mother took the cutting from him as if it were a 'get out of jail free' card and she was behind bars and starving. Aunt Aida looked at my mother and the neighbour in silence. My mother was already thinking about the suitcase she would have to buy and the other things she would need for a new life abroad. Her imagination was running riot, though of course she didn't yet have a job. Before she had time to build up her hopes, the neighbour with the cutting added a cautionary 'but . . .' Everyone fell silent for him to finish his sentence. 'You have to give the agent some money to accept your application,' he said. He went on to talk about the details and how much money was required. Everyone was stunned when he said how much, because the family couldn't possibly raise such an amount. Aunt Aida went off to her room and my mother burst into tears from disappointment.

'Stop crying!' my grandfather shouted. 'You know I've arranged some work for you here. Live with it.'

The neighbour left and my grandfather lay on his back on the shabby old sofa. My mother sat on the floor lamenting her fate.

My Aunt Aida came out of her room after a while, carrying Merla on her hip and holding an envelope that she handed to her younger sister. 'My father had started to snore,' my mother said later, recalling the moment. 'Aida came up to me and whispered, "This is some money I'd saved for Merla. You can do what you like with it, Josephine."

'My father stopped snoring,' my mother went on. 'He opened one eye and raised his eyebrow, then sat up like a corpse that had suddenly come back to life. "While the elders sleep, the children whisper secrets!" he said.

'He lunged towards Aida with his eyes shooting sparks. I was still on the floor. He twisted Aida's arm in an attempt to wrest the envelope from her hand.

'"Josephine, take Merla!" she shouted. Merla was about to fall but I caught her and stood in the corner watching Aida push my father, swearing at him as he punched and kicked her. Aida was crazy. Who else would dare do that?

'I was begging them to stop and Merla was crying in alarm. Despite the pushing and the punching, Aida and my father kept talking.

'"Aren't you satisfied with selling me to men and . . ." said Aida.

'"Shut up," my father interrupted, pulling her hair and slapping her on the mouth.

'He pushed her hard against the wall. With her front pressed to the wall, he pulled her head back by the hair.

'"Merla," he whispered in her ear with a snarl. I imagined his lips parting to reveal fangs and a forked tongue. "A whore's daughter, with an unknown father."

'Aida couldn't speak but her eyes were wide open in a silent scream. He continued to hiss at her.

'"I'll kill her if she keeps bringing trouble to this house," he said.

'"Trouble?" Aida asked, then burst out laughing. She looked like a madwoman, with her clothes torn and her hair dishevelled.'

My mother stopped and looked down, then turned her face towards me. 'Do I have to tell you all these things, José?' she asked.

I nodded and urged her to continue, so she went on. 'I swear my father almost pissed in his pants at the sight of Aida. He took his fingers out of her hair. She moved slowly towards the door leading to the yard outside. My father followed her, and I went after, carrying Merla. Close to the low bamboo fence around the pen where he kept his cocks, under the big banana tree, Aida stopped. I stood behind my father at the back door of the house. "It's you betting on these cockfights that's the real trouble," Aida said, in a voice that was hardly audible.

'My father didn't say a word, and Aida continued. "You're all cockerels!" she said.

'"It looks like your sister's gone mad," my father whispered to me.

'I didn't say a word, because she really did look mad.

'"You're a cockerel," Aida said, pointing her finger at my father. "All the men I gave my body to were cockerels," she added.

'My father's face showed a trace of remorse, or maybe fear, but he didn't move an inch.

'"Ah, ah, Aida!" he said. All he did was say her name.

'But Aida didn't hear him and she continued. "And I'm fed up with playing the role of hen!" she said.

She hitched up her dress above her knees and stepped over the low bamboo fence around the pen. She stood in the middle of the pen, puffed out her chest and looked up to the sky.

"Cockadoodledoo!" she crowed.

'Then she pounced on the cocks and began to rip their heads off one by one with her bare hands. She threw the four lifeless bodies towards my father, who almost collapsed in a faint. Aida stood upright, facing us, her hands covered in blood. "Next time it'll be your head," she said, pointing at our father.

'The next morning Father left home early with Aida's envelope. He came back a few hours later carrying a wicker cage with four new cocks inside.'

4

My mother continued her story. 'Aida and I ran into Father with his cage of birds in the narrow passageway that leads to the lane at the end of the front yard. He didn't look in our direction. He'd been avoiding looking at Aida since the incident with the cocks. As soon as she came into sight, he looked aside as if he thought she had some eye disease and he was frightened of catching it. Aida had freed herself from slavery and put a stop to my father's tyranny. I wanted to escape from slavery too, but I'm not Aida. That morning she took me to the grocer's shop at the end of the lane. The grocer knew us well and had often lent us small sums of money when my mother was alive. Aida told him the whole story. She said I needed money to work abroad as a maid. The man was sympathetic, as he usually was with us, but he said he was sorry he couldn't provide that amount. As we were about to give up and go home, he said, "I can vouch for you with the Indians. They trust me. I've been dealing with them for years."

'Dealing with the Indians meant setting in motion an endless cycle of debt. It meant obediently making regular payments to people who took advantage of your poverty and then watching with your own eyes as the money you paid multiplied and went into other people's pockets.

'The shopkeeper arranged a meeting between us and one of the Indian moneylenders,' my mother continued. 'We knew the Indians because we'd had dealings with them years earlier. We'd bought a cooker and a television and some ceiling fans and floor fans from them on credit. It took us ages to pay back all the money we owed. They were greedy then, but the terms when we bought all those things from them were better than the terms they asked for giving me a loan to go abroad. The shopkeeper tried to explain my circumstances to them, but they still doubled the interest rate. They took advantage of my urgent need for cash.'

My mother shook her head sadly, then continued. 'We had no choice but to accept. We would have done anything to save ourselves in the short term, even if it meant more trouble down the road.

'In the employment agency in central Manila the next day I had to stand in a long queue that started at the door to the little office and ran along the pavement, down the street and far into the distance.

'Hours later I managed to meet the clerk. I paid him half the amount and started to fill in the forms. On my next visit, after my application was accepted,

I paid the rest of the money. The clerk told me I would be working in Kuwait, and that was the first time I had ever heard of the country. I cheerfully got ready to leave, though I knew I would have to give half of what I earned abroad to the Indians and the other half to my family. I willingly agreed to let them share out my money between them, in exchange for leaving me free to do what I liked with my body, free to give it to whoever I chose.'

5

When my mother came to work here in Kuwait, she was completely ignorant of the local culture. The people here are not like people in the Philippines. They look different and speak a different language. Even the way they look at each other can have connotations that she wasn't aware of. The climate in Kuwait is nothing like the climate in the Philippines, except that the sun does shine by day and the moon comes out at night. 'Even the sun,' my mother said. 'At first I doubted it was the same sun that I knew.'

My mother worked in a large house where a widow in her mid-fifties lived with her son and three daughters. The widow, Ghanima, would later become my grandmother. The old lady, as my mother called her, was strict and neurotic most of the time. Although she seemed to be sensible and to have a strong personality, she was also superstitious and firmly believed what she saw in her dreams. She thought that every dream was a message that she couldn't ignore, however trivial or incomprehensible it might seem. She spent much of her time looking for an explanation for the things she had dreamed and if she was unable to do so herself she would seek out people who interpret dreams. Although the various interpretations she obtained from these people were different, sometimes even contradictory, she believed everything they said and expected the things she dreamed to take place in real life. On top of that, she saw everything that happened, however banal, as a sign that she shouldn't take lightly. Once, when I was with my mother and my Aunt Aida in the little sitting room in our house in the Philippines, my mother said, 'I don't know how that woman could live like that, keeping tabs on everything that happened, every coincidence that came her way. Once she was invited to a wedding with her daughters and they came back only half an hour after leaving home. "That party finished quickly, madam," I told her.

'The old lady went straight upstairs without looking at me. Hind, her youngest daughter, took up my question and replied, "The car broke down halfway there."

'I thought of all the cars lined up in front of the house. "What about the other cars?" I asked her.

'"My mother thinks that if the car hadn't broken down halfway, then at the end of the journey the angel of death would have reaped our souls," she said, wiping her lipstick off with a handkerchief.

'"What do you mean?" I asked her in surprise.

'"My mother thought some disaster was in store for us," she replied, bending down to take off her shoes.'

It was a vast house my mother was working in, compared with houses in the Philippines. In fact one house in Kuwait is ten or more times bigger than the houses where my mother came from. My mother arrived in Kuwait at a sensitive time. My grandmother thought her arrival was a very bad omen, and it showed on her face whenever she saw my mother. My father had an explanation for that. 'You came to our house, Josephine, around the same time a bomb went off near the Emir's motorcade,' he said. 'Without divine intervention it would have killed him. So my mother saw your arrival as a sign of bad luck.'

My father was four years older than my mother. My grandmother mistreated her, and so did my father's sisters, except for the youngest one, who was temperamental. Only my father was always kind and gentle to her and he often disagreed with his mother and his sisters over how they treated my mother.

I was almost ten when my mother started telling me these stories about things that had happened before I was born. She was paving the way for me to leave the Philippines and go back to Kuwait. In the sitting room of our little house she read me some of the letters my father had sent her after we left Kuwait. Before I went back to Kuwait as my father had promised, she told me all the details of her relationship with him. Every now and then she made a special effort to remind me that I belonged to another, better place. When I first started speaking, she taught me some Arabic words, such as greetings, how to count and how to say 'tea' and 'coffee' and so on. When I was older, she tried her best to give me a good impression of my father, who I couldn't remember.

I would sit in front of my mother in our house in the Philippines, listening to her as she told me stories about him. Aunt Aida would usually dismiss her stories impatiently. 'I loved him, and I still do,' my mother said. 'I don't know how or why. Perhaps it was because he was nice to me when everyone else treated me badly. Or perhaps because he was the only person in the old lady's house who spoke to me, other than to give me orders, or because he was handsome, or because he was a young writer and was well-educated and had dreams of writing his first novel, and I loved reading novels.'

She smiled as she spoke to me and, strangely, she often came close to tears, as if the events in the story had just taken place.

'He said he was happy with me because, like him, I liked reading. He told me that whenever he was about to start writing his novel, something always came up to distract him. He kept being dragged into the thick of political events in the region. He wrote a weekly article for a newspaper but it was rarely published because of the censors in Kuwait. He was one of the few writers who opposed the Kuwaiti government's decision to take sides in the Iran-Iraq war. Imagine how crazy your father was! He used to talk to his maid about literature and art and the political affairs of his country, at a time when no one else even spoke to their servants, except to give orders: bring this, wash that, sweep the floor, wipe the table, get the food ready, come here and so on.'

Aunt Aida grumbled and fidgeted in her seat but my mother continued. 'I washed and swept and mopped all day long, just so at the end of the day, when the women of the house had gone to bed, I'd be free to chat with your father in the study. I tried to keep up with him when he talked about politics, and impress him by showing off my meagre political knowledge. One day I told him how happy I was that Corazon Aquino had won the presidential elections. She was the first woman to rule the Philippines and had restored democratic government after leading the opposition that brought down the dictatorship of Ferdinand Marcos.

'Your father was unusually interested in what I had to say. "So you put a woman in power!" he said. "Five months ago, on 25 February," I said proudly. Your father burst out laughing, then checked himself in case he woke up his mother and his sisters. "That was the same day we were celebrating our national day," he said. He paused. Then, tapping his fingertips on the desk and as if speaking to himself, he said, "Which of us is the master of the other?" I didn't understand what he was driving at. He talked to me about the denial of women's rights, as he put it, because in his country women don't have the right to take part in politics. He looked very sad, then he tried to involve me by talking about the Kuwaiti parliament, which had been suspended by the Emir of Kuwait at the time. Although I didn't much care about what he was saying, I listened to his voice and took great interest in how he felt.'

'Why was he talking to you about these things, Mama?' I cut in.

'Because the people around him dismissed his ideas? Maybe,' she replied, spontaneously but sceptically. 'He was an idealist, I thought, and I'm sure everyone else thought so too. His mother gave him special treatment, saying he was the only man in the house. He was quiet and rarely raised his voice. He spent most of his time reading or writing in the study. Those were his main interests, apart from fishing and travelling abroad with Ghassan and Walid, the only friends who came to visit him, either in the study to discuss some book or to talk about literature and art and politics, or in the little *diwaniya* in the annex if Ghassan had brought his oud along. Ghassan was an artist, a poet, sensitive, although he was also a soldier in the army.

'At the time the countries in southeast Asia, especially Thailand, were popular destinations for young Kuwaiti men. Your father often spoke to me about going there with his friends. When he was talking about Thailand one day he looked me straight in the eye and said, "You look like a Thai girl." Did I really look like one, or was he hinting at something else? I wasn't sure.

'It was depressing in the old lady's big house when he went away with Ghassan and Walid. I would count the days till they came back and got together again and made some noise for a change in the house or in the *diwaniya*.'

My mother suddenly stopped a moment and looked at the floor. 'I used to watch them in the courtyard from the kitchen window, laughing and getting their gear ready for a fishing trip,' she said. 'They'd be gone for hours and I'd wait for your father to come back so that I could put his fish in the freezer and wash the fish smell out of his clothes.'

She turned to me and said, 'I hope you find friends like Ghassan and Walid, José, if you go back to Kuwait.'

'Tell me more, Mama. What about Grandma?'

'The old lady worried about her son and the way he spent his time. She often told him she was worried that either his books would drive him mad or the sea would sweep him away. She often walked in on him in the study and begged him to stop reading and writing and turn his attention to things that would do him good. But he insisted that writing was the only thing he was good at. He loved the sea as well as his library. He adored the smell of fish as much as his mother liked her incense and Arabian perfumes.'

My mother closed her eyes and took a deep breath as if she was smelling something she loved.

'Your grandmother was always worrying about your father, not just because he was her only son but because he was the only remaining man in the family and only he could pass on the family name. Most of his male ancestors had disappeared long ago. Some of them were sailors who disappeared at sea and others in other ways. Those who survived only had daughters. The old lady said this was because long ago a jealous woman from a humble family had cast a spell so that only the women in the family would survive. Your father didn't believe in such things, but your grandmother was totally convinced. In those distant days your grandfather and his brother, Shahin, were the only surviving males in the family. Shahin died young before marrying. Isa married your grandmother, Ghanima, late and they had your father, Rashid, and when Rashid's father died Rashid was the only male left in the family.'

My imagination ran riot: people dying at sea, sailing ships fighting giant waves, a woman casting spells in a dark room, the males dying out one by one because of magic. My mother's stories made my family sound like characters in some legend.

'He was the only reason I had the patience to stay in the old lady's house and put up with the way she mistreated me,' my mother continued. 'He offered me words of sympathy at night, when everyone else was asleep. He used to slip his hand into his pocket, pull out banknotes and give them to me – one dinar, or two or three. Then he would leave. I wasn't interested in the money of course.'

Aunt Aida interrupted her. 'All men are bastards,' she said.

My mother and I turned towards her. 'However much they don't appear to be,' she added.

My mother replied with two words: 'Except Rashid.'

'One evening in the kitchen, he put his hand on my shoulder and whispered, "Don't be angry with my mother. She's an old woman and she doesn't mean what she says. She's neurotic, but well-meaning." I didn't want him to take his hand away. I forgot all the insults from the old lady. After that I deliberately made her angry every now and then. I'd drop a glass on the kitchen floor and leave the pieces lying around

27

till the next morning, or I'd leave a tap running all night and making noise, or I'd leave a window open on a windy day so that all the dust came in and landed on the floor and the furniture. When the old lady got up in the morning, she would throw a fit. Everyone in the house would wake up to her shouting and calling out "Joza!", the name she had given me because she thought Josephine was too hard to pronounce. She would curse and yell and swear, and I would just sweep up the pieces of glass from the kitchen floor or spend the whole day dusting and cleaning the place in the hope that when night came it would bring your father's gentle hand to touch my shoulder.'

She took out a handkerchief and wiped the tears from her eyes. 'One day he was writing his weekly article in the study,' she continued, 'resting his left elbow on the large file that contained a draft of his first novel. I put a cup of coffee down in front of him and said, "I like watching you write, sir."

'"Can't you call me something other than 'sir'?" he said.

'I didn't know what to say. I couldn't imagine ever calling him Rashid, like his mother and his sisters.'

'"Isn't there anything else you like, other than watching me write?" he asked.

'"Anything else?" I said.

'He put his pen down, locked his fingers together and rested his chin on his hands. "Something, or maybe someone?" he said.

'After that I was sure I was in love with him, or almost, although to him I was no more than someone who would listen without objecting whenever he wanted to explain his ideas and beliefs. Since I was certain he hadn't fallen in love with me and never would, I was content to love him in return for his interest and his sympathy.

'When I came to work in their house, your father was just getting over a love affair. He had had a relationship with the girl since he was a student. He wanted to marry her but, because of prejudices I know nothing about, the old lady prevented the marriage. So love alone is not enough to bring you together with the girl of your dreams. Before you fall in love, or so I understood from Rashid, you have to choose carefully the woman to fall in love with. You can't leave anything to chance. Apparently some names bring shame on others, and that's what happened with Rashid. As soon as his mother heard the girl's family name she rejected the idea of Rashid marrying the girl. Some time later the girl married another man.

'The relationship between your father and me continued like this. When the old lady was asleep in the afternoon or at night, and the sisters were busy at university or watching television upstairs, I would take the opportunity to make tea or coffee for Rashid, and spend as much time as possible with him, listening to stories that mattered less to me in themselves than as a reason just to be in his company in his study.'

6

My mother's intuition was quite right about his remark on how she looked like a Thai girl. My father was hinting at something. He didn't say it straight out, but there was an insinuation. My mother didn't tell me all the details, but he must have been clear about what he wanted, because she answered him firmly. 'Sir, I left my country to get away from things like that,' she told him. As time passed, his hints became more explicit but my mother stood her ground.

Then one day he said, 'Shall we get married?' and she finally relented. She must have been very pleased, because she accepted the marriage, which wasn't really much of a marriage.

It was the summer of 1987 and my mother had been in Kuwait for about two years. As my mother told me, and as I later experienced for myself, the summers in Kuwait are brutal. Rashid's family spent the weekends in their beach house on the coast south of Kuwait City. The house is still there and the family gathers there from time to time.

My grandmother and my aunts had gone there with the Indian driver, on the understanding that my father would drive my mother and the cook there and join them. He set off later the same day but he didn't go straight to the beach house. He stopped the car in front of an old building not far away. He and my mother got out, while the cook stayed in the car.

'It was old and in bad shape,' my mother said, talking about the building. 'Apparently it was housing for foreign workers. There were clothes hanging on lines in the courtyard and in the windows. It didn't look like a woman had been near the place in years. There were tyres of various sizes piled up in the corners of the courtyard, and abandoned planks of wood, old wardrobes and cupboards covered in dust and thrown aside any old how. There were coils of wire and mattresses that were torn and faded by the sun. Instead of going in through the front door your father took a narrow passageway to the left towards an outer room. There was a man waiting for us there. He looked like an Arab, with a long bushy beard and a dark mark in the middle of his forehead. He was wearing an Arab gown and an Arab headdress but without the black band that Kuwaitis usually wear to hold the headdress in place. The man called in two other men, who apparently lived there. We didn't stay long. We sat down in front of the man, who started talking with your father in Arabic. He turned to me and asked, "Have you been married before?"

I said no. He asked your father something in Arabic and he answered yes. Then he turned back to me and asked, "Do you accept Rashid as your husband?"

'He wrote out a piece of paper after we agreed. We signed it, Rashid and me. Then the other two men signed it too. Then it was "Congratulations."

'On the way back to the car, I was rather sceptical. "Is that all it takes to get married?" I asked.

'He nodded and said, "It's simple."

I was hesitant and I didn't feel any different towards your father. When we got out of the car he was my master, and when we got back in again, he was still my master. "Are you sure?" I asked again.

He took the piece of paper out of his pocket. "This piece of paper proves it." He put his hand out, offering me the paper. "You can keep it," he said. I asked him about the old lady and his sisters. "Everything in good time," he replied casually. I shut up. I wasn't convinced we were really man and wife, but because of the way I felt towards your father I accepted it.

'We got back in the car and drove off to the beach house. The cook didn't say anything but he was looking at me suspiciously.'

★ ★ ★

I doubt my father did what he did because he really wanted to marry my mother. Perhaps he just wanted to have his way with her. Anyway, it was good of him to go through with this strange marriage.

That same night they had a secret rendezvous at a time set by my father. After midnight my grandmother and my aunts went to sleep. When the lights in the house had gone out one by one, my mother slipped out and walked along the beach in the cold sand.

'Josephine,' my father whispered. He was launching the boat into the water. 'Yes, sir,' she said.

'You shouldn't call me that any longer,' he replied. 'Come closer,' he beckoned, 'so I don't have to raise my voice and people notice.'

My mother went up to him and stood there while he launched the boat and jumped in.

'Has everyone gone to bed?' he asked.

'Just now. The old lady and the girls have gone to their rooms.'

He put out his hand to her. 'Come,' he said.

She was confused. 'Where to?' She asked.

He was still holding out one hand to her. With his other hand he pointed out to sea at a red light that was flashing.

'Near there,' he said. 'We won't be long. An hour, or two hours at the most.'

She looked behind her at the beach house. 'But, sir, I . . .'

'If you insist on calling me "sir", then I, as your master, order you to come with me.'

My mother took a few hesitant steps towards the boat. She left her shoes in the sand and started to wade deeper and deeper into the water. The water rose above her waist. She grabbed my father's hand and he put his arm around her waist to lift her into the boat.

He pushed off from shore with a long wooden pole, then started the engine as soon as they were out of easy earshot, while my mother sat next to him with her knees folded up against her chest, hiding the contours of her body, which would have shown through her wet clothes.

Then and there, far from shore and close to the flashing red light, as the boat rocked in the calm sea, I made my first journey, leaving my father's body and settling deep inside my mother.

7

As the months passed my mother's belly expanded to make room for me as I grew. The rounded bulge stuck out and she couldn't hide it forever under her loose clothes. She hid it from my father at first. 'It was a strange marriage,' my mother said. 'It didn't seem real, especially after he had fulfilled his objective. He was still my master, in spite of everything that had happened. So I kept you secretly inside me because I was frightened he might try to make me have an abortion if he found out.' Like Aunt Aida, she didn't tell my father she was pregnant till it would have been impossible to have an abortion.

My father didn't believe it at first. He didn't know what to do when he realised she was serious. He told her off for keeping quiet about it for so long. 'That was when I realised that this wasn't a real marriage,' she said. He hinted at the idea of an abortion. When he understood it was too late he promised her he would act at the right time. As time passed the changes were obvious – the way she looked and the way she moved, her complexion, her nose, her lips, her swollen fingers and the way she walked. It wasn't hard to tell, especially as the lady of the house was the father's mother. One day in the kitchen, in the presence of the Indian cook, Grandmother sprang the question on her. 'Who did it?' she asked, expecting my mother to confess that she had slept with the cook. My mother burst into tears, and the cook fell to his knees, kissed Grandmother's hands and assured her he had never gone anywhere near Josephine.

My father heard his mother shouting in the kitchen. He left the study and headed towards all the noise. My father sent the cook off with a wave of his hand. He turned to his mother and, casually and rebelliously, he said, 'It's me.'

There was a heavy silence, then my grandmother said, 'Yes, you, the man of the house. You'll deal with that bastard, won't you?'

She was sure the cook had done it, so my father had to explain. 'No, it was me who did it, Mother,' he said.

She clasped her chest with the palm of her hand, as if her heart had sunk and she had to hold it in place. She put her hands over her ears and then over her face. 'She'll have to leave,' she said, in a voice that was hardly audible.

'I'm not in the habit of going back on what I say or do, and sometimes there's no going back anyway,' my father answered coldly.

His mother was about to collapse. Despite appearances, my father was also close to collapse. She took her hands off her face, sat down and pounded the dining table with her fist.

'You can write stuff like that for your crazy readers, but not for me,' she shouted.

'I made a mistake when I made this baby,' my father replied. 'But I don't want to make a bigger mistake by abandoning it.' My mother said she had never heard him raise his voice so loud, and this was at his mother!

My three aunts had gathered at the kitchen door after hearing all the noise. They didn't dare come closer.

'That slut Josephine must leave the country tomorrow,' Grandmother said.

My mother clasped her hands together in front of her face and wept.

'Yes, yes, madam, I'll leave tomorrow,' she said.

My father silenced her with his hand. 'She won't leave as long as she's carrying a part of me in her womb,' he said.

His mother stood up straight, her hands resting on the table in front of her. 'The girl at college, the one who . . . I'll arrange the engagement, tomorrow if you like,' she said.

My father shook his head. 'It's too late for that, Mother,' he said.

'It's a disaster, a scandal,' she shouted between sobs.

She pointed at my aunts at the door. 'Your sisters, you selfish, despicable man. Who'll marry them after what you've done with the maid?'

Rashid had nothing to say in response.

'Get out of my house, and take that slut with you. Those crazy books have ruined your mind!'

For a whole week, my mother kept asking my father questions about what had happened in the kitchen that day. 'Why was she pointing at your sisters?' she asked. 'She was talking about books. What was she saying? What were you saying when you shouted in your mother's face?'

'He acted out the scene for me and translated the conversation so that I could understand. I cried. Your father made me cry many times, José.'

My mother cried that day because my father hadn't been open with his mother about the marriage. She cried even more because she knew my father hadn't rebelled against his mother to protect her or because he wanted to stay with her, but rather to protect me, his unborn child. And although he managed to protect me while I was in my mother's womb, he couldn't do so when I came out.

If only he had done what his mother wanted.

If only he had kicked my mother in the stomach and I had ended up a small lump of matter swimming in her blood on the kitchen floor.

8

Rashid and Josephine lived together in a small flat, a flat my father could afford on his modest salary. The only regular visitors were Ghassan and Walid, who were witnesses to an official marriage after the couple moved to their new home.

One day when my mother, Aida and I were sitting around talking, my mother took a copy of her official marriage certificate from the briefcase where she kept her papers, which are now in my possession along with my father's letters. She pointed to the bottom of the certificate, which neither she nor I could read.

'This is Ghassan's signature,' she said.

She moved her finger to the next signature. She said nothing for a while then, sadly, she said, 'His signature is crazy, much like him.'

I examined the second signature, the one she called crazy. 'Whose signature is that, Mama?' I asked.

'Walid's,' she said, smiling and folding up the certificate.

Then she took two pictures out of the briefcase, including one of my father. He was smiling, very thin with a thick moustache and small eyes behind a pair of glasses, wearing a loose white thobe and a white cap on his head like the ones the Muslims wear in old Manila and the Chinese quarter. I don't know what made my mother think my father was handsome. The second picture was of two young men on a boat. My mother pointed at one of them. He wasn't looking at the camera because he was busy doing something. 'That's Ghassan. He's fixing the bait to the fish hook,' my mother said. Then she pointed at the other man, who was looking straight at the camera. 'That's Walid,' she said. The picture caught my attention. He had a childish face, apparently much younger than my father or Ghassan, and he looked cheerful.

'He was crazy, unlike Rashid and Ghassan,' my mother said. 'He loved racing cars and motorcycles.

He was daring, reckless, argumentative. He loved travelling though he had a phobia about planes. When he had to fly he took sleeping pills before take-off and slept like a log. He didn't wake up till the wheels hit the runway.'

I liked his character, from his picture and from what my mother said about him. I stared at the picture. He was holding a plastic bag in one hand and my mother said it contained chicken guts, which my father liked to use as fish bait. He was wearing dark sunglasses and was holding his nose because of the foul smell coming from the bag.

'The smell must have been horrible, Mama,' I said, pulling a face in disgust.

'Yes, the smell of guts is really nasty, but the smell of fish on Rashid's clothes . . .'

She left her sentence unfinished, closed her eyes and took a deep breath until her chest expanded. 'I miss him so much,' she sighed.

Aunt Aida pointed to the kitchen door and said, 'In the upper section of the fridge, José, there are ten galunggong fish. Bring two of them.' Aida stuck a finger up each nostril, then continued in a hushed voice. 'Let's put them up your mother's nose!' she said.

My mother ignored her and went on talking about herself and my father when they were together.

My father stayed away from his mother's house while my mother was pregnant. He was stubborn, she said, or pretended not to care, while inside he badly missed the old lady. I was sure he felt remorse, even if he didn't show it. He didn't visit her at all during that period, maybe because he was embarrassed. He did try to contact her but his sisters told him she didn't want to hear his voice and so none of them made any attempt to get in touch with him.

My father was sure that as soon as I came into the world his mother's attitude would change. He thought she would take me into her arms as soon as she saw him carrying me, as soon as she realised she had now become a grandmother. He had taken a decision to call me Isa after his father if I was a boy, or Ghanima after his mother if I was a girl.

My mother had no regrets about anything in her life, including marrying my father and getting pregnant with me. She believed and still believes in her own private philosophy: 'Everything happens for a reason and for a purpose.' The couple lived in isolation until I was born – the moment my father had been counting on. In the maternity hospital on 3 April 1988, the doctor gave my father the news that I had arrived. 'Your wife has given birth to a baby boy, and they're both in good health,' the doctor said.

My father picked me up in his arms and took a long look at my face. 'Maybe he was looking for just one thing that you two had in common,' my mother said. For sure, what he saw was a face with elements taken from other faces, but not from his own. My features were a mixture of my mother's, Aunt Aida's and my grandfather's.

As soon as we three – my father and mother and I – were out of hospital, my father drove to his mother's house. When we arrived my father asked my mother to stay where she was in the car, because his mother might not be able to handle the sight of her just then, whereas her grandson, me that is, might make it possible for her to accept my mother as time passed. My mother waited in the car while my father carried me in to his mother.

My father tried to open the front door but his mother had changed the locks so that he couldn't come in if he ever thought of coming back. When he rang the bell a new Indian maid opened the door. He spoke with her a while, then pushed the door to go in and disappeared out of sight of my mother. A few minutes later my mother saw a car drive up to my grandmother's house. She lay low in her seat so that no one would see her. The car stopped at the kerb outside the house and four women got out. One of them rang the bell and the servant opened the door. It didn't take long. As soon as they disappeared behind the door, the garage door at the side of the house opened and my father appeared, carrying me in his arms and heading for the car in silence.

'Your father changed after he visited the old lady's house,' my mother said with a sad look. 'He didn't speak much and he was always thinking about something. He spent more time reading and writing. I tried to persuade him to go out boating several times but he always refused. He said Ghassan and Walid were busy getting ready for a trip abroad. I begged him to go abroad with them but he refused.

'Two days after you were born, they did go abroad, but if only they hadn't!

'Ghassan and Walid were passengers aboard the Kuwaiti plane that was hijacked by a pro-Iranian extremist group on its way to Thailand. Your father went crazy. He was glued to the television screen most of the time. If he wasn't watching television, he was reading the newspapers or calling his remaining friends in search of news, but all they knew was the same as the news on television. Things got worse. Two of the passengers were killed and people were horrified. Your father broke down when he saw television pictures of the body of one of the passengers being thrown from the plane door at Larnaca airport. He wept his heart out when an ambulance took the body away from under the plane. I'll never forget how Rashid looked when he heard the news. He started beating his chest with his fist and shouted, "They didn't kill him. It was us who did it. It was us who did it. We shouldn't have supported Iraq." I don't understand, even now, how someone could cry with such feeling over the death of someone he'd never met, and how someone could accuse himself of committing a murder when he hadn't done it.

'After that there were rumours that a third Kuwaiti had been killed, but it wasn't officially confirmed. Rashid followed the news. Through friends who worked in the newspapers and television, he confirmed it was true. Someone had died on the plane after being hit. He had had a fit and his condition had deteriorated. Without medical attention he had died of a heart attack.

'It was Walid. Fear of flying hadn't killed him but it may have played a part. Your father sobbed and sobbed. All I could do was fall on the floor and grieve for my husband and his friend, but I couldn't do anything about it.

'After Walid's death, the old lady agreed for the first time to have contact with your father by telephone. "I didn't really want to speak to you, but I just wanted to let you know that you're in for a run of bad luck. Look what happened to your friend after that horrible thing was born. It's a curse, like its mother," she told him.

'Your father bit his lip and floods of tears rolled down his cheeks. "Throw them out and see how your luck changes," his mother concluded. "Then come home and you'll find I have a mother's heart and I've forgiven you the horrible thing you've done."

'My grandmother hung up. Rashid bowed his head. With the receiver still in his hand, fighting back his tears, he said, "My mother says . . ."

As soon as my father had arranged a birth certificate for me, with the name Isa, he contacted a travel agency and asked them to book a seat on any plane going to Manila, so long as it wasn't on Kuwaiti Airways.

A few days later I made my second move, but this time it was from my father's country to my mother's country.

PART 2

Isa . . . After His Birth

'He who does not know how to look back at where
he came from will never get to his destination.'
José Rizal

I

From Kuwait we flew to the Philippines to live in the land of my grandfather, from whom I took the name José Mendoza. Mendoza was really my grandfather's family name but people often called him by that name alone.

I grew up on a piece of land of no more than 2,000 square metres in Valenzuela City in northern Manila. There were three small houses there, one of which, the largest of the three, had two storeys. That was where we lived, piled on top of each other – my mother and I, Aunt Aida and Merla, Uncle Pedro and his wife and their children. Another house, which was very small and separated from the larger house by a watercourse a metre wide, was where Grandfather Mendoza lived. The watercourse between the two houses was not a stream or a branch of a river, but rather a drain where waste water collected along with our rubbish, which made the smell unbearable, especially on humid days.

Far from those two houses, in a corner overlooking the road and under a giant mango tree, stood the third house, which was made of bamboo stalks and was the smallest of the three. My grandfather had built it many years earlier for a poor, single woman called Choleng. We didn't know where she'd come from. Before she came to live near us her only home was the pavement. We didn't know anything about her but her name, to which we added the title *inang*, or 'mother', out of respect for her age. His decision to let her stay on his land for free was one of the paradoxes about my grandfather, who was usually greedy and mean. She was very old. The way she looked frightened the neighbourhood children. Her back was hunched and she had a grey moustache. The white hair on her head covered only bits and pieces of her scalp; the rest of her scalp had sores and red patches. Children made up frightening myths about her, which made it impossible to walk past her house, especially after dark. Inang Choleng was the local witch. She ate children and would never die, they said.

The empty spaces around the three houses were planted with trees – mangoes, bananas, guavas, papaya and jackfruit – and the land was surrounded on all sides by stands of bamboo that formed a high wall.

Shortly before my mother came back from Kuwait my family's financial position had improved a little. They would have been able to live better if Mendoza hadn't been so reckless and wasn't addicted to betting on cockfights. Addiction doesn't just apply to drugs: gambling and betting ran in his blood. My grandfather, Aunt Aida and Merla, and even Uncle Pedro and his family, had basically depended on the money my mother sent at the end of each month when she was working as a maid, and their situation improved greatly when she had paid off the money owed to the Indian moneylenders and started sending all her salary. This meant my grandfather could buy a fridge, because Aida had asked for one and he was frightened of her, though most of the time the fridge had no food in it.

My mother relayed Pedro's account of the event. 'I wish you had been here,' he said. 'The welcome ceremonies when the fridge arrived were amazing! It was like we were welcoming a warship home from victory in battle. All the men, women and children in the neighbourhood gathered around the house to watch the workers carry the fridge from the company truck to inside the house. It was a wonderful feeling, Josephine!'

A few weeks after the fridge arrived, the family found a way to supplement their livelihood, fortunately not in the form of cash or else my grandfather Mendoza would have taken it all for himself. Aida agreed to let the neighbours store their food in our fridge in exchange for a small portion of the food,

2

When we arrived home and my mother opened the door, I was wrapped in a sling strapped to her back. Grandfather Mendoza was asleep on the sofa in the sitting room, as usual at midday. He rarely went to his own house nearby, other than to sleep at night.

My mother pushed the door and went inside. 'I stood stock–still in front of him,' she said, referring to my grandfather. 'Father was in front of me and the door behind me. I didn't expect to go to my room until I'd had my share of insults, and maybe a beating! I was going to show respect by bending down, picking up his hand and holding the back of his hand against my forehead. But then I remembered how he had slapped Aida some years back.'

'"Father!" I called.

'He didn't wake up so I raised my voice and tried again. "Father."

'He opened one eye, then sat up. '"If you had finished the year . . ." he said with a smile.

'He left the sentence unfinished and kept smiling.

'*If he knew what I'm carrying on my back*, I thought to myself. "Three years," I said. "I think that's enough, Father."

'As soon as I finished my sentence I heard Pedro's voice from outside. "Whose suitcase is that?" he asked.

'Pedro pushed the door behind me to bring in the suitcase I had left at the door before coming in. He stopped at the door and the first thing your uncle Pedro saw was you, strapped to my back.

'"Who's that?" he asked.

'I heard him behind me. My father, who was still sitting on the sofa in front of me, burst out laughing.

"It's Josephine, you idiot," he said.

'Pedro came past me, stood between me and my father and looked back at me in amazement. "I meant what she's carrying on her back!" he said.

'My father left the scruffy sofa and scowled as soon as he heard what Pedro said. He walked towards me with his eyes wide open. He went past me. I stood where I was without moving, ready to take a blow from behind. He stood up straight behind me and whispered in my ear, "Another bastard!"

'He pulled my hair back. My head banged against your little head and you burst out crying, while I was about to . . .

"If you did your whoring here instead of—" he said.

"He's not a bastard," I interrupted. "His father's my husband."

'He gripped my hair tight, then shouted at Pedro: "You, shut the door quickly."

'I knew he was thinking about his cocks but I wasn't as brave as Aida was that time when she broke their necks.'

3

The way my grandfather treated my mother was different from that day on. Although he was angry, he showed her a respect to which she wasn't accustomed. And although she had let him down by coming back with a child, at least she was married. My mother was the child closest to him, even if he sometimes gave the opposite impression, because she was the one who looked after him and who treated him as a father, however cruel he was to her. She brought him food and took the trouble to clean up his little room. She even gave him half of what my father sent her from Kuwait, although she and I needed the money.

My mother said, 'As far as possible I've tried to get along with your grandfather as well as your grandmother did. He's irritable because he was a soldier and had a hard time when he was young, or so your grandmother said. His addiction to gambling is just a way of venting his anger, or maybe it's an attempt to get revenge on old adversaries by defeating rival cocks.

'We women,' she continued with a smile, 'need to understand the male temperament and make allowances for the things men do. That means we have to put up with their mistakes, if only to preserve something that's more important.'

She gave a little laugh, then continued, 'If I tried to resist him, I would end up suffering the same fate as Aida. I would end up with a hardened expression on my face and eyes that didn't show any emotion, heading straight to my destination like a train, with marijuana smoke blowing out of my nostrils.'

No one but my mother could handle my grandfather properly, because dealing with Mendoza meant dealing with several men, each with his own style, his own tastes and even his own way of thinking. I don't know what set my mother apart from everyone else. Maybe she was more patient, maybe more intelligent.

Mendoza was someone I never managed to understand through all the years I was there. I wasn't sure which of the personalities that he switched between was his real personality. You could have written a novel about him. My mother once said, 'If you come across a man with more than one personality, you can be sure he's looking for himself in one of them, because he has no character.' But I think she was wrong, because Mendoza, despite his many personalities, did have a real personality. It only came to light in the evening when he drank *tuba*, fermented coconut milk. His other personalities were merely attempts to conceal that real personality. He was crying inside but he suppressed it. And when the drink began to take effect, I could hear him raving at night, saying, 'I'm weak, I'm lonely.'

In 1966 my grandfather had joined the Philippine Army, which was allied at the time with South Korea, Thailand, Australia and New Zealand under US leadership to fight North Vietnam in the Vietnam war. He was in one of the units that helped provide medical and logistical services there. 'In the mountains of Vietnam the Viet Cong stole my father's humanity,' my mother said. 'He never told us what he saw, but he must have gone through indescribable things, to come back at the end of the war in the state you can see him in now.' When I was growing up I hated my grandfather with a vengeance and wished him dead, whatever excuses my mother made for him. If I complained that he'd been cruel to me, she would say, 'We went through the same thing – me and Aida and Pedro. We used to complain to your grandmother when he flew into a temper and snapped at us, but she would always say, "It's the war. It's still raging inside him."'

My grandfather came home in 1973 with traumatic memories we knew nothing about and with a small US government pension for the rest of his life. The pension money didn't count as income for the family, because it was just enough to buy a new cock every month, and if the cock was killed by a more aggressive cock, then it meant the loss of a month's income. If the cock defeated its rival, my grandfather would take his winnings and buy another cock. Whatever money was left he spent on food, stimulants and expensive vitamins for the cocks. Either way the money would fly away like the feathers of the fighting cocks and no one in the family had the right to object. The only solace if my grandfather's cock did win was that he would come home carrying a cage with three cocks in it: the winner, a new cock, and the loser, which would usually be dead or on the point of death, as a feast for the hungry family.

4

My mother somewhat neglected my religious education in the belief that my future was to be a Muslim in my father's country. My father had whispered the Muslim call to prayer in my right ear as soon as he held me in his arms in hospital after I was born, but that didn't stop my mother from taking me to the small local church as soon as we arrived in Manila to baptise me in holy water as a Catholic. Apparently she wasn't yet fully convinced at that stage that I would go back.

If only my parents could have given me a single, clear identity, instead of making me grope my way alone through life in search of one. Then I would have just one name that would make me turn when someone called me. I would have just one native country. I would learn its national anthem. Its trees and streets would shape my memories and in the end I could lie at rest in its soil. I would have one religion I could believe in instead of having to set myself up as the prophet of a religion that was mine alone.

Sometimes I think of those minutes Rashid and Josephine spent on that boat when they became my father and mother. It's madness that their minutes of pleasure should make my whole life such a misery.

If I had been born Muslim to a Kuwaiti father and a Kuwaiti mother, I would be living in a big house with a spacious room on the upper floor, with a forty-six-inch television, a walk-in closet and an en suite bathroom. I would wake up every morning to go to a job I had chosen myself, wearing a loose white thobe and a traditional headdress, at ease in my surroundings, instead of looking like an extra playing the role of an Arab in some Hollywood movie. I could look at the people around me and I wouldn't need to look up to the sky to address them, and they wouldn't need to look down to the ground to notice I was there among them. I could sit in expensive cafés and restaurants without people grumbling in whispers that people like me shouldn't be in such fancy places. I could go to young people's parties in the evening and have lots of Kuwaiti friends, friends like Ghassan and Walid. I could meet them in the *diwaniya* and go boating with them. I could go to the mosque on Fridays and listen to the man standing in the pulpit and understand what he was saying, instead of just raising my hands, imitating the men around me and repeating 'Amen, amen' like a parrot.

Or . . .

If I had been born to a Filipino father and a Filipina mother, two of a kind, then I would be a Christian, comfortably off, living with my family in Manila,

63

venturing every day into a mass of humanity, exposing my lungs and the pores of my skin to vehicle exhaust fumes. Or I might be a poor Muslim living at peace among my people in Mindanao in the south despite hunger and harassment by the government, or a rich kid living in a fancy house in wealthy Forbes Park in Makati City and going to a school that only the rich can afford, or a Buddhist of Chinese origin, working with my father in a shop in the Chinese quarter of Manila, burning incense in front of a statue of Buddha every morning because it's good for business. Or if I had been born to Ifugao parents in the north of Luzon island, I would wear nothing but a loincloth all day. I would work in the terraced rice paddies in the mountains and sleep at night in a thatched house on stilts, guarded from evil spirits by statues of the anito. If I had been born a mestizo, I would have had my physical appearance as a feature to exploit, and I could have become a film star or a model in advertisements or a famous singer.

Or . . .

If I'd hatched from the egg of a house fly, I would have zipped around the house and grown old in ten days, then given up the ghost within two weeks at the most.

If I were something clearly defined, anything. If if if . . .

What a puzzle it is!

Did my baptism make me a Christian? Did I really embrace Christianity at that ceremony, which I attended at an age when I couldn't even remember anything?

We all have our own private religions. We take from religions the parts we believe in and ignore the parts that our minds can't grasp. We pretend to believe, we perform rituals we don't understand for fear of losing something we are trying to believe in.

Despite all the wrongs I have suffered, I usually forgive people when they do me harm. I turn my left cheek to those who slap me on the right. I once loved Jesus Christ so much that I started seeing him in my dreams. He smiled and patted me on the head with a hand that still showed traces of the nail that went through it on the day he was crucified. So am I a Christian? But what about the times when I discovered myself through meditation? What about my constant desire to commune with the natural world around me? I used to sit under the trees on Grandfather Mendoza's land, leaning against the tree trunks, until I hardly felt any sensations, which the Buddha says in his teachings are sources of suffering. I loved reading those teachings so much that I became like Ananda, the Buddha's closest and most beloved disciple. Might I be a Buddhist without knowing it? What about my belief in the existence of one supreme and eternal god, unbegotten and without offspring? Am I a Muslim by default?

What am I?

It's my destiny to spend my life looking for a name, a religion and a country. I won't however deny my parents credit for helping me, unintentionally, to discover my creator, in my own way.

5

There was nothing special about my relationship with the Church in the Philippines. My visits were very infrequent. After I was baptised I didn't go again till I was twelve. On that occasion I went with Aida and Pedro and his wife for my confirmation ceremony, the third sacrament I had undergone, after baptism and confession.

First confession had been organised by the school. Schools usually call in a priest to meet the third-grade children and take their confessions. I was nine when the priest came to see us and perform this rite. We lined up outside the classroom and the priest sat inside receiving the children one after another. The sins they confessed were what you would expect from children of that age – fairly insignificant, nothing more than 'Once I lied to the teacher' or 'I disobeyed my mother' or 'I stole a pen (or a doll) from so-and-so'. But my sin was different, not a small sin you'd expect from someone as small as me. It seemed like a big sin to me, as big as Inang Choleng was old.

When I think back to my grandfather Mendoza's land, I can't help remembering three sets of creatures that shared the small piece of land with the family.

There was Whitey, my grandfather's dog, there were his cocks and then there was Inang Choleng. She lived alone and I never saw her outside her little house. All I ever saw of her was her upper half when she appeared behind her front door examining her daily bowl of food. My mother cleaned the old woman's house once a week when grandmother was ill and after she died, because grandmother had done the cleaning before her. When my mother was away, Aunt Aida did it. The other women in the neighbourhood used to put bowls of food at her front door every morning and evening. When I was seven I was walking past Inang Choleng's house one day on the way home from school and I was ravenously hungry. I saw a woman putting a bowl of food in front of Inang Choleng's house. Usually the bowls would contain white rice and pieces of fruit or fried plantain, but that day I saw half a chicken lying in the bowl by the door. It made my mouth water. I stopped in front of her house, just a short distance away, but I didn't dare go closer because I was afraid of the old woman. I stared at the bowl. All I could hear was the rustling of the leaves and the buzzing of the bees in the giant hive they had built in the branches of the mango tree over the witch's house. I look around hesitantly. *Should I do it?* I wondered.

I looked at the handle of the wooden door.

What if she suddenly appears and drags me inside?

I started biting my fingernails.

I'd run off before she could catch me.

I took a step forwards.

What if she starves to death?

I looked down at the bowl on the ground by the door.

It looks delicious.

From somewhere nearby I heard a dog barking. It must have been Whitey.

The dog will beat me to it if I don't . . .

I took another step forward, torn between the thought that the dog would get there first and my fear that Inang Choleng would drag me inside. My hunger drove me to take another step forward. Then I stopped and thought about the old woman starving to death, then the barking grew louder and drew closer. The bees were still buzzing. I felt a knot in my stomach. I made a dash to Inang Choleng's door, closed my little fist around the half chicken lying in the bowl on the ground and ran off, leaving her an empty bowl.

In the classroom, two years after the incident, alone with the priest, I confessed I had stolen the old woman's food, even if I didn't eat it in the end.

'First repent of your sin,' he said.

I nodded. 'I will, Father, but . . .'

'Pray for the Lord Jesus twenty times and for the Virgin.'

The priest smiled, a sign that the ritual was over.

'But is there any way I can get the bee out of my head, Father?' I asked.

The priest looked surprised.

'When I ran away from Inang Choleng's house,' I explained, 'a bee followed me.'

Now he looked interested. He nodded his head, encouraging me to continue.

'I was running and the buzzing was right by my ear and I was frightened.'

I started thrashing the air around my face to explain what had happened.

'I tried to shoo it away, but it was insisting on something. It hit my ear.'

I hit my ear with my finger, continuing my little reenactment.

'I hit it, but I dropped the chicken and it fell to the ground, then . . .'

I put my hands over my ear and stared into the priest's face.

'Suddenly the buzzing outside stopped. But then I could hear it inside my head instead.'

The priest smiled. His smile gradually faded. He was thinking about something else but he wasn't silent for long. 'That's guilt,' he said.

'The Lord will forgive you if you pray, and the buzzing will disappear.'

I prayed and prayed, but the bee chose to stay in my head for ages.

6

My mother never stopped talking about my father and Kuwait and the life that awaited me. I used to cry when the subject of Kuwait came up. It was a country I knew nothing about and I couldn't imagine myself anywhere other than on my grandfather Mendoza's land in Valenzuela. I got annoyed when I heard the name Rashid, because my mother never stopped mentioning him. But because life was hard and my mother painted a picture of the paradise that awaited me, I ended up looking forward to the day when I would be rich and I could get whatever I wanted without having to work for it. If I was impressed by an advertisement for an expensive car, my mother would say, 'You can have one of those if you go back to Kuwait.' If I pointed to something in the shops that my mother couldn't afford, she would say, 'In Kuwait Rashid will buy you one like that.' I imagined myself as Alice in Wonderland, running after my mother's promises instead of the rabbit's and falling down a hole that led to Kuwait, the Wonderland. My mother convinced me that we were living in hell and that Kuwait was the heaven I deserved.

I had learned to read English, and one day my mother gave me my father's first letter to her to read. He had sent it after we left Kuwait, when I was four months old.

In his letter my father wrote:

Dear Josephine,

It's been three months since you left and you still haven't asked why I abandoned you and Isa so mysteriously.

I handed the letter back to her and sighed. 'I hate the name Isa,' I said.

She frowned. 'But Isa's a beautiful name,' she said reproachfully. 'It's Arabic for Jesus,' she added, patting my head.

'If you choose your mother's religion, then Isa is the son of God, and if you choose your father's religion then Isa's a prophet sent by God. In either case you should be proud of your name.'

I didn't respond.

'Go on reading, José,' my mother said with a smile.

I continued, mainly because she called me José: *I know you won't ask, because you're the one who was always saying that everything happens for a reason and for some purpose and you're not the kind of woman who looks for explanations.*

We know, or rather we admit, you and I, that getting married and what we did later on that crazy night on that boat was reckless.

I looked up at my mother's face.

'What happened on the boat, Mama?' I asked.

'You'll find out one day,' she replied, a look of irritation on her face.

I read on: *That's why we accepted the consequences and lived with them in the beginning. But afterwards I must admit I couldn't take it and in my weakness I put all the responsibility on to you.*

I was sure that Isa would soften my mother's heart in her anger, because before I admitted our relationship to her she never stopped saying she wanted to see me have children before she died. But that night, after we came out of the hospital and went to visit her with Isa, I felt she would rather have died than see the child.

She was so angry she had changed the locks on the doors so that I couldn't come in if I ever thought of coming back. I wasn't happy about the way she behaved and I know how much she loves me, but although I couldn't open the door to the house, I thought I held another key with which I could open her heart, a key called Isa.

I looked at my mother with a frown. She laughed.

'Very good, keep on reading,' she said.

The smell of incense was the first thing that hit me when the servant opened the door. Was my mother burning incense to celebrate my possible return, I wondered. I stepped inside, impatient to see my mother's face after months apart. The servant followed me, asking, 'Who are you? What do you want?' I didn't reply. I asked for my mother. She pointed to the stairs and said, 'She's upstairs.' All the lights in the house were on, something that only happened on special occasions. I headed for the stairs and had gone one step up when my mother appeared at the top, about to come down.

I stood stock–still on the first step. She hesitated at first. She was about to back away as soon as she saw me but she resisted the impulse. My mother wasn't one to run away. She looked me in the face, eye to eye. At first she looked angry and severe, but with every step I took up the stairs she mellowed and softened. I kissed her hand and her forehead. I held out the baby boy for her in my arms. 'Isa,' I said.

I gritted my teeth with irritation at the name Isa, without looking at my mother's face this time.

Did her eyes water at the sight of the baby? Did she have visions of my father when I said the name Isa to her?

She took the baby into her arms and walked slowly downstairs, while I stood on the top step, watching as she stared into the baby's face and tried to hold back her tears. She sat down on a sofa at the bottom of the stairs and I watched them from the top. I could see them between the crystal pendants in the large chandelier hanging from the middle of the ceiling. Isa started crying in her arms. My mother held him close, then burst into tears as I had never seen her cry, except years ago when she heard that my father had died. My eyes filled with tears as I watched my mother and my son, in the house where I grew up, surrounded by lights and the smell of incense. The smell reminded me of the question in the back of my mind: why the incense? Had she had a premonition about this day in particular?

I walked downstairs to where she was sitting on the sofa and knelt on the floor in front of her, with my hand pressing hard on her knee. Although my mother and the baby were both crying I heard the doorbell ring. The servant arrived a few seconds later. 'Madam, there are four women outside asking for you,' she said. My mother pushed the baby towards me as if it were a bomb about to explode. 'The suitor's family! The suitor's family!' she said. She wiped away her tears, stood upright in front of the mirror to restore the hard look that the baby had softened. Without turning towards me she pointed to the back door that led to the garage. 'Take your son and get out of here,' she said. I was stunned by the change in her mood. 'Mother!' I shouted, over the sound of Isa crying. 'Mother, please,' I added. She stepped towards the back door and opened it. 'Get out. Now,' she said, emphasising the words. Then she pointed to the baby. 'And mind you never bring that thing back here again,' she said.

I left through the back door, carrying the curse of Isa with me, so that good fortune could enter the house through the front door. My mother had an appointment to meet the family of a man who wanted to marry Awatif, my eldest sister.

Josephine, there's more to this than you imagine. I won't keep playing a game when I don't know the rules. I completed

76

the divorce procedures a few hours before writing this letter.
Believe me, this will be best for me and for you. As for Isa,
I promise I won't abandon him. I'll take care of all his needs
and I'll send him whatever money he needs at the end of
each month until the time comes when I can take him back.
I promise I will do that when the time is right.

   Rashid

   Kuwait, September 1988

My mother cried when I read out the words 'I completed the divorce procedures', despite the fact that she had read the letter years before and had married another man after Rashid. I cried too, but that was when I read about my grandmother saying 'Mind you never bring that thing back here again.'

'Why does Grandmother hate me, Mama?' I asked. My mother was busy mopping up my tears with a handkerchief that was already soaked with her own.

'As Jesus said, even prophets are strangers in their own country,' she said.

'So I'm a prophet?' I asked her in surprise.

'God alone knows,' she said, looking away towards the window.

Frightened, I took her hands. 'Mama, if I grow up and go to my father's country as a prophet, won't they crucify me there?' I asked.

7

My mother said she was stunned when she read the letter for the first time, not because of the divorce, which was how she expected the relationship to end ('The decision wasn't your father's. A whole society stood behind him,' she said), but because she was afraid of his promise. She couldn't imagine being able to give me up to my father under any circumstances. That was at the beginning, but when she thought about it hard, unemotionally, she realised that everyone in the Philippines dreamed of living abroad in a country that provided stability and a decent life. Women gave up everything to marry Western men who would take them off to their countries, for the sake of an opportunity to live well and have a family, but men found it hard to fulfil this dream. In the Philippines it's the dream of every man and woman to emigrate and settle in Europe, America or Canada, giving up everything – their past, their country and even their family.

My mother realised that a secure future, of a kind rarely available to men, awaited me there in Kuwait, where the state provides citizens (and I was a citizen) with much more than even the most developed countries provide. My mother accepted my father's promise, expected it to be fulfilled and prepared me for it. Although he had let her down and abandoned her by divorcing her, she would still say, 'I never loved anyone as much as your father.' Despite that love, about two years later my mother married Alberto. He was about ten years older than her and he lived in our neighbourhood. He worked on merchant ships and sailed the oceans for eight months a year. He spent the other months with her in his little house near my grandfather's land. My mother had a better life with her new husband and when he was in the Philippines she left me in the care of my Aunt Aida. My mother almost went back to work as a servant in the Gulf at about this time so that she could secure her own future and that of her new husband, but she dropped the idea after my father intervened.

In a letter he sent more than two years after we left, he wrote:

Dear Josephine,

How are you? And how is Isa?

I received your last letter and read what was in it. I hope that being married is not distracting you from bringing up the boy, and also that you'll give up the idea of coming to work in the Gulf again. I'll send you enough money so you won't need to go abroad. Just stay close to Isa. I don't want him to grow up separated from his mother. What his father has done is already quite enough.

In a few days I'm going to marry a nice girl, Iman, who loves me very much. She follows what I write and it's good to have her read it. I've told her about our son and she didn't object when I told her that he would come back to live with me once my three sisters have married. She's going to move in and live with me in my mother's house until things improve and we can go and live in a new house and start our own family.

Keep well, you and Isa,
Rashid
Kuwait, May 1990

At first it was my mother who asked me to read my father's letters to her, but then his letters started to get me interested and I asked her to show me more of them.

'I don't have any more, José,' she replied, putting the letters back in the briefcase. 'He stopped sending letters and the money transfers stopped after that letter because of the war over Kuwait.'

8

My grandfather began to hate me. When my father's transfers stopped arriving, he no longer bothered to hide his feelings towards me. 'You'll settle down in Alberto's house one day,' he told my mother, 'and I don't want that boy staying here.' But Aida stepped in. 'I'll look after him,' she said, silencing my grandfather.

When the money stopped coming it had a big effect on Mendoza, although he still had a faint hope that the war would soon end and the monthly transfers would resume. But deep down he doubted this would ever happen.

'I hope he doesn't go missing in the war,' he said, addressing no one in particular, while my mother rapped her knuckles on the wooden part of the sofa for good luck.

'Or the war doesn't drive him crazy,' Mendoza added.

It was an implicit admission on the part of Mendoza, who had experience of war, a suggestion that his own mind was disturbed.

'War's like that,' he added.

He wasn't talking to anyone in particular. He was staring blankly as if looking at mental images of his own.

'War isn't just the fighting on the battlefield,' he continued, 'but also the war that's fought in the minds of those who take part. The first ends, the second goes on and on.'

His eyes were frozen still. My mother said his eyes glistened as if he was about to cry. He turned his face towards the door and headed towards his house next door. He shook his head and said in a low voice, 'That man will never come back, never come back.'

My mother said that before he went out, she heard three knocks on the wooden door that led outside.

9

The war in Kuwait ended in February 1991 but even then no letter arrived from my father. My mother called my grandmother's house several times but all she received was insults and shouts, and then the usual tone you get when the line is disconnected. She asked women working in Kuwait to look out for any news of my father but nothing came of that. She asked after him in the Kuwaiti embassy in Manila but there was no response from the people working there. She waited a long time, but he seemed to have disappeared.

The first person to gloat, my mother said, was Aunt Aida.

'All men are like that. They're all bastards,' she said.

From that day on my mother would reply with her favourite expression: 'Except Rashid.'

The days passed, but my mother's faith that I would go back to Kuwait one day never wavered, even when no letters or news of him arrived.

Although I was still young, Mendoza became openly hostile towards me. 'If there was any good in this boy, his family there wouldn't have abandoned him,' he said.

My mother held her tongue and he continued: 'If he was older, we could make use of him.'

My mother was in the first months of pregnancy by Alberto at that time. When she had her son Adrian I was about three and a half. My mother decided to move into Alberto's house, whereas previously she had stayed there only four months a year, when Alberto was on leave in the Philippines. She visited our house every now and then to ask after me and give Mendoza some money, and once a week to clean Inang Choleng's house.

My mother hadn't settled there long before she started thinking about going abroad again because her financial needs had increased. When Adrian was six months old she went off to work in Bahrain, leaving me and my brother in the care of Aunt Aida for three years.

It can't have been anything but poverty that persuaded her to leave her children with Aida, who always had bloodshot eyes from smoking too much marijuana.

In a letter she wrote to Aida one year after she left, my mother said:

How are you, my crazy sister?

And how are the kids?

A few hours ago I sent you my whole salary. Please make sure that none of it goes to my father and that it's shared out to José and Adrian and you and Merla. I'll try to save some money to help Pedro with his new building project.

Alberto called me a few days ago and told me he would be back in a few weeks. Please clean his house before he comes back and don't forget to take Adrian to him every day because, as you know, Alberto doesn't like to visit our house because father harasses him and is always pressing him with demands for money. I don't want to lose this man, even if all men are bastards.

Tell José I miss him very much and I'm working in a country close to his father's country. I wish I could swim across the sea to meet Rashid or find out what happened to him, so that I could feel confident about José's future.

I'm well. Bahrain isn't like Kuwait when it comes to the standard of living. Although the family I work for is well off, some people are poor. Simple people.

Bahrainis do all kinds of work. They wash cars, work as porters in hotels and sell stuff in shops. Even the woman I work for very often shares the housework with me. I like the people very much.

The people are kind. Tell José that. Kindness seems to be the most obvious feature of the poor. The poverty here is not like the poverty we have but, even for people who are relatively better off, it's still poverty.

Josephine

March 1993

Aida told me that my mother loved me and missed me very much.

I don't remember that. I was five years old. But definitely she did.

Did she kiss Adrian? Did Adrian feel my mother's kiss through Aida's lips?

If only your letter had come earlier, Mother.

★   ★   ★

That year Uncle Pedro finished building his new house on Mendoza's land and bought a used car. He had found work driving trucks for various companies, paid by the day. The great advantage for me was that for the first time in years I had my own room in the house, after Uncle Pedro left. A room that encapsulated my life in the Philippines. It was a small room with blue walls, a bed, a ceiling fan and a window that looked out on the window of my grandfather's little house next door. The distance between the two windows was no more than two metres and the watercourse ran through the gap below. Along the banks thin stalks of bamboo grew. There was nothing to disturb my peace of mind when I was in my room, except for Grandfather's nocturnal ravings under the influence of *tuba*, which I could hear through his window, or his constant calls of 'José!!!' during the day.

10

I was five years old and Adrian had started walking a few months earlier. He was in the middle of his second year. I looked after my little brother if Aida was busy. I didn't look after him in the full sense: all I did was keep an eye on him and stop him going outside or into the kitchen. He was chubby and very pretty, with small eyes and a flat nose squashed between his plump cheeks. 'That's what legitimate children look like,' Mendoza told Aida.

One night Aida asked me to look after Adrian while she went off to help Uncle Pedro sort out his new house. Merla was asleep upstairs. I was alone with him in the little sitting room. All I remember of what happened are some disjointed images that Aida pieced together for me when I was older. She explained to me the implications of one image that still flickers indistinctly in my memory.

It's dark and raining heavily. Thunder and lightning. Aunt Aida, in the rain, shouting, 'Adrian! Adrian!' Uncle Pedro's children moving around outside. Men and women carrying flashlights, searching Grandfather's land. Uncle Pedro running between the trees shouting, 'Adrian! Adrian!' Their clothes soaked and sticking to their bodies. The rain lashing down. The beams of the flashlights. Straight lines criss-crossing and never resting on one spot. All I remember are the voices and the images frozen by the sudden flashes of lightning.

'Here, here,' shouted Pedro's wife. Then Merla screamed and Aunt Aida wailed. All the flashlights pointed to one spot. Everyone running to somewhere between our house and my grandfather's house. I followed them. Pedro jumped into the watercourse, picked up something and put it on the bank between the bamboo stalks, which were leaning over because of the rainwater. A flash of lightning lit up the scene. Everyone dispersed, with shock on their faces. People made the sign of the cross. Uncle Pedro holding Adrian's face in both hands. It was dark blue. There was a thick black liquid running from his mouth and nose. Uncle Pedro pressed the boy's chest and kept pressing, locking his fingers, pushing down on Adrian's chest. Hitting, hitting. He pressed his lips to the lips of my little brother and blew. Then he burst into tears.

* * *

We should be able to forget the mistakes we make in childhood, but if the victim of your mistake is still there, right in front of your eyes, and grows up with you, and the effects of the mistake still show, then how can you forget?

I often make excuses for myself. I say I was just a child that didn't understand, that I couldn't be held responsible, that it wasn't my fault.

The excuses are persuasive, but if you try to convince both your head and your heart at the same time, one of them refuses to believe.

I borrow my mother's saying: 'Everything happens for a reason, and for some purpose.' Resorting to faith, by its very nature, requires faith.

But what if the faith is all a pretence?

With the passage of time everything new becomes old. But Adrian's face seems new whenever I see it.

He sits in front of me in his favourite corner, his mouth open, drooling constantly, reminding me of something I want to forget: a crippling sense of guilt about a mistake I can't even remember happening.

'Aida, isn't there any way to cure him?' I ask my aunt.

She gives her usual answer: 'No. That's what they told us in the hospital, after the incident, years ago.'

Although she's told me to my face dozens of times over the years what the doctor said, I still ask. 'What did the doctor say?'

I hear the same answer as always. 'It's because the oxygen didn't get to his brain. Damage to the cells.'

I'm always deeply disappointed, as if I expect a different answer every time I ask.

After nearly drowning, Adrian was in a coma for weeks. After that he gradually regained weight and recovered his health.

He recovered everything, except his mind.

11

At first no one dared tell my mother in Bahrain what had happened to Adrian and they were hoping they wouldn't have to because he would recover before she came home. But two years later, after they had lost hope, Aida phoned my mother to tell her all about the accident, leaving aside the permanent damage it had done to him. Alberto had come back from one of his trips a few weeks after the incident. He was horrified at what had happened. He spent most of his four months' leave in the bar close to his house, then disappeared to sea again.

After Aunt Aida called her, my mother came straight back from Bahrain. That was in the middle of 1995. We waited for her at home – Aunt Aida, Merla, Adrian and me, Pedro and his children.

Tragedy leaves deep scars on the walls of memory, whereas happiness paints pictures on them in bright colours. Time acts on the walls like rain: it washes away the colours but leaves the scars.

Uncle Pedro pulled the door open just as my mother was about to come in. I jumped up and she hugged me. 'You've grown into a man, José!' she said, overjoyed. Everyone exchanged kisses and greetings with her. Everyone was awaiting the inevitable confrontation. The group moved apart around her. My mother looked at Adrian in his corner and went up to him. 'Three years,' she said with a big smile. 'Enough for you to forget your mother.'

Her smile faded.

'What's wrong with him, looking at me like that?' she asked.

Uncle Pedro wrapped his arms around her and Aunt Aida took her hand. 'Sit down, first sit down, Josephine,' my aunt said. My mother's face changed.

'What's going on here?' she asked.

Slobber was pouring from Adrian's open mouth. My mother clasped her hand to her mouth and sat down between her sister and her brother.

Aunt Aida began to explain, stumbling for words. Uncle Pedro joined in, also explaining. My mother's face was frozen and only her eyebrows showed signs of her anguish. She burst into tears. She went to Adrian and hugged him tight but he pushed her away. She turned to Aunt Aida, her eyes throwing sparks, and began to insult her between sobs. 'You bitch, you bitch!' she said.

She raised her arm and brought it down on Aida's face.

'What kind of future can my son expect now, all because of you,' she shouted, slapping Aida around the face. Aida stood up but she didn't try to push her away or protect her face with her arms.

'I wish I hadn't come back,' said my mother. 'Why do all these things happen to me?'

My mother went on hitting Aida, while I put my hands over my face, the sound of the slaps ringing in my ears.

'I wish I hadn't come back, I wish I hadn't come back,' she continued.

Then she stopped slapping her sister and hugged her tight. Aida burst out crying too.

'Josephine! Enough,' said Uncle Pedro, pushing my mother towards my room.

It was the first time I had seen Aunt Aida cry.

Something inside me told me that no one but I deserved all those slaps. Although it was Aida's face that received them, I could feel the sting of them.

My mother spent a week crying over Adrian. Once she had exhausted all her sadness and all her reserves of tears, she called everyone into the sitting room. She sat on the ground with her suitcase open in front of her and gave out the presents she had brought from Bahrain for the members of the family, as if nothing had happened.

I wonder if she believed that what happened to Adrian happened for a reason, and for some purpose.

12

In one of her letters from Bahrain, my mother said she wanted to swim across the sea to Kuwait to meet my father or at least find out what had happened to him after the war. She didn't know that all she needed to do was come home to the Philippines and find out there.

One night in 1996, or about a year after my mother came back from Bahrain, I was lying on the sofa in the sitting room of our little house, after an exhausting day at work with my grandfather. Aunt Aida and Merla were watching television and my mother was with Adrian in my room because there was a power cut at her husband's house. Suddenly we heard Uncle Pedro calling 'Aida, Aida!' from outside. He opened the door and, clearly bursting to share some news, he asked, 'Where's Josephine? I went to her house and there was no one there.'

Aida pointed to the door of my room. 'She's in José's room,' she said. 'What's up?' Without answering, Pedro headed off to my room. My curiosity was aroused and I followed him.

When Pedro opened the door, letting light into the dark room, my mother put a finger to her lips. 'Shhh,' she said. 'Don't wake up the boy. I'll come and join you in a minute.'

In the small sitting room my mother sat down between Aida and Merla, while I stood next to Pedro.

'I delivered some goods to a company today,' he said.

Mother looked at his face with interest, her eyes half-closed.

'The company belongs to a Kuwaiti businessman,' Pedro continued.

Now her eyes opened wide. 'Go on. And then what?' she said.

'One of the staff said the man's well-known in Kuwait,' he continued, looking Mother straight in the face.

Mother stared back. 'A writer, a novelist, or something like that,' Pedro added.

Mother stood up straight. 'Do you think . . .?' she said.

* * *

Since my father had been writing for a Kuwaiti newspaper, my mother hoped it might be possible to get some information from this man, something that would lead her to him, or maybe she hoped that the man himself would turn out to be Rashid.

Pedro decided to take my mother to see the man the next day to ask him if he had heard of my father or if he could help us reach him or find out what had become of him.

My mother didn't sleep that night. She woke me up early in the morning and asked me to get changed and join her with Uncle Pedro.

'What's a Kuwaiti businessman doing in the Philippines?' my mother asked Pedro while we were on our way to meet the man.

'The people who work there say he's been living here for five years. But that's none of our business,' said Pedro.

At the man's office one of the staff told us he was away in Bahrain.

'Will he be staying there long?' Pedro asked.

'Two weeks at the most,' the man said. 'He has a play on there.'

Uncle Pedro turned to my mother and said, 'Well our little play here seems to be over.'

Mother turned to me and said, 'The man's in Bahrain.'

She paused a moment, then continued, 'He was here when I was in Bahrain, and today he's in Bahrain and I'm here.'

We went back to the car. My mother was speaking to herself: 'Everything happens for a reason, and for some purpose.'

She opened the car door and sat in the seat. 'I'd very much like to meet this man,' she said.

We went back later in the hope of meeting the Kuwaiti man when he was back from his trip. My mother pinned many hopes on meeting him. 'He's bound to know Rashid,' she said. 'Or perhaps he knows at least how we can get in touch with him. Fate has something in store for us.'

When we were almost home, in the narrow lane leading to Mendoza's land, Uncle Pedro stopped his truck to make way for a vehicle that had just come out.

When we asked Mendoza about the vehicle, he beamed with delight. 'Those guys were representatives from Smart Communications,' he said, taking a piece of paper out of his pocket. 'I've just signed a contract with them. They're renting six square metres of the land to set up a relay tower. They're going to pay rent every month.'

My mother looked away from Mendoza and waved her hand dismissively. 'A cockerel every month, more likely,' she said.

13

I really loved the piece of land I grew up on. I spent so much time alone there, looking at the things around me, that sometimes I thought I myself was one of the trees that grew there. I didn't rule out the possibility that my head might sprout leaves or that mangoes might grow behind my ears, or that if I lifted my arms a bunch of bananas would appear under my armpits. Sometimes I imagined myself as a humble pebble on the same piece of land. It might shift position, it might be buried by sand and then the rain might uncover it, but it would stay there, never crossing the bamboo fence that surrounded the land. I loved the green, the colour of life, with all its shades, and in the end I sometimes thought it was the only colour in the universe. And yet, though I loved the green on Mendoza's land, I hated Mendoza.

Even the land wasn't spared his greed. He destroyed the only thing of beauty I thought he had created. Despite his greed, there was one thing that had made me see him in a more favourable light – his interest in the land, the trees, his dog Whitey and his gang of cocks. I respected his interest in natural things, even if he didn't himself take the trouble to look after them. Instead his interest took the form of giving me orders to look after them for him. But when he agreed to let them put up that monstrosity of a tower on the land that I loved, crowding out the trees, I could no longer believe there was a good side to his character.

Often, mostly at night, I would lean my back against the trunk of the biggest tree on Mendoza's land, with a piece of flat land stretched out in front of me towards Inang Choleng's house. I would watch everything around me, except for the old woman's house in case the bee in my head stirred and started buzzing again. In that space I had another life. I would sit on the damp ground. The place would be shrouded in darkness, except for the light that slipped through from the windows of the four houses arranged around me – our house, Mendoza's house, Uncle Pedro's house and Inang Choleng's house.

The frogs croaking, the crickets chirping, Whitey barking and the other dogs in the neighbourhood barking back, and other noises I couldn't identify. The noises, coupled with the smell of the earth, would make me want to stay longer. If my mother couldn't find me at night before she went back to Alberto's house, she knew I would be sitting under my usual tree. She would open the window and shout, 'José! Come on! Come inside!' I would stand up and head back, with a feeling that the trees were bending their branches behind me and trying to grab me. The croaking of the frogs and the buzzing of the insects grew louder, and I sometimes imagined that among all the noises something was calling my name. The weeds caught my feet and made it hard to walk. I wasn't afraid of leaving these things behind me because I knew I would soon meet them again. By sunset the next day I would have prepared myself to meet my friends again.

As soon as I was home, Aida would comment, 'Ah, the Lord Buddha's back.'

I don't know why Mother would be upset that I was sitting under the trees. Perhaps she was worried I would strike roots so deep into the ground that I would never go back to my father's country. But even roots don't mean much sometimes.

I was more like a bamboo plant, which doesn't belong anywhere in particular. You can cut off a piece of the stalk and plant it without roots in any piece of ground. Before long the stalk sprouts new roots and starts to grow again in the new ground, with no past, no memory. It doesn't notice that people have different names for it – *kawayan* in the Philippines, *khaizuran* in Kuwait, and bamboo in many places.

Once the relay tower had been put up in the clearing in front of my favourite tree, I began to sit

14

One morning, about ten days after the relay tower went up on Mendoza's land, I was in my room when I heard Uncle Pedro honking the horn of his truck outside. I opened the window and shouted, 'Need any help, Uncle?' He gestured for me to come out.

My mother was sitting in the seat next to him. She opened the door and my little brother stepped down. 'José, take Adrian to Aida and you come back and come with us,' she said.

Off we went to the office of the Kuwaiti businessman.

'He's not coming today. You can come back tomorrow,' one of the staff told Uncle Pedro, but my mother insisted on meeting the man. The worker turned to a colleague and didn't say anything. His colleague picked up the phone and made a call. 'You can visit him at home at this address,' she said, writing it out on a piece of paper. 'If it's really so important.'

Uncle Pedro pulled up in front of a simple house, not much different from the one we lived in. 'Are you sure of the address?' my mother asked.

Pedro pointed towards the door of the truck. 'Go and check for yourself,' he said.

'This couldn't possibly be a Kuwaiti's house, Pedro,' she said.

Pedro didn't answer. She opened the door and turned to me. 'Come along, José,' she said.

I followed her while Pedro stayed in the truck waiting for us. Mother knocked on the door. We didn't have to wait long. 'Welcome, come in,' the man said in English.

He was a man in his forties. He seemed simple, perhaps compared with the image that went with Pedro's description of him as a Kuwaiti businessman. He was of medium height, thin, greying a little on the temples, calm-looking, and with a distinctive pointed moustache that drooped on the sides of his mouth, and black eyebrows that seemed to be thicker than they should be.

In his little sitting room, which was full of books, he asked us to sit in front of a small desk covered in papers and well-sharpened pencils.

'My name is Ismail,' he said, sitting behind the desk. I later found out that he was the Kuwaiti writer Ismail Fahd Ismail, who lived in the Philippines for six years after the liberation of Kuwait.

'I'm Josephine, sir,' said Mother.

Then she pointed at me. 'And this is Isa, my . . .'

'José!' I said, interrupting her.

'José. My son,' mother said, correcting herself.

'Pleased to meet you,' the man said with a smile, then paused, waiting for my mother to speak.

'Sir,' she said. 'I want to ask you about a man.'

The man's calm face showed signs of interest. 'I thought you needed a job!' he said.

'What I need is more important, sir,' she said.

The man nodded, encouraging her to continue.

'Sir, do you know a Kuwaiti man called Rashid?'

He gave a gentle smile. 'Thousands of Kuwaitis have this name,' he said.

'Rashid al-Tarouf, sir,' said my mother, more specifically.

The man raised an eyebrow.

'A writer,' my mother continued, 'who lives in . . .'

'Qortuba?' the man interjected.

'Yes, yes, sir,' said my mother in surprise.

There was silence for a few seconds.

'Do you know him, sir? Please.'

The man nodded.

'Do you know him personally?' she asked.

The man kept nodding and my mother went on talking. 'I used to work in his mother's house in Kuwait. We haven't had any news of him since the war.'

The man looked calm again.

'Do you know what's happened to him? Where is he now, sir?'

He didn't answer. He seemed uncertain and thoughtful. He pointed at a large stack of papers on the desk in front of him and said, 'He's here.'

My mother's eyes almost popped out of her head. She turned to me and whispered to me in Filipino so that the man wouldn't understand, 'Damn Pedro. The man seems to be crazy.'

The man smiled. 'I'm not mad,' he said in Filipino.

My mother blushed and the man continued in English. 'I was in Kuwait during the war. We were part of a resistance group and Rashid was one of the members.'

My mother stared at the man's face as he went on: 'You look surprised, but I'm even more surprised than you.'

The man put his hand on the large stack of paper. 'This is an account of our activities and the events that took place during the seven months of occupation. I started writing it more than five years ago, and the strange thing is . . .'

The man hesitated before continuing.

'Yesterday evening . . .'

My mother nodded, pressing him to go on.

'Only yesterday evening, Rashid's role in it came to an end when he fell into the hands of the occupation forces.'

When the man had finished, my mother didn't say a word. She was silent in the truck too and at home. After meeting the Kuwaiti man all my mother had come up with was the news that my father had been captured, and an envelope full of money that the man had given her before we left his house. My mother hadn't told him that she was Rashid's wife, or that I was his only son.

15

After the Kuwaiti man told us that my father had been captured in the war, Kuwait no longer meant anything to me. I automatically stopped thinking about going back to my father's country. But my mother on the other hand continued to bring it up from time to time. 'The promise will be fulfilled,' she would say.

'And what if Rashid is . . .' Aunt Aida started to ask her, but then she stopped and left the rest of the question hanging. Both of them knocked on the wooden part of the sofa.

'Even if Rashid is dead, his promise won't die,' my mother said.

I felt sorry for my mother. What kind of faith could she have that didn't waver through all those years? She was still building hopes on a man who went missing in war ages ago. I had lost interest and no longer had hopes of going to Wonderland, despite my mother's faith.

What if the promise was fulfilled, I wondered. What if the man called Rashid did reappear? Could I really be replanted, like a bamboo stalk?

★ ★ ★

In 1997, my mother began looking for work and the first person she thought she could ask for help was Ismail, the Kuwaiti man. But by that time he had wrapped up all his business in the Philippines and gone back to Kuwait.

After some effort my mother did manage to find a job as a servant to a rich family that lived in Forbes Park in Makati. She spent the whole day working in their house, came back at the end of the day, had dinner with us and then went off to her own house with Adrian.

I felt my mother gradually growing apart from me. She was away at work and busy with Adrian and his special needs. She was often in a bad mood and always absent-minded, and I no longer saw her smile. She had changed a lot but I understood the reasons for all that and I didn't hold it against her.

While my mother grew distant, my relationship with Aida and Merla grew stronger. I was close to both of them, despite the distance between them. I never heard Merla calling Aida 'Mama'. Instead she called her by her name: Aida. She went out without asking permission and came back late at night. She went on trips to places far out of Manila and Aunt Aida couldn't stop her. Although my aunt treated her daughter well, sometimes too well, and although she always tried to please her, Merla reacted in the opposite way and never treated her mother well.

The way Merla mistreated Aida made me sympathise with my aunt. One evening I heard her complaining to my mother that Merla never called her 'Mama'. From then on I started calling her 'Mama Aida'. It had quite an effect on the way my aunt behaved.

When someone ends up having two mothers, you can be sure they're equally confused about their names, their country and their religion.

16

I had my twelfth birthday in 2000 and I had to go to church to be confirmed.

'Josephine!' Mama Aida said. 'José is twelve now.'

We were sitting around the dining table in the kitchen.

'You go smoke your poisons, Aida, and let José go his own way,' Mother replied.

'I've given up smoking marijuana,' Mama Aida retorted sharply.

'Since when?' asked Mother with interest.

'From today,' answered Mama Aida, without looking at my mother.

Mother didn't comment, but went to feed Adrian. Mama Aida continued, 'We have to take José to church, Josephine.'

Adrian automatically made the sign of the cross in the air as soon as Mama Aida mentioned the church.

'Sooner or later José will turn Muslim in his father's country,' Mother said. 'If you're such a believer . . .' she resumed, then paused a moment. 'Then your daughter is now sixteen. Make her behave properly, then take *her* to church, or to hell.'

Mama Aida didn't say a word.

★ ★ ★

My first visit to the Manila Cathedral was with Mama Aida, who insisted I be confirmed in the cathedral rather than just in the little parish church where I was baptised years earlier. Mama Aida asked Uncle Pedro and his wife to come and witness the rite and to join her as my sponsors. The two agreed, but my mother stuck to her position – 'He'll embrace Islam sooner or later' – and she didn't attend.

We went through the big wooden door – Mama Aida, Pedro and his wife, and me. We stopped in front of the statue of an angel carrying a font of holy water. Everyone dipped the tips of their fingers into the water and made the sign of the cross, and I did likewise.

The cathedral certainly gave me a sense of awe, but I wasn't sure if that was because of faith. Maybe the candles, the statues and the icons played a part too.

Mama Aida, Uncle Pedro and his wife sat down and started saying prayers, while I stood in the middle on a long red carpet, wooden pews on my left and right. I had a new sensation I hadn't known before this visit – complete serenity. There was a decorated ceiling held up by eight marble columns, large crosses on the walls and stained-glass windows. The sunbeams threw the colours of the glass on to the marble floor, and a statue of the Virgin Mary, in a white dress and a blue cloak, stood above the altar, surrounded on all sides by bouquets of flowers.

In the front seats there were lots of boys about my age, accompanied by their parents, waiting for the bishop to conduct the ceremony. Mama Aida's excitement was a ritual in itself.

We finished the confirmation ceremony and the bishop blessed us with holy water after we had answered 'I do' to his questions: 'Do you reject Satan and all his works, and all his empty promises?' 'Do you believe in God the Father almighty, creator of heaven and earth?' 'Do you believe in Jesus Christ, his only Son, our Lord?' 'Do you believe in the holy Catholic Church, the communion of saints, the forgiveness of sins, the resurrection of the body, and life everlasting?'

What difficult questions you ask, Father! And how easy it is to say, 'I do, I do.'

Lucky Adrian. These questions don't give him any trouble. He has no doubt and no faith. No uncertainty and no fear. If only it had been me who nearly drowned that night, so that my brain cells would be damaged, instead of his.

Before we left the cathedral Mama Aida gave me a crucifix on a chain. Her happiness that day was the most beautiful part of the confirmation ceremony.

17

'José, José, José . . .'

I heard the call dozens of times a day from my grandfather, and although I longed for a real name, it made me want not to have a name at all, at least when Grandfather was around, so that he couldn't call me. The reason for the constant summoning wasn't that he wanted to talk to me. When Mendoza called my name, an order was bound to follow. 'Fill the trough with water for the cocks.' 'Clean out the pen.' 'Take the scraps to Whitey.' 'Climb the mango tree and pick some mangoes.' 'Warm up the oil and follow me.'

No one but me obeyed Mendoza, especially after my mother moved to her husband's house and had Adrian. She insisted on staying with Adrian in a better environment, away from her father's house, even if her new place was just a little house at the end of the sandy lane that ran past my grandfather's land.

Ironically, while Mother wanted Adrian to grow up in a better environment, Adrian himself, the lucky boy, knew nothing of what was happening around him.

My mother won her freedom through marriage. Years earlier Mama Aida had won her freedom by rebelling. In Merla's case, her freedom and salvation lay, leaving aside her personality, in her association with Mama Aida. This made all of them invisible to Mendoza, so all he could see was me, because I had not yet won my freedom. I hated my name when it came from his dark lips, through the gaps in his brown teeth, from a mouth that smelled of tobacco. I had visions of him dropping down dead as soon as he shouted out his usual summons – 'Joséeeeee!' – in a voice that grated like nails on a blackboard. I would run to him, I would bow down, I would take his hand and press the back of his hand to my forehead in a show of respect, but inside me I heaped curses on him.

He was short, dark-skinned, with deep lines in his forehead and cheeks. His eyes were sunken, almost buried under his bushy eyebrows. He coughed constantly as if he were about to cough up his lungs. Ever since I was young I'd thought that Mendoza was at death's door, but the dying went on many years. I could easily imagine what he would look like dead, because it wouldn't have been very different from the way he looked before he died: he was just a bony skeleton covered in wrinkled skin.

In his little house he lay on his wooden bed all day with his face buried in his smelly pillow. His upper part was naked. Although I was young at the time, I had enough experience to work as a professional masseur, since I played that role every day. I would sit on Mendoza's buttocks, which were as hard as his wooden bed, and let a thin trickle of cheap warm oil stream on to his back from the plastic bottle in my hand. I would press my hands against the small of his back and work my way up the bony vertebrae as far as his neck. 'Aahh,' he would groan. 'Keep pressing.' I was terrified his skin might come undone, exposing his backbone underneath. Like a bird waiting for day to break so it could fly off into the trees, I waited for the signal of liberation that would release me from this arduous task. As soon as he was breathing regularly I would gradually reduce the pressure on his back, switching from my palms to my fingertips, until he began his snoring concerto and I could slip away to Merla.

18

Merla is four years older than me. The only thing that kept me away from her was being summoned by Mendoza. How I envied her. My grandfather was so frightened of Aida that he didn't dare give Merla any chores to do. Her personality also played a role in it, which added to the burden on me because I had to obey his constant requests.

Merla has a strong personality. She's been clever and a natural leader ever since she was a child. Boys were frightened of her. She didn't often use her tongue, as other girls did, but her hands went into action automatically if she was angry.

She was slim and relatively tall, with a pale, slightly pink complexion. Her hair was brown and wavy. Her eyes were blue, which made her a classic mestiza, though she hated the label. Her beauty reminded her of the unknown European father she hated. Because of him she absolutely detested the way she looked and everything European.

We grew close after Mama Aida began to look after me in the four months that my mother spent at her husband's house every year, before she settled permanently in her new house.

I missed Merla terribly when I was in Kuwait, far from the Philippines.

I longed for her as much as I longed for the colour green, which was hard to find in Kuwait. I missed her like I missed the smell of grass after a downpour, when the wet soil gives off refreshing vapours that bathe the human spirit.

I wish we could bring back the days that are gone with those whose paths have now diverged from ours, and live them again with other people, but no one in this world can replace anyone else. And how much more so if that someone is Merla? I loved to be with her.

She was always a mystery, despite all the time I spent with her, because she hid an aspect of herself that I was not aware of. One day she came home with the letters *MM* tattooed on her arm and I started pestering her with questions about it.

"'M' for Merla,' she explained. 'And because I love myself so much, a single "M" wouldn't be enough.'

She was strikingly beautiful, powerfully feminine, with a sculpted body, wild hair and full lips, but I didn't notice any of that until I saw her in a new light, later. I had just turned fourteen when I first dreamed about her. In my wet dream she was adventurous, and I was too. When I woke up I couldn't believe that the dream hadn't been real. It happened again and again as I shed the mantle of boyhood and grew into a man. The sensations I had in my dream – the touch, the taste, the smell and the effect the dream had – came back to me whenever Merla appeared. She was the same girl who had grown up in the same house as me. Nothing in her had changed. It was the way I saw her that was different. It's not the way a woman looks and behaves that arouses a man's instinct, so much as the image he has of her in his head. And inside my head, when I looked at Merla, I only saw her the way she looked in my dreams.

But there were limits to where our relationship could go because, apart from the age difference, which seemed big to me, Merla was my cousin.

Once, when I was six and Merla was ten, I said to my mother, 'Mama, I want to marry Merla.'

My mother burst out laughing. 'It looks like you're going to turn Muslim quicker than I imagined,' she said.

Mama Aida also looked surprised. 'Are Muslims allowed to marry their cousins?' she asked.

Mother nodded, and I said, 'In that case I'm a Muslim!'

Mama Aida put her hand to her breast and said, 'Perish the thought. My daughter and I are Catholics.' She roared with laughter and pointed at me threateningly. 'Go back to your father's country, and marry your grandmother if you want,' she said.

That day I was upset that there was something to prevent me marrying Merla. I was in love with her and very jealous, but all those were childish dreams that soon faded. It came back years later in a different form, in dreams that were different from the dreams of childhood.

Merla, her boldness, her rebelliousness, her crazy talk, hanging out on the streets of Manila – the mestiza girl and the Arab boy, drinking iced tea in front of the juice stands on the pavement, visiting Fort Santiago, the old Spanish citadel, our trips up the mountains and down the valleys and into the Biak-no-Bato caves, sitting by the lake with a view of the famous Taal volcano and watching the boats with fishermen seared by the sun.

On those trips, we had fun for free, as Merla put it. We only spent a minimal amount on transport and sometimes, but rarely, some of the places charged a fee to enter a world that seemed infinite. Everything except the train or the bus or the Jeepny and the entrance charge, if there was one, was free. No one tries to charge for the hours you spend looking at the volcano. No one tells you your time is up when you're sitting under a giant tree that has grown out of the heart of a massive boulder. No one tells you not to float on the surface of the lake, looking up at the clouds and counting them. There's nothing to stop you reaching out and picking a delicious fruit, and sharing it with the one you love.

'Have you noticed? Nature gives us happiness for free,' Merla said.

'But we bought tickets to go in,' I said, stuffing my hand into the pocket of my shorts and taking out two pieces of yellow paper. 'Do you think they have the right to make us pay?' I asked.

Merla looked at the sky, then the trees and the rocks around us. 'It's not nature's fault if people charge for things they don't own,' she said.

She paused and then continued. 'Besides, we bought the tickets just to get through the gate, and after that everything is free.'

I didn't comment on what she said even if I wasn't convinced, since because of our age difference, which seemed massive, I thought that Merla was wise and understood everything. I also wanted to avoid getting into an argument with her, because I would lose in the end as usual, and because, as a boy of fourteen at the time, I voluntarily deferred to the judgment of a girl of eighteen.

We were in Biak-no-Bato that day, some time in 2002. It's an awesome place on a giant scale, with massive trees that reach the sky and giant boulders overhanging steep cliffs. It was my first trip with Merla so far from home. I looked like the travellers I had seen on television. Like an explorer, I had a backpack with everything I needed for the trip. I wore shorts that went just below my knees and that looked baggy because they had so many pockets, and high boots that were good for walking on rough, stony ground. Merla carried a flashlight that we used when it was dark in the caves. She wore a white blouse with short sleeves and very skimpy denim shorts, and tied her hair back. Damn her! If only she weren't my cousin.

Obviously she was my guide, because she had visited the place before, and she asked the official guide not to come inside with us. I followed her, listening to her explanation. 'Many years ago the heroes of the revolution stayed in these caves,' she said, 'making their plans for revolution out of sight of the Spanish occupiers.'

She talked a lot about the history of the place. When the path was clear I listened, but I ignored what she was saying when the going was tough, for example when we had to climb steps through clefts in the rock. When I felt dizzy halfway across a wooden suspension bridge I asked her to stop talking. She made fun of me: 'These bridges and stairways were made for people like you, you wimp!' she said. She pushed me on, urged me to keep walking. 'These bridges and stairways didn't exist when the heroes of the revolution stayed here,' she added.

'So how did they move from one cave to another?' I asked.

'They were heroes and . . .' she said, sticking out her tongue to make fun of me.

'And what?' I asked, wondering why she hadn't finished her sentence and impatient to hear her answer.

She pointed at the massive boulders. 'The rocks must have been in league with them when they let them stay inside the caves,' she whispered, as if she didn't want the rocks to hear her.

With my cousin Merla even ordinary stories became fantasies. She had an amazing ability to turn the simplest of stories into myths. She was a magician, Merla.

She was walking along, and I was following, looking at her body from behind – its curves, the way she swayed when she walked, the softness of her legs, the *MM* tattoo on her arm. I wanted to remove one of the *M*s and put a *J* in its place. The dream I had had a few days earlier was very much on my mind as I watched her. The only thing that distracted me from my fantasies was the feeling of claustrophobia when the path took us up between massive boulders and the tangled branches above us blocked out the sunlight and the breeze.

Halfway across one big wooden bridge between two bluffs on either side of a large lake, Merla stopped and pointed down.

'Lots of workers drowned in this lake when they were building this bridge,' she said.

I held tight to the ropes on the side of the bridge. I plucked up courage and tried to look down, but it was no use.

'They say this bridge couldn't have been built here without some sacrifices,' Merla continued.

She put her hand on my shoulder. A strange, unexpected feeling came over me. She slowly brought her face close to mine. I shivered with pleasure and closed my eyes. I moved my face closer to hers, but suddenly she hit me on the head with her flashlight.

'What are you doing, you idiot?' she shouted.

Confused, with the palm of my hand I rubbed the spot at the front of my head where she had hit me. I didn't say anything because it was obvious what I had been about to do. Merla got over what had happened, as if nothing had happened. She opened her eyes wide and finished off what she had been saying before I had closed my eyes.

'The workers who drowned,' she whispered, 'were sacrificial offerings to the spirit of the place, to persuade them to let humans build the bridge.'

She shook her head sadly. 'They must have been good people,' she said.

And because I didn't pay much attention to what she was saying, she carried on explaining. 'Rizal said the victim must be pure and spotless if the sacrifice is to be acceptable,' she said.

I wasn't thinking about the tragedy of the dead workers when they built the bridge, or about what Rizal said. I was too busy thinking about the bump that had started to form on my head and Merla's expression 'the spirit of the place'. My mind wandered. I looked around at the big rocks, the giant trees and the vast caves. I swear I could hear the rocks groaning around me, the leaves rustling, the trickling of the water, everything whispering something in languages I did not understand.

Ever since that day I've believed that everything has a spirit. Everything. Looking at the lake below the hanging bridge, Merla said, 'I'd like to end my life by jumping from this bridge.'

I looked at her suspiciously and said, 'But my mother says only cowards who can't face up to life try to commit suicide.' She didn't hear me, or perhaps she just pretended not to hear.

While we were on the bridge, the birds in the sky suddenly disappeared. 'Follow me,' said Merla as she headed deeper into the forest. We could hear the birds twittering and making other calls from somewhere in the trees. As we walked along, Merla said, 'Hurry up. It's going to rain.' I looked at the sky through the tangle of branches but I couldn't see any sign of clouds.

'How can you tell that, Merla?' I asked.

She pointed to the trees. 'See how the birds have hidden away,' she said.

Then she turned to a wall of rock on her left. 'Look here,' she said.

Thousands of ants were climbing the wall.

'What's that got to do with rain?' I asked.

'You don't understand anything,' she answered irritably.

I hated the way she boasted that she knew everything. Sometimes I had questions to which I didn't know the answers. I would be about to ask my cousin, who had more experience than me, but I would hold back in case she gave me her usual answer: 'You don't understand anything.'

We kept walking along the narrow paths that overlooked the deep valleys between the massive rocks. Clouds gathered and within minutes they blocked out the rays of the sun. Claps of thunder started to shake the place, and torrential rain soon followed. The clouds just dumped all the water they were carrying, proving to me that I really didn't understand anything.

We ran between the boulders and took shelter in the largest cave. We sat together on a big rock inside the cave. All we could see through the entrance to the cave was the rain pouring down in sheets and a dark green haze. The place was very damp inside and the combined smell of wet earth and bat droppings gave me a strange feeling. Merla turned on her flashlight and swept the beam over the rocks above us. There were hundreds of bats hanging head down from the rocks.

I was right next to Merla. My leg was touching her wet, bare leg. I had various feelings, but not fear. I would never be frightened in Merla's presence, even if we faced death together.

I remembered the dream. A sense of numbness began to seep into my body from the part that was touching her leg. I could feel the pulse in my temples, and the humidity, wherever it came from, added to my sense of confusion.

'What are you thinking about?' asked Merla.

'Nothing,' I replied without thinking, as if on the defensive against some implied accusation.

Who was I trying to lie to, I wonder. Merla didn't wait long before hitting back. 'Don't imagine that I don't understand you,' she said.

The raindrops pounded the rocky ground outside the cave with a staccato rhythm matched by my heartbeats. 'For some time now, the way you look at me, the way you behave,' Merla continued.

She moved her face close to mine. I could feel her breath. The air she breathed out went into my lungs as I breathed in. Her eyes stared into my eyes. My eyes, open this time, were fixed on her flashlight. The blood throbbed under the bruise on my head.

'What you're thinking is impossible, José,' she said.

I felt a fear I had never known in her presence. 'Yes, yes, impossible,' I agreed.

We were still face to face. 'Why is it impossible?' she asked. 'Do you know why?'

I looked straight into her eyes. 'Because you're my cousin,' I said.

She smiled a strange half-hearted smile. 'A silly reason like that wouldn't stop me doing something that I really wanted,' she said.

She turned to face the entrance to the cave. 'There's another reason that prevents me,' she said.

She switched off the flashlight. The light was so faint I could hardly see her face. 'If you weren't a man . . .' she continued.

19

'José, José, José.'

I was fed up with being summoned by my grandfather. The grievance rankled, but it rarely came to the surface and never passed my lips.

When my mother talked about how she had suffered, psychologically at least, when working for the old lady in Kuwait, I didn't understand what she meant until I found myself working so hard for Mendoza.

After a long, exhausting day, I would leave my window open to hear the sound of the crickets, but that was rarely the only thing I heard.

'Damn you, bastards!' Mendoza's drunken voice, alongside the sound of the crickets. 'Merla.' He said Merla's name in a hushed voice, then shouted out my name: 'José!'

I didn't answer.

'You bastards.'

I opened my eyes. The shadows of the bamboo plants danced on the walls of my room, cast by the flickering candlelight that shone through Grandfather's window.

'José!'

I stuck my fingers in my ears. The silence was unbearable. I took my fingers out. I listened carefully. The crickets came back, and . . .

'José!'

I pretended to be asleep.

'I know you can hear me.'

The sound of wood knocking against wood. A cup of *tuba* on the table.

'I hate bastards!' shouted Mendoza.

I jumped to the window, put my arms through the iron bars and imagined I had my hands around his neck.

'I'm not a bastard,' I said.

Mendoza didn't respond. Might he perhaps come through the door behind me? He didn't stay silent for long.

'Can you prove that?' he said, and burst out laughing, then started to cough.

'Curse these crickets. I wish they'd come and live in my room, so that I could hear them and close the window at the same time.'

I brought our brief conversation to an end by slamming the window shut.

★   ★   ★

'José!'

Now it was the next morning. 'Bring me a banana.'

'A yellow banana,' he added after a moment's pause.

Of course the banana should be yellow, so why did my grandfather insist on saying what colour. Ah! He knew the banana trees around our house only had bunches of small green bananas that weren't ready to pick yet. *I hate you, Mendoza.*

'The bananas are still green, Grandfather.'

He pretended to be angry. 'You must be able to find a yellow banana,' he answered in his annoying voice.

'No, there aren't any,' I replied, my patience exhausted.

'Are you sure?'

'Yes, I'm sure,' I said, though I knew what he was planning to say.

'OK, I hope you grow a thousand eyes so that you can see things clearly,' he said, raising his voice.

'I'll pray to the Lord to make your wish come true, Grandfather,' I answered him calmly.

He didn't reply. I was sure he was about to explode with anger.

I was fourteen then, and Mendoza's wish still frightened me as much as it always had.

★   ★   ★

For years I used to wake up every morning to the alarm clock next door: 'José!' As soon as I opened my eyes, I would run my hand over my face, and thank the Lord when I had checked it was still covered with skin.

Grandfather was cunning. He knew the effect the old legend had had on me since I was a child – the legend of Pinya.

He had fun frightening me with a fate similar to that of the girl in the legend. If he couldn't think of any other tasks for me to perform, he would ask me to bring him something – anything from anywhere. Because he knew that the thing wasn't where he sent me to find it, he would be waiting impatiently for me to come back empty-handed. Then he would spring his malicious little curse on me: 'I hope you grow a thousand eyes so you can see things clearly.'

I wasn't yet seven when Mendoza started frightening me with this wish of his. As soon as he said the words I would be off, running in fear like a mad thing, looking for whatever it was in the place he suggested, and in other places too, while he roared with laughter behind my back.

★   ★   ★

The story of Pinya was one of many that my mother and Mama Aida used to tell me before I went to sleep. I would ask them to repeat the stories and I enjoyed them every time as if I were hearing them for the first time, except for the legend of Pinya. I hated that one from the first time I heard it, and I asked Mama Aida not to repeat it. Even so, I couldn't forget it.

★　★　★

Once upon a time, in a certain village, there lived a woman with a beautiful daughter. The daughter was spoilt because she was an only child. She was badly behaved and lazy and she had no initiative. Her mother met all her demands anyway, because there was nothing in the world she loved more than Pinya.

Pinya was well-known in the village and the other children envied the advantages she enjoyed that weren't available to them. One day Pinya's mother fell ill. She wanted to get well as soon as possible so she could look after Pinya, but for the moment it was the mother who needed looking after.

'Pinya, Pinya,' she called weakly, unable to get out of bed. 'Come here, my girl. I need you for something,' she added.

Pinya was busy playing in the backyard.

'OK, Mama. What is it?' asked Pinya, standing at the foot of her mother's bed.

'I'm exhausted. I can't get up,' her mother said. 'I'm hungry but I can't eat anything solid. I'd like you to bring me a bowl of congee.'

Pinya was surprised.

'It's very simple, Pinya,' her mother continued. 'Put a little rice in a pot. Add some water and a little sugar, then leave it to simmer for a while.'

'That's really hard to do, Mama,' Pinya said impatiently.

'You have to do it, Pinya,' her mother said weakly. 'What will your poor mother eat if you don't?'

Pinya dragged her feet downstairs to the kitchen.

She got the pot ready, and the rice, the sugar and the water, but she couldn't find the big spoon. 'How can I stir it without the spoon?' she wondered. She shouted up to her mother, 'Mama, where can I find the big spoon?'

'It's with the other kitchen stuff,' her mother groaned. 'You know where I put it, Pinya!'

But Pinya couldn't find the spoon with the other utensils and didn't take the trouble to look for it anywhere else.

'I can't find it, Mama,' she shouted, 'and I can't make you congee without it.'

'Oh, the lazy child,' her mother sighed, half in despair and half in anger. 'You haven't even looked anywhere else,' she shouted down. 'I hope you grow a thousand eyes so you can see things,' she added angrily.

As soon as she uttered the words, the house fell silent. There was no more clattering of plates in the kitchen. 'Perhaps she's started cooking,' said Pinya's mother, trying to reassure herself.

A long time passed, and all was still in the house. There was no sound of pots and pans in the kitchen, and no smells of cooking from downstairs. The mother grew seriously worried about Pinya. With all the strength she had left, she shouted out, 'Pinya! Pinya!' But Pinya didn't answer.

The neighbours noticed that Pinya's mother was calling her and crying. 'Oh! You know how Pinya behaves. Don't worry. She must be off playing with her friends somewhere,' said one of the neighbours, trying to reassure her. 'Perhaps she's upset you asked her to make congee. She'll come back soon,' he added.

Pinya's mother was comforted by what the neighbour said but the feeling didn't last long. She struggled out of bed to look for Pinya in the village and ask people if they had seen her, but there was no trace of the girl. Her mother was exhausted. She cried and sobbed, but Pinya still couldn't be found.

One sunny day, as Pinya's mother was sweeping the backyard, she spotted a strange and unfamiliar fruit, about the size of a small child's head and with thick green leaves sprouting from the top. Surprised, she went up to it and ran her fingers over the outside of the fruit. 'It feels strange. It has a thousand eyes,' she said. Then she repeated that last sentence to herself and suddenly remembered the wish she had made for her daughter.

Pinya's mother was convinced that Pinya had turned into the fruit and now had a thousand eyes, as she had wished, but none of the eyes could see or shed tears.

Because Pinya's mother still loved her more than anything else in the world, she tended the fruit and, faithful to Pinya's memory, made a vow to collect the seeds of the strange fruit and replant them. The plants multiplied in her backyard and she started giving some of them to her neighbours and to the other villagers, who called them piña, pineapple, after the unfortunate girl.

This myth no longer frightened me, even when Mendoza kept saying, within earshot of me, that he wished I would grow a thousand eyes. But even so, ever since I heard the legend, I haven't been able to eat pineapple.

Something inside me tells me a pineapple was once a person, Pinya the little Filipina girl.

20

In 2004 Maria appeared in our lives. She was Merla's closest friend, and now I had an explanation for the tattoo with which Merla had adorned, or disfigured, her silky arm: *MM*.

Maria was a weird girl. I had heard her name from Merla for some time but I had never seen her till then. When she started visiting us at home, no one in the family warmed to her. She visited often and spent plenty of time with Merla in her room. Mama Aida didn't hide her feelings towards Maria: she received her with a frown, and this caused many problems between Mama Aida and Merla. Mama Aida warned Merla about Maria all the time and told her frankly that she wasn't comfortable about her. There were repeated arguments. Merla did what she wanted. The day would end with Mama Aida crying in bed before going to sleep.

I didn't have any hostile feelings towards Maria because of what Mama Aida thought. Despite her strange appearance – the little hairs that showed on her temples, her short hair, her loose clothes and her way of walking, which was inappropriate for a girl – the reason I didn't take a liking to her was that she had imposed her will on my cousin.

Merla kept her distance from me and we had absolutely nothing in common any more. We no longer spent the evenings together in my room or went on trips to faraway places. Nothing that made my relationship with Merla special was left after Maria got hold of her. Merla wasn't even satisfied with the time she spent with her weird friend outside or at home; she installed a phone line in her room so they could chat all night.

Although I was attached to Mama Aida and loved her, and she looked after me, our house was no longer what it had been once Merla started staying out till the early hours. She chatted with Maria on the phone, woke up late and spent the rest of the day outside with her friend.

Every day, when I was working with Grandfather, I would see Merla heading to the sandy lane at the end of Mendoza's land, jumping on the back of Maria's motorcycle and wrapping her arms around Maria's waist. Then they would set off for an unknown destination.

In my dreams Merla was mine, but in real life she was Maria's.

But I couldn't get Merla out of my heart. Religion didn't stop me wanting to have her and her preference for her own gender didn't stop me thinking about her in my sleep and in my daydreams.

* * *

One time that year I woke up in the middle of the night. Mama Aida was shouting and pounding on one of the doors upstairs. I was still in bed.

'Keep quiet! Keep quiet, you whores!' Mendoza shouted through his window nearby. 'Get up, you son of a whore, and go and see what's happening upstairs,' he added, speaking to me.

'You get up and go see, if you dare,' I muttered to myself.

On the upper floor Mama Aida was kicking the door of Merla's room and pounding on it with her fists like a madwoman.

'What's happening, Mama?' I asked, pushing her back from the door.

'Can't you smell it? That girl is crazy,' she said.

I could smell cigarette smoke from Merla's room.

'What's new about that, Mama? You know Merla smokes,' I said.

She pushed me away and attacked the door again, pounding on it hysterically. 'That's not cigarettes,' she said.

She kicked the door with her foot. 'Open the door or else!'

'Merla's smoking marijuana,' she added, turning to face me.

Mama Aida, so assertive upstairs, was weaker than I had ever seen her once we were in the sitting room downstairs.

As Maria started up her motorcycle, breaking the silence of the night outside, Mama Aida was sobbing inside. She took her daughter's hands and kissed them.

'Please, I beg you, don't go,' she said.

Merla looked away, towards the front door, and picked up her bag of clothes.

'Merla, I beg you. Merla, don't do it.'

Mama Aida locked the door and stood leaning back against it.

'Get out of the way, Aida,' Merla said. 'Your begging won't do any good.'

Mama Aida slumped to the ground, her energy spent, her back still against the door. 'This isn't the life I want for you, Merla, please.' She covered her face with her hands and sobbed. 'I want you to have a real life. A house, a husband and children.'

'That's enough!' shouted Merla. 'You said a husband and children!'

I cried because Mama Aida was crying, while Merla went out shouting: 'After everything you've said about men you want me to have a husband and children!' But suddenly Merla's voice cracked. 'Look at me,' she said. 'Look what's happened to me! Where's my father?'

She burst out crying and, trying to fight back her sobs, she continued, 'Look at yourself. At your drunken father in his house. Look what's happened to him. Look what's happened to yourself.'

She pointed at me. 'Look at him! Look at everyone here!'

Merla rushed to the door, grabbed the door handle and pulled on it with all her might.

'No, no, Merla, I beg you,' said Mama Aida, her face covered in tears and snot, as she pressed her back against the door to keep it closed, but as usual Merla proved to be stronger.

The sound of the motorcycle faded into the distance and disappeared.

PART 3

Isa . . . The First Wandering

'To doubt God is to doubt one's own conscience,
and in consequence it would be to doubt
everything.'
José Rizal

I

Now that Merla had left home, there was nothing left to persuade me to stay. If Mama Aida had been a reason to stay, she wasn't any longer, especially when she went back to drinking and smoking after the fight with Merla.

I was sixteen. I left school. My mother was upset, but I had taken my decision. 'I'm going to look for a job,' I said.

When I took this decision I had only intended to break free of subjugation to Mendoza and the demands that had become intolerable after he fell ill. I was prepared to do the same kind of work that he gave me to do, provided it was somewhere else and provided I was paid for it. Once the things were gone that had me feel at peace on Mendoza's plot of land – Aida's good behaviour and Merla's company – I no longer had any reason to stay. Mama Aida's faith had made me feel that I wasn't alone, and I had started to draw some peace of mind from her faith. When she abandoned her faith, I lost that sense, and my own weak faith was shaken. For the first time I felt I was alone and that I held my own fate in my hands. I was terrified when I realised that all I had to fall back on was my own resources.

My mother tried to dissuade me. She begged me. She warned me and threatened me. She sent Alberto to see me several times, but I had learned from Merla how to be stubborn and persistent. Only Uncle Pedro stood by me in my decision. He lent me some money and gave me a mobile phone. 'Stay in touch,' he said.

He arranged for me to meet a man he knew who sold bananas and said the man would help me. He put his hand on my head and said, 'Listen, José. I don't like to give advice, since I very much need it myself, but . . .' He took his hand off my head and put it on my shoulder. 'If you want to avoid problems at work, make sure you're on good terms with your boss. If you want to avoid problems in life, make sure you're on good terms with the Lord.'

★ ★ ★

My grandfather's health had deteriorated by this time and he made many more demands. He raved more at night, whether he'd been drinking *tuba* or not. The daily massage sessions, which once took one hour, now took several hours. The shouting at night, which I couldn't stand, had changed into monologues addressed to his dead wife. He started shouting names I'd never heard before and when I asked Mama Aida about them, she said they were the names of people in our family who had died long before. Then he stopped the monologues and started shrieking frightening things like 'Help! Help! He's looking at me.' I jumped out of bed, went to his house, and looked in the corner by the ceiling where he was looking, but there was nothing there. 'Look at him, José,' he said. 'Can you see him? He's pointing at me and telling me to go with him.' He covered his face with his hands. 'Help! Save me. I don't want to go.'

'There's nothing, Grandfather. Nothing there,' I said. I would have felt sorry for him if it wasn't for my memories of how he had treated me.

With his hand over his face, he moved his fingers apart and peeked out between them. 'Look at him! He's there!' he shrieked in terror.

I went over to the corner and waved my hands in the air. 'There's nothing there, Grandfather,' I said.

'Go closer, José. Go closer.'

At his insistence I went further into the corner. 'Take him!' he shouted, addressing no one. 'Take him instead of me, please.'

My grandfather was as shameless in moments of weakness as he was in moments of strength.

I moved a small table up to the wall and stood on it, so that I could get my head right into the top corner of the room.

'See, Grandfather. There's nothing here,' I said.

He pulled up the bed cover and hid under it. 'Damn you!' he sobbed. 'I hope you grow a thousand eyes so you can see things clearly.'

I jumped off the table and went to the fruit basket in our kitchen. I picked up a pineapple and took it back to Grandfather's house. He was still under the cover. I put the pineapple on the small table I'd been standing on and left, closing the door behind me.

★   ★   ★

I spent the whole day behind a cart selling bananas in Manila's Chinatown. All I earned from my work was a commission on sales, which varied from day to day. But even on Saturdays and Sundays, the busiest days, it was hardly worth anything.

On the pavement opposite where I parked my cart, Cheng parked his cart, with the narrow street between us. Cheng was a Buddhist of Chinese origin, born in the year of the tiger, 4683 according to the Chinese calendar. He was eighteen at the time and worked for the same banana merchant. His commission was more than my commission and he sold twice as many bananas as me because of his experience in this work and because he knew so many customers. When I asked him if we could share a place to live, he asked me when I was born. I told him I was born on 3 April

1988. He closed his eyes, thought a while and counted on his fingers. 'Year 4685, the year of the dragon,' he said. 'That's excellent. We both have wood as our element.' If I had been born in the year of the snake, the horse or the sheep, Cheng wouldn't have let me share his room, because they have fire as their element, and wood and fire don't go together, he said. Chinese astrology is complicated and Cheng didn't trouble himself with the details. He just looked at the basic elements, such as earth, fire, water, wood and metal, and took his decision on that basis. It was the kind of madness that my Kuwaiti grandmother went in for when she decided whether things were good or bad omens, or so my mother had told me.

For a small amount, Cheng made space for me to share his little room on the second floor of an old building in a street close to Chinatown. The room had one window, which looked out on the Seng Guan Temple. When we spread our mattresses on the floor at night, there was only just room for a small fridge in which we kept our food in plastic containers. On my first night in his room I asked him why he had agreed to let me move in, given that the room was so small. 'I need a voice to listen to, other than my own,' he replied.

I pointed to behind the door, where there was a guzheng, or Chinese zither, leaning against the wall.

2

When Cheng was asleep at night, I looked out at the Seng Guan Temple through the window of our room. It looked awesome, dark grey, with a tiled roof in the style of Chinese houses and with lots of decorative reliefs on the walls. There was a statue of a Chinese dragon and one of a bald old man with a smile on his face and a long beard. Above the arched doorway there was a plaque with an inscription in Chinese, and under that plaque, inside the arch, it said *Seng Guan Temple* in English. I loved the place and grew curious to find out what went on inside, but although I was curious I never thought of going into the temple.

Instead of visiting the temple, my curiosity led me to the shelves above Cheng's fridge. I pulled out one of his books and from that night on I started reading by candlelight when he was asleep. I read the teachings of the Buddha, about his life and his disciples and how he sat in the lotus position under the fig tree, and the story of his enlightenment.

I found his personality fascinating. *If I had stayed sitting under my favourite tree on Mendoza's land, would I have become a Buddha*, I wondered. Damn that relay tower.

Cheng noticed I was interested in his books, especially as I asked him many questions about his religion and the rituals. After that he started telling me about the Buddha every night and in return he would ask me about Jesus Christ. We compared them, noticed the similarities in how they were born and how they lived, their disciples and all the things that happened to them.

They were great men, I thought.

Would I be betraying one of them if I followed the teachings of the other?

Both of them advocate love and peace, tolerance, charity and treating other people well.

* * *

One day Cheng invited me to go to the temple with him. I hesitated at first, thinking it might not be allowed, but he assured me the temple let in Buddhists and non-Buddhists. 'You'll feel serene inside,' he said.

Shortly before sunset, when we'd finished work, Cheng and I went to the temple. It was nothing like a church, but the feeling was the same.

'Watch me, and do what I do,' Cheng said, and when he realised I was confused, he added, 'Or you can just sit there', pointing to some red leather cushions on the ground. There were six rows of ten cushions side by side, each no more than a foot off the ground. I sat in the middle, on the fifth cushion in the fourth row. The light was low. In front of me there were three large glass enclosures with a life-sized golden statue of the Buddha in each one. In the middle enclosure the Buddha was standing upright surrounded by golden decoration in relief against a dark red background. In the other two enclosures the Buddha was sitting cross-legged.

Cheng and I were the only people in the temple. Cheng went up to the glass enclosure in the middle with his hands pressed together under his chin. He bowed his head and started to pray.

All my senses were on high alert. Many things can be discovered and experienced for free, as Merla said. I was impressed by everything: the incense smoke that hung in the air like a thick fog, the smell of jasmine flowers in all the corners. And the silence. Silence in itself can give rise to voices inside us that seem to be the voices of people that we feel we can trust. The voices show us the way to unfamiliar places and we hurry off confidently.

Cheng finished praying. He walked over to a large bronze bowl, lit an incense stick and stuck it in the soft sand in the bowl.

Before Cheng prepared to leave, I went up to the glass enclosure, leaving the red cushion behind me. I stood in front of the statue with the tranquil face. I bowed and made the sign of the cross. When I looked up, I found the expression on the Buddha's face was just as tranquil, with no disapproval of what I had done.

I went to the bronze bowl, lit an incense stick and planted it in the soft sand. Then Cheng and I left together.

★   ★   ★

In the evening, after we'd spread our mattresses on the floor, Cheng sat cross-legged on his mattress. He rubbed his hands together like a fly. 'Could you pass me the guzheng, please?' he asked.

I went to the corner behind the door, where he left his instrument propped up against the wall. I picked it up carefully with both hands as if it were a child. It looked magical. It was made of ivory inlaid with tortoise shell. The twenty-one strings were carefully tuned. I passed it to him. He put it on his legs, then took off his shirt.

'Are you going to breastfeed it?' I asked him. He laughed at my joke.

'I'm used to playing naked. If you weren't here,' he said.

I burst out laughing. 'OK, OK, that's quite far enough,' I added.

He fixed little rings on his fingertips, with prongs like claws on them, and looked serious. 'Before you sit down, José, switch that light off and light those candles on top of the fridge,' he said.

I switched the main light off and lit the candles. And then . . . but how can I convey here the sound that instrument made?

'*Jasmine Fragrance*,' said Cheng, referring to the piece he was about to play.

The fingers of his right hand strummed three strings at extraordinary speed, repeating the same chord, while the fingers of his other hand skipped from string to string, filling the room with magical music. The hair on the back of my neck stood on end and I felt my entire body respond to what I was hearing. I leaned back against the wall and closed my eyes. It was obvious that the instrument could make music. But how the strings produced the fragrance of jasmine, now that I can't explain.

As soon as he'd finished plucking the strings he handed the guzheng back to me and pointed to the corner behind the door without saying a word.

'What magic that instrument produces!' I said as I put it back in its place. He smiled and didn't say anything. He stuck his legs under the cover and lay on his mattress. I blew out the candles and lay on my mattress, waiting for him to start the usual bedtime conversation, but he didn't speak.

'Aren't you going to chat tonight?' I asked.

He adjusted his position, turning his back to me.

'I just said everything I have to say. Everything,' he said.

3

Late one night Cheng woke me up. 'José!' he said.

'What's up, Cheng?'

He was lying on his front on top of his mattress.

'Heat up the oil and do your work,' he said.

'It's nothing to laugh about,' I replied angrily. 'It was because of words like that that I left Mendoza's land.'

Cheng tried to make amends. 'I wasn't joking. Didn't you tell me you were willing to do the jobs your grandfather made you do, as long as it was somewhere else and you got paid for it?'

I sat up straight. 'And will you pay me?' I asked.

'Don't be stupid, José. Do your work first and I'll tell you later.'

I gave in without understanding what he meant.

'I need some oil,' I said.

He pointed to the corner of the room. 'On top of the shelf there.'

Within half an hour my massage had Cheng fast asleep.

'Cheng! Cheng!' I said, waking him up.

'Tomorrow, José, please, tomorrow,' he said, like someone who has been disturbed in mid-dream and doesn't want to miss the rest of it.

I gave his shoulders a firm shake. 'You're not going to cheat me, Cheng, understand?' I said angrily.

He sat up. 'Selling bananas isn't the right job for you, you idiot,' he said, his eyes still half-closed.

'It was my only option.'

'Look, José,' interrupted Cheng. 'I'll take you to the Chinese centre tomorrow morning, at the street corner behind the temple.'

'But I can't speak Chinese,' I said.

He laughed so much that his eyes closed. He pointed at my hands. 'But your fingertips do,' he said.

Cheng was talking about the Chinese physiotherapy and massage centre. To be a physiotherapist, you needed a professional diploma. 'But to be a masseur, all you need is magic fingers like yours,' said Cheng.

★　★　★

At the Chinese centre they gave me a test. 'Not bad,' the man in charge said, 'but it's not enough.'

He got up off the couch and walked towards a wooden screen around a shower stall. He disappeared behind the screen to wash the oil off his body. He had to raise his voice to be heard above the sound of the shower water. 'You'll need some practical training in Chinese massage, traditional massage, Thai massage, dry massage and massage with hot stones,' he said.

I signed a contract with the Chinese centre as soon as I passed the training course. It said I would work for a fixed monthly salary plus commission for the services I provided. The most important part wasn't mentioned in the contract – the tips the customers pressed into my hand if the service met with their approval. This gave me an income several times the amount I earned by selling bananas in Chinatown.

I proved myself in the job despite the difficulties I faced at the beginning. Being a man in itself reduced my chances of finding clients, because in this line of work, as in others, women had better luck. But as time passed this was no longer a problem: I had serious clients who visited the centre after a hard day's work or after strenuous physical exercise to enjoy an hour of real massage, without any of the services that some masseuses provided in the closed rooms at the centre.

4

After a month selling bananas in Chinatown and a month working at the Chinese centre, I decided to visit our house in Valenzuela City. I was homesick for the place and I had two envelopes of money in my backpack, one for Mama Aida and the other for my mother and Adrian.

On the bus there were more people standing than sitting. Some of them slept standing up, like horses, their faces pale from exhaustion. The bodies were crammed together and there was a medley of smells, some of which I could make out – the leather of the seats, the humidity from the air conditioning, sweat, fruit, cheap perfume – and others I didn't recognise.

I studied all the faces, looking for something among them: there were workmen tanned by the sun, office workers in uniform, nurses wearing white like a sports team, a mother nursing her baby, children jostling for space at the windows, pressing their faces against the glass, making condensation with their breath and then drawing their little fantasies in the water with their fingertips. People made way for an old man with a walking stick. They helped an old woman to an empty seat and carried a paper bag full of fruit for her. The conductor slipped between the passengers like quicksilver. I admired his ability to identify the new passengers in the crowd. He asked each new face where they were going, took their fares and gave them tickets. Then he weaved his way through again, back to where he stood at the front of the bus.

The bus shook and the heads swayed in time. It suddenly stopped and took on new passengers, adding to the crush. The bus swallowed up many but spat out few, then set off again. I was mesmerised by the stories behind the faces around me. I didn't need to guess what the stories were, because every face told its own story. I looked into every face and read it, taking advantage of my sunglasses with the mirrored lenses. If people tried to see my eyes, all they could see was their own faces reflected in the lenses.

I couldn't find a trace of a smile on the bus, except in the happy faces of the children. All I saw in the other faces was a mixture of fear, sadness, anger and resignation.

I was like someone in the middle of the bridge between two towns – the town of happy childhood and the town where men and women struggled with life.

I was halfway across that bridge and I had to keep walking, weighed down by my sixteen years of life. I could hear the children singing and laughing in the town behind me as I walked away. The further I walked, the fainter the sound of laughter. The songs disappear. I keep walking, I grow tired, I cough. My back is bent and I grow old. I hear other sounds in the distance, growing closer: crying, begging, complaining, praying, swearing, sobbing.

I took off my sunglasses and held them out in front of my face. I could see my face in the mirror lenses. It no longer looked like the children, and soon it would turn into one of those pale faces I could see around me on the bus.

I was horrified. *What fate awaits me here*, I wondered.

I wanted Alice's white rabbit to appear halfway across the bridge and take me to a hole that led to my father's country, to Wonderland, before I reached the town at the other end of the bridge and my face turned into one of those faces.

★   ★   ★

'Promise me, Mama Aida, that you won't spend any of that money on things that damage your health,' I said.

She put her hand out and took the envelope from my hand. 'I promise you,' she said.

How could I believe her when her eyes were already bloodshot and her impassive face showed that she was in another world when she gave the promise?

I turned to Mother. 'Are you still angry?' I asked.

'Not at all, José. I've never been angry with you.' She looked at my face sadly. 'It's just that I worry about you. I don't want anything to stop you going to your father's country, when the time comes,' she said.

'Mama!' I broke in.

'José!' she interrupted. 'I've been preparing myself for that day for ages. Do you understand?' She was fighting back tears. 'I love you, José,' she continued. 'But you weren't made to live here. I've been preparing myself, so that I didn't get too attached to you. I moved to Alberto's house without you and gave Adrian my attention, but not because I didn't love you.'

She wiped her tears away with the back of her hand and continued. 'It was because I was frightened about getting too attached to you. I left you here in the house with Aida and Merla so that when the time came your departure would be easier to bear.'

I looked at my watch as a sign to my mother that my visit was over. I put my backpack on my back. As I was about to leave, she asked, 'Aren't you going to visit your grandfather?'

'I will,' I said with a nod.

I stopped at the door to Grandfather's house and hesitated. The smell of the place was unbearable. My mother had told me that Mendoza had been bed-bound recently and never got up. He urinated and defecated wherever he was lying. At night he was still shouting scary stuff and having conversations with his dead ancestors. 'He seems to have lost his mind,' my mother said.

I turned away from Mendoza's door without going in. I'd seen enough of this man and I didn't need to see any more of him. But as I was walking along the path that led to the sandy lane along the side of my grandfather's land I heard his voice from the half-open door behind me.

'José turned into a pineapple. José turned into a pineapple,' he said.

I stopped as soon as I heard what he said. *My God*, I thought. *Has Mendoza gone mad because of me?* Before I had a chance to walk on, I heard him calling for help behind me. 'Josephine! Pedro! Aida! Merla!' he shouted.

Aida and Merla! Since when had grandfather been calling Aida and Merla? Now he was crying bitterly like a child. 'José turned into a pineapple. José turned . . .' he was shouting.

Tears welled up in my eyes. *Should I go back and reassure him that I hadn't really turned into a pineapple*, I wondered. I hesitated, then walked on. I came up to Inang Choleng's house and the bee buzzed inside my head. The buzzing grew louder. I hurried past the bamboo fence that surrounded Mendoza's land and left everything behind – our house and Grandfather's cries: 'José, forgive me, I'm sorry. José, can you hear me? I'm sorry. José. José. José.'

5

Less than six months after I started my new job the manager of the Chinese centre told me I would have to look for a new job and he was giving me one week's notice before my contract with them ended.

The law in the Philippines requires employers to give workers redundancy pay if they lay them off after more than six months in the job. Employers often lay workers off before the six months are up, so that they don't have to make redundancy payments, and also because contracts are usually renewed automatically after the six-month period. Workers are always available, so it's in the employer's interest to terminate contracts before the six-month threshold and find new staff to replace those who are leaving. This may be why Filipinos rapidly acquire experience in a variety of trades, because the system keeps them moving from one job to another all the time.

Before my last week at the centre was over I had come up with a new job at a tourist hotel on the island of Boracay, south of Manila. I got it through one of my customers at the centre, who worked in a tourism company. It was a pathetic job, with a salary that would hardly keep me alive till the end of the month, but the man assured me that the tips from tourists would guarantee me a reasonable income. 'That's the most I can offer to a young man who hasn't even graduated from senior school,' he said.

When would my father's promise be fulfilled, I wondered. *When?*

In the Philippines the doors had started to close in my face, one after another. All the doors left were only half-open. I could hardly slip through them, hardly make even a temporary living.

★ ★ ★

Before I set off for Boracay on the longest journey I had made since I was a baby, I passed by the family home and prepared the things I would need.

I felt as if I was trying out every possible means of transport that existed in the Philippines, all in a single day. I took a tricycle, a Jeepney, a bus, a train, a plane and finally a boat.

It was on the same boat that I began working. It was a small boat, with one man standing behind the rudder and another man helping him. I wasn't lucky enough to be one of those two. I was the third man and my job was to stand in the bow with a long bamboo cane that I used to check whether we were approaching shallow water and to keep the bow away from rocks when we came into harbour. When we arrived I threw the painter and tied the boat to one of the bollards with a thick rope. Then I had to put the gangplank in place so that the passengers could embark or disembark. Then I followed after them, carrying their bags to the vehicle that took them to the hotel.

Every hotel in Boracay had one or more of these boats to bring the tourists over from the much larger island of Panay where there is a small airport at Caticlan. I spent the whole day going back and forth between the two islands, mostly standing at the bow. It was ten minutes there and ten minutes back. The boats, each marked with the name of its hotel, set off towards Panay as soon as we received word that a plane had landed. There would be dozens of boats heading for the same destination at the same time. The quality of the boats varied: some were luxurious, some were average and others were basic. The quality of the boat indicated the quality of the hotel it belonged to. When they set sail for the big island, the men working on the boats hoped to find plenty of tourists so they would stand a better chance of receiving more tips for their services.

My skin changed colour. The skin on my shoulders and my nose peeled off because of the salty water and the rays of the sun. I soon looked very different.

In Boracay I really missed the colour green. But I liked blue too. For all those years I had never seen how magical it was. In Boracay the world was an infinite expanse of blue. When I looked up at the blueness of the sky, I could imagine my eyes soaring like a pair of seagulls, their wings touching the white of the clouds. If they tired of flying I could imagine my eyes as a couple of fish in the sea, swimming through the endless blueness. I fell in love with the blue of the sky and the sea, whereas before I had noticed it only in Merla's eyes.

In my work at Boracay I saw Kuwaitis again, for the first time since our meeting with Ismail in Manila. Newly married couples came on their honeymoons, as well as groups of young men in high spirits, six or more at a time. They came to the island when Kuwait had its long summer holiday. They were so happy. I loved the atmosphere they created wherever they went. They were crazy. They made lots of noise in the boat, singing together in my father's language, which I didn't understand. They were really good at clapping in rhythm. They formed a circle around one man, or two men facing each other, and started by clapping softly. They clapped louder and louder till it sounded like a hundred men, while the man in the middle of the circle did some weird dancing. He leaned forward and shook his shoulders, bending his legs and putting his hands on his head to hold his hat in place, then leapt up in the air as the circle around him broke up. They went on clapping while the man in the middle stayed where he was, swaying from side to side, then started moving his arms as if he were pulling on an invisible rope.

I loved them. I jumped for joy if I found out there were young Kuwaitis on the boat. At first I could only identify tourists as Arabs but later I could tell which of them were Kuwaitis. I tried to convince myself it was because I was one of them.

Their clothes, their shoes, their hats, their sunglasses, the perfumes they used – none of it was appropriate for the place they were visiting. Their clothes made them look rich but the way they behaved made them seem simple and naïve.

In return for a smile or for helping them across the gangplank between the boat and the quay, some gave me good tips. Money didn't seem to mean anything to them. When they got into the jeep with the captain and his assistant and set off for the hotel, I looked at myself in the bow, holding the long stick, and wished the stick would change into a magic wand that could turn me into one of them.

I wanted to follow them and call out to them saying, 'Hi! Stop! My name's Isa. I'm one of you. Wait for me.'

The jeep drove off and their laughter faded into the distance. I sat on the ground not far from the boat, looking at it, imagining my father and mother aboard in those moments when I began my journey before I was born. I closed my eyes, then opened them again. I saw my father in his white cap with Ghassan, throwing their lines in the water, and Walid looking at me cross-eyed, sticking his tongue out at me. I went up to the boat. Walid vanished. I moved closer. My father disappeared. I stopped there in case the third man vanished too.

★ ★ ★

I lived in a small staff annex, next to the hotel and with a door that opened on to a narrow dusty lane between our hotel and the high wall of another hotel. If you walked to the right, you came to the beach and if you walked to the left you came to the street that ran parallel to the shoreline and went past the other hotels.

I only went to the staff annex to sleep. Before going to bed I often spent some time smoking cigarettes in the narrow lane or sitting on the beach nearby.

Off the beach there was a small island surrounded by water most of the time and known as Willy's Rock, with a palm tree on it and two other trees I never identified. Under one of the trees there was a niche made of pebbles, with a statue of the Virgin Mary inside, facing the beach. Her face was at peace and beautiful and her hands were clasped in prayer. She had a golden halo around her head.

When the tide was out people could walk to the rock but when the tide was in they had to swim out. Then they would climb some stairs, stand in front of the niche, pray and light a candle.

I went out to Willy's Rock one night in the middle of 2005. I left my shirt, my shoes and my packet of cigarettes on the beach. The tide was so high that it was above the stairs. The only parts of the rock that were visible were the niche and the three trees. I walked into the water until it was up to my waist. Then I held my lighter between my teeth and started to swim out to the island.

It was late and the only people on the beach were the guards and a group of guests sitting in the dark in a semi-circle like ghosts. Only their white shirts were visible. The lights in the hotel rooms behind me weren't on, which made the stars look brighter. I went up the stairs and stood in front of the statue of the Virgin Mary. I put my hands together and began to pray. The sound of the waves around me was loud but it gave me a sense of calm. The waves were crashing on the rock, spraying salt water on my face. I wiped them away with the back of my hand.

'I'm not crying, Mother Mary,' I said.

I looked up into her face. 'Those were drops of seawater. Don't worry,' I continued.

She didn't look at me. She was looking at something behind me in the distance. I climbed the last step, which brought me to the same level as her. I leaned over her left shoulder and whispered in her ear. 'But I will cry if I have to stay here too long,' I told her.

I wrapped my arms around her with my eyes closed. Then I heard a sound alongside the sound of the waves, rather like a piece of guzheng music. The hairs on my arms stood on end. I looked at the Virgin Mary's face. Her eyes were still looking into the distance. I turned to see where she was looking. There was a group of guests sitting on the sandy beach. They were swaying from side to side. One of them was playing strange music on an instrument I didn't recognise.

I lit a candle. I clenched my teeth on the lighter and went down into the water to swim back to shore.

6

They were Kuwaitis, young men, five of them, sitting on the beach in a semi-circle. The one in the middle was holding an instrument that looked like a guitar. He was playing and singing while the other four listened in silence. He sang louder and the guard came over. 'Sir,' he said. 'You'll disturb the other guests.'

The Kuwaitis looked at him without saying a word.

'You can sit over there,' the guard added, pointing to the compound next door, which was dark because it was being renovated. 'That hotel's empty, as you can see.'

The man in the middle stood up with his instrument and walked off. The others followed him, each of them carrying something.

I was sitting close by, between them and the sea, level with Willy's Rock, listening to what they were saying. When they had moved and started singing again in the other compound, under a towering coconut tree, I could no longer resist going to join them.

'*As-salam aleekum*,' I said, greeting them the way my mother had taught me. They looked at each other, then at me, and then they answered in unison, '*Wa alaeekum as-salam.*'

I was worried they might be drunk, but apart from one of them they weren't. 'You're from Kuwait, aren't you?' I said with a smile.

They looked at each other in surprise. 'Yes,' said the man in the middle. 'How did you know?'

'I can tell, sir.'

They spoke among themselves but I didn't understand what they were saying. Then one of them, a man with a glass in his hand, said in perfect English, 'Please, have a seat.'

'Can I really, sir?'

'Yes, yes, of course,' they all said, pointing at the ground.

I sat down with them. One of them reached over and offered me a cigarette from his packet. I took my own packet out of the pocket of my shorts. 'Thanks, sir. I have one,' I said.

He took my cigarettes out of my hand and examined them. He handed them back and insisted I smoke one of his Davidoffs. 'Have one of these,' he said. 'It will clear your chest out.'

His friends laughed. The man with the glass reached for a brown bottle with a red label. 'Would you like a drink?' he asked, offering me his glass.

'Legally I'm not allowed to drink,' I said. 'I'm only seventeen. But I have already tried it.' He was about to put the glass back in its place. 'But I'd be delighted to accept your invitation,' I added. I took the glass from his hand. 'They say that Red Horse beer is powerful stuff. Is that true?' I asked him.

He downed the rest of his glass and grimaced as if he had bitten into a lemon. 'Try it for yourself,' he said.

I drank a whole glass in one gulp and everyone laughed. The man poured me another glass and I asked the man in the middle, 'Aren't you going to play the . . .' I hesitated, then asked, 'By the way, what's that instrument called?'

'It's an oud,' the young man said. The name reminded me of the stories my mother used to tell about Ghassan, who played the same instrument.

The man started plucking the strings with a small piece of black plastic.

'Sir, what's the name of the piece you're going to play? I asked.

'This is a song by my favourite singer in Kuwait,' he said, continuing to strum. Then he stopped, put the piece of plastic between his nose and his upper lip like a moustache and said, 'It's called . . .'

I don't in fact remember the name he gave but I do remember that his friends burst out laughing. He laughed too, then started to play again. 'His thick moustache makes him different from all the other singers in Kuwait, as well as his voice,' he said.

Then he began to sing. He moved his head around, sometimes looking up to the sky and sometimes resting his head on the instrument. I wanted to understand the words.

I drank glass after glass and my head started to feel heavy. The music went on, and the singing couldn't have been more beautiful.

I stood up, with the world spinning around me. 'Stop, stop,' I said. The man in the middle stopped singing and all five of them looked at me.

'Look, you guys. I'm going to tell you a secret,' I said. No one said anything, so I continued. 'I'm Kuwaiti,' I said.

I looked up with difficulty to see their faces. They looked surprised.

'My name's Isa,' I added.

They exchanged glances.

'If you don't believe me, I'll prove it to you.'

The man in the middle put his oud upside down on his lap and looked at me with interest.

'Could you all clap please?' I said. They started clapping, still looking surprised. 'No, no, not like that,' I said, and they stopped and looked at me.

The man with the glass banged his feet together. 'Like this?' he asked, making fun of me.

'No, sir. Clap the way the Kuwaitis clap,' I said.

This time they smiled and said things to each other I couldn't understand. They started clapping in that crazy way. I shook my shoulders and my body swayed back and forth. Their surprise, their big smiles and the effect of the beer all encouraged me to continue. I leaned my shoulders forward, put my hands on my head to hold an imaginary hat. The man who was drinking stood up too and came towards me. He started moving his shoulders back and forth like me. The others began to show interest. I bent my legs, then leapt into the air. The man stood beside me, shoulder to shoulder. 'No, not like that. Do what I'm doing,' he said. He planted his feet firmly on the ground. I did the same. We went on shaking our shoulders slowly. I started pulling on that invisible rope with my hands, with my legs apart.

They burst out laughing. They roared. They rolled on their backs. 'Yes, you're right. You really are a Kuwaiti, but Made in the Philippines,' one of them said.

They went on laughing at the top of their voices.

The guard came running over. 'Please! Please!' he cried.

The session broke up.

7

'José, José, José.' It wasn't Mendoza calling me this time. It was my mother on the phone, calling me after midnight, crying and struggling to say my name.

'José, José.'

She caught her breath and tried to put together the words to tell her news. 'My father's just died,' she said.

She went on crying. She sobbed and wailed. 'Come at once. You have to be here,' she told me.

★ ★ ★

When I took the ten-minute boat ride from Boracay to the airport on the other island, the young Kuwaitis were on the boat too. This time I wasn't the man who stood on the bow. I was one of the people leaving the island, even if I thought I would be back after no more than a week of unpaid leave.

The Kuwaitis were as cheerful as ever, singing and laughing and playing tricks on each other. They were just as crazy on the boat as they were in the hotel or later on the plane.

On domestic flights the airline crew usually organises amusements for the passengers, such as competitions. They ask general knowledge questions and give the winners token prizes. But on that flight with the Kuwaitis the cabin crew didn't know what to do. Nobody paid any attention to them and the activities they were trying to organise because everyone was focused on the crazy Kuwaitis, who were singing and clapping in their traditional way.

One of them stood up in the middle of the aisle and addressed the passengers. 'Ladies and gentlemen,' he said. Pointing to the passengers sitting on the right, he said, 'You clap like this' and began clapping. 'That's the beat,' he explained.

Then, turning to the passengers on the left, he said, 'And you, clap like this – tak, tak, tak . . . tak, tak, tak. Is that clear?'

He went back to his seat and shouted out, 'One, two, three, now!'

The man with the oud played a piece with a rapid tempo and the others sang.

It was crazy the difference those Kuwaitis made to the flight: the smiling faces, the laughter, the cameras recording everything.

It was such fun that I forgot I was going to the funeral in the church near Mendoza's land. I didn't feel sad at losing my grandfather, but when the plane landed at the domestic airport I did feel sad that these crazy Kuwaitis were going off to my father's country without me.

At the airport gate I was about to get in a taxi when one of them called me. 'Isa! Isa!' But the name didn't catch my attention. It was just another noise in my head, along with the noise of the cars and the horns blaring, the people in the crowds and other noises.

One of them grabbed me by the shoulder. 'Isn't your name Isa?' he asked.

It was the man who had been drinking beer.

'Yes, sir,' I replied.

He pointed to his friends in a van nearby. They were looking at me from behind the windows and smiling. 'Me and my friends,' he said hesitantly, 'we're going to Ninoy Aquino International Airport to go back to Kuwait.' He put out his hand with a large wad of cash. 'We didn't have time to spend this money. It's yours,' he added.

'But that's a lot, sir.'

He ignored what I said and looked into my face. 'I'm not sure that what you said was true, about being Kuwaiti, but . . .' He paused. I wanted to swear to him that my father was Kuwaiti and I was born there and I had papers to prove it, but I let him go on with what he wanted to say: 'But whatever you are, don't even think of going there unless you're a real Kuwaiti.'

He turned away and headed back towards his friends in the van. I looked after them, the money in my hand and a puzzled look on my face. Before getting into the van, he looked back and said, 'Stay here, my friend, and drink Red Horse.'

'I can drink it there,' I said in surprise.

'The Red Horse there won't accept you. It'll crush you under its hoofs, my friend,' he said. He rubbed his foot against the ground as if stubbing out a cigarette butt, then pulled the sliding door open and plunged in among his friends packed into the van.

As the van drove off into the traffic, the man with the oud leaned out of the side window. 'We don't know what that drunk was telling you,' he shouted, so loud that people turned towards me to see what was happening. 'But come back to Kuwait if you're telling the truth. You'll find you have lots of rights there.'

People were looking at me. The taxi driver asked me to get in. Through the back window of the van, the man who had been drinking shook his head and wagged his finger as if to say, 'Mind what I say.'

The van disappeared into the traffic. The crazies were gone, leaving me a pile of cash and a head full of uncertainties.

8

In the small church where I had been baptised years earlier, the family received condolences on Grandfather's death. Many people had come from places far and near to console us and say goodbye to Mendoza after he was gone. It's strange to say your farewells after someone's departure.

I sat next to Mama Aida, who turned up reluctantly after my mother and Uncle Pedro insisted. She told me how she had learned of her father's death. 'It was horrible, horrible, José,' she said, looking towards the coffin where Mendoza lay. 'I was in my room smoking, late at night. The old dog Whitey started barking. The barking soon changed into a howl like a wailing. My head felt numb and I felt an itching like ants in my scalp. I shook my head like someone trying to wake up from a bad dream. But Whitey didn't stop wailing and then one of the cocks started crowing. Can you imagine the sound they made – the dog howling and the cock crowing at the same time? The cocks never dared to crow when Whitey was barking but this time they were crowing non-stop. One would stop for a rest and another one would take up where the other left off, and Whitey kept howling horribly.'

Mama Aida ran her hands along her arms, as if trying to stop her hair standing on end. 'I ran downstairs in my nightclothes and went out without shoes,' she continued, crossing herself. 'Whitey was crouching at the door of Father's house, howling at the sky. Someone had undone the collar that was tied to his kennel. The cocks were still crowing. But what really scared me and sent a shiver down my spine, José, was seeing Inang Choleng stooped at the window of her house in the darkness. She was topless and had her arms crossed under her shrivelled breasts. She was looking down, as if she had something in her arms.'

Aida leaned forward, put her elbows on her knees and covered her face with her hands. 'I didn't dare go near my father's house. I hadn't gone inside for years. I ran off to Pedro's house without looking back at Inang Choleng's house. I knocked on his door with both fists. Pedro asked what had come over me. "Father's dead, Pedro, he's dead in bed," I told him. "Who told you that, Aida?" he asked, because he was sure I wouldn't have gone inside. I pointed to the patio outside father's house. "Whitey and the cocks," I said.'

Uncle Pedro came and sat down on the other side of me and his sister left straight away. 'I'm going home,' she said. 'Enough. I can't bear to stay here any longer.' My uncle didn't look at her, but he picked up the story where she left off.

'After Aida told me I ran to Father's house and opened the door. Whitey beat me inside. It smelled like the candles had been blown out only a short while ago. I pressed the light switch but nothing happened. I lit my lighter and found my father lying naked on his side, with his knees folded up against his chest, like the foetal position. He had covered his face with his hands like someone who doesn't want to look at something horrible.'

★   ★   ★

Merla arrived three days after Grandfather died. The family had decided that his body should stay in the church for five days so that all the family members could see it before he was buried.

Merla came to the church with Maria, who sat in the back row near the door while Merla came forward to the front row. She greeted us and said, 'I'm sorry to hear the news.' Uncle Pedro made room for her next to me and she sat down.

The family members and the guests started to leave one by one and by sunset Merla and I were the only ones left inside. She turned to me and looked me in the face. 'You hypocrite!' she said. 'Don't pretend to be sad to lose him, José.'

I put my hand on her knee and looked towards the coffin where the body was lying. 'In fact I am sad,

Merla,' I said. 'I had never looked at his face till now.'
I squeezed her knee. 'If I had seen him again before
he died, I would have told him I forgive him.'

I took my hand off her knee. She stood up and
walked towards the coffin. 'What matters is that you've
forgiven him. That's up to you, not up to him,' she
said.

'What do you mean?' I asked. Her back was towards
me and her face towards the coffin, which was just a
few metres away.

'We're not rewarding others when we forgive them
their sins,' she said. 'We're rewarding ourselves. They
call it catharsis.'

My silence didn't mean I agreed with what Merla
believed, but I wasn't going to argue with someone
crazy right now. I wanted Mendoza to be absolved of
his sins against me before he was buried, and when he
was absolved, I would have a clear conscience too.

'Aren't you going to have a last look at Mendoza,
José?' Merla asked, without turning towards me. Merla
stepped towards the coffin and I followed with heavy
feet.

The coffin was at the front of the church, open on a
table covered with a piece of white silk. It was
surrounded by white flowers in silver vases. The coffin
was white with decorative touches in purple and golden
handles on all four sides. There was a crucifix hanging

above it on the wall. To the right there was a picture of Mendoza in a frame on a wooden stand and some basic information about him – Sixto Philip Mendoza, born 6 April 1925, died 21 June 2005, aged 80.

I stepped towards the coffin, where Merla was standing praying. Grandfather was lying under the glass cover with his eyes closed. His face was grey and the powder they had put on it didn't hide the pallor. He looked respectable in a way he hadn't looked when he was alive. He was wearing black trousers and a white shirt with vertical black stripes.

I looked at the inside of the coffin lid at the end where his head would be. My mother had attached strips of purple cloth to it, each with the name of a close family member: Aida, Josephine, Pedro and his wife and children, Alberto and Adrian, Merla and José. When the lid was closed the names would be on the ceiling of the coffin, in front of Mendoza's face, so he would be reminded of his family in the other world.

'Let's go, José,' said Merla. We crossed ourselves over the body and left him in the tranquillity of the church.

On the way home, I asked Merla to go on ahead. 'I have something to do. I'll join you later,' I said.

I went back to the church. The man in charge had switched off the lights and was about to close up. I asked him for a little more time to pray for my grandfather. 'I'll be back in five minutes,' he said. He went to a table, took a candle and lit it. He gave it to me before leaving.

Holding the candle I went to Grandfather's body and looked at his face. His eyes, his nose, his lips and the other parts of his face all seemed to be moving because of the candle flame flickering in the dark. I turned to the coffin lid, reached out, and with my thumb and index finger I pulled off the strip of cloth that had my name on it.

'Sorry, Grandfather,' I said, looking at his face behind the glass. I closed the coffin lid and walked down the short corridor that led outside, with the candle in one hand and the strip of cloth in my other hand. 'That way you won't be reminded you have a grandson called José,' I said to myself as I walked away, leaving the coffin behind me.

At the door I stopped and turned, facing the coffin. I rounded my lips to blow out the candle, confident that I would never again hear that call of Mendoza's: 'José, José, José.'

9

The White Rabbit appeared without warning five days after Mendoza died. Maybe it had been waiting for him to die.

I had been waiting a long time, rabbit, for you to appear in front of me. I would follow you, trip up and fall down a hole that leads to my father's country. But apparently falling down a hole isn't as easy as I imagined.

* * *

At noon on the fifth day after his death a luxury limousine, decorated with vast quantities of flowers, carried away the body of my grandfather Mendoza. He who had never travelled in such a car in his lifetime did so in death, on his journey to the cemetery near his piece of land.

The wheels of the limousine turned slowly. The family and the many other mourners walked behind it, carrying wreaths of flowers and umbrellas to keep off the sun, as they took Mendoza to his final resting place.

Meanwhile the White Rabbit was waiting for me somewhere, wearing his famous waistcoat, holding his pocket watch and counting the time.

A week before Mendoza's funeral the White Rabbit had been at another funeral, saying his own last farewells to a friend, after a separation that had lasted fifteen years.

★   ★   ★

Mama Aida was at home. She hadn't come to the burial with us. Although my mother and Uncle Pedro had tried to persuade her, she flatly refused to come. 'As far as I'm concerned, my father died a long time ago,' she said, 'when we were children. The only new thing today is that you're throwing his body in a dark hole like the hole he pushed me into when I was seventeen. Off you go and take the children with you.'

When the burial was over and we were together at home, Mama Aida said someone had called to ask after Mother. 'I asked him to call back in two hours,' she said. Right on time, the rabbit called.

'Yes, I'm Josephine,' my mother told the caller. She jumped to her feet in surprise. 'How could I not remember you? Of course I remember you, Ghassan.'

Ghassan. The name hit me like an electric shock. My father's friend. The fisherman. The soldier. The poet who played the oud.

The memories teemed in my head and all my senses came to life: the music I had heard in Boracay, the smell of fish and other disgusting smells, maybe the

190

smell of the bait in the plastic bag that Walid was carrying in the old photograph.

As soon as my mother said the name Ghassan, I couldn't help rushing upstairs to Merla's room, where there was another telephone. I picked up the receiver and put it to my ear to hear their conversation – my mother and Ghassan.

'I imagine it's time for him to come back,' said Ghassan in a rough voice that was nothing like that of a poet, maybe the voice of a soldier. 'That's what Rashid wanted, fifteen years ago,' he continued.

My mother breathed faster when she heard my father's name.

'I asked Rashid to look after my mother if anything bad happened to me. In return he asked me to look after Isa if anything happened to him,' said Ghassan.

'Rashid? Something bad?' my mother said, so quietly I could hardly hear her.

'I had great hopes he'd be released from detention,' said Ghassan, his voice gentler now and hesitant. 'I'm sorry but . . .' he continued. The soldier's voice was gone and he went on in the voice of a poet. 'One week ago the Tarouf family received the remains of Rashid from a mass grave in southern Iraq.'

My mother didn't say a word.

'Doesn't he want to come back to Kuwait?' Ghassan asked.

My mother started crying and I answered on the other line. 'Yes, I want to go back, I want to go back,' I said.

Ghassan promised us he would look after everything. 'I know people who can help us bring him back,' he told my mother. To me he said, 'Give me some time to prepare your papers and get you a Kuwaiti passport.' He said he'd like to come to the Philippines to bring me back to Kuwait himself but there was a reason why he couldn't do that.

'I'll be in touch,' the rabbit concluded.

10

Death is strange. It comes and then lingers, moving slowly and looking for someone else whose life it can snatch. As long as it's passing this way, why bother to go away only to come back later?

Five days after Mendoza died we received the news of Rashid's death. A week after the burial of Mendoza, death went off with the soul of Inang Choleng.

The neighbours noticed that the bowls of food outside the old woman's door hadn't been touched since the morning. 'It looks like Inang Choleng is ill,' one of them told Mama Aida. Aida went to the old woman's house and came back minutes later with her face frozen in shock. With dry, trembling lips she picked up the phone. 'Josephine, come quickly,' she said, then burst into tears. 'The old woman's dead.'

She threw down the phone, then threw herself on to the sofa crying hysterically. I was so shocked I was tongue-tied and couldn't think straight. She didn't cry when her father died, I thought. Uncle Pedro came in looking pale and my mother arrived leaning on Alberto's arm, followed by Adrian with his mouth open and large drool stains on his shirt. Mother sat down next to Mama Aida, covering her face with her hands and crying. 'The poor woman's died after waiting so long,' she sobbed. 'She died when her only hope died.' *What's going on here*, I wondered. I looked around at their faces: Mama Aida sobbing, my mother in tears, Uncle Pedro sad, Alberto silent, Adrian in his own world and the neighbour puzzled.

I went upstairs to Merla's room, sat on her bed and picked up the phone. 'Inang Choleng's dead,' I told Merla.

'That's sad, but what's wrong with your voice, José? The woman was close to a hundred, maybe more. Did you believe the children when they talked about Inang Choleng as the witch who would never die?' Maybe I did believe in the legends about the old woman, but it wasn't her death or the legends about her that puzzled me.

'Hello? Hello? José!' Merla shouted, breaking my train of thought.

'Come, Merla,' I said at the end of our conversation. 'Something strange is going on downstairs with my mother, Mama Aida and Pedro.'

★ ★ ★

Everyone but me went to Inang Choleng's house. I sat waiting for Merla and as soon as she arrived, she asked where everyone had gone.

'To the old woman's house,' I answered. She looked at me in surprise.

'José, you frightened me. What's going on?' she asked.

I shrugged my shoulders. 'I don't know,' I said uncertainly, 'but . . .'

I didn't finish the sentence. She took my hand and pulled me away. 'Let's have our first and last look at the inside of the old woman's house,' she said.

I didn't want to let go of her soft hand but I did. 'Are you mad?' I said. 'You're going to go inside the witch's house?'

She looked at me in surprise. 'So why did you ask me to come, José?'

I didn't know what to say because I didn't know what had made me do it.

'I don't know, Merla. But your mother was really sad, my mother and Uncle Pedro too. Their reaction when they heard the news was weird.'

'Everything's weird in Mendozaland, everything,' she commented.

'But my mother said the old woman had waited a long time,' I said, interrupting her.

'Don't be silly, José,' said Merla, interrupting me this time. 'What else would a woman her age be waiting for, other than death?'

I didn't say a word.

'So let's go and see the old woman's shack.'

The neighbours were gathered outside Inang Choleng's house, at least the men and the women. The children were watching warily from a distance. Uncle Pedro's wife and children were outside. My stepfather Alberto was sitting on a rock nearby. When Merla and I approached, Uncle Pedro's wife said, 'Pedro and Josephine and Aida are with the priest inside. Aren't you going in?'

Merla looked at me and waited for me to reply.

'No, there's no need for us to go in,' I said.

Alberto came up to us and said, 'Merla, José, you have to go inside.'

Merla came close and whispered, 'I was planning to go in, but the way they're insisting has made me worried.'

Pedro's wife went to the door of the house, opened it and beckoned us in. Merla went first, reluctantly, and I followed her, even more reluctantly. The house was small on the outside and seemed even smaller inside. There was a bedroom, a bathroom, a small kitchen in the corner open to the main room. It smelled of damp, rotten food and death. I felt sick. At the wooden bed my mother and Mama Aida were solemnly saying prayers, while Uncle Pedro sat on a chair nearby.

Inang Choleng was lying on the bed under a white cover, with only her head and shoulders visible. There were three pillows supporting her hunched back. The priest was anointing her forehead with holy oil and saying prayers. He was incredibly brave. Her mouth was wide open, showing a few teeth here and there. I was dripping with sweat as I waited for the priest to finish his task. I half-expected the old woman to spring into life and dig her remaining teeth into his hand.

I was frightened. My guilt about stealing her food years before was encouraging the bee in my head to start buzzing again. My mother and Mama Aida crying, the buzzing in my head, my heart throbbing in my temples, and my limbs shaking – everything encouraged me to leave. Before I could do so, Merla nudged me with her elbow. I looked at her. She was looking at one of the walls. I looked in the same direction and my eyes popped out in disbelief. There were black and white photographs of Mendoza on the wall. One of them I had seen before on his army identity card. In another one he was standing with a group of men in military uniform. In a third he was sitting on a bench with a woman, two girls and a boy between them. There were other old photos of Mendoza I hadn't seen before. I looked to Merla for an explanation for the photos. She leaned over and

whispered in my ear: 'You don't understand anything.'
She knew that what she said would hurt me. I looked
at her disapprovingly. 'Our wily grandfather had
admirers!' she said.

'But I never saw him go anywhere near her house,'
I replied, completely mystified.

The priest left after he'd performed the rites. As
soon as he was through the door, Merla asked the
question in a low voice. 'Why are there pictures of
Grandfather on the wall of Inang Choleng's house?'

Uncle Pedro went out after the priest. My mother
pretended to be busy clearing the place up. Only
Mama Aida spoke and even she didn't look at us.
'Nothing strange about a mother putting pictures of
her only son on the wall,' she said.

Merla and I looked at each other in disbelief. 'So
Inang Choleng was Mendoza's mother?' I asked Mama
Aida.

She nodded, and floods of tears rolled down her
cheeks. My mother turned her back and pretended to
be doing something. Her shoulders were shaking
from crying. I went over to her and looked in her eyes
but she looked away. 'That old woman was Mendoza's
mother. So who was his father?' I asked her.

She looked at me with tears in her eyes. 'He didn't
have a father,' she said. The words were like a slap in
the face.

The bee in my head stopped. The buzzing disappeared. I closed my eyes and tried to detect it but it had left my head to join a hive of other bees, in Mendoza's head.

11

Six months after Ghassan's first phone call, and after months of bureaucracy, I finally picked up my passport from the Kuwaiti embassy in Manila. I went straight from the embassy to the cathedral. Now that I was certain to be travelling, I felt confused and afraid of the unknown.

In the cathedral I sat in the front row. I put my hand on the cross hanging round my neck, the one Mama Aida had given me after my confirmation ceremony years earlier. I started to pray: 'Our Father who art in Heaven, Hallowed be thy name; Thy kingdom come, Thy will be done, On earth as it is in heaven. Give us this day our daily bread; And forgive us our trespasses, As we forgive those who trespass against us; And lead us not into temptation, But deliver us from evil. Amen.

'Our Father, I am going back to where I was born, to the land of the father I have never known, to a destiny known only to You. My mother says a beautiful life awaits me there but no one but You knows what really awaits me. Our Father who art in Heaven, in my hand I have a blue passport and in my heart I have a faith I fear I may not be able to preserve. Help me to believe in You. Abide with me on my journey. Guide me to what is good and dispel my doubts. Our Father who art in Heaven, are You really in Heaven? Answer me, in the name of Your angels and in the name of Your son the Messiah and of the Virgin.'

* * *

From the cathedral I walked towards Chinatown as far as the Seng Guan Temple. It took me two hours, mostly on foot, simply because I wanted to walk among ordinary people in Manila one last time, breathing in the thick exhaust fumes and trying to look at the sun, which doesn't look like the sun in Kuwait, and looking at the trees on the sides of the street, with their branches hanging heavy with fruit. I looked into the faces of the people around me and missed them even before I had left them. I wanted to apologise to them all, saying that despite the years I had spent amongst them I did not belong with them.

I stopped three quarters of the way from the cathedral to the temple. I felt tired. I hailed a taxi. 'To the Seng Guan Temple, please,' I said.

The driver was surprised. 'It's very close to here,' he said, pointing towards it.

'I know, but will you take me?' I replied.

The traffic was heavy and I would have arrived sooner if I had carried on walking to the temple. In the taxi I could see out of the window on my left and through the front window. I saw things as if I were looking at them for the first time. I was finding it hard to breathe, maybe because of all the traffic around me, or maybe because of the tangle of emotions that I felt. I could see misery in many of its guises through the taxi window: the misery on the faces of the vendors, the dirty clothes, the child beggars following anyone who looked clean, the Muslim boys in their caps that had once been white, offering pirated DVDs of pornography and the most popular Hollywood films. On the pavements there were people with carts selling bananas, including Cheng. He looked happy. People were crowding around his cart as though there were a festival on. Yellow and blue were the colours around him: the yellow of the bananas and the blue of his plastic bags.

The driver had a wooden crucifix hanging on a chain from the rear-view mirror, and behind the steering wheel there was a little statue of the Buddha sitting cross-legged with prayer beads in his hand.

'Why do you have the cross?' I asked the driver.

He turned and looked at me suspiciously. 'Because I'm Christian,' he said.

'And why the other statue?' I asked, looking at the Buddha.

He smiled, as if he knew what I was driving at. 'It brings in business,' he said.

The taxi stopped outside the Seng Guan Temple and I started to get out. 'I see you have a cross around your neck. Why?' the driver said.

I opened the door and got out. 'It's something my aunt chose for me,' I said with a smile.

He pointed to the temple gate and smiled broadly. 'And Seng Guan, why?' he asked.

While he waited for me to answer, I closed the taxi door and turned my back on him. But I could hear him through the window. 'Hey!' he said. 'I answered you when you asked me a question.'

I kept walking towards the temple gate. 'Hey, be fair!' the driver shouted. 'Why?'

I stopped at the gate and turned to face the taxi. The man was still waiting for me to reply. I looked up and scratched my head to indicate I was trying to think of an answer. 'It does something for me, but I don't know what it is,' I said.

★ ★ ★

I stood in front of the glass enclosure in the middle, where there was a golden statue of the Buddha standing. There was a man with prayer beads sitting on one of the low cushions and there was an old woman standing in front of the glass enclosure in the middle praying devoutly. I stood next to her, facing the Buddha statue.

'Buddha, I don't know how to pray to you. But if you really are the one who will save mankind from its ordeals and afflictions, then you will hear me and accept my prayer as it is. I don't know how to pray with prayer beads like the man sitting over there. I don't see the need to put my hands together and move them up and down in front of your statue like that old woman next to me. But I know how to light an incense stick and plant it in the bowl of soft sand, even if I don't know why I'm doing it. Help me to believe in you, in your message, your disciples and your virgin mother, Maya, who bore you inside her on the day when her womb radiated light and you were visible inside it before you were born. If you are a god, a prophet or a saint, guide me, be my helper so that, through you, I can see the light.'

PART 4

Isa . . . The Second Wandering

'The tyranny of some is possible only through the
cowardice of others.'
José Rizal

Kuwait airport looked very gloomy when the plane landed on Sunday, 15 January 2006. People's faces were much the same – gloomy in a way for which I could see no justification. The passengers formed lines in front of the immigration officers who stamped their passports. There were signs above the front of each line, some of them saying *GCC Citizens* and others saying *Citizens of Other Countries*. I stood there, uncertain which line to stand in. Should I go to the line where the Filipinos from my flight were standing? Or the line with the people who didn't look like me?

Under a *No Smoking* sign attached to one of the columns, a man in military uniform was standing, leaning against the column. I went up to him and asked him which line I should stand in. 'Sir,' I said, 'does *GCC Citizens* include Kuwaitis?'

He threw his cigarette on the floor and crushed it with his boot. He spread his arms, shook his head and said, 'No English.' I went over to where they were stamping passports, carrying my briefcase of valuables: old pictures of my father and my identity papers. I stood in one of the GCC lines behind men wearing loose gowns and Arab headgear. *They must be Kuwaitis like me*, I thought.

The officer stamped their passports one by one until my turn came. I put my hand in my trouser pocket but before I could take out my passport the officer shouted at me so rudely I was shocked. He waved me towards the other line, where the Filipinos and people of other nationalities were standing. He said something I didn't understand. I hurried to the other line, while the officer went on talking loudly and pointed at the sign above him. He sounded angry. Then he pointed a finger at his ear and made that gesture that meant he thought I was crazy. I was shaking and people were looking at me. Was it forbidden to stand in that line? Was it a military zone?

In the other line, a young Filipino said to me, 'You were standing in the wrong place. That line's for Kuwaitis and people from the other Gulf states.'

I nodded gratefully and muttered to myself, 'He turned me away when he saw my face, even before he had a chance to see my passport.'

I crossed the yellow line on the floor and presented my blue Kuwaiti passport to the officer. He took it, leafed though the pages and examined my face. 'Sorry about my colleague,' he said with a smile. 'I could stamp your passport here, but would you mind going back to my colleague?' I looked over at the scowling officer and shook my head. 'Please, you have a right to stand there, even if it does take you longer,' he said. He handed my passport back without stamping it and said with a smile, 'Welcome to your country, but not through the gate for foreigners.'

I crossed the yellow line a third time and submitted my passport to the angry officer. The fact that my passport was blue made his face turn red. Without checking my face or making any comment, he stamped the passport. I turned to his colleague with the smile as soon as I was through the gate. He was looking at me, still smiling. He gave me a wink and a thumbs-up sign, then went back to work stamping foreigners' passports, letting people into the country in the proper lane.

The shops, restaurants and cafés at the airport were closed. The lights were off and the chairs were upside down on the tables. It was really depressing. I turned and looked at the faces of the various people who had come to meet arriving passengers. If the faces weren't sad, they were blank and silent. *If they weren't in a good mood, what made them come out to meet people coming back from their travels*, I wondered.

Ghassan was standing in the crowd. I wouldn't have recognised him if he hadn't been holding a sign with my Arabic name, or my Filipino number, on it – Isa. He was wearing a dark Arab thobe and nothing on his head. His moustache, like his hair, was silver, or rather a mixture of black and white, which made it difficult to guess how old he was. His eyes were sad in a way I hadn't seen before. If someone were ever to ask me what sadness looked like, I would say, 'Ghassan's face.'

It was cold outside, not as my mother had described it in our conversations about Kuwait. When we came out of the airport I took a close look at the streets. Beautiful trees and flowers were planted on the verges and the roundabouts but the scenery grew less and less green as we drove away from the airport, until in the end it was mostly yellow. On that day there were flags at half mast along the road too.

'The way we put up flags is different from your way,' I said to Ghassan. 'In the Philippines we put the flag at the top of the mast.'

Ghassan nodded and in English with a strange accent he replied, 'In Kuwait too, and everywhere else, but the country's in mourning.'

'Mourning?' I asked him, expecting an explanation.

'The flags are at half mast because the Emir died this morning,' he said.

2

Ghassan told me he was supposed to take me straight from the airport to Grandmother's house, but the country was in mourning, people were upset and, most importantly, it wasn't clear how Grandmother felt about me coming back. What would she think about me arriving just as the Emir had died? Hadn't my mother and I caused enough trouble in the past? My mother had arrived at the time of the attack on the Emir's motorcade in the mid-1980s, I was born at the time of the plane hijacking, and we left Kuwait when the passengers were released. The fact that I had arrived at just that moment confirmed my grandmother's belief in the curse of Josephine, Ghassan said. So my meeting with Grandmother had been postponed for a month.

Just because I took a liking to Ghassan and trusted him didn't mean I took a liking to the place where he lived. It was a small flat in the district of Jabriya, the same name as the plane that was hijacked years earlier with Ghassan and Walid on board. Both took their name from Jabir, the first name of the Emir that people were mourning on the day I arrived.

We didn't go out of the flat for the first three days. Ghassan didn't need to go to work because government offices and most companies and other offices were closed for the period of mourning. Ghassan was busy watching television. He would speak to me a little, then go back to watching and occasionally crying. He wiped away his tears with the back of his hand. The television showed the Emir carried on people's shoulders, wrapped in the Kuwaiti flag, and thousands of people around him in a cemetery in the desert. The presenter sounded sad but I couldn't understand what he was saying. He would stop his commentary whenever he was about to cry. I said nothing. Ghassan seemed to be performing some religious rite and I didn't want to interrupt him. On television the camera switched to another place that was packed with women with black tattoo marks. They were weeping bitterly. There were girls carrying pictures of the late Emir and old women crying on the pavement. Amazingly some of them had come in wheelchairs.

I was surprised at how the sadness affected everything. Seeing sad faces is only to be expected on some occasions, but for everything to be sad – the streets, the houses, the land, the sky – all at the death of one person, seemed a little too much.

Sadness is something colourless and invisible that a person projects and that then infects everything around them. The effect is evident on everything they touch, even if the sadness itself remains invisible. That's how Kuwait was in the first days after I arrived. People were projecting their grief; the ground, the sky and the air, everything soaked it up.

The television went on broadcasting shots of the late Emir at various ceremonies, with the voice of a man singing unaccompanied. Or perhaps he was praying or reading the Qur'an. I wasn't sure.

If Ghassan hadn't told me that the man on the screen was the late Emir I would have thought he was a major religious figure. His simplicity, his humility and the way people jostled to be near him suggested that people had an unusually warm relationship with him. There were shots of him stepping out of a black Mercedes in a black cloak and shaking hands with old men who looked overjoyed to see him. In other footage, which Ghassan said dated from when he came back to Kuwait after the liberation from Iraq, he was in a brown cloak on the steps of a plane, with his hands raised in the same way as at Friday prayers. He kissed the ground as soon as he set foot on Kuwaiti soil again. The black band that held his white headdress in place fell off when he bent down. He stood up, put it back on his head and then kissed a red book that some men presented to him. In another shot he was on a red carpet greeting men in military uniform, and in one he was without a gown, sitting with many men around a meal laid out on the floor. Finally he appeared on a flat piece of desert turning his head right and then left, with a line of men behind him following his lead in communal prayers. Far from the scenes on television, in the sitting room where I was sitting, Ghassan was in another world.

★　★　★

'Sir, the first time you called you told my mother there was a reason why you couldn't go abroad,' I said to Ghassan a few days after I arrived.

'Isa! Ghassan isn't a hard name to say,' he replied disapprovingly. 'Why do you insist on calling me "sir"?' He paused a while, then continued, 'Yes, I can't go abroad, because I'm not Kuwaiti.'

In everything I had heard about Ghassan from my mother, she had never told me he wasn't Kuwaiti. Besides, I couldn't see what not being Kuwaiti had to do with not being able to go abroad.

'So where are you from then?' I asked inquisitively.

'Bidoon,' he answered straight off.

'Really? I thought you were Kuwaiti,' I said, uncertain what he meant. He didn't offer any further explanation. 'Bidoon? I've never heard of that country,' I added.

Ghassan still didn't speak. 'Is Bidoon one of the GCC states?' I asked with my usual stupidity.

Ghassan laughed, but it sounded like crying.

Through Ghassan I met a new and special type of person. A rare species. I discovered people who were stranger than the tribes of the Amazon or those African tribes that are discovered from time to time. They were people who belonged where they didn't belong, or didn't belong where they did belong. The idea was hard for me to grasp. I tired Ghassan out in my quest for an explanation. After many attempts to simplify the concept, my mind managed with difficulty to digest it.

'But you went abroad on that plane that was hijacked that day!' I told him.

'Things were rather less complicated in those days than they are now,' he replied, with a smile that I couldn't explain.

I went over all the information I had heard about Ghassan from my mother. 'But you're a soldier,' I said, pressing him to explain.

'I was, once upon a time,' he replied.

I pestered Ghassan with questions till I knew everything about him, though that doesn't necessarily mean I understood everything. The sadness on his face was because of a label that had been stuck on him and that he couldn't shake off. He was a bidoon – a term I grew to hate. I didn't really understand the term even after Ghassan translated it for me. 'Without nationality,' he said, 'born that way.' If he had been a sardine born in the Atlantic, he would have been an Atlantic sardine. If he had been a bird in the forests of the Amazon basin, he would have been an Amazonian bird. But although Ghassan's parents were born in Kuwait, and he too was born in Kuwait, although he knew no other country, had served in the army and defended the country when it was under occupation, he was still a bidoon.

Bidoon. He had five Kuwaiti brothers and sisters. They had escaped while he had fallen down some legal crack.

'For God's sake, Ghassan, what's the complication?' I asked. He laughed, as if his experience was nothing to cry about. 'You and your parents were born here. Your brothers and sisters are all Kuwaiti. You had a job in the army. You helped my father, a Kuwaiti, defend Kuwait, and yesterday, and I apologise for intruding, I saw you crying at the death of the Emir. And in spite of all that . . .'

'Isa!' he broke in. 'All these questions of yours have stopped you asking about your father.'

I didn't say a word. I didn't have any feelings for my father that mattered.

'Rashid loved you, Isa. He was always talking about you,' Ghassan said.

Deep inside me, a strange feeling for my father stirred. 'Was my father really like that?' I asked.

'More than you imagine.'

I hesitated before asking my next question. 'So why didn't he let me stay? Why did he get rid of me?'

Ghassan smiled. The man had a strange face. When you find a smile on a sad face it's impossible to predict what the person plans to say. 'OK,' he said. He was still smiling. He also gave a long sigh. 'There's someone you care about, someone you love and worry about, and that person faces two options and for some reason he doesn't have the right to choose,' he said, turning to me and pointing at me with his finger. 'You, only you, can decide.'

I nodded and Ghassan continued. 'Either he's going to be thrown into Hell or into a bed of thorns. Which would you choose for him?'

'The thorns of course,' I answered without thinking.

Like someone who has just won a bet, Ghassan gave me the thumbs-up sign. 'That's what Rashid did,' he said.

3

Ghassan and I built up a close relationship in the month I spent in his little flat, where I felt so claustrophobic. I wasn't used to living like that. In Cheng's flat, although it was tiny and quiet, I at least had the window overlooking the Seng Guan Temple. But from among the windows in Ghassan's flat, although there were plenty of them, I never found one that looked out on anything interesting, other than that bitter feeling of alienation towards the country and the people.

Ghassan went to work every morning while I stayed at home looking for ways to kill time. All the books on the shelves on the wall were in Arabic. The newspapers and magazines that Ghassan kept were also in Arabic. One morning I started browsing through them, looking at the pictures. In every magazine and every newspaper there was always one or more photos of Ghassan. That's why he had kept those copies. There was plenty of writing under the pictures and I wondered what it said, what was written about him. He told me later that these newspapers and magazines were like his personal archives, including some of his poems and reviews of them, newspaper interviews he had given and press coverage of seminars and discussions in which he had taken part.

One evening I asked him to read me something he had written. He looked at my face with interest. 'Read you one of my poems? In English? I never thought of that,' he said. I was delighted when he pulled a piece of paper out of his desk and put his glasses on the end of his nose. 'That sounds like a wonderful idea. Just give me some time, Isa. I'll translate a small passage,' he said. He started writing on the paper with a pencil. It didn't take him long. He lit a cigarette. 'I can't talk without some smoke to go with my words,' he joked. He cleared his throat, then started reading in English in a beautiful voice, softly at times and sometimes more loudly. He was waving his arms around melodramatically and using facial expressions to reinforce the effect.

I was very moved by Ghassan's performance and was almost crying. He finished reading and looked at me. 'What do you think?' he said.

I was embarrassed. The words of his poem were indeed English but they didn't include a single meaningful sentence.

'To be honest,' I began, hesitantly. 'I didn't understand anything.'

Ghassan nodded his head. 'If you had said anything different, I would have known you were lying,' he said, then paused. 'Because I didn't understand anything of what I said either,' he added.

He roared with laughter, blowing cigarette smoke from his mouth and nostrils. I laughed too, and examined his face.

I wished I could read what Ghassan had written, or understand it when it was read, as easily as I could read his face.

★ ★ ★

'There are lots of pictures of your father in that drawer,' Ghassan said one morning before leaving for work, pointing at the drawer of his desk. Then he took ten dinars out of his pocket and gave them to me. 'On the top of the desk, you'll find the telephone numbers of some restaurants, if you don't like what I have in my kitchen,' he added.

I had never thought about whether I liked a particular food or not. As far as I was concerned, the function of food was just to stave off hunger. White rice and soya sauce served the purpose. My only problem at the time was with the water. It had a different taste from the water I was used to drinking in the Philippines. Ghassan laughed when I said one day, 'The water there is nicer.' He bought me two bottles of mineral water but it still wasn't as nice as the drinking water I was used to.

When Ghassan went out, I kept thinking about the drawer where he said the pictures of my father were.

Years earlier, when my mother used to show me pictures, she had been trying to help me find out about a man I was going to meet one day. Now that the man was dead, I had a strange feeling about seeing pictures of him. I was very reluctant to open the drawer, especially after Ghassan told me my father was always talking about me, which made me feel drawn to him. I didn't want to love this man now that it was impossible to meet him, but how much longer could I resist looking inside the drawer?

Despite all the clutter in the sitting room, it was the drawer that interested me most. The pictures of my father that I had in my briefcase didn't seem to be enough. I kept myself busy watching the English-speaking channels on television. There was nothing in Ghassan's flat to help me kill time other than the television. I looked out of the window from time to time but I didn't see anything outside that would encourage me to go out.

★   ★   ★

I couldn't walk down the street in Kuwait without noticing the cars. For an ordinary Filipino the cheapest, most basic car you could find in Kuwait would be like an impossible dream. The same with the houses. The smallest of them would be considered a mansion in the parts of town where I grew up.

The weather was so cold that for the first time in my life I could see my breath condensing in the air. I shivered as I walked the streets and watched the air I breathed out turn to mist. I had the strange feeling of being in a new climate, in a winter unlike the winters I had known in the past.

One day as I was walking along some backstreet, a car pulled up against the pavement and a man wearing traditional dress and headgear got out. He waved his identity card in my face. It was similar to the one I had. 'Police,' he said.

I was caught off guard and tongue-tied. The man continued angrily. 'Show me your identity papers,' he said.

I put my hand in the back pocket of my trousers and took out my wallet. He took it out of my hand before I had a chance to get the identity card out for him. I stood still and watched him. He began to look through it. He pulled out the ten dinars Ghassan had given me and put them in his pocket. He threw the wallet in my face without looking at my identity card, got in his car and drove off at speed. I stood there, unsure what to do, with the wallet at my feet.

If the police are thieves, what do the thieves do, I wondered.

A policeman? Without a police car or even a police uniform! I didn't understand anything.

4

After dinner one evening, I said to Ghassan, 'I've never seen you playing the musical instrument, the one my mother told me about.'

He looked at my face in surprise. 'Do you mean the oud?' he asked.

'Yes,' I said. He was silent for a while, as if thinking about something. He went out of the sitting room for a few minutes, then came back with the oud in a black leather cover that was the same shape as the instrument. In his other hand he held a damp cloth.

Ghassan sat cross-legged on the ground, with his back against the sofa behind him. Without thinking I slipped off the sofa and sat on the ground like him. With the damp cloth, he started removing the dust that had gathered on the leather cover. As he worked, he said, 'Josephine seems to have told you everything.'

Ghassan put the instrument on his legs without taking it out of the cover.

'You know, Isa,' he began, with a sad look on his face. 'The last time I played this instrument was during our activities under the occupation.'

'I thought you resisted the Iraqi army with weapons!' I said disapprovingly.

'Each of us resisted in his own way. Everyone had his weapon.'

While my father joined the Abu al-Fuhoud group, along with Ismail al-Kuwaiti and others, Ghassan was resisting the Iraqis elsewhere, using a different approach. He was writing patriotic poems and setting them to music, then recording them for distribution to the public, with the aim of inspiring people with the will to resist. Ghassan soon stopping doing that and started working with Abu Faris, who was writing a patriotic operetta that became known as *al-Sumoud* (*Steadfastness*). Ghassan sang in the chorus with other young men from the resistance. He also helped distribute the operetta in the form of cassettes, which were widely circulated during the Iraqi occupation.

Ghassan said that after the secret meetings where they rehearsed for the patriotic choral work, far from the eyes of the Iraqi forces, he no longer had any desire to play the oud, especially after Abu Faris and the man who wrote the music for the operetta were captured by the Iraqis.

Ghassan took the oud out of the leather cover. The colour and shine of the wood made it look new, untouched. He picked up the small piece of plastic and strummed the strings. He smiled at me. I prepared to hear him play. He reached out to the keys to tune the strings. He turned one of the keys and plucked the string to test the pitch. Suddenly the string snapped.

'See? Even the strings refuse to play,' he said, putting the oud back in its cover.

Ghassan went to his bedroom while I stayed in the sitting room. I kept thinking about the drawer that held the pictures of my father, but at first I was hesitant to open it. I didn't hesitate for long. I sat in the chair at the desk and gently pulled it open.

There were dozens of photographs from different periods of his life. Pictures of him with a thin moustache, others with a thick moustache. Pictures of him wearing glasses and others of him without. If he had looked sad in the pictures, the fact of his death would have had less impact, but in all the pictures he looked so happy that it brought a lump to my throat to think he had died so young. Every picture showed that my father had been full of life. There was a picture of him in the beach house with a large fish hanging from one raised arm, and his other arm bent to show off his biceps, as if to say, 'It was me who caught it.' Walid was standing next to him, with his arm raised high too, but with a fish only the size of a finger, and with his other arm bent like my father's. There was another picture taken in London, with my father standing under Big Ben in a smart grey suit and a dark red tie, next to a woman who appeared to be Kuwaiti, wearing a long brown coat, a short checked skirt, knee-length boots and an elegant hat that made her look like an English princess. There was another picture of him and Walid in Thailand, wearing short-sleeved shirts. My father was bowing, his hands folded, in the traditional Thai greeting, as was a young woman standing beside him. Walid was behind them, sticking out his tongue as always and making V-signs with two fingers of each hand behind their heads. It looked like a peace sign but that definitely wasn't what Walid meant. There was a picture of my father with Ghassan, with Ghassan in goalkeeper's kit and my father standing with a ball between his feet. He had such long hair that he looked like a tree. He was wearing black shorts and a yellow T-shirt with the number nine. Ghassan told me later that was the number of my father's favourite player. There was another picture in which my father appeared with his head shaved and a piece of white cloth wrapped around his body, baring his right shoulder and part of his chest. In the corner of the same picture Walid is wearing the same type of cloth, submitting to a man who is shaving his head with a razor. In one picture I couldn't easily make out my father. He had a long beard and was wearing a white gown and the traditional headdress any old how without the black headband. I later found

5

Kuwait was beautiful. That's what I thought when Ghassan took me out to the shopping malls and the restaurants. The streets were remarkably clean. They had to be, because the cars that drove on them weren't ordinary cars. Each building and house was different, and each had some special feature – the colours, the design and so on. And the cars parked outside were so beautiful!

I was particularly struck by the way men kissed each other as a form of greeting. In fact it wasn't really a kiss, but it came close to one. The man brushed his cheek against the other man's cheek as they shook hands. I heard from Ghassan that it was the traditional form of greeting here, and not just between men. In fact the women did the same when they greeted each other.

One man walked past us and whispered '*As-salam aleekum*' and kept walking as Ghassan replied, '*Wa aleekum as-salam*.' I turned to Ghassan and asked if he knew the man. He shook his head. Before I had time to ask more questions, he was saying '*As-salam aleekum*' to one of the men at the door to the lift in the shopping mall. 'Do you know *him*?' I asked him again. He shook his head. *So why did they greet each other*, I wondered.

People looked and dressed so differently from each other, sometimes the complete opposite. I pointed to one man whose appearance caught my attention and asked Ghassan where he was from. 'He's Kuwaiti,' he said.

'And that one?'

'Kuwaiti.'

'No, no, I don't mean that one, I mean that one.'

'They're both Kuwaiti.'

'And the one standing there?'

'Kuwaiti.'

'And the girl who's wearing the . . .'

'Kuwaiti too.'

And so on, and so on.

Some people wore clothes that followed the latest fashions. Others wore traditional clothes. There were people in shorts, in T-shirts or in jeans. There were young men with long hair visible under their headdresses. There were people in clothes that would be tight even on thin people. There were young people who had bizarre hairstyles that I really liked, while others wore hats. Some had white headdresses and others wore red ones. There were burly athletic bodies and others that were very thin. There were lots of girls, with different hairstyles, nice clothes, some short skirts and some long, and bright colours. Some of them covered their hair with headscarves of various kinds – beehive-style scarves, scarves that showed a wisp of hair on the forehead, scarves that covered all the hair and others that also covered part of the chin. Black thobes, some of them so tight that they showed details of the woman's body, others loose. There were young women who looked like Hollywood stars, others with so much powder on their faces that they looked like geishas. Sharp noses, unnaturally full lips. There were women who covered their faces with pieces of black cloth that only showed the eyes. Black hair, blonde hair. Brown people, white people, black people.

With so many differences, I found reason to hope. *You'll be invisible among all these people*, I told myself.

★ ★ ★

I stayed as Ghassan's guest for more than a month. During that time Kuwait gradually cheered up. At the end of January the new Emir took office and his picture started to spread in the newspapers, on the streets and on cars. By the last week of February Kuwait was completely changed. I wouldn't be exaggerating if I said I saw Kuwait dancing for joy on 25 February.

Ghassan took me out for a ride in what he called his 'beloved', his white Mitsubishi Lancer, to the streets near the sea. The air was cold although it was sunny. It grew more crowded as we drove closer to the area on the coast. Cars were flying flags of all sizes and playing loud patriotic songs with the windows down. The car horns competed with each other. There was clapping and cheering and people looked happy. On national holidays Kuwaitis fire water pistols and foam sprays at each other, so it's like a giant washing machine. That's what I felt. People were singing and dancing soaked in water and covered in foam, as if they were washing in a communal bath. Ghassan made sure all the car doors were locked, saying that some people wouldn't hesitate to open car doors and spray the passengers with water and foam.

I remembered the crazy young men I used to see at Boracay and realised they were only a small sample of those who were dancing in the street on National Day.

I looked into people's faces, examining them closely. There must surely be a place for me in this mixture, which blended together well despite the diversity.

My musings were interrupted by a strange noise. A woman had put her hand close to her mouth and was flapping her tongue up and down, making a noise rather like the war cries of the American–Indians.

I was struck by how people interacted. The deep sadness on the day I arrived had changed in record time into enthusiastic celebration.

'Did you – my father, Walid and you – celebrate like this?' I asked.

'Not at all,' said Ghassan, as if I had made some accusation.

'We celebrated our love for Kuwait in here,' he said, pointing to his heart.

6

'Are you prepared to meet your grandmother tomorrow?' Ghassan asked me on the evening of the day he took me to the National Day celebrations.

'I don't know,' I answered hesitantly. 'She used to hate me.'

I watched Ghassan's face, expecting some encouragement from him, but he didn't say anything. 'Do you think she still feels the same way?' I continued.

'I've no idea, Isa, but . . .' Ghassan began, then paused. 'Don't think it will be easy,' he continued.

The next morning, a little after eleven thirty, I was shaking and sweating. I sat next to Ghassan in his beloved car. He parked outside my grandmother's house and looked at me. 'Isa! What's wrong?' he said.

'Take me back to Jabriya, please.'

He took a paper handkerchief out of the box in front of him and passed it to me. 'Isa, take it easy,' he said. 'Don't be . . .'

I hated myself when I couldn't stop myself looking so weak. I cried like a child who was about to be thrown down a dark hole. Ghassan was shaken. He started patting me on the shoulder. 'Take it easy, take it easy,' he said.

He opened the car door and said, 'You stay here. I'll go and see your grandmother alone.' He closed the car door, then put his elbows on the window sill and put his head and shoulders through the hole. 'I'll talk to her about you, and then I'll come and invite you in,' he said. 'Be brave,' he added with a broad smile.

I wiped my tears away with the handkerchief and watched him ring the doorbell. He spoke to a maid who looked Indian. She went off for a while, then came back to let him in. Ghassan disappeared into the house, but the door remained open.

Which door would he come out through, I wondered. Would he come out of the garage door with his tail between his legs, like my father years earlier? I looked at the big house and imagined my mother working inside. How did she manage to look after such a big house all by herself?

'*Allahu akbar, Allahu akbar*,' called the muezzin from a small mosque about fifty metres from Grandmother's house, followed by other calls to prayer from far and near: '*Allahu akbar, Allahu akbar*.' It was the first time I had heard the call so clearly and so close up. I had a strange feeling. Something about it reassured me. The words sounded familiar even though I didn't know the language. Something still inside me started to stir.

It was the same call that my father had whispered in my right ear just after I was born. That was the first human voice I ever heard. Did the call to prayer perhaps stir a subliminal memory of the words my father whispered? It was a sound that made me curious to go into the mosque near my grandmother's house – a curiosity I had never felt when I went past the Golden Mosque or the Green Mosque in Quiapo in Manila.

I had a strange, vague impression of Islam. For me it was associated with certain symbols, like any religion or civilisation or idea. If the symbol worked well, it left a good impression of the thing it symbolised. If the symbol was a failure, it sent the wrong message.

When I was young, I looked on Islam with some bewilderment, mixed with respect when I found out how highly people regarded Lapu-Lapu, the famous sultan of Mactan, seen by Filipinos as one of their most important national heroes because he resisted colonialism in the sixteenth century. There are giant statues and other memorials to him in main squares across the country, portraying him with long hair, bare-chested, with his hands resting on the hilt of a sword planted in the ground. I remembered everything about this Muslim sultan. My classmates at school skipped this lesson and jumped on to the next lessons, but I read on until I reached the description of what happened on the morning of 27 April 1521, when Lapu-Lapu came out at the head of 1,500 warriors armed with *barong* knives, lances, *kampilan* swords and *kalasag* shields, in the famous battle of Mactan against Portuguese invader and explorer Ferdinand Magellan, who organised the first expedition to sail around the world. Magellan had sailed to Mactan in command of a force of more than 500 troops armed with muskets, on a mission to convert the sultan of the island to Christianity after successfully converting the ruler of a nearby island. Lapu-Lapu refused to meet Magellan's demands and sprang to the defence of the island. They managed to kill Magellan with a poisoned arrow at the end of the battle.

Lapu-Lapu was the only Muslim icon I knew. I saw him and his men as mythical heroes and I thought my Muslim father was a distant descendant of his lineage. Because of him I had a positive image of Islam. But later this image was severely challenged by another Muslim icon that undermined my earlier impressions. That was the Abu Sayyaf group, which financed its activities by robbery, assassinations and blackmailing companies and rich businessmen. I had heard plenty about them when I was in the Philippines but I didn't pay them much attention because I was young and I wasn't interested in details of their movement at the time. Then they carried out their famous kidnapping in the middle of 2001. Everyone in the Philippines followed the news of the hostages, among them three Americans – two men and the wife of one of them. The news was horrifying. Twelve Filipino hostages were killed and the body of one of the American men was found with his head cut off. The hostages were held for more than a year before the army made an attempt to rescue them and the other American man and a Filipino nurse were killed. The Muslims in Mindanao are no doubt kind and peace-loving, like poor people everywhere, but people abroad only know them through the Abu Sayyaf group.

The heroism and life story of Sultan Lapu-Lapu, and the way ordinary people in the Philippines, regardless of religion, admired him and recognised his role in resisting invasion, were positive images that made me feel close to Islam. But the Abu Sayyaf group, by killing missionaries and other innocent people, very much alienated me from Islam.

★   ★   ★

The call to prayer was over and quiet returned. I was still in the car outside keeping an eye on Grandmother's house. The curtain on one of the upstairs windows moved. I caught sight of a young woman looking down at me. She disappeared behind the curtain a few seconds later. I looked down to the front door, where Ghassan was coming out. His face left no room for guesswork.

He closed the car door, put on his seatbelt and lit a cigarette. 'Never mind. We'll try again another time,' he said, without turning to face me.

I didn't say anything, just like my mother years earlier when my father came out of the same house carrying me in his arms. I preferred not to speak, and I prepared myself for a return to Mendoza's piece of land once again.

★   ★   ★

'What's the point of trying again, Ghassan?' I asked when we were back in his flat.

'Because your grandmother is bound to change her mind,' Ghassan said. He stopped, as if trying to remember something. 'She's not sure what to do.' He looked me right in the face. 'It would be easier if she wasn't so worried about what people might say,' he added.

'What have other people got to do with my family accepting me? How would they know about me?' I asked naively.

Ghassan shook his head in frustration. 'Gossip rules here,' he said. 'And besides, it's not about you, it's about the Tarouf family. Everyone will know about it. Kuwait's a small place.'

'So small there's no room for me,' I added sadly.

★   ★   ★

When my grandfather Isa died, he left my grandmother with three girls and a boy – Rashid, my father. My grandmother gave Rashid special treatment because he was the only son and the man of the house. That's what my mother told me. But what was more important was that my father was the only child whose children could inherit the family name. My grandmother had wanted to see Rashid have children, particularly males who might ensure the survival of the Tarouf name, especially as Isa my grandfather had been the last of the Tarouf clan since the death of his brother Shahin. My grandfather had my father to carry the family name after him. But when my father was killed during the Iraqi occupation without leaving a son (bearing in mind that I was just a 'thing', as my grandmother once put it), it became impossible for the Tarouf family name to survive. But now, with my sudden reappearance, my grandmother started thinking about that 'thing' – the only person left who could guarantee that the name of his father and grandfather continued and who could pass on the family name to his offspring.

'What does the Filipina's boy look like?' she asked Ghassan at that meeting.

'Like a Filipino,' he answered.

'That old woman is impressive,' said Ghassan, although I hadn't asked him for details of the meeting. 'You don't know what Rashid meant to Auntie Ghanima, and despite the way you look, you are his only son. Do you understand?'

'No, I don't understand.'

'OK,' said Ghassan, shrugging his shoulders. 'Pass me that packet of cigarettes so I can explain.'

I passed him the packet. He took out a cigarette and lit it. 'Listen,' he said, blowing out the smoke. 'Khawla is the last person whose family name is Tarouf. One day she'll get married and her children will take her husband's name.' He thought a while and then continued. 'Apart from you, Auntie Ghanima has two other grandsons with the first name of their grandfather, Isa. But they don't bear the family name because both of them have taken their family names from their fathers. Now that you're back,' he said, pointing at me with his index finger, 'no one but you can guarantee that the Tarouf name will continue.'

I was looking at him like an idiot. I showed no interest in what he was saying. 'Who's Khawla?' I asked.

★ ★ ★

Khawla was born six months after the end of the war over Kuwait and so her father never saw her. She too was never lucky enough to be able to say 'papa'. But I suddenly realised that I did have one advantage over my sister. In spite of everything that had happened, at least my father had carried me in his arms. I also bore the name that he had chosen, his own father's name. He had looked into my face and kissed me, even if I remember nothing about it. Poor Khawla. Father never whispered the call to prayer in her right ear after she was born. He didn't carry her in his arms and Khawla wasn't the name he had chosen for her.

My father had married again in the middle of 1990, this time to Iman. He didn't spend much time with her because he was captured by Iraqi forces. His wife gave birth to my sister the year Kuwait was liberated and the two of them lived in Grandmother's house until Iman married another man some years later. She moved to his house and left Khawla in the care of Grandmother, who treated her better than she did my three aunts – Awatif, Nouriya and Hind.

In Grandmother's house, my sister was Khawla, the daughter of Rashid, and nothing she asked for was withheld. She was Grandmother's precious darling. Grandmother was anxious to protect her from both other people and from the *djinn*. Ghassan said that every night Grandmother put her hand on Khawla's forehead and recited verses from the Qur'an. She prayed to God to protect Khawla and keep her safe from envious people. In the morning she gave her holy water to drink – water over which she had recited Qur'anic verses.

Ghassan often talked to me about Khawla. He was fond of her, and she of him. She saw him as a substitute for the father she had never seen. 'She's a wonderful girl,' Ghassan said of her. 'She's intelligent. Make friends with her, Isa. She needs a brother as much as you need a sister.'

Khawla had her problems too. She was fatherless, of course, and her mother had abandoned her for her new husband. These things didn't seem to have had a negative effect on her however. She wasn't like other girls of her generation. She was almost a copy of her father in the way she spent hours reading his books in his study. She dreamed of finishing off the novel my father had started writing but hadn't finished when he died. She didn't have many friends. Ghassan and her Aunt Hind were her closest friends.

'I'm proud of her. She's like a daughter to me,' said Ghassan.

What Ghassan said about me being the only person who could ensure the survival of the family name made me feel like a legitimate king who had just come back from a long journey to reclaim his kingdom. But legitimacy alone wasn't enough to secure recognition. *Should I fight for it?* Kings lose legitimacy when people reject them and I had been rejected, and I wasn't even a king.

I didn't understand what continuing the family name meant. What would happen if the family name didn't continue? And what did the way I looked have to do with it?

I later found out that Grandmother didn't know what to do the night after her meeting with Ghassan. I was her grandson – Isa Rashid Isa al-Tarouf, a name that brought honour. But I had a face that brought shame. I was Isa, the son of Rashid who died defending his country, but at the same time I was Isa, the son of the Filipina maid.

7

It was thanks to Khawla, Grandmother's favourite, that I was accepted into the Tarouf household, albeit under duress. My sister told Grandmother that she insisted I be allowed to visit.

'It would just be a visit, Grandmother, please,' she said. 'And afterwards you can decide.'

Grandmother gave in to Khawla's entreaties. 'I don't know why, but I've been pressing Grandmother to let you visit our house,' Khawla told me at our first meeting. 'Maybe it was curiosity, or maybe because I was happy to have a new brother suddenly appear in my life.'

Ghassan and I had been in the sitting room in his flat when the phone rang. Ghassan had picked it up, and after a short conversation put it down again. 'You're lucky,' he said. 'You have a brave sister.'

★　★　★

Everything happens for a reason, and for a purpose. I like my mother's faith. Her saying reminds me day after day that chance has no place in our destiny. My father married Iman to pave the way for Khawla, who spoke up for me in the Tarouf household. If it hadn't been for her I would never have had a chance to come close to that house. But what if Khawla had been born a boy – a boy who had his grandfather's name, Isa, and the family name that was about to die out, and who could pass it on to his children, who could then reproduce and act as an extension of generations that carried the name many years ago, people who built walls around their ancient city and who were no less proud of having built them than the Chinese were to have built the Great Wall of China?

Thank God for Khawla.

* * *

After sunset on the day after Khawla's phone call, Ghassan rang the bell at Grandmother's house, while I stood in fear behind him – in fear of being thrown out, of being humiliated and of not being accepted.

The door opened. 'Welcome,' said a female voice. The voice and the accent aroused my curiosity. I stood on tiptoes to look over Ghassan's shoulder, and there was a young Filipina maid dressed in white from head to toe – the headscarf, the uniform, the apron and the shoes. She looked like a nurse. I squeezed Ghassan's shoulder with my hand. I was overjoyed to see a face that looked like mine.

'Filipina?' I asked her.

Ghassan turned around and gave me a disapproving look. 'Isa, she's the maid!' he said.

'Luza, Luza, who is it?' asked a voice from inside, speaking in perfect English.

'It's Mr Ghassan,' said the maid, waving us in. As soon as we were through the door, we were warmly welcomed.

'*Salamuuu alekooom*,' someone said.

I looked around to see who was speaking and found a parrot in a beautiful gilt cage fixed to the wall opposite the door. Ghassan laughed. The parrot raised its voice and started repeating the maid's name: 'Luza, Luza.' Then it shouted a word I couldn't make out. The maid came towards the cage, waved her arms in the air and said, 'Shhhhh.' The parrot shut up and Ghassan went on laughing.

'Come in, come in,' said Khawla, who was waiting for us. I knew who she was at first sight. She looked older than her sixteen years. She was brown-skinned and taller than me. She had covered her hair with a black *hijab*. She had a sharp and prominent nose, thin lips and white teeth that were strikingly regular. She was pretty and she looked charming when she smiled. She spoke with Ghassan in Arabic, then turned to me. 'So you're Isa,' she said cheerfully.

I smiled at her and nodded.

'Come on in, come on in,' she continued.

We followed her in, and she kept turning to me with a broad smile that showed how pleased she was. She invited us inside and asked us to sit down and wait. Then she went upstairs, looking back at me all the way up. *Nice house*, I said to myself. But I wondered how people found time to deal with all the details – matching the colours, the furniture, the marble floors, the fine rugs, the decorative touches on the walls, the chandeliers, the plush velvet curtains, the little wooden tables with tablecloths decorated with shiny beads that looked like pearls or precious stones, the vases of various sizes holding bamboo stalks. I loved the place even though I was cowering in my seat for fear of damaging something unintentionally. The Filipino face that met us at the door and the bamboo stalks made me feel more at home, even if the bamboo looked out of place in those expensive vases, rather like me in the Tarouf household.

Another maid came in, older than the first, wearing the same white uniform. She looked Indian. She offered us some fruit juice, then withdrew. Then a woman came down from the first floor, apparently in her late thirties. She looked serious and practical. She had black hair, cut short like a boy's. She put out her hand to shake Ghassan's hand, then she shook mine and sat down opposite us with her legs crossed.

'This is your youngest aunt, Hind,' said Ghassan as he introduced me to her.

I nodded and said, 'Pleased to meet you, madam.'

She nodded but didn't quite smile. She and Ghassan spoke in Arabic, while I watched their expressions and noticed how serious they looked. She raised her eyebrows when she was speaking to Ghassan. She snatched a glance at me, adjusted her glasses with her finger, then went back to chatting with Ghassan. I noticed that he didn't look at her when they were talking. I was silent, looking from one to the other. I felt like I was watching a film in a language I didn't understand, with no subtitles. Although Ghassan and my aunt gave nothing away through their facial expressions, I interpreted their conversation the way I wanted it to be. I imagined her saying, 'We promise him a private room when he comes to live here with us' or 'We're very happy he's come back to his country and his family.'

Then an old woman appeared at the top of the stairs, leaning on Khawla's arm and holding the banister with her other hand. She had to be my grandmother, Ghanima. She wasn't looking at us in the sitting room. Her eyes were on the steps by her feet. She was having trouble bending her legs and was coming down slowly. She had covered her hair loosely with a thin black shawl, quite different from Khawla's *hijab*. Some of her hair showed from under the shawl. Because she was concentrating on making her way down the stairs, I had an opportunity to take a long look at her face without her seeing me. With every step she took I discovered something new in her face. She was old – the wrinkles in her dark skin showed that. Her lips were thin, or she didn't have lips, if I can say that – just a horizontal slit under her nose. She had thick eyebrows and a large, protruding nose that was hooked at the end. Her eyes were small and bright, with black pupils so large that hardly any white was visible around them. She had a keen gaze, as if she could see through things. Her crooked nose and her bright eyes gave her the look of a golden eagle.

As my grandmother approached, leaning on Khawla's arm, Ghassan and my Aunt Hind stood up respectfully for her. I stood up too. She nodded in greeting to Ghassan. I was at a loss. I didn't know what my role was or what I should do. Should I bow, take her hand and press it to my forehead as we do in the Philippines? In her presence I stood there confused, like someone meeting the leader of a tribe and ignorant of the social conventions. Ghassan turned to me and said, 'Kiss your grandmother on her forehead.'

My heart raced. I looked at her forehead as if I were about to kiss a hot piece of metal. She wasn't looking at me. I stepped towards her, encouraged by Ghassan's smile and the happiness on Khawla's face. I was standing in front of her, but as soon as I moved my face towards her forehead she raised her hand, which was stained dark brown with henna presumably, and put it on my shoulder, preventing me from coming any closer. I pulled back. She looked me straight in the eyes. My lips began to tremble and I bowed my head. She took her hand off my shoulder and involuntarily I examined the part of my shirt where her hand had rested, in case the tribal leader had left a mark there as part of a ritual recognising me as a member of her tribe. But nothing in this little fantasy of mine came true. I looked up to her face. She was still staring at my face. Her eyes were glistening – was it a sign of intelligence or did it mean that tears were gathering and about to flow? I bowed my head again.

'Kiss her forehead, Isa,' Ghassan repeated. The hot piece of metal seemed even hotter now. My lips were trembling even more than before. I moved my face towards the metal to kiss it, but my grandmother turned her face away towards one of the sofas in the corner and asked Khawla to help her reach it. Grandmother sat down, after resting her hands on her knees and bending her legs with difficulty. Khawla brought her a stool on which to rest her legs, and everyone but me sat too.

Khawla looked at me standing there. 'Please sit down,' she said.

The Filipina maid came in with a tray of tiny glasses for tea, rather like shot glasses but with handles and little saucers. I didn't look at the maid. I didn't smile. I didn't utter a word. Even when she gave me a glass of tea, on a saucer with a tiny golden spoon and two cubes of sugar, I found I couldn't say 'thank you', though everyone else did. Grandmother was looking around, sometimes at me and the maid, sometimes at Ghassan and Hind, examining our faces with her keen gaze. She was on guard and I didn't feel comfortable in her presence. Sitting in front of an interrogator as a suspect makes you feel uncomfortable, even if you're innocent. How much more so if you're a rat in the presence of an eagle?

'*Salamuuu alekooom*,' cried the parrot. Then two women came in, one in *hijab* and the other without. They greeted Ghassan and kissed Hind and Khawla. then bent down to kiss Grandmother's forehead. Khawla introduced me to them: 'My Aunt Awatif and my Aunt Nouriya.' They sat down next to each other on a sofa in a corner of the large sitting room. They didn't look a bit like each other. Awatif, the eldest, was wearing a black cloak and was clutching her handbag with both hands. Her legs were pressed together. She wasn't wearing any make-up and she had a pleasant face, though she wasn't pretty like Khawla and Hind. She was smiling all the time and seemed friendly. She had big eyes set far apart and a broad and prominent forehead. All in all, including her cheerful face, she reminded me of a dolphin. Nouriya was the complete opposite. She sat with her legs crossed and seemed very self-confident. She had a fair amount of make-up on and was noticeably elegant, with sharp features. She held her chin up and raised her eyebrows when she spoke. She seemed arrogant. I looked from one to the other, making a quick comparison. *How did a dolphin and a shark come from the same womb*, I wondered.

They were talking, each in her own way, while Grandmother watched them quietly. She looked at Hind if Ghassan was speaking, and then switched to Ghassan if Hind was speaking. They talked loudly and interrupted each other. Sometimes they looked at me and sometimes they pointed at me. Khawla was looking at me with the same smile she had had since she came into the room with Ghassan. They had a discussion that went on more than an hour. Ghassan nodded. Hind was tense, swinging one of her legs and speaking quietly. The dolphin smiled naively. The shark spoke excitably. The old eagle silenced everyone with a shake

8

When we were back in Ghassan's flat after the visit to Grandmother's house, I finally found out what had happened in the meeting. Ghassan had two options: either to hand over his charge, in other words me, to the Tarouf household, thereby fulfilling my father's wishes, or to make arrangements for me to go back to my mother's country. Khawla was happy to have discovered her new brother because, as she put it, if her mother had another child with her second husband her new brother or sister wouldn't be as close to her in age as I was, so she insisted on me staying. 'I'll teach him Arabic and I'll look after him. Don't you worry about him, Grandmother,' she had said.

Awatif, my eldest aunt, was very happy. She didn't see a problem, and she was enthusiastic about me staying in Grandmother's house because, as she put it, 'He's our son.' Although the others ignored her opinion, she had insisted on recognising me. 'He's my brother's son. God wouldn't like it if we disowned him,' she had said. Ghassan made me happy when he told me what she said. I was delighted to hear that God was present at the meeting to hear what was going on. Even if I hadn't seen Him, I was reassured that He was present in Awatif's heart, because that meant He was nearby. I asked God to enter my heart as well.

Nouriya was totally opposed to me being around and had got angry with Awatif and warned her of what might happen if her husband, Ahmad, found out about me. Awatif wavered a while when her husband was discussed but she later relented. 'My husband is a God-fearing man and would not take a negative position if he found out,' she said. Nouriya had grown angrier and raised her voice. She said that, if there was no other way out, my full name should be just Isa Rashid Isa and the Tarouf name should be removed from my official papers. They should look for somewhere that could put me up, away from the Tarouf house, or settle the matter by offering me some money and sending me back to the Philippines, she added. She lost her temper. 'Kuwait's a small place and word spreads fast,' she said. 'If my husband and his family find out about this boy, it will change the way my husband sees me. I'll lose the respect of the Adil family and I'll be the laughing stock of Faisal's sisters and sisters-in-law.' Angrily, she had picked up her handbag to leave. Before she stormed out, she said, 'I have a son and a daughter of marriageable age and I won't allow this Filipino to wreck their prospects.'

I didn't understand what Ghassan said about Nouriya's attitude. Why was she so upset? What was it that threatened her reputation and made her the laughing stock of her husband's family? Why did my presence complicate marriage for her son and her daughter? Those were the same words Grandmother had said to my father years earlier when she found out my mother was pregnant: 'And your sisters, you selfish, despicable man. Who'll marry them after what you've done with the maid?' These were things I didn't understand. When I was in the Philippines my mother couldn't explain them to me. I asked Ghassan what it all meant.

'It's impossible to explain such things to you, Isa,' he replied, 'and it's hard for you to understand.' I was in a difficult position, caught between support from Khawla and Awatif, and categorical rejection by Nouriya.

Hind was unsure where she stood. She was a rights activist, well-known as Hind al-Tarouf. 'My credibility is on the line and so is my name,' she had said. She would have to sacrifice one of them – either her credibility or her name. If she upheld my rights as a human being when people found out that her war hero brother, Rashid al-Tarouf, had married a Filipina maid, she would have to sacrifice the way people saw her illustrious name. Sacrificing her principles and taking a stand against my human rights would preserve the prestige of her name and society's respect for her. Or she could try to preserve both her own reputation as a person of principle and the reputation of her family by sacrificing me before anyone found out about me. But would it be any sacrifice on their part if they disowned me and turned me away? If that was the case, I would have been happy, because choosing to sacrifice me would mean that I had some value in their eyes. Real sacrifice means giving up things we value, something irreplaceable, for the sake of something else. But as far as I knew I had no value. They didn't need me. If I disappeared it would be no loss to them, and they wouldn't need anything to make up for my disappearance.

'And my grandmother, Ghassan, my grandmother, what did she think?' I asked, after he had briefed me on the conversation I couldn't understand when I was with them. He blew out some cigarette smoke and said, 'Auntie Ghanima has the first say, and the last say.' Then he paused to think.

I looked at his face with interest. 'And what did she decide?' I asked.

'Did you hear her say anything at the meeting?' he asked.

'No, she was silent, just looking at people's faces all the time,' I replied.

He stubbed his cigarette out in the ashtray and looked at me. 'Why ask me now what she thinks? Maybe she needs some time to think,' he said.

He paused, and smiled to reassure me. 'Leave things to Khawla,' he added.

★　★　★

There were many things my mother hadn't told me about the paradise I was promised. She told me a lot about making dreams come true, securing a safe future and many opportunities that weren't available to anyone in the Philippines. For years I had lived on Mendoza's land listening to what my mother had to say: 'One day you'll go back to your father's country.' Yet when I did go back to my father's country I found that I posed a dilemma for his family. They wanted me but didn't want me. Some of them were happy I'd come back. Others were undecided and others wanted to pay me off and ask me to go back to the Philippines. In the meantime I was in a country I didn't know, looking for somewhere that would take me in, torn between Kuwait and the Philippines.

As soon as I learned to live with my new name, Isa al-Tarouf, and shook off my old names and nicknames – José, 'the Arabo' and 'the bastard' – I found there were people who were offended that I shared their name. I'm not Mendoza, who didn't have a father. I'm Isa, and I have a father called Rashid al-Tarouf.

9

Three days after the family meeting I was in Ghassan's flat feeling cold, though the weather was mild as far as he was concerned. I was wrapping my hands around a cup of coffee, toasting my feet in thick socks against an electric fire and watching one of the foreign film channels. Ghassan was reading a book. His mobile phone rang. He put the book upside down on his knees and looked at the screen of his phone. 'It's a call from your family,' he said.

In a single leap I was on the sofa where he was sitting. 'My mother? Or Mama Aida?' I asked impatiently.

He didn't answer. He put the phone to his ear and said, '*Wa aleekum as-salam.*' The conversation went on for more than ten minutes, and throughout it Ghassan didn't say a single word. He just nodded and murmured 'Mmm' every now and then. Then the conversation ended.

'Listen, Isa,' he said. 'You're going to go and live in your grandmother's house.'

As soon as he said the words I couldn't help jumping up and down in the middle of the sitting room, punching my fists in the air and shouting, 'Yes, yes, yes!' I felt that the ground was shaking under my feet.

'Isa!' Ghassan said in annoyance. 'Stop jumping. We're on the fourth floor and there are people beneath us.'

I went back to the sofa where he was sitting and looked straight into his eyes. 'Beneath us?' I asked. 'But we're the lowest of the low, you and me,' I said, shaking my head.

Ghassan laughed so much that he was shaking all over. 'I'll miss you, you crazy,' he said.

Jabriya is not far from Qortuba, where my grandmother lived. But I suddenly felt sorry for Ghassan, though he had lived alone all his life. I felt that by moving to my grandmother's house I was abandoning him. I remembered my father and Walid and when they were with Ghassan and my mother's stories about the three friends – their private world, their conversations, their singing, their travels abroad and their boating trips. The man must feel very lonely in his small, claustrophobic flat in a building full of a mixture of migrant workers – Egyptians, Syrians, Indians and Pakistanis.

'Ghassan,' I said.

He stopped laughing and looked at me.

'Why haven't you got married yet?' I asked.

His face reverted to the face of the Ghassan I knew. He took the book off his knees and put it on the sofa beside him. He was about to say something but he stopped. I picked up his packet of cigarettes, took one out, lit it and offered it to him.

'Go on, spit it out with the cigarette smoke,' I said.

He took a deep puff. The end of the cigarette glowed bright red and bits of ash fell off. 'I don't want to have children who would curse me after I die, Isa,' he said as he exhaled the smoke. He leaned back in the sofa and locked his hands behind his head, with the cigarette hanging on his lip. 'All I could pass on to my children would be a label that has stuck to me all my life,' he continued, then stopped and looked at me. 'Being a bidoon, Isa,' he said, 'is like having a damaged gene. Some genes malfunction but are not passed on, or they only recur in later generations. But this malignant gene never misses. It passes from one generation to the next without fail, destroying the hopes of those who carry it.'

Ghassan stubbed out his cigarette in the ashtray, then withdrew to his room.

★   ★   ★

While I was in the sitting room late that night, Ghassan came out of his room with his face swollen and his eyes half-shut. He passed me his mobile. 'A call from . . .' he said, opening his mouth wide in a big yawn, 'your sister Khawla.' I took the phone. Ghassan turned and walked robotically back to his room.

'Hello.'

'Hi, Isa. I hope I haven't woken you up.'

'No, no. I hadn't gone to sleep yet.'

Khawla told me they had prepared a room for me in the annex with everything I would need. My heart skipped for joy. 'You'll find everything in the room,' she said and began listing all the contents.

'That's too much,' I said, interrupting her. 'Far too much, Khawla.' She stopped. I looked at the phone screen to make sure I was still connected.

'Hello, Khawla?'

'Yes, I'm still here.'

'Thank you for everything you've done for me.'

'But . . .' She stopped again, then continued hesitantly. 'Are you sure you're happy about that?' she asked.

'Very much. It's better than I'd dreamed of,' I said.

'Isn't staying in the annex a bit . . .' she trailed off, as if looking for the right word. 'Look, I did my best to make sure you could stay with us more properly,' she continued, 'but let's wait and see. Maybe Grandmother will change her mind and let you live with us inside the house.'

I realised then that Grandmother had only partially accepted me. The annex wasn't the house itself. It was

264

somewhere separate in the inner courtyard where the cook and the driver lived. Only the owners lived inside the house itself, and the maids on the top floor. I accepted the arrangement with good grace, partly because my room in the annex had once been the *diwaniya* where my father met his friends.

'Hello, Isa, are you still there?'

'Yes, yes, I can hear you.'

'There are some other things I want you to know before you come.'

Before I moved to Grandmother's house I had to be told several things. I mustn't talk to the servants about who I was, especially the cook and the driver, because there were lots of neighbours and every house had a cook or a driver, or perhaps both. Servants in general don't keep the secrets of the houses they work in. They gossip among themselves, which means that secrets are liable to come out in the neighbours' houses. Khawla said a lot about this in our conversation and I concluded that I would be living in secret in Grandmother's house, or the annex, and my presence must not be disclosed to others.

'If any of the neighbours or their servants ask, then you're the new cook. This is temporary until we find a way around the problem,' Khawla said.

10

'Will we meet again?' I asked Ghassan as I got out of his car with my bags, in front of Grandmother's house.

'Many times, you crazy,' he replied.

I turned and headed for the door. 'Isa!' Ghassan called out. 'Take this,' he said, reaching out through the car window. I left my clothes bag and went back to him, carrying with me the briefcase with all my documents.

'What is it?' I asked.

'It's the key to my flat, so you can come any time. I might not be there, but you'll have the key,' he said.

Even you're not sure I'll stay in Grandmother's house, Ghassan, I said to myself. I thanked him and went back to my clothes bag by the door.

Even before I pressed the bell, Khawla opened the door and said, 'Hi, Isa.' She'd been waiting for me behind the door. Ghassan said goodbye by honking his horn, then drove off in his beloved Lancer, leaving me in the company of my sister. '*Salamuuu aleekooom,*' said the parrot, as usual whenever the door was opened. I was about to go in, but Khawla stopped me hesitantly. She looked at the houses next door and said, 'That way,' pointing to the side entrance. 'Your room's over there, Isa, and from there you can come into the main house through the courtyard.'

I went in through the side door, the door through which my father and I were evicted years earlier. The door led to the annex and Khawla was waiting for me there. She asked me to follow her and stopped in front of an aluminium door. She pointed to the door and said, 'This was my father's *diwaniya*. He used to meet his friends here.' She opened the door and stood aside. 'In you go. This is your room,' she said.

All this for me? It was a room way beyond my dreams. I would never need to go out. I couldn't believe what I saw. It was twice the size of my old room. A large carpet covered the whole floor. There was a large double bed with pillows and a fancy white cover, a big-screen television and a small table with a laptop computer. There was a fridge, a heater and air conditioning. 'Are you happy with this?' Khawla asked me.

'More than you can imagine,' I said, comparing it with my wretched room in the Philippines.

She asked me to leave my bags and follow her. In the courtyard she pointed to a door near to the door to my room. 'That's Babu and Raju's room, the cook and the driver,' she said. She pointed to a glass door with a steel frame right opposite my room. 'That's the way to the big sitting room where we were sitting last time. You won't have to meet the parrot if you come in through this door,' she said with a laugh. She pointed to a window on the upper floor, above the glass door. 'That's the window of Grandmother's room,' she said. She looked at her watch. 'It's almost ten o'clock. Shall I leave you to go to sleep?'

'No, no, it's still early,' I replied.

'Get changed now, and I'll visit you later.'

'Won't I be allowed to go into the main house?' I asked.

She gave the sweetest of smiles. But was it a real smile or just the way she shaped her lips? She nodded and said, 'Oh yes, Isa, but don't be impatient.'

Fully dressed and without even taking off my shoes, I lay down on my big new bed. Before long I heard a light tapping on the door. I sat up. Before I even went to the door, my Aunt Hind opened it, but she didn't take a step inside. She looked around, inspecting the room. 'Is everything as it should be?' she asked.

I was standing by the bed. 'Yes, madam,' I replied, without looking at her.

There were some seconds of silence. When she spoke again, her tone had changed. 'That's strange,' she said.

I looked at her, expecting her to explain what she thought was strange. 'You have Rashid's voice. It's like you're him but with a different face,' she said.

'Really, madam?' I said, pleased at what she had said.

'Why do you call me "madam"? I'm your aunt.'

I smiled and nodded without speaking. She nodded too. 'If you need anything,' she said, putting her hand into her little bag and handing me a mobile phone, 'this is for you. You'll find some numbers on it that might be important to you. Ghassan's number, Khawla's number and the phone number of the house.' She turned away and, as she walked towards the glass door that led to the sitting room, she looked back towards me and said, 'And my number too.'

★ ★ ★

After about an hour, Khawla came back and I opened the door for her. 'Come in,' I said, but she shook her head to say no.

'Follow me,' she said. 'I want to show you something.'

I followed her but when we reached the glass door, I felt I couldn't walk any further. 'Where are we going?' I asked.

She turned to me with her finger on her lips, asking me to keep quiet. Then I followed her. We went through the sitting room to a short corridor. We walked past the parrot's cage, which was covered with a piece of cloth. At the end of the corridor we came to a wooden door. Khawla pushed on it and said, 'In you go.'

It was a small room. Bookshelves covered most of the wall space. There was a wooden desk in one of the corners and a few pictures in gilt frames hanging where there was space on the wall. 'This is my father's study,' said Khawla.

Amazed by the number of books, I asked, 'And did Father read all these books?' Khawla smiled. I recalled all the conversations in which my mother had spoken to me about this room. This is where she and Rashid chatted when Grandmother and my aunts had gone to sleep. This is where my mother brought my father cups of coffee. It felt strange, like being in a museum that contained relics of our ancestors.

I went up to a picture on one of the walls, a black-and-white picture of an old man with a very high forehead, unkempt hair, bushy eyebrows, a white moustache and a long, forked white beard that reached halfway down his chest. 'I think I know who that is,' I said, turning to Khawla.

She came over to me by the picture. 'You should recognise him, Isa,' she said.

I looked at her with a broad grin. 'That's Grandfather Isa, right?' I said.

Khawla wanted to laugh but held it back. She rushed to the door of the room and locked it. Then she burst out laughing. 'That's Tolstoy, Isa,' she said. 'The famous Russian writer.'

I laughed with her to hide my embarrassment. To make amends for my mistake I pointed at another picture, of a man with the traditional headdress. The black ring on his head looked unusually thick. He was wearing a dark green coat and had a black, Hitler-style moustache. His eyes were covered by black glasses with round lenses. 'Now this man doesn't look Russian at all,' I said, looking at Khawla, 'even if he is wearing a Russian general's coat. Would he be Grandfather?'

She covered her mouth with her hand to hold back her giggles and shook her head to say I wasn't right this time either. 'No, that's an old Kuwaiti poet, a great poet,' she said.

Although I was happy she was laughing, I was also embarrassed. 'I won't guess any more,' I said firmly. 'You tell me who the people in the pictures are.'

I pointed at a picture of a large man, taken in profile, wearing traditional Kuwait dress with a brown cloak. He had a small white beard in the middle of his chin. 'Who's that?' I asked.

'One of the emirs of Kuwait, the Father of the Constitution,' she said.

I moved on to the next picture in the hope of finding my grandfather or some other member of my family, whose past I knew nothing about. On top of the desk I found a small picture in a wooden frame. I picked it up and while I was examining it, Khawla said, 'I'll tell you the story of the man in that picture. That young man . . .' she began.

'I know, Khawla,' I said, interrupting her. 'I liked him without even meeting him. I've seen many pictures of him, and I know what finally happened to him when that plane was hijacked. It's Walid.'

'You seem to know a lot.'

'My mother told me some things.' I pointed to a picture of a woman in sunglasses with her mouth open singing into a microphone, her arms spread, carrying a handkerchief in one hand. 'Who would that be?' I asked my sister.

She showed no interest in my question but rushed over to one of the shelves, saying, 'If you want to see a picture of Isa al-Tarouf, our grandfather.' She took out an enormous book and offered it to me. I took hold of it and looked at the picture on the cover. It was a very old picture of two men. I think it was originally in black and white and had been coloured by hand later. One of the men had a short beard like the Emir who had died on the day I arrived, but he didn't have the Emir's smile. The other man had neither beard nor moustache. The one with the small beard was wearing traditional dress under a cloak, while the other was wearing a white thobe under a black waistcoat, with a small chain that was probably connected to a watch in his pocket. The rings holding their headdresses in place on their heads didn't look like the black rings they use these days. They had black blocks linked together by thick yellow cord to look something like a crown. Khawla pointed to the man with the small beard. 'That's Papa Isa, our grandfather,' she said. She moved her finger to the other man. 'And that's his younger brother, Shahin,' she added. It was an enormous book, with high-quality paper and many pictures of old maps, wooden ships and houses made of mud.

'What does the book say about grandfather and his brother?' I asked.

Before she had time to answer, the study door flew open and slammed against the wall. I shuddered at the sight of Grandmother leaning on the Indian maid with one arm and holding the door frame with her other hand. She was scowling and, without looking at me, she scolded Khawla with words I didn't understand. Khawla blushed, then took Grandmother's arm to support her in place of the maid. She turned to me in embarrassment and said, 'You'd better go back to your room, Isa.'

II

On the morning of the next day, I woke up early to a voice calling the two maids: 'Miri, Luza, Miri, Luza.' I didn't hear either answering. The same voice started angrily calling someone else, but I couldn't make out the other name. I went to the bathroom, which was between my room and the room of Raju and Babu. Old Babu was looking at me through the kitchen window. I ignored him. In the inner courtyard Raju was holding a hose and spraying water on the floor to wash it. He looked at me too. They both looked suspicious of me, as if to say 'Who's this intruder?' My self-confidence replied, 'I'm one of the family.' I felt that even the door of the bathroom I shared with Raju and Babu saw me as an intruder on their space. Neither of them approached me to talk to me, and I didn't take the initiative either. The instructions not to mix seemed to have reached them too. I washed my face and brushed my teeth, but so early in the morning I couldn't bring myself to have a shower when it was so cold outside.

Back in my room I didn't know what to do. *What next?* I thought. I began switching the television from channel to channel. Nothing interesting. I sat down at the laptop and browsed the Internet. My stomach told me it was empty. I was hungry. They hadn't offered me anything for supper the previous night. Had they perhaps prepared this fully equipped room for me but forgotten that I needed to eat? I opened the little fridge in the corner. Tins of milk, orange juice, mango, soft drinks, mineral water, fruit, apples, oranges and pineapple. As soon as I caught sight of the pineapple I shut the fridge door, with memories of the story of Pinya and Mendoza's ranting.

I picked up the phone that Hind had given me. It was a new Nokia with one camera at the front and one at the back. I was reluctant to call Khawla and ask her for something to eat. Just as I was calling Ghassan to ask him what I should do there was a knocking on the door and I called off. I opened the door and there was Babu looking dour. '*Taal*,' he said, then turned his back and walked towards the kitchen. The word wasn't new to me at all. Taal was the name of the famous volcano in Batangas province. I stood in the doorway, unsure what the old Indian might have meant. Did he really mean the Batangas volcano? He went back to the kitchen without looking back. I was still standing there looking towards the kitchen, which was next to the annex. Babu leaned out of the window, beckoned me and shouted, '*Taal*!' Apparently the volcano was about to spew lava. I went to where he was beckoning. He pulled back a chair at a small table and put a glass of milk down among various dishes: fried eggs, boiled eggs, cheese, olives, slices of tomato and cucumber. He gestured to me to sit down, then turned to the stove, where he resumed his work.

I began to eat in silence. *I wish Khawla could eat with me*, I said to myself.

Before I'd finished, Luza, the Filipina maid, came in with a large round tray carrying the remains of a meal not much different from what I had been offered. The maid smiled at me. 'How are you?' she asked in my language, which I missed.

'I'm well,' I said. Babu turned to us, hiding a smile, rather different from the person who had been frowning when he invited me to eat. He pointed at me, then spoke to the maid in Arabic. She burst out laughing. 'What did he say?' I asked her.

'He said the old lady used to make fun of us when she saw us watching Indian movies. "How can you believe these stories?" she would say. And now her grandson turns up, just like in an Indian movie!' said the maid.

I was taken aback when she said 'her grandson', which contradicted what Khawla had told me about the servants not knowing who I was.

'And how do you know about me?' I asked.

277

She pulled out a chair and sat opposite me at the table. 'Don't you be like them too!' she said. 'They treat us as if we have no feelings and don't understand anything.'

'You mean it was just a feeling you had that led you to the truth?' I said.

She shook her head. Before she could continue the old Indian maid came in smiling. She was holding a broom and a plastic basket. The Filipina maid pointed to the cook and said, 'Many years ago the old lady accused Babu of getting Josephine pregnant.'

I was stunned. All the things my mother had told me came back. She pointed at the Indian maid and introduced us. 'Lakshmi, Babu's wife, is the maid who replaced your mother after she and your father were thrown out,' she said. 'She was the first person to see you in your father's arms when he came to visit the old lady after the months he lived outside the house.'

Everyone was smiling.

'Does the family know that you know all this?' I asked.

'No, we have no feelings and we understand nothing,' said the Filipina.

Babu took the plates off the table. 'Miri, Luza,' someone called from outside. It was Grandmother calling. Lakshmi went off and the Filipina maid prepared to follow her.

'Thank you, Luza,' I said. 'And by the way, that's an odd name,' I added.

She stopped at the kitchen door and turned. 'My name's Luzviminda. The old lady didn't like it, so she took off some of the letters and kept the rest.'

'Luza, Luza,' Grandmother called again, then followed it up with a word similar to the word the parrot cried whenever it called the same name.

'Coming, Madam,' Luzviminda replied, hurrying off. I pushed my chair back to get up. Luzviminda stuck her head round the kitchen door, saying, 'The old lady didn't like the name Lakshmi either. You can call her Miri like your grandmother does.'

She laughed and hurried off. I thanked old Babu for the delicious breakfast and left the kitchen. I stretched out on the bed in my room, repeating to myself: 'Luzviminda, Luzviminda, Luz Vi Minda.' That was a purely Filipino name. Why didn't the maid have a Spanish or English name like many Filipinas? Teresa or Mercedes or Marilyn or Angeline?

The name was a composite of the first part of the name of each of the three main island groups in the Philippines – Luzon in the north, Visayas in the centre and Mindanao in the south. At first I decided to call her Luza, the name my grandmother had chosen for her, so that I wouldn't think of the map of the Philippines every time I called her, since I very much needed to discover a new geography. But then I remembered how confused I myself could be about names and I had pangs of conscience. So I went back on my decision and stuck to Luzviminda, unchanged.

12

That's how I spent the first months in my grandmother's house, having three meals a day in the kitchen. The servants avoided me and wouldn't speak to me in the courtyard but they changed completely once we were together in the kitchen, out of sight of the others. They chatted away and treated me well, except for Raju the driver, who avoided me. He was the only one who didn't know anything about me, and he wasn't on good terms with the other servants, who often warned me about him. I began to pick up some simple words of Arabic. I understood some and I would sometimes use Arabic in the same way as the servants in their dealings with the family or among themselves, when they spoke a mixture of English and broken Arabic.

In my room I spent the time watching television or films on DVD or browsing the Internet. I opened an email account for Merla and sent her the address and password by SMS, so then it was easy to communicate with her. I really missed her. Merla, my forbidden love. I spent lots of time writing to her or answering her messages.

At sunset I would go out for a walk in the neighbourhood. I would go to the central market and hang out in the shops nearby, then spend about an hour in the pedestrian street that ran parallel to the main street. The pedestrian street was long, with nothing to distinguish it. There were large houses on both sides, and on the other side lay the main road. On one part of the road, a stretch of no more than 200 metres, there were beautiful trees on both sides of the road. That was my favourite spot. I used to sit under a big blue sign that read *Damascus Street*, with my back to one of those water coolers that were common on the pedestrian street. People install them for charitable purposes, to quench the thirst of pedestrians or workmen on hot days. I would sit on the ground facing the main street, with a sandy area behind me without any houses. The cars on the main street would drive fast and make an irritating noise but I had to put up with the din in order to be close to the trees. It was the best place of all, compared with the others. I looked at the sandy area behind me and spoke to myself. 'If it was mine,' I said, 'I would plant it with mango and jackfruit trees, pineapple and banana and all the other trees that grew on Mendoza's land.'

Khawla visited me every day but she didn't come into my room. She just stood at the door, sometimes chatting for hours like that, without either of us approaching the other. While Khawla and I were chatting, from time to time I could hear the upper-floor window sliding up and down in its frame. It was Grandmother looking out from her room, monitoring us and making sure that Khawla didn't come into my room. Khawla didn't go out much. She went to school in the morning. Sometimes she went out shopping or to cafés with Hind. She rarely saw her mother because Grandmother was uneasy about her granddaughter being in her stepfather's house and Iman's husband wouldn't let Iman visit the home of her former husband. All Khawla had was the phone or quick meetings with her mother outside.

Hind decided to give me her share of the pension my father's relatives were awarded because of his work in the resistance. It had been shared among her, Grandmother and Khawla. Although some of the pension should have been mine, I hadn't asked for it. Hind would also send the servants every now and then with presents and clothes and phone top-up cards so that I could stay in touch with my family in the Philippines. I sent her an SMS by mobile whenever the servants brought me presents from her: *Thanks, Auntie Hind*. She would answer with just one word: *Welcome*. One day she took me to a government department that deals with official papers. She submitted some papers to them and was given some other papers. On a later visit to the same place we got a nationality certificate. It was a little booklet with four pages and a black cover with Arabic words in gold. In the middle there was an emblem like the one on the banknotes. On the second page there was a picture of me and underneath it said in Arabic: *You are officially Kuwaiti.* That's what Hind told me, without turning to look at me, as she drove home. I said to myself, *Yes, but what am I as far as the family's concerned?* I only met Hind very rarely, mostly by chance in the courtyard, but I saw her now and then on television, talking about things I didn't understand.

Awatif and Nouriya, my other aunts, visited my grandmother every week with their husbands and children. When they were visiting I was forbidden to leave my room in case my uncles, Ahmad and Faisal, found out about me. Although Awatif had shown some sympathy for me at first, she later deferred to her sister Nouriya, who said, 'Ahmad and Faisal are friends and if Ahmad found out about the Filipino, word might reach my husband. You'd only blame yourself if that were to happen.' Awatif was weak. One day she gave me, through Khawla, a copy of the Qur'an in English and a prayer mat. After that she disappeared under orders from Nouriya, but I gathered from Khawla that she was always asking whether I prayed. I kept away from all of them. The answer was for me to go out on the day they visited, so their family visits coincided with my visits to Ghassan. He came to pick me up from the house. We either ate out or sometimes in his flat.

In the summer Grandmother spent the weekend, Thursday and Friday, in the beach house with Hind and Khawla. She let me go with them if she knew that none of her other grandchildren would be coming. Grandmother wouldn't let her other grandchildren have any contact with me, or even know about me, because one rotten fish spoils the rest, as they say. I don't know, should I find fault with Khawla for telling me everything Grandmother said about me, or should I thank her? She was honest with me, but her honesty was hurtful.

The family gave me a separate suite in the beach house, on the side away from the sea. I wasn't allowed to go into the main part of the house or go close to the sea, especially if Nouriya was there. The weekly trip to the beach house was like going to prison. We would set off in two cars, one with Grandmother and Khawla, driven by Hind, and the other with Babu, Lakshmi and Luzviminda, driven by Raju. I don't need to say which car I went in.

The sea was beautiful at night. In fact I never saw it at any other time to compare, because I spent the whole day confined to my miserable room, killing time on the laptop. At night one weekend I left my room and headed for the sea. I walked past three big awnings. Under the first one there was a big generator for when there was a power cut. Under the second there was an old Jeep so covered in dust that it was impossible to make out what colour it was. The third awning was over a small boat. I stood there and examined it. *It must be the one!* I thought. All the incidents this old boat had witnessed, all the people it had carried – my father, Ghassan, Walid, many fish, chicken guts, and my mother.

I turned my back on the boat, trying to escape memories of events I played no part in making. I hurried to the beach. The air was humid and the sand was cold. The tide was going out, leaving the sand clean and level. If it wasn't for the tide, my mother's footprints might still have been there – testimony to the beginning of my tragedy.

I sat down on the wet sand. The calm, the darkness, the sound of the waves in the distance and the humid air took me back to Boracay. The darkness turned everything black. Those days seemed very distant. Distance and space have dimensions we are not aware of. Time runs through them, and the further we move away, the more time recedes into the distance, or so we feel. I could scarcely believe at that moment that it was less than a year since I had been at Boracay. I looked deep into the darkness, where there was no dividing line between the sea and the sky, as if I were looking for Willy's Rock at Boracay. Nothing disturbed the darkness but the red flashing light towards which my father had sailed one night. I left the beach and went back to my room.

13

One day Khawla knocked on the door of my room in the annex. She said Raju had told Grandmother I was often talking to the servants, and so she was very angry. 'How can I avoid them when I eat in the kitchen?' I asked.

'You mustn't mix with them,' she said with a smile. 'So Grandmother's decided you'll eat with us inside.'

I gave her a big smile. *Thank God you're such a snitch, Raju*, I thought to myself.

Raju was mad about this and asked the other servants why I was in the house, but they pretended to be as ignorant about me as he was.

At my first lunch with Grandmother, Hind and Khawla, I found I couldn't put anything in my mouth. Khawla was offering me dishes, serving yellow rice from a large bowl and putting it on my plate. She gave me a piece of chicken, tomato sauce, salad, little triangles stuffed with cheese and vegetables and meat, something like mashed rice coloured orange, and various other dishes. Grandmother never looked in my direction. It was as if I didn't exist. She was rolling the rice into balls with the tips of her fingers and eating in silence. I was daydreaming about Mama

Aida, my mother and Adrian, white rice, soy sauce, grilled bananas and crispy chicken's feet. Poor people's food is delicious because it's salted and spiced by the good cheer and warmth that bring you together around it. Rich people's food has no flavour when they sit there with silent faces. Hind brought me down to earth: 'Why aren't you eating?' she asked.

I was flustered. I had been asking myself the same question: what was stopping me from eating when I was starving? 'I don't feel hungry, Auntie,' I said. This was the first time I had spoken in the presence of Grandmother. Without looking at me, Grandmother opened her eyes wide and took her hand off the bowl of rice in front of her. I thought she must have seen an insect in her bowl. She put her elbows on the table, locked her hands together and rested her forehead on her hands. I didn't know what to make of it. Khawla and Hind looked at me. 'I hope I didn't say something that upset her,' I said.

As soon as I spoke, Grandmother grabbed the end of the shawl thrown carelessly round her neck and covered her face with it. She began to cry silently. Her body was shaking violently. Hind pushed her chair back, stood up, put a hand on Grandmother's shoulder and spoke to her gently. Grandmother answered her between sobs, still covering her face with the shawl. Hind smiled, kissed Grandmother's head and patted her on the back. Khawla was smiling and wiping her tears away with the back of her hand. Hind looked towards me: her nose was red and her eyes were glistening with tears. 'My mother says you have your father's voice,' she said.

Khawla deliberately spoke to me so that I would answer her and Grandmother could hear Rashid's voice in my own voice. Grandmother picked up the glass of water to drink as she listened, but she didn't look towards me and she didn't understand what I was saying in English. She stared into space, or maybe she was looking at the face of her only son in her imagination. The glass of water was still in her hand. She shook her head sadly, with a bitter look on her face, and with her left hand she began to wipe away her tears. She wiped everything away except the sobs she tried to suppress.

Everyone but me finished eating. Grandmother went off to the sitting room, leaning on Hind's arm. She sat on her sofa in the corner and put her legs on her footstool. Now I started eating and I found that the food tasted completely different. It was delicious. I was watching Grandmother in her corner. 'Why does she put her legs on the stool like that?' I asked Khawla.

'Poor Grandma,' she said. 'She has arthritis and problems with her knee joints.'

When I went back to my room after lunch, I asked Lakshmi to bring me two small towels and a bowl of hot water. About half an hour after lunch I called Khawla and asked her to tell Grandmother that I wanted to see her about something. Khawla opened the glass door for me and I found myself standing in front of her with the bowl of hot water and towels in my hands. 'If you want to wash the car, it's under the awning over there,' she said. Khawla was crazy, quick-witted, smart and full of fun. I asked her to bring me some oil. 'What do you want to do, Isa?' she said in surprise.

'You'll find out later,' I replied.

She was looking at me suspiciously. 'Where would I find you some oil?' she asked, then paused a moment. 'Would cooking oil do?' I looked at her in disappointment, and she had second thoughts. 'Olive oil?' she asked. I agreed to her last suggestion. Khawla called the maid: 'Luza, Luza!!!' and from the other end of the sitting room, near the main entrance, came the sound of the parrot. As soon as it heard the maid's name, it cried out the word that it always attached to Luza's name.

'Grandmother and the parrot always shout the same word after they call Luzviminda,' I said to Khawla. 'But what does that word mean?'

Khawla blushed. She put her hand behind her head and scowled. Still blushing, she said, 'It's *himara*. It means donkey.' I repeated the word as she said it in Arabic: *himara*.

'Yes, madam?' Luzviminda said from behind me, asking Khawla what she needed. She asked her to bring the bottle of olive oil from the kitchen.

★ ★ ★

Grandmother refused at first but Khawla insisted. She accepted reluctantly. She stretched out her legs on the stool. I sat on the ground near her knees. I soaked the towels in hot water, then wrapped them around her legs. I began to press with both hands on top of the towels. She was looking at me uncomfortably. I asked Khawla to put one of the cushions behind Grandmother's head and ask her to lean back and close her eyes. I kept squeezing until the last drop of water dripped from the towels. I removed the stool, put one of her feet on my knees and the other one on my shoulder like a grenade launcher. Grandmother took hold of the end of her shawl and covered her face with it. 'Grandmother's embarrassed,' Khawla whispered in my ear, suppressing her giggles. I took the bottle of oil out of the bowl of hot water. I poured just enough of it on to the leg that was on my shoulder. I laced my fingers together and wrapped my hands around her leg, pressing gently, starting with her ankle, then her calf and then her arthritic knee. I massaged it gently with my fingertips. I took her leg off my shoulder and put it on my knee. I took hold of her foot with my hands, pressing the sole with my thumbs. I put my fingers between her toes. I gripped tight and kept pressing. Grandmother started to snore gently. I pulled the stool towards me and rested her leg on it. The snoring stopped. She said something I didn't understand. I looked at Khawla for an explanation. 'Grandmother says don't forget her other leg,' she said.

I nodded happily. 'Of course, of course,' I said. If massaging her legs could have brought me closer to her, I would have spent my whole life doing it.

14

On 20 June 2006, Ghassan called me and asked me to go somewhere with him. 'Get changed. I'll come and pick you up in a few minutes,' he said. I got changed quickly and waited for him to come to my room. He didn't take long. I got in the car and he drove off towards the place he wanted to take me. 'Do you remember that Abu Faris that I told you about?' he asked me on the way. I remembered the name immediately. He was the poet who was captured during the Iraqi occupation because of the poems and songs he wrote urging people to resist. Ghassan told me he was going to say his last farewells to Abu Faris, whose remains had been found in a mass grave near Karbala in Iraq and were now going to be buried in Kuwait. I couldn't see any reason why this called for Ghassan to take me along with him. Why? I didn't ask him, but he answered my unspoken question himself anyway. 'I want you to see how your father was given a hero's welcome a few months ago. It will also be a chance to visit his tomb,' he said.

I felt a tightness in my chest. Why did I have to keep hanging on to memories of this man? Why did I have to love him more than I did already? Why now, when he was no longer here? Why was I tormenting myself over a man I had seen only in the days before I remembered anything? Of course I was proud of him, but my sadness overwhelmed all other feelings.

The place was similar to the place where I had seen large crowds on television for the funeral of the Emir on the day after I arrived in Kuwait. It was where they buried the remains of people who had been captured by the Iraqis and had died in captivity. A large sandy area, with gravestones arranged in horizontal lines. Many people had come to say farewell to their loved ones. They were all men in military uniform, with not a woman among them. There were some prominent people, apparently – the ones in traditional dress with cloaks of various colours – black, brown, grey – all edged in gold cloth. The remains of the dead were covered with the Kuwaiti flag, as the Emir had been the day I arrived. I asked Ghassan if my father's remains had been covered with the Kuwaiti flag like them and he nodded. I liked the flag and from that moment I felt that the Kuwaiti flag was my flag too.

Ghassan's face was sad enough already, but when he cried it was even sadder and the sadness spread to me like an infection. Lots of people were looking at me and whispering to each other, apparently surprised that I was there. Damn my face! I had so many names but my face stayed unchanged, alarming the people around me.

One of them held out his hand to shake hands with Ghassan. One of them kissed it. One of them hugged him, his body trembling as he tried to hold back his tears. *Do they really cry for their dead after all those years?*

The burial ceremonies ended and the men dispersed one by one. Ghassan pointed to a place not far off. 'Rashid will be pleased to meet you. I swear he can hear our footsteps now as we approach,' he said. I shivered. I felt as if ants were crawling on me, from my neck up to my forehead. We walked towards my father's grave with heavy steps. At the grave Ghassan crouched and prayed. When he'd finished he said, 'I'll drive over to visit the grave of my mother and father. I won't be long.'

Suddenly I was alone in my father's presence. I looked back to see Ghassan stepping carefully between the graves towards his car. Of course he looked sad when all those he loved were in their graves.

I sat on the ground next to the grave. I put my hand down and picked up a handful of soil. 'Papa,' I said. If I hadn't started like that, I would have burst out crying. I was choking on my words. All the pictures of him I had seen – in Ghassan's drawer and in my mother's briefcase – passed through my mind. I thought of all the happiness, all the fun, all the love and bravery that lay buried in that grave. My lips trembled. 'Papa,' I repeated, and because I have my father's voice, I unintentionally answered myself: 'Is that you, Isa?' Tearfully I nodded. 'Yes, it's me. I've come back to Kuwait, Papa,' I said. 'I'm lying in peace now, my son.' Tears poured from my eyes and I wiped them away with my dusty hand. The tears turned to mud on my face. I was crying so much I couldn't speak. I couldn't say anything. I didn't tell him that I loved him and needed him, that I was an outcast, that my grandmother didn't know what to do with me, that my aunts didn't want to recognise that I existed, that I was alone and weak. I wasn't able to say all that or, since he couldn't do anything about it, to say I wanted him just to rest in peace.

Ghassan's beloved car called and I got to my feet. I turned my back on the grave and headed to the car without looking back. On the way I tried in vain to control my sobbing. Ghassan didn't say anything until we were close to Grandmother's house. 'Are you OK?' he asked.

'Yes, I'm fine,' I replied.

He looked down at my hand. 'Why are you clenching your fist like that?' he said.

I opened my hand. 'A handful of my father's dust,' I said.

Ghassan stroked my head as if I were a pet dog.

15

'Isa, Isa, Isa.'

The calls came almost every day. They came from the window of Grandmother's room on the upper floor, then crossed the courtyard and filtered into my room. Grandmother had become more accepting of me than at first. The change apparently began from below, from her feet, and then moved up her legs to her knees. *That's good, to some extent*, I told myself. Soon I would move past her knees and reach her heart. If only I could massage that, maybe it would soften. I didn't want anything more than that. I had plenty of money, plenty. My grandmother had decided to give me a monthly allowance of 200 dinars. That was apart from the money I received from Hind through the servants. I started to send my mother and Mama Aida money every month. I bought my mother a computer to make it easier to stay in touch with her through emails and chats and webcam conversations. Grandmother was generous, lavishing money on me without me asking.

Grandmother had another personality that she didn't usually display. One day, by chance and without her noticing I was there, I saw an aspect of her that I will never forget. This severe, overbearing woman, who never let a smile cross her lips, had a strange passion for music. Not the music that I'm familiar with, but a kind of folk music called something like samurai. Khawla told me about it one day. She laughed when I asked her if it was Japanese and she made fun of my ignorance. 'You don't understand anything!' she said, the very same expression Merla used to use whenever I asked her about anything I didn't know. It was actually called Samiri, and it involved poetry as well as music.

I was walking past the glass door on my way to the kitchen. The door was half-open and through the gap I saw Grandmother behaving strangely. I went up to the door and peaked through. The television was broadcasting one of these songs. There was an old man sitting cross-legged on the floor, which was spread with red carpets. His face was smooth and soft and he was wearing a white headdress held in place with a thin black ring and a bright blue jacket over the traditional white thobe. He was holding an oud. He was wearing dark glasses although he was indoors in a studio. To his right there was a man playing the fiddle and to his left a man playing an instrument that looked like a guzheng. Around him sat men in white thobes and women wearing strange-looking dresses, each one a different colour but all of them with gold embroidery across the bodice. There were other women wearing black abayas like the ones Grandmother wore when she went out. The musicians played and the chorus sang. Some of them were clapping, while others were singing behind the man in the blue jacket and others were holding strange-looking drums. Grandmother was completely carried away by the song. She was holding her black shawl between her fingers to cover the lower half of her face. Her upper body was swaying rhythmically in time with the song, while her lower half was immobile. Her legs were stretched out on the footstool as always. Her head was bent forwards and swaying in time with her shoulders. She leaned her torso to one side, then slowly reversed and leaned it to the other side, completely enthralled by the song, like a cobra by the flute of a snake-charmer. An extraordinary woman. Even when she danced, she had an awesome presence. All I could do was hold my breath and watch her perform her ritual.

* * *

At first I could only go into the sitting room and the dining room, which opened on to the sitting room, but now I started going into Grandmother's room every day. She covered her face with her black shawl and lay down on her bed, leaving me to massage her legs. I would spend up to an hour there. Then she would start snoring and I withdrew. I spent the rest of the time in the sitting room with Khawla.

Once I was at the top of the stairs and about to go down. Khawla was lying in the sitting room and I could hear her talking on the phone in English, as usual when she spoke to her friends. I went downstairs quietly and as soon as I stepped foot on the ground floor Khawla realised I was there. She screamed. She picked up a cushion that was next to her on the sofa and covered her head with it. 'Isa! Wait, wait!' she shouted. I turned away as if I had invaded her bedroom when she was changing. 'OK, you can come now,' she said after putting on her *hijab*. It was the first time I had seen her long black hair uncovered. My sister was beautiful and looked very much like Hind. I sat down next to her on the sofa. 'Does Islam say I can't see you with your head uncovered?' I asked her.

She locked her fingers together and started to wave her legs in the air like a child. 'In fact Islam doesn't say that in the case of a *mahram*,' she said.

'A *mahram*?'

'Yes, a *mahram*. The husband or people that the woman wouldn't be able to marry – her father, her grandfather, her brother, her son and some special cases,' she said.

301

I locked my fingers together and started waving my legs in the air like her. 'Well then! There's no need for this *hijab*, because I'm your brother,' I said.

She stopped waving her legs and pursed her lips. 'Not yet,' she said. 'It's still too early for me to feel we're brother and sister.'

I stopped waving my legs. She turned to me and continued, 'Even if Father were still alive, he'd need time to accept you as his son.'

I was annoyed by what she said. 'That's not true,' I said.

She nodded assertively. 'Marquez says people don't love their children because they're their children but because of the friendship that develops when they bring them up.'

I looked at her like an idiot.

'Who's Marquez?' I asked.

She opened her eyes wide and, as usual, made fun of my ignorance. 'You don't understand anything,' she said.

★   ★   ★

When I was young, I learned a lot from Merla and I put that down to the fact that she was four years older than me. But now that I had grown up, how come I was learning from Khawla, who was two years younger than me? Was I really so slow at understanding things? When I liked the things she said or her answers to my questions, I would say, 'Khawla! Where do you get these answers from?' She would point to Father's study. 'From there,' she would say confidently.

'If only I could read Arabic!' I said sadly.

Her mobile phone rang. She put it to her ear and started speaking in English. When she'd finished her conversation, I asked her why she'd been speaking English. 'I like it for conversation, more than Arabic,' she replied immediately.

I took the opportunity to show off my knowledge. 'José Rizal says that anyone who doesn't like his mother tongue is worse than a rotten fish,' I said.

She frowned. 'And who would José Rizal be?' she asked inquisitively.

I shook my head, pretending to be shocked. 'You don't understand anything,' I said.

Khawla wouldn't leave me alone that day till I'd told her everything about the national hero of the Philippines. 'He made that remark when he noticed that Filipinos had started to abandon their own language and adopt the language of the colonisers,' I told her. She showed so much interest that I was encouraged to continue. 'He was a doctor, a writer, an artist and a great thinker. He was familiar with twenty-two languages. He believed that freedom was life. He criticised Spanish colonialism and called for reforms. He incited revolution against the colonialists. He wrote a famous novel called *Noli Me Tangere* in which he exposed the practices of the Spanish and their appalling violations of the rights of the Filipino people. He followed that up with a novel called *El Filibusterismo*. He wanted to rouse the Filipinos from their subservience to Spain. People related to him and the Spanish resented that. They arrested him. He had been in prison a long time when he was executed. The people revolted and the Filipinos managed to throw out the colonisers within two years and declare independence. Freedom has a price and that price was Rizal.' I looked at Khawla with pride. 'In the Philippines they called me José, after him.'

Khawla was enthralled by the story of Rizal and listened to me with interest. When I'd said what I had to say, she said, 'When Father said he wanted to change reality by writing, he wasn't crazy like Grandmother says.' She bowed her head, then continued, 'If only he'd finished his novel before he was captured.' She looked at my face thoughtfully. 'If only people here read,' she added.

★   ★   ★

The fact that I had good relationships with Khawla and Ghassan didn't stop me from feeling lonely. A kind of barrier stood between us, even if it was a barrier full of gaps. Khawla had the same feeling. She felt alone although she was surrounded by Grandmother and our aunts. When I asked her one day how she fought against this feeling of hers, she surprised me with her answer. 'Whenever I feel the need for someone to talk to, I open a book,' she said.

I thought a while, then I said, 'But books don't listen.'

'When I was little, Miri was the person closest to me. She always listened to me even if she wasn't able to do anything,' she replied. 'That didn't last long,' she added, bowing her head. 'My relationship with Miri upset Grandmother. She forbade me from talking to her.' Her smile returned. 'But I found an alternative,' she continued.

I looked at her inquiringly, encouraging her to continue.

'If I need to tell someone all the things I'm too embarrassed to reveal . . .' She stopped and smiled and winked at me. 'Then I tell Aziza,' she continued, 'she's the one who listens to me best.'

'Aziza? Who's she?' I asked her in puzzlement.

Khawla walked towards the glass door. 'Wait a moment,' she said. 'It's a good opportunity to introduce you to her.'

She came back a minute later with a lettuce leaf in her hand and put it on the carpet in the middle of the sitting room. Then she sat on the sofa. 'Let's wait a while. She's rather slow,' she said.

We didn't have to wait more than three minutes before a tortoise appeared from under one of the sofas in the corner, the size of an average soup bowl. It walked slowly towards the lettuce leaf in the middle of the carpet. Khawla pointed to the tortoise, turned to me and said, 'Aziza.'

I nodded in delight. 'Pleased to meet you,' I said.

16

On 24 September 2006, Ramadan began. I really suffered during the month – the hunger, the thirst and the people.

Since I was Muslim as far as my family was concerned, I had to fast. And because I was willing to perform any ritual that might bring me close to God, even if I didn't know what religion I was, I had to fast. I envied the Muslims their ability to tolerate the hunger and thirst. It's admirable. But for me it was impossible. I managed to fast five hours the first day, six hours the second day and eight hours the third day. Then I fasted the whole of the fourth day. I jumped for joy when I heard the call to prayer at sunset from the local mosques and on the telephone – '*Allahu akbar, Allahu akbar*' – marking the end of the fast for the day.

After *iftar* on the first day I fell fast asleep on my bed, almost unconscious. No one inside the house talked. Khawla, Hind and Grandmother sat for hours in front of the television, moving from their seats only to pray. I hadn't noticed they were so interested in television until it was Ramadan. There was also a lot of praying in the month. Even late at night I saw light from the window of Grandmother's room. Khawla said Grandmother prayed all night.

Ghassan had strange rituals in Ramadan. He didn't like to stay in his flat during the day. He would call me after he came out of work. 'Get changed. I'm on my way,' he would say. We spent the time before *iftar* in a different place every day: the Mubarakiya souk, the fish market, the meat and fruit and vegetable market, the Friday market, the pet and bird market, the market for Iranian goods.

As usual I looked at people's faces and facial expressions. During the day in Ramadan they looked different. People were tense when driving and honked their horns for the slightest reason. They put their arms out of the windows and waved them angrily. They looked sullen. 'Ghassan?' I said one day. He turned to me. 'Does smiling during the day in Ramadan mean you're not fasting?' I asked.

One day, a little before sunset, Ghassan and I were in the pet and bird market and I saw a tortoise just like Aziza. I bought it without thinking. I held it in my hands and began to strike up a friendship. I had a strange need for animals at that time. There were so many animals on Mendoza's land — the old dog Whitey, the cocks, the cats, the birds, the frogs and the lizards, but I hadn't before felt how important these creatures are.

At home I was with the tortoise in my room. '*Allahu akbar, Allahu akbar.*' It was the call to prayer and time to break the fast. I'd forgotten I was hungry and what time it was. Khawla knocked on the door. 'Aren't you fasting?' she asked, pushing in the door of my room. 'It's time to eat.' She gaped in amazement when she saw the tortoise.

'How did Aziza get into your room?' she asked.

I shook my head. 'That's not Aziza,' I corrected her.

The tortoise had to have a name, so I made one up on the spot. 'That's Inang Choleng.'

★ ★ ★

If I got bored in Grandmother's house, and I often did, I would meet the servants secretly in the kitchen and chat with them, on my guard against being discovered.

When I saw the conditions the servants worked under in the house I felt sorry for my mother and wondered how she had put up with it years ago. But compared with the fate that awaited her in the Philippines, the hardship of working in Kuwait must have counted as luxury. The servants worked from six in the morning to ten o'clock at night. Babu said that in some of the houses nearby they didn't have set work hours. The hours depended on the needs of the household. Any time someone in the family needed something, they had to be fully prepared to respond. Wily Raju was the one who worked least. All he did was drive Grandmother around if she had to go out, which didn't happen often, and sometimes go out to buy stuff from the central market. In the morning he washed the car and the courtyard and watered the trees in the area opposite the house. I noticed that Raju enjoyed a weekly day off. Babu and his wife Lakshmi had a day off once a month while Luzviminda worked every day.

In one of my furtive meetings with them in the kitchen, I asked Luzviminda why she worked like an automaton without a single day off outside the house. She replied, 'When I asked the old lady that, her argument was "If I let you go out, how can I be sure you won't come back pregnant within months." She didn't realise that if I wanted I could do that here, in her house.' Then she started criticising Grandmother.

Babu didn't like Luzviminda criticising, and neither did Lakshmi. Babu said, 'Mama Ghanima is an old woman, like my mother. If she was that bad I wouldn't have stayed in her house close to twenty years.' His wife agreed with him, so Luzviminda held her tongue.

17

One evening during Ramadan, just before the middle
of the month, the family gathered at Grandmother's
house for a special meal that comes between the *iftar*
at sunset and the *suhour* before dawn. They called it
the *ghabqa*. I was in my room with Inang Choleng.
From behind the curtain over the window I could see
the kids in the courtyard – the children of Awatif and
Nouriya. In the meantime everyone else was inside –
Awatif and her husband Ahmad, Nouriya and her
husband Faisal, Hind, Khawla, Grandmother and her
older grandchildren. The doorbell rang every now
and then. Lots of children gathered at the door,
wearing special clothes. The boys were wearing
traditional white thobes with sleeveless jackets; some
had skullcaps on while others wore the same white
headdress as the men. The girls were wearing different
clothes: a light piece of cloth with golden decoration
covering their heads and the top half of their bodies.
All the children, boys and girls, had cloth bags hanging
round their necks. Hind stood at the door with
Lakshmi and Luzviminda on either side carrying large
bags of nuts and sweets. The children sang in unison
and clapped at the door. The songs ended with

generous donations of nuts and sweets to go into their bags. The children kept coming to Grandmother's door for three days in succession.

A handsome young man, about my age or a little younger, dressed in a white thobe, walked past the children, kissed Hind and greeted Khawla in the outer courtyard, then walked inside. As soon as he walked through the wooden door, there were cries of 'cololoooosh', a strange sound rather like the war cries of the American Indians – a shrill, high-pitched sound like a referee's whistle. Khawla told me later that he was Nouriya's eldest son and Grandmother's first grandson. She always celebrated his visits by making this sound and in her prayers she asked God to give her a long life so that she could live to see him married.

The family members disappeared inside. I was still behind the curtain, with Inang Choleng in my hands. Thank God her shell was too hard to break under the pressure of my hands as I watched my family with a heavy heart from my exile in the annex. Just being with them would have been enough. Their voices sounded loud and close by despite the distance: their laughter, the words I didn't understand, the 'cololoooosh' rang in my ears.

The glass door opposite the door to my room opened. It was Nouriya in a strange outfit, maybe special for the occasion: a dress with wide sleeves, blood-red with shiny yellow decoration. 'Isa! Isa!' she started shouting.

I dropped Inang Choleng and didn't notice she had hit the floor between my feet. Nouriya wrapped up her call with a '*Taal*' and then went inside. I knew that word well. How could I forget it? She was inviting me into the sitting room to join in the party. Nouriya, who hated me, was calling me by name and inviting me in! I jumped for joy.

I don't remember the aluminium door to my room, or the inner courtyard or even the glass door that led to the sitting room. I just remember standing inside the sitting room with the door behind me. They stopped chatting and a sudden hush fell on the room. I felt as if I had been struck deaf. All eyes were pinned on me. Grandmother took hold of the shawl thrown loosely over her shoulders and threw it on to her head. Hind and Khawla looked at each other in amazement. Awatif was aghast. Ahmad, her husband with the long beard, sprang to his feet and looked at me with sparks flying from his eyes. Faisal looked at his wife, Nouriya, as if seeking an explanation for what was happening. '*Salamuuu alekooom*,' cried the parrot. Then through the front door Nouriya's maid came in carrying a young boy. 'Here's Isa, madam,' she told my aunt. Faisal stood up to take the boy.

Nouriya was flustered but handled the situation well. She passed me some silver bowls, then held out Faisal's car key and asked me, as if I were a servant, to put the bowls in the car. I took the objects with trembling hands and before I left Ahmad suddenly shouted some words at me that I didn't understand. He was waving his hands angrily and pointing at my aunts, but I couldn't make out a word of what he was shouting. Khawla ran towards the stairs. Awatif looked horrified. Speaking in English that wasn't very clear and that I understood only in part, she said something like, 'You mustn't come in like that when there are women present. Next time knock on the door and wait outside. That isn't right. Do you understand?'

I nodded and said, 'Very well, madam.' I went out into the inner courtyard carrying Nouriya's bowls. Babu, Lakshmi and Luzviminda were watching me in anguish from behind the kitchen window. I bowed my head and choked back my tears.

As I was putting the bowls in the trunk of Faisal's car, Nouriya came up to me, her eyebrows raised and her face flushed. She glanced behind to the door of the main house. No one there. She grabbed my shirt and pulled on it. She clenched her teeth and said, 'Listen. This time I saved you by pretending you're a servant. Next time I'll leave you to Awatif's husband and he'll slit your throat.'

314

I was so frightened my mouth was dry. I was trembling. The curtain on the upper-floor window overlooking the street moved. It was Khawla watching us from upstairs. Nouriya tightened her grip on my shirt and shook me. With great effort, I said, 'But it was you who called me, Auntie.'

'Shut up. I'm not your auntie,' she said.

I got the message. I dropped the word 'aunt' before Nouriya's name ever since that night on the pavement outside Grandmother's house, or perhaps it fell into the boot of the car before I closed it on the bowls. Nouriya looked back again, checking that no one was there. 'I was calling Isa my son, you idiot,' she said. She let go of my shirt and gave her parting shot: 'Don't you ever speak unless you're spoken to, you Filipino!'

The trick took in Ahmad and Faisal, although they were surprised that Grandmother had brought a male servant from the Philippines, since it was customary in Kuwait for people to have male servants from India or Bangladesh.

In my room, I hugged Inang Choleng. I wept like a child in front of the small bottle I had filled half-full with the soil I had brought from my father's grave the day I visited the cemetery. I looked at the bottle as if asking the soil to bear witness to what was happening. I threw myself down on my bed and nodded off. I don't remember how long I slept but I remember I was woken up by the sound of the dawn call to prayer. I had been close to death in a horrible dream. I was in Mindanao and my arms were tied behind my back and my face was to the ground. Nouriya and Awatif were holding down my shoulders, pinning me to the ground. Grandmother was sitting at a distance under the tropical trees with tears in her eyes but motionless. I was about to call out, to ask her for help, but someone pulled my head back by the hair. I looked straight into his eyes. It was Ahmad, Awatif's husband, and he was holding a knife. 'Grand . . .' I shouted, but Ahmad slit my throat before I could finish saying Grandmother's name.

18

'*Allahu akbar, Allahu akbar.*'

Besides being the start of the call to prayer, that's also the signal that it's time to start fasting. I woke up terrified, repeating, 'Grandmother, Grandmother.' I was desperate for a drink of water. My throat was dry and I could feel my heart throbbing in my temples. I felt my throat with my fingers. No sign of blood. It was a nightmare, a sequel to the living nightmare that had taken place in the sitting room when I burst in without permission. I took a bottle of mineral water from the bedside table and gulped it down without stopping till I finished the bottle.

'*Allahu akbar, Allahu akbar.*'

When she first translated the words of the call to prayer for me, Khawla said they meant that God is greater than everything else in existence and mightier than anything you can imagine. *So if that's how God is, I should give up complaining to Inang Choleng and telling her my sorrows.* I picked the tortoise up from the bed and put it on the floor. I wanted to get closer to God, and as far as I knew, God resided in Awatif's heart, and at that time Awatif was far away in her own house with her husband Ahmad. But could God be far away too? *How can I open my heart to God?* I asked myself. '*Allahu akbar, Allahu akbar.*' The phrase was repeated towards the end of the call to prayer.

I picked up my mobile phone and called Khawla. 'I want to go to the mosque,' I said. Khawla had just woken up to pray as well. 'It's only a few steps from the house. Go before the prayers start,' she said.

'Do I need one of those dresses that you and Grandmother and Hind wear when you pray?' I asked.

She burst out in giggles. 'Go as you are, man,' she said. 'But make sure you've done your ablutions.'

I didn't know how to wash before praying. In fact I didn't even know how to perform Muslim prayers. I stood by the wall of the house looking at the mosque. It was a small mosque in the courtyard in front of a large building that looked like a school. There were many cars parked in lines outside it. People pray in Ramadan more than at any other time. 'I'll wait till it's less crowded,' I said, and because I didn't know how to wash for prayers, I had a complete shower. I wanted to do my ablutions properly, as Khawla had suggested. I came out of the bathroom with my body in a state of ritual purity. But what about my soul?

All the cars were gone from the open space opposite the mosque, except for one or two. I walked slowly towards the door. There were shoes and sandals piled on top of each other at the foot of the door, and others arranged neatly on special racks. I stuck my head through the door. The people inside were barefoot. I took off my shoes and put them on one of the racks. As soon as I went in my bare feet felt a draught of cold air. I felt lighter than I had even been. I was almost flying. *Is this the mosque?* I wondered uncertainly. The floor was covered with carpets – light green carpets with dark green lines. There was a large chandelier hanging from the ceiling and although the mosque was air-conditioned there were fans attached to the walls. I stood in the middle looking around me. In front of me was the *mihrab*, a sort of alcove or niche like an arched doorway in the middle of the back wall. The area around it was highly decorated, maybe with Arabic writing. The mosque didn't have as much detail as you would find in a cathedral or a Buddhist temple. I was struck by how plain it was. There were some people sitting in a circle, talking in low voices. Some people were praying, bowing, pressing their foreheads to the floor as though they were kissing it. Other people were reading the Qur'an. In one corner there was a young man kneeling with his hands open in front of his face as he looked down. The feeling I had had in my feet when I went in came back as I walked towards the

statues. We don't need that because we are in Your presence and because You are God, the greatest.'

Someone's hand touched me on the shoulder. I turned around. It was a young Filipino who looked like he was in his early thirties. He asked me something in Arabic. I shook my head to show I didn't understand. 'Are you Filipino?' he asked in Filipino. I nodded without thinking. 'My name is Ibrahim Salam,' he said, introducing himself.

'*Wa aleekum as-salam*,' I answered automatically. He laughed, then suppressed his laughter when he realised we were in a mosque.

'What are you doing in the *mihrab*?' he asked me, as if it was a strange thing to do. 'I was praying,' I said, full of confidence. The young man laughed, took my hand and led me over into a corner. He and I were the only people there, other than an old man reading the Qur'an in another corner.

He was a young Filipino in his thirties who had lived in Kuwait a long time. He had studied in the religious institute to which the mosque was attached. He had graduated in Kuwait and, although he no longer lived in the student residence halls near the mosque but had moved out to another area, he still prayed in the institute mosque because after prayers he was in the habit of meeting Filipinos, Indonesians and Africans who were studying at the institute.

He was active in promoting Islam and worked as a translator at the Philippine embassy and as a correspondent for Filipino newspapers, sending them news from the Kuwaiti press about the Filipino community.

He sat with me a long time that dawn. He showed an interest in me. He told me about himself and, without thinking about the warnings from my family, I couldn't help revealing everything about myself to him. He tried to reassure me. 'Kuwait's wonderful,' he said. 'The people here are kind.'

I paid close attention to what he said. I almost said, 'That's because you're not a Kuwaiti who looks like a Filipino!' but I decided against it. After sunrise he said he had to go off to work and asked if we could meet up again in the same place. He stood up from the ground and put out his hand to shake mine. I put out my hand too and while I was standing up my chain slipped out from under my shirt, revealing the cross on the chain. I was flustered. I grabbed the cross with my fist to hide it.

Ibrahim smiled. 'Don't worry,' he said. 'You're seeking the path to God. One day you'll abandon things like that.'

'But I love Jesus,' I replied.

'We love him too,' he said spontaneously, to my surprise. 'We believe in him and in the Virgin Mary.'

I liked what he said. 'And do you pray to Jesus and to the Virgin Mary, like you pray to the Prophet Muhammad?' I asked him.

He shook his head. 'We don't pray to the Prophet Muhammad, Peace Be Upon Him. We pray directly to God,' he said. He looked at his watch and picked up his mobile phone. Before making a phone call, he said, 'Before I go, I'm going to lend you something.'

He spoke on the phone with a friend of his who was living in the residence halls at the religious institute. Within five minutes his friend came in. He was a young Filipino who appeared to be in his early twenties. His hair was uncombed and his face was puffy from sleeping. He gave Ibrahim a small package and then left. While we were walking to the main door, Ibrahim passed the package to me. It was a DVD case with a picture of Anthony Quinn in a black turban on the cover, and at the top the title of the film: *The Message*. Just as we reached the door someone asked us to wait. It was the old man who had been reading the Qur'an in the corner. He hurried over towards us. 'The mosque is for praying, not for exchanging films,' he said angrily. 'That's *haram*.' He pulled the film rudely out of my hands and started to examine the cover, back and front. He gave it back to me without saying a word. He patted me on the shoulder, then turned his back on us and left the mosque.

I liked the film very much. I watched it several times. I liked the Prophet Muhammad, even though he didn't appear in the film. I liked Hamza, the Prophet's uncle. I liked the companions of the Prophet and their conversation with the Negus of Abyssinia. The conversation provided answers to many of the questions I had been thinking about. The film was not enough however: it made me interested in doing more research and finding out more. I started researching on the Internet. The first thing I read about was *The Message,* its crew, how it was filmed and how audiences responded. I was particularly interested in the director. I saw a picture of him on one website, smartly dressed in a suit and a black tie. I was stunned to read the news under the picture. It said that two months before I came back to Kuwait the director, Moustapha Akkad, and his daughter were killed in an Amman hotel in a bombing carried out by an Islamist group.

I left the laptop on the table and, puzzled, I went to lie down on my bed. Which one of the two was Islam? Was it what I had seen in *The Message*? Or was it what had put an end to the life of the director? Was it the Islam of Lapu-Lapu, the sultan of Mactan? Or the Islam of the Abu Sayyaf group in Mindanao? I was filled with confusion, fear and doubt. I wondered whether Satan had taken root in my mind while I was preparing a house for God in my heart.

Sometimes I really wished I could swap brains with my little brother Adrian, so that I could atone for a mistake that I don't even remember and spare my heart the uncertainty that I had in my mind.

19

Ramadan ended and it was Eid al-Fitr, the feast that follows the month of fasting. I spent the first day behind the curtain in my room, spying on the people visiting the family whose lives I had complicated. No one asked after me. No one sent me any festive greetings apart from Ghassan, who sent me a text message saying *Eid Mubarak*. The women were in their best clothes and had had their hair done. They came into the house through the inner courtyard. The men wore the usual traditional dress and had shiny new shoes on. Even the little boys, my aunts' children, were wearing traditional dress with headdresses just like the men. The servants were also celebrating the occasion by wearing new clothes. Through the glass door, which was half open, I could see Grandmother with her legs stretched out as usual. The children were kissing her on the forehead. She stuck her hand in her bag and gave out money to them. Happy, they went out into the inner courtyard and counted the money they had received from the grown-ups. The servants also received their share of presents for Eid and were very happy with them.

I was alone in my room. I imagined myself wearing white and kissing Grandmother on the head to wish her a happy Eid. But then I drove the idea out of my mind, tired of idle fantasies. I turned my back on the curtain and looked around the room for Inang Choleng. I found her withdrawn into her shell under the bed. I lay on my stomach under the bed. I picked her up and stood up with her in my hands. I brought her face close to my forehead so that she could plant a kiss on it. She didn't do so. I made a kissing sound with my lips to trick myself into thinking that the tortoise had kissed me. I put her on the floor, then went to the small fridge in the corner. I came back with an Eid present for her – a lovely, succulent lettuce leaf. I brought her face close to mine and whispered, 'Happy Eid.'

*   *   *

Around noon, after the Eid well-wishers had gone, Khawla knocked on the door of my room, which was half open. She pushed it open and stayed where she was in the doorway, without stepping over the threshold. 'Happy Eid,' I said, beating her to it. She wished me well with a friendly smile, but she had nothing in her hand.

'Aren't you going to come in and wish Grandmother a happy Eid?' she asked me. 'After everyone's gone?

Once she's sure no one will see the face that brings shame on the family?' I said. The words just slipped out of my mouth, involuntarily. I was pointing at my own face as I spoke. 'Khawla!' I said angrily. 'Why do they treat me this way?'

She was still smiling, though there was no longer anything to smile about. 'It's not easy, Isa,' she said, looking at the ground.

'Grandmother and Awatif are religious people,' I said excitedly. 'They pray a lot. Is God against me too?' Khawla didn't answer. I walked towards the door where she was standing.

'The Buddha says in his teachings that people are equal and that no one is better than anyone else, other than in their knowledge and their ability to control their desires,' I said.

'We're not Buddhists,' she said, shaking her head.

I took the chain with the cross from the drawer near my bed. 'And in the Bible, St Paul the Apostle says there's no longer any difference between Jews and non-Jews, between slaves and those who are free, between men and women. They are all one in Jesus Christ,' I told her.

She cast a suspicious look at me. She was about to answer but I didn't give her time. 'I know, I know, you're not Christians.'

I went to my laptop and turned the screen for her to see a website page that I had left open since the night before. 'The Prophet Muhammad, in his farewell sermon, said, "All mankind is from Adam and Eve. An Arab is not superior to a non-Arab nor is a non-Arab superior to an Arab; also a white person is not superior to a black person nor a black person to a white person, other then in piety and good deeds."'

I folded the screen down on to the keyboard. 'I'm not *that* evil,' I added.

'Enough!' said Khawla, and her raised voice shut me up.

'I'm sorry,' she added, and she did look remorseful. 'But this has nothing to do with religion.'

It's hard to explain what I gathered from Khawla. Perhaps that's what Ghassan meant by things that are hard to explain and hard to understand. My existence, Khawla explained, reduced the family's status in society. Other families of the same class might not agree to marry into our family because of me. They would look at our family with contempt. 'If you recognised me, would that make you bidoon?' I asked her in my usual stupidity. My question surprised her.

'Did Ghassan tell you about the bidoon?' she asked. 'Anyway, that's not what this is about,' she added before I had time to answer. Khawla explained to me what Ghassan had failed to explain. In Kuwait, I gathered, people didn't set much store by the word *Kuwaiti*, even if they were Kuwaiti, because it didn't mean much. There were different kinds of Kuwaitis, different levels, different classes that distinguished themselves from other classes. I don't mean to exaggerate. This doesn't happen only in Kuwait. In the Philippines as well rich families have similar attitudes. I didn't argue with her on the question of intermarriage, because every family is free to choose, and it was nothing new to me. Filipinos of Chinese origin, for example, don't intermarry with ordinary people in the Philippines, for reasons of their own. They prefer to marry their own kind. But they don't put other people in categories in this way, outside their own circles, as either above them or below them. But I saw absolutely no justification for what Khawla said about people despising each other.

Khawla said, 'In his unfinished novel, my father said we're Kuwaitis only in times of need. We become Kuwaitis when there's a crisis, but we soon go back to that horrible putting people in categories as soon as things calm down.'

I really needed to learn Arabic to read what my father had written. 'What did Father want to say in his novel?' I asked Khawla.

She pursed her lips, uncertain how to answer. 'I don't know, because the novel's full of contradictions.

I dream about rewriting it one of these days,' she finally said.

I thought of saying, 'It's no surprise it's like that if he was describing his surroundings,' but I held my tongue.

Khawla elaborated: 'On the first page he says that one hand can't clap, but in the body of the story he calls on people to be as one hand. I can't understand why he calls on people to be as one hand when he's so sure that one hand couldn't clap.'

'One hand can't clap, but it can slap. Some people don't need hands clapping for them. They need a good slap to wake them up,' I said.

'Isa, I don't like the way you talk!'

That wasn't really my style, nor the way I thought, but that was what I concluded my father wanted to say. Khawla said I might be right in what I said and that kind of talk might be acceptable from an insider, but no one would accept me coming from outside and criticising the situation in Kuwait. To change the subject, she asked about people in the Philippines. I told her in turn about the variety there, the mestizo families with Spanish or European roots, the families of Chinese origin, the northern tribes such as the Ifugao, the Aeta and many others. What I said about tribes caught her interest. 'You have tribes too?' she asked.

'We have lots,' I said. 'The Ifugao, for example, have been famous for growing rice since ancient times.'

I went to the laptop to look for some pictures of them, half-naked on the terraced rice fields or in their traditional costume on special occasions. I turned the screen towards her. She nodded with interest at the pictures, still standing in the doorway. I was proud when I talked about people in the Philippines, and I wished I could have talked about people in Kuwait with the same enthusiasm. But that would only happen if I became one of them, and they refused to let me become one of them. And if I did manage to become one of them, where would they place me in their complicated social hierarchy? If they put me on the bottom level, would I talk about them so enthusiastically? Again, when times are hard, I wish I had Adrian's brain.

Khawla was still looking at the pictures I was showing her. 'Our tribes are known for growing rice,' I said. 'What are the tribes here famous for?'

'For eating rice,' she said without thinking.

She laughed out loud as soon she spoke the words, delighted with her own comment as though she was laughing at a joke.

'You seem to think they're ridiculous,' I said.

'And they think we are too,' she replied.

I don't claim that such things don't exist in the Philippines, but people there are busy with more important things. Some people may look on others with contempt but it happens on a limited scale, and it's not as important as Khawla suggested it is in Kuwait. In Kuwait, my sister explained, some people boast that their ancestors built a wall around the old city, although all that's left of the wall is two gates, and others boast about events that took place many years ago around a red fort somewhere in Kuwait. Both groups claim they love their country, Khawla said, and both deny the existence of the other group. It was like watching a match between two teams. Large crowds of supporters, with me in the middle of them, on neither side.

I remembered the Philippines and wondered whether, if life there was as easy as it was in Kuwait, people would have time to make these social distinctions. Perhaps poverty brings advantages we aren't aware of.

There was something complicated in Kuwait that I didn't understand. All the social classes looked for a lower class on whose back they could ride, even if they had to create one. Then they would climb on to the shoulders of those in the class below, humiliate them and use them to ease the pressure from the class above.

20

Merla seemed to be going through a rough patch. The tough, stubborn, carefree Merla of old was hardly recognisable now. My cousin's emails suggested she was having psychological problems. The messages were troubling, full of gibberish I couldn't understand. In one of my emails I asked her to turn her webcam on so that we could chat. *I want to see you*, I wrote. She refused. I begged her. I insisted. A week went by, more or less. Then she sent a message saying, *I want to see you.*

About one year after leaving the Philippines, I saw a Merla who didn't look like Merla. There she was on the screen. The surroundings suggested she was in an Internet café. The picture was clear at first but gradually faded. We tried again. We turned off the camera and restarted it whenever the picture faded. Even when the picture was clear and crisp, Merla's face looked pale. There were dark rings around her eyes. Her lips were almost the same colour as her pale skin. But despite all that, she was still attractive. 'Hello, hello, can you hear me?' I said.

She nodded. Then she used the keyboard and wrote, *This place . . .* She looked around her, and continued: *as you can see, is very crowded. I will use the keyboard instead of the microphone.*

She got busy writing but it took much longer than it should have. Minutes passed, with the promise of plenty of words. She shook her head irritably. She stopped a while, then resumed writing. My heart raced as I waited for her words. Time passed. Three, four, even five minutes. Her eyes sparkled and her fingertips worked away on the keyboard. She looked up at the screen. Meanwhile I was impatient to write my news. She sent her words, then covered her face with her hands and cried. I read what she had written: *I feel useless.* I brought the microphone close to my mouth and whispered, 'That's not what you spent five minutes writing, Merla.' Merla turned off the camera and vanished.

The same evening I received an email from her, nothing like the previous nonsense.

José,

I hesitated a long time before sending you this message. I don't know why you in particular. You're the only man I don't feel hostile towards. Maybe we're similar to a large extent. We're both looking for something. You seem to have found it, or you're about to. But me, not yet, and I don't think I will find it. In twenty-two years I still haven't found myself. I'm still looking. There are things I have overcome and things that have overcome me and there are things I am still struggling with. When I had MM tattooed on my arm a few years back, I was deceiving myself. Everyone, including you, interpreted it as a combination of my initial and Maria's, and no one but me knew that I was really asserting a connection to a grandfather who hated me – Merla Mendoza.

People aren't interested in my story, and the fact that I'm illegitimate doesn't detract from my worth because my beauty is the only thing that people look at and it distracts them from everything else. But in my beauty all I see is a sign that marks me out from those around me and reminds me of my mother's past and the fact that my father was some despicable European bastard. I find myself compensating for my own inadequacy by loving the Philippines and everything that is Filipino, as if with this love I can erase the traces left on my face by my European father. I love the things that represent the Philippines, its heritage and culture. On the other hand I've developed a hatred for Europe and Europeans, the ones who occupied our country years ago. Although they have gone, they have left things that bear witness to the fact that they passed this way. The country still has the name they gave it, after their King Philip II, and not many years ago a European man took possession of Aida's body. He disappeared but he left proof that he passed this way – me.

I have adopted Rizalism. It looks interesting, if only because it is a purely Filipino religion, unlike Christianity, which the colonialists imposed on us. Although José Rizal did not preach this religion, and although it only appeared in the early 20th century, after he was executed, it's the religion that best deserves to be adopted.

Did you know that I've got over everything except the things inside me that I'm not aware of? My need for a man to reject is suffocating me. I want one and I don't want one. I arouse them. I amuse myself by making them submit. I thrive on their thirst. I put the glass close to their lips. They kiss it and feel it with their fingertips but I don't let a single drop of water wet their lips. It gives me pure pleasure when they bow down to kiss my feet. When they bow down, I see them as just pathetic chickens looking for worms between my toes. I examine them closely, and feel a deep sense of satisfaction. Although I need more, I make do with that. I get dressed. I turn my back on them and take pleasure in their pleas, without letting them get anything out of me.

José,

Don't bother about the way you look. I don't bother about the way I look. Prove to yourself who you are before you prove it to others. Believe in yourself, and those around you will believe in you, and if they don't believe that's their problem, not yours.

I don't know whether you've turned Muslim in Kuwait or whether you're adrift, looking for God in other religions. In any case, pray for me. Ask your Lord to wipe away the sins of Merla, your loving cousin.

338

I want to be pure because Rizal says the victim must be pure and spotless if the sacrifice is to be acceptable.
MM

When I'd finished reading Merla's message, I was grateful that my television was turned on. The silent picture took me away from Merla's sad and mysterious message to another, distant world. I picked up the remote control to raise the volume. It was a group of musicians with more than twenty-five men. They were arranged in lines wearing traditional clothes rather different from what I was used to seeing. The hems of their thobes and collars were embroidered in various colours. They had very wide, loose sleeves. Behind them there was a model of a wooden ship rather like the Kuwaiti emblem on the banknotes, and behind them there were Kuwaiti flags attached to the wall. The men in the middle row were holding tambourines and facing the camera. To their right there was a line of men facing a line to their left, clapping in the traditional style that I like. One of the men was moving freely between the lines holding a drum hanging from a strap around his neck. The line on the left and the line on the right moved towards each other till they were almost touching. The men were clapping and singing in unison. Then the two lines moved apart by stepping back, the men in each line holding hands with their neighbours. The songs changed. They made way for several men dancing those dances that I know well. They swung their shoulders forward, put their hands on their headdresses, which were thrown any old how, and jumped in the air. Then they turned backwards swaying. Their laughter was infectious and I laughed too. As they danced I left the laptop table for the middle of the room and ended up imitating their dance with a big smile on my face. With the men on the television screen, I had the same feeling I had had when I was with those crazy Kuwaitis in Boracay. I began clapping the same way as them. I swung my shoulders and did a turn. The men went back into their lines and the man with the drum appeared alone, prancing around between the lines of men. I went on dancing till I noticed that my phone was ringing.

'Hello. Isa?'

'Hi, Khawla.'

'Could you turn down the music, Grandmother says.'

21

Eid al-Adha comes about two months after the feast at the end of Ramadan. I woke up early to the sound of the sheep in the inner courtyard. It was bleating, and the sheep in the neighbours' houses bleated back, as if they were exchanging festive greetings or perhaps saying goodbye to each other before the mass slaughter in the morning, when their blood would flow into the street, to be washed away with water and disappear through the grating in the gutter nearby.

It was half past six in the morning. Before people started visiting Grandmother I had already finished having a shower in order to meet her, kiss her forehead, and wish her well on the occasion of the feast. I put on the new clothes I had bought specially for the occasion from the menswear shop near the central market: a white thobe, long white pants to go underneath, a white cap and a white headdress. Everything about me was white that morning, except for my shoes and my head ring, which were black. I stood in front of the mirror to look at myself. The only thing I recognised was my face.

I pushed the glass door. Grandmother was alone in the sitting room in front of the television screen, which was showing the same man in the bright blue jacket, apparently singing a different song from the one that had so excited Grandmother the previous time. I went up to her. She turned to me and looked into my face in disbelief. I bent down and kissed her forehead. The black ring fell off my head. I was flustered. I remembered the scene when the old Emir of Kuwait bent down to kiss the soil of Kuwait and his head ring fell off. It was a simple matter, no need to be flustered. I ignored the head ring and in my own special Arabic I said, 'Happy Eid, Grandmother.' She nodded but didn't say anything. She was looking alternately at the wooden door at the front of the house and the glass door on the side. She was worried some visitor might come in and see me or that the servants might notice my clothes and their curiosity might lead them to realise who I really was. When I massaged her legs, she was careful to close the doors in case someone visited unexpectedly. And now it was Eid, so there might be many visitors.

I picked up the black head ring from the floor. I turned away from Grandmother now that I had fulfilled my wish to kiss her forehead, as I had seen my cousins do at the feast after Ramadan. 'Isa!' she called from behind me. I turned towards her. She beckoned me over, saying, 'Come, come' in English. Of course she could have said '*Taal*' and I would have understood just as well. I walked back to her. She slipped her hand into her handbag and handed me twenty dinars, then waved me away as if anxious I should leave in a hurry. 'Go, go,' she said, also in English.

I took off my new clothes and called Ghassan and Ibrahim Salam to wish them a happy Eid. I sent greetings messages to Khawla and Hind. Then I lay on my bed and watched television. At half past eight, I received a text message from Khawla. *Happy Eid, I want to see you about something*, it said.

When it came to despicable behaviour Raju was a real professional. He had been gossiping maliciously about me to the servants in the houses nearby. Some of the servants had clearly passed on the gossip to their employers. Umm Jabir, the owner of the house next door, phoned on the morning of the Eid to wish Grandmother well and ask if she could borrow what she called 'the Filipino man who works at your place'. 'Raju says he's a good worker. The men are going to meet for lunch in the *diwaniya* today and the cook's busy. I need someone who can serve tea and coffee and juice,' she said. Khawla said it was very bad for Grandmother. Umm Jabir was known in the neighbourhood for being nosy and gossiping in the women's meetings that Grandmother was careful not to attend. Umm Jabir had recently retired from her job and she didn't have anything to do but call up this

343

or that neighbour and pass on news from here or there. She had no scruples about adding whatever details she felt like adding.

Grandmother tried to fob her off. She suggested Babu as an alternative to me.

'No,' said Umm Jabir.

'Then Raju.'

'No, no, the Filipino looks well-behaved,' Umm Jabir said.

'But he's not good at serving.'

'It's easy. All he has to do is hold a tray and take it round to the guests.' Umm Jabir's insistence raised doubts in Grandmother's mind. She did however send Khawla to tell me about it, not to consult me but to ask me to go and serve at Umm Jabir's.

Khawla was angry. 'Whatever Grandmother has done, make sure you don't agree.'

I listened to her and thought to myself: 'When I accepted Grandmother's request that I hide my identity in front of the servants, it was because I understood it was temporary. When I promised not to say anything in front of Ahmad and Faisal, as if I was a servant, that was to save Nouriya and Awatif from disaster if their husbands found out. But to take it this far, that's too much!'

'I'm Isa Rashid al-Tarouf. I'm Isa Rashid al-Tarouf, whether you like it or not. That's what I inherited from my father. When it comes to my mother, even if I did inherit her appearance I certainly didn't inherit her old job in this house, where she was Josephine the servant.' I was furious.

Khawla was standing still at the door watching me. I kicked the tortoise. I pushed the little table, throwing the laptop onto the ground. I grabbed my headdress in one hand and the black ring in the other and shouted, 'What can I do to make them recognise me?'

Khawla bent down and picked up Inang Choleng, who was upside down on her shell. Grandmother appeared behind her. She had come alone without leaning on anyone's arm. She leaned against the door frame of my room. Her fear of scandal had relieved her arthritis. Khawla looked back into the inner courtyard, to left and to right, hoping to find out who had helped the old lady up the three steps to the glass door. But then she realised it was fear that had given her the strength to come.

Grandmother was murmuring and crying. She pointed towards the sky with both hands. All I managed to catch was the name Ghassan. 'What's she saying? What's she saying?' I asked Khawla angrily. Grandmother was venting all her wrath on Ghassan for bringing me back to Kuwait without consulting anyone. 'All Ghassan did was carry out my father's wishes!' I told her. 'Ghassan did what you should have done.' Grandmother was tired. She held on to Khawla's shoulder for support. Her voice was fading but she did keep talking and I caught the names Ghassan and Hind now and then. 'What's she saying?' I asked Khawla angrily again. I was insistent.

She turned away to help Grandmother back inside but she answered me anyway. 'She says Ghassan brought you back to get revenge on our family because she refused to let him marry Hind,' she said. With that she went off with Grandmother on her arm and with Inang Choleng in her other hand.

I sat down on my bed, too shocked to think. So Ghassan with the sad face had played a dirty trick – a trick that was out of character with his face. He had waited all these years. He had made all the arrangements for me to come back from the Philippines. He had put me up in his flat. He had treated me kindly, but only to satisfy his own sick desire for revenge.

★ ★ ★

Ghassan called me many times that day but I didn't answer. He must have called Khawla as well to find out why I wasn't answering his calls. In the evening he sent me a message saying, *I found out why you're not answering my calls*. That's all it said. Ghassan disappeared and I don't know which of us gave up on the other. His grave offence and the fact that he had been exposed must have persuaded him to avoid confrontation, rather than try to defend himself. Khawla took a neutral position, which left me the task of trying to work out whether Ghassan really had duped me. Khawla said this was what Grandmother thought, whereas Hind dismissed it. As for Khawla, she had no opinion on the subject.

* * *

From the time my father was captured and until years after the liberation of Kuwait, Ghassan was a frequent visitor to Grandmother's house as a friend of Rashid's. He asked after them and always reminded them that Rashid's disappearance did not mean the end of the relationship between him and a house where he felt at home and with people he saw as family. He was in touch with Iman, Khawla's mother, to ask after Rashid's daughter. He felt he had to keep the promise he had made to the memory of his late friend. Everyone in the Tarouf household welcomed him because he 'brought a whiff of Rashid', as Grandmother put it. But that factor faded with the passage of time. After Awatif and Nouriya got married, Ghassan felt confident there were others looking after the family's affairs. He gradually grew more distant, but in the meantime a vague relationship had developed between him and Hind. She was the only person who asked after him if he didn't come, because when he didn't come she felt the absence of her brother, Rashid, she said. Khawla was young at the time and wouldn't have known about these things unless her mother had told her. Hind stayed in touch with Ghassan by telephone. Their relationship led to a love affair. Hind kept her feelings a secret from everyone except Iman, who was close to her at the time, until eventually it was no longer possible to continue in the same way. Ghassan proposed to Hind. Grandmother said to him, 'You're almost family and we hold you in the highest regard but when it comes to marriage, I pray to God to provide you with a woman who is better than Hind.' Khawla said she understood why Grandmother turned Ghassan down: she didn't want her grandchildren to be bidoons like their father – social and legal outcasts.

Ghassan stayed away from Grandmother's house and went off in his own world, while Hind went through a period of emptiness, which she filled with her interest in human rights. She wrote on behalf of people who had been mistreated, asserting their rights, and took part in public meetings as an activist in the field. Through seminars, television discussions and interviews with newspapers, she became known for defending people regardless of their gender, religion or affiliation. She was famous in Kuwait. People knew her name – Hind al-Tarouf. But what no one know was that the only thing she was defending was a love that wasn't destined to last long, love for one of those whose cause she had dedicated her life to defend – a cause that became her cause.

I looked at myself caught in all these crosscurrents and waited for recognition from my family. I was horrified. I didn't want to suffer a fate similar to that of Ghassan. I didn't want to take revenge on my family even if they didn't recognise me. I looked around for Inang Choleng. I remembered seeing her upside down on her shell at the door with Khawla bending down to pick her up. I remembered what had happened in my room that same morning: Khawla standing by the door, talking about Umm Jabir and Grandmother's fears, my rebellion against my weakness and my fears. *I'm Isa Rashid al-Tarouf. I'm Isa Rashid al-Tarouf. Do I need them to recognise me, once I've recognised myself?*

Not after that day, because the time had come for me to set myself free – Kuwait was more than the Tarouf household.

PART 5

Isa . . . On The Margins Of The Country

'It is a useless life that is not consecrated to a great ideal. It is like a stone wasted in the field without becoming part of an edifice.'

José Rizal

On the afternoon of the first day of Eid al-Adha, Iman visited the Tarouf house for the first time in ages to wish Grandmother well on the Eid. Her husband mustn't have known about this forbidden visit. She hadn't visited Grandmother in Ramadan or at Eid al-Fitr, so what exactly was it that brought her this time? It never rains but it pours, as they say.

Khawla knocked on the door of my room and as usual she didn't come past the doorway. She told me that Umm Jabir had called Grandmother again and when Grandmother said she couldn't send me over Umm Jabir asked her, 'Is the Filipino really called Isa?' Grandmother almost had a breakdown in response to Umm Jabir's insinuation. Raju must have been behind this.

I shook my head indifferently and said, 'So what?'.

Khawla's eyes were bathed in tears. She told me that her mother, Iman, had had a call from Umm Jabir asking her about the Filipino who was living in the home of her former husband's family. Iman found out about me without our inquisitive neighbour finding out anything, then came over immediately to ask Grandmother to let her take Khawla to live in her other grandmother's house, because she didn't want her daughter living in a house where I was living. I remembered a letter my father sent to my mother in which he said that his new wife would have no problem if I went back to Kuwait. What had changed? Khawla didn't respond but just wiped away her tears.

'I'll cut out Umm Jabir's tongue,' I said. 'I will not be the cause of you leaving the house you love so I've decided to leave.'

Although she was sad, Khawla didn't insist I stay. Slightly shocked, she just said, 'To the Philippines?'

'To Kuwait,' I replied. For the first time since I'd come to her house, Grandmother gave me a big hug as soon as she heard of my decision, and almost suffocated me. She let go of me after planting a kiss on my cheek. She turned to Khawla and asked her to translate what she was going to say. Highly embarrassed, Khawla said that on top of the 200 dinars a month, Grandmother would now give me another 200, so now I would have a monthly allowance of 400 dinars. I nodded gratefully.

Grandmother talked again to Khawla, who then turned to me. 'She'll also give you her share of Father's pension,' she added. Both of them were red in the face, out of embarrassment in the case of Khawla, out of happiness in the case of Grandmother. I turned my back on them and went back to my room, which would soon no longer be my room.

* * *

On the evening of the second day of the Eid, Ibrahim Salam was waiting for me outside in his car. As I was picking up my suitcase, Khawla opened the door to my room and for the first time she took a few hesitant steps inside. The fact that she came in like that disconcerted me. I left my suitcase on the floor and watched her. She stood in front of me, examining my face. I was so anxious my throat felt dry. Her face was completely expressionless. I tried in vain to smile but I couldn't because I was so taken aback that Khawla had ventured into the danger zone. She put her hands under her chin and fiddled with something and her *hijab* came loose. She grabbed it from the part nearest her forehead, took it off her hair and let it fall to her shoulders. She shook her head and tossed her hair free. She looked straight into my eyes. I almost burst into tears. She wrapped her arms around me and buried her face in my shoulder. 'I'll miss you, brother,' she said.

My arms hung down and I didn't reciprocate. My heart was pounding. She kissed me on the cheek, then turned and went back where she had come from, covering her hair with her *hijab*. Her words rang in my ears. The word 'brother' continued to echo even after she had left the room.

It was the first time Khawla had called me brother and, just one day earlier, Grandmother had embraced me and kissed me, also for the first time. If I had known that would happen I would have left the Tarouf house much earlier. I picked up my suitcase and turned off the lights. In the outer courtyard I looked towards the kitchen. Babu, Lakshmi and Luzviminda were behind the window watching me. They waved sadly. I left Grandmother's house behind me. As I was putting my suitcase in the boot of Ibrahim's car, Raju appeared from behind the garage door. He threw a cigarette end on to the floor and crushed it with his foot. He turned to me and said, 'Goodbye', then closed the door.

Hind's car was in its usual spot under the awning. She was at home but she didn't come out to say goodbye. I understood her attitude: how could she say goodbye to me when she had failed to play the role she should have played in my case?

I'm not blaming her, because, as my mother said of my father one day, 'The decision is out of one's hands if a whole society stands behind it.'

2

Ibrahim Salam shared his room with me temporarily, until I could find somewhere permanent to live. 'Why do you have to live in Jabriya?' I asked Ibrahim, since I had only painful feelings about the area. My father's friend had died in a plane with the same name and it was in the same area that the friend who had betrayed him lived. 'Because it's close to my work in the Philippine embassy,' Ibrahim explained.

One night I asked him to tell me about the Prophet Muhammad in return for me telling him about Jesus Christ, rather like those bedtime conversations that Cheng and I used to have about Jesus and the Buddha. 'I'll tell you about the Prophet Muhammad, but you don't need to tell me about Jesus,' he replied. When I asked why not, he answered confidently, 'I'm sure I know more about Christ than you do.'

He often spoke to me about Islam. I was interested in some of the similarities between the Qur'an and the Bible. Was Islam a new religion, as I had thought, or a supplement to religions that predated it? Ibrahim told me about the previous holy books that the Qur'an refers to. When I asked him about those books, he picked up a copy of the Qur'an and translated some passages, including one I remember from the chapter called 'Women': *'Behold, We have inspired you, just as We inspired Noah and all the prophets after him – as We inspired Abraham, and Ishmael, and Isaac, and Jacob, and their descendants, including Jesus and Job, and Jonah, and Aaron, and Solomon; and as We vouchsafed unto David a book of divine wisdom.'* I understood from what he said that Islam didn't dismiss the religions that came before it, because the Qur'an refers to the earlier religions, mentions the prophets by name and tells us they were all sent to mankind by God. Ibrahim switched some lights on in my head but turned out others. When he saw I was confused, he seemed more interested than me in the subject. I don't know if he was trying to convince me or convince himself. He closed the Qur'an and put it back in its place in a drawer near his bed. He told me about miracles I had never heard of. Clouds that spelt out the word 'Allah' in the sky, a watermelon with seeds arranged to form the name of the Prophet Muhammad, a fish with stripes that could be read as Allah, and other stories like the ones I used to hear in the Philippines about statues of the Virgin Mary that shed tears or about the Virgin Mary appearing in some place, which would soon become a shrine. Ibrahim amazed me and it showed on my face. In response to my amazement he would ask confidently, 'So? What do you think?'

I was amazed in the sense of being underwhelmed, but Ibrahim read it the opposite way. 'These are just fantasies,' I told him in the end. He turned pale. 'If only you'd stick to reading the Qur'an,' I added.

He took a folded piece of paper out of the drawer where he kept the Qur'an. 'I'm going to show you a miracle,' he said. I had goosebumps. Although I don't believe in such things, he was so enthusiastic that I braced myself to see something new.

'It happened more than two years ago, in December 2004,' he said.

The date brought back memories of disaster and I interrupted him. 'That was when the tsunami hit several countries in East Asia,' I said.

He nodded. 'That's right, brother,' he said.

'The waves hit one particular island,' he continued, unfolding the piece of paper. 'It flattened the whole area but saved the . . .' He left the sentence open so that the piece of paper could finish off what he wanted to say. It was a big glossy colour picture of a white mosque standing intact amid the devastation.

'Where's the miracle?' I asked him, as amazed as ever.

'Look. There's nothing left of the houses around the mosque. Everything was swept away by the waves and only the mosque survived.'

My goosebumps disappeared with disappointment. 'Ibrahim!' I said. 'The houses around the mosque were made of wood and corrugated iron, while the mosque had foundations that went deep into the ground and was build of concrete, with concrete pillars.'

'Are you casting doubt on Islam?'

I shook my head. 'No. But I am casting doubt on your ridiculous miracles. Would God send a tsunami to destroy the houses of the faithful around the mosque just so that people who didn't believe in God will see that this is the true religion?'

For the first time, I was confident of what I was saying. God couldn't be promoted in this way because, as I had started to feel, God is greater, God is mightier and much deeper than that. I didn't say much because Ibrahim looked upset and I didn't want to sleep in the street. I pointed to my heart and said, 'Faith lies here, but with this missionary activity of yours, you're trying to put it here.' I pointed to my head. 'But faith doesn't stay there long.'

'What do you mean?' he asked, a sceptical look in his eyes.

'The only place for faith is in your heart,' I said with unusual confidence.

He looked at me in silence and I continued: 'Look at yourself in the mirror and you'll find enough miracles there to dispel your doubts, because you're a miracle in yourself.'

I pointed to the drawer next to his bed. 'Get the Qur'an out and translate some of it for me instead of offering feeble proofs that weaken your case.'

Religions are bigger than their adherents. That's what I've concluded. Devotion to tangible things no longer matters as far as I'm concerned. I don't want to be like my mother, who can only pray to a cross, as if God lived in it. I don't want to be like one of the Ifugao and never take a step unless it's sanctioned by the anito statues, which help my work prosper, protect my crops and save me from the evil spirits at night. I don't want to be like Inang Choleng, tying my relationship with God to a favourite statue of the Buddha. I don't want to seek *baraka* from a statue of a white horse with wings and the head of a woman, as some Muslims do in the south of the Philippines. I remember that statue well, when I once asked a Muslim boy at school if he had a statue or an icon of the Prophet Muhammad. He came back the next day and told me that drawing pictures or making statues of the Prophet was forbidden in Islam. But then he put his hand in his satchel and took out this statue. I was amazed at the way it looked and when I asked him what it was, he said, 'It's Buraq.' I forgot about Buraq until I saw it again later in various sizes, some as large as a small foal, in the National Museum of the Philippines. On a rectangular plaque on the glass case it said, *Buraq: the animal that the Prophet of Islam rode on his Night Journey from Mecca to Jerusalem and to Heaven.*

The statue of Buraq, the cross, the Buddha, the anito, imaginary miracles and other such things help to reinforce people's faith. People aren't satisfied with the miracles that took place in distant times and that were the monopoly of prophets when religions were in their infancy. So everyone who wants to find faith goes looking for miracles that don't exist. They make them up and believe in them, but their belief only shows how much doubt they still have.

I was sitting in front of Ibrahim. He was silent, as was I. In my right ear I heard the call to prayer, in my left ear the ringing of church bells. The smell of incense from the Buddhist temples hit my nostrils. I ignored the sounds and the smell. I focused on my steady heartbeat and I knew that God was there.

3

With Ibrahim's help I found a flat that suited me on the third floor of an old building in Jabriya, an area I hated, about a ten-minute walk from where Ibrahim lived. The building had no families at all because the usual practice in Kuwait is that families live in special buildings where unmarried young men are not allowed to live. Where I lived there were no women or children at all. It was like a prison or a military camp. Migrants of various nationalities lived in the flats and some of them housed more than ten people. Most of the flats in the buildings were empty during the week but were noticeably full of young men on Thursday and Friday nights and on religious and official holidays. Only then would I hear women's voices in the building. On the third floor, where my flat was, there were three other flats. One of them had five young Filipinos, in another there was an Arab man more than fifty years old, and the third was rented by a group of young men who came only at weekends, when they would make a lot of noise after midnight with laughing, singing and rowdy activity.

Renting the flat was a luxury I hadn't dreamt of. I had two bedrooms, a sitting room, a bathroom and a kitchen all to myself. Moving was easy because the only things I had that needed moving would fit in three bags – a large one for my clothes, a small one for the laptop and, most important of all, the briefcase where I kept my documents. Ibrahim lent me a mattress and a duvet and brought them over in his car. Khawla was constantly in touch, tracking my move. 'I feel guilty. I was one of the reasons why you left our house,' she said. She said that Grandmother missed me. *Her knees must be in a bad way*, I thought. Hind didn't call but she sent me a text message asking for my new address. I sent her the address and a few hours later a pick-up truck arrived with my bed, my fridge, the wardrobe, the television and a small cardboard box. The workers brought the things up, then left. I opened the cardboard box and there was my tortoise, hiding in her shell. There was a crack in the top of the shell that I hadn't noticed before. I remembered kicking her a few days earlier in an angry outburst and I felt bitter remorse. I found a small piece of paper inside the cardboard box. In beautiful handwriting, Khawla had written: *Aziza was jealous of your tortoise and denounced her to Grandmother, who got angry and evicted her, ;p*. A cruel joke but I laughed, in the knowledge that Khawla wanted to make me laugh.

Late that evening, after I had arranged the flat, my mobile rang. I thought it would be Ibrahim but in fact it was from Hind, asking me about him.

'What's that young man like, the one that Khawla told me about?' she asked. What does he look like? How old is he? Where does he live? Does he belong to some organisation? Lots of questions, rather like an interrogation. I answered them to the best of my knowledge, and when I had done so, she gave me a warning. 'Isa,' she said, 'beware of those backward people.' I was tongue-tied. 'In Kuwait,' she continued, 'there are many types of people who are better to make friends with than those people you're about to get involved with. I'm here if you need anything, but keep your distance from these dubious characters.'

★   ★   ★

Isolation is like a little corner where you're alone with your mind and you can't avoid looking it in the face. My mind would probably have wasted away like an unused muscle if I hadn't pushed it to the limits when I was alone. I hadn't planned to use it because I didn't trust it and it made me sceptical about everything. Perhaps my mind acted of its own accord. It felt neglected and sprang into action. How is it that ideas have this ability to distract us from everything else? Hours went by without me noticing that my stomach was empty or that I needed to sleep. Maybe my head was so stuffed that I lost my appetite, or perhaps my mind was so distracted all the time that I might as well have been asleep. I would look out of the window at the street and say, 'I haven't been outside for three days.' I suddenly realised I had been in the flat all that time. Without feeling it, it was as if I were in mourning. It was a mourning without flags at half mast, without the people outside wearing the sad faces I saw on the day I arrived in Kuwait. How did I spend all my time? I'm trying to remember. I didn't watch television. I didn't read a word. I never called anyone. Apart from thinking, what was I doing?

For the first time in my life, I felt useless. My old dream had come true, I had the paradise I was promised, I had travelled to Kuwait and I had more money than I needed. What next? In the Philippines all I had was my family. In Kuwait I had everything except a family.

I soon found it demeaning and embarrassing to take the money I received every month in return for being lazy. I felt increasingly useless now that a dream that had once seemed distant had come true. The truth about our dreams becomes clear to us the closer we get to them. We mortgage our lives for the sake of achieving them. The years pass. We grow older while the dreams stay as they were when we were young. We finally make them come true, and then we find that we have outgrown our dreams, which are the dreams of the young and not worth the trouble of waiting years for.

Giving without love has no value. Taking without gratitude has no savour. That's what I have discovered. I looked at the floor in the middle of the sitting room. I imagined my mother there, sitting cross-legged by her suitcase a week after coming back from Bahrain. The family were around her on the sofas, everyone waiting for their present. 'Pedro!' Mother shouted, throwing him a cigarette lighter as blue as Merla's eyes. Pedro was delighted with the present because it was a present. 'Aida!' – a pair of rubber shoes. 'Merla' – two pairs of underwear. Pedro's wife – a bra. Pedro's children – a bag of sweets and chocolates. 'José' – a pen and a school bag. Then Mother picked up a white hat, went to Adrian in his favourite corner and put it on his head.

I can still remember how happy everyone looked. Why wasn't I as happy with the presents from my Kuwaiti family as Uncle Pedro was with a cigarette lighter that wasn't worth more than 100 fils? It's love that makes things valuable.

In my isolation I found I had a morbid longing for my family in the Philippines. I was nostalgic for home although I had started to become familiar with some of the things in my father's country. The taste of the water still irritated me as much as when I first arrived. The water in the Philippines tastes better. I was no longer surprised when I saw men kissing when they greeted each other. I was no longer suspicious of strangers if they said hello to me as they walked past me. I even took the initiative and said '*As-salam aleekum*' to them as I went past. It made me feel as if I knew everyone in the country, especially when Ibrahim explained to me that the word *salam*, which was also the name of his father, meant peace. What a beautiful greeting! It provided me with an outlet, however small, through which I could share something with Kuwaitis. But whenever I tightened my grip on the hem of Kuwait's thobe, it slipped out of my grasp. I called Kuwait and it turned its back on me and I ran to the Philippines to complain.

It was hard for me to get used to my new country. I tried to focus narrowly on the people I loved there, but the aspects of Kuwait that they brought with them let me down. My father's death left me adrift. Ghassan's betrayal disappointed me. Grandmother and her incomplete love. Awatif's weakness, rejection by Nouriya, Hind's silence and my sister's fatalistic attitude. How could I approach a country which had so many faces if, whenever I approached any one of them, it looked away?

My spacious flat seemed cramped. Talking to the dumb tortoise grew boring. I put on a coat to keep out the cold and set off headlong into the outside world. In the corridor outside my flat I waited for the lift. The lift door opened and a young Filipino who lived in the flat next door was there, carrying some plastic bags, some of them under his arms and some clutched to his chest. His face was barely visible behind them. 'Hi, are you the new tenant?' he asked. I nodded. 'Before you go, please,' he said with a laugh, 'could you get my keys out of my coat pocket?' I put my hand into the pocket and gave him the keys. 'Could you open the door please?' he said with a smile. I turned the key in the lock and pushed the door open. The man went in, leaving me at the door. He disappeared into one of the other rooms while I stood there, looking around the small sitting room. It had soft lighting, wallpaper on the wall, boxes of pastries, soft drinks and the smell of cooking. In one of the corners near the window there was a Christmas tree and a big sign above it saying *Happy New Year 2007*. 'What are your plans for this evening?' the man asked from inside one of the rooms.

'Nothing,' I said.

He stuck his head out from one of the rooms. 'You can come over and spend the evening with us,' he said. 'We'll meet at ten.'

I accepted his invitation and my heart jumped for joy. I said goodbye, on the understanding that we'd meet again at ten.

I hung about in the street. It was about eight o'clock in the evening and bitterly cold. I looked around and then broke off three or four small green leaves. No one had noticed me. I closed my fist on them and crumbled them up between my fingers and thumb until I could feel the sticky sap on the palm of my hand. I brought my hand to my nose, closed my eyes and took a deep breath that filled my lungs with the smell. I opened my hand and the green leaves were still there. I had a close look. Mendoza's piece of land, the four houses, Whitey the dog, the cocks and the frogs were all there on my trembling palm, fenced in by the bamboo plants. That alone got rid of half the homesickness I had felt in my seclusion. I needed to do something else to cure the rest of it. I looked around. There was a bus stop not far off, but there were some boys there. I waited till they had finished their senseless ritual: they were standing on the pavement by the roadway with stones ready in their hands, waiting to throw the stones at buses as they went past. Buses did go past: some stopped and others went past the bus stop without stopping. The boys kept trying until one of them had a good hit. The windscreen of the bus shattered and the boys took to their legs, disappearing down dark, narrow alleyways.

When the coast was clear, I hurried to the bus stop. There was a blue pole sticking out of the pavement. At the top there was a white metal sign with the logo of the bus company. I leaned against the pole as I waited for the bus. It didn't matter what number bus it was. I didn't need to know the destination. The only thing about the bus that mattered was the filthy black smoke that its engine would spew into the air around me. That would cure my homesickness. I closed my eyes and leaned back against the post. One bus after another went past. The thick black diesel exhaust rose in the air. I filled my lungs with it. I could smell the streets of Manila. A bus went past leaving a cloud of black smoke and punching holes in the ozone layer. One of the holes fell from the sky and landed on the ground. From the hole came the noise of car engines and horns. The sound of people speaking in Filipino and English. I stuck my head into the hole. Jeepneys and motor tricycles jostled for space in the street. Buses, trucks and motorbikes. Rain fell on the streets with all the might the clouds could muster. The smell of diesel vanished. The noises receded into the distance. The image of Manila faded, the hole shrank, and there I was – in a Jabriya street, leaning against a post, free of the homesickness I had felt a few moments earlier.

to sing along with him for his girlfriend, who was listening to us on the telephone. A girlish young man in a tight short-sleeved shirt and shorts showed off his legs as he pranced around to our songs in a way that made people laugh. A man with a camera wouldn't stop taking pictures. One man drank reluctantly, cursing the state of affairs that forced him to work in Kuwait and complaining with every sip that he missed the taste of Red Horse, Heineken, Budweiser and the other beers he was used to. Some of them stuffed themselves with food. Others spent the time watching silent images on the television screen. Others formed small circles, sharing food, drink and conversation.

I moved over to the window overlooking the street with a drink in my hand. I watched the young men in the car park outside the building. They were getting out of their cars and coming to the door of the building alone or in small groups. One of them was with a friend, another with a woman. They looked around warily, like thieves preparing for their first burglary. The others noticed I was standing apart and came over to join me. They looked out of the window like me. One of them made fun of the young Kuwaitis. The guy with the baseball cap laughed and kept making jokes about people in Kuwait. The man who had been complaining knocked back the rest of his drink in one swig and spoke angrily about Kuwaitis, saying derogatory things about them. I remembered my father and imagined his remains, draped with the Kuwaiti flag and carried on his friends' shoulders. 'They're arrogant,' said the bald man. The glass shook in my hand. 'But the young men here are sexy,' said the effeminate one, licking his lips. Some of them burst out laughing. The man with the camera defended the Kuwaitis: 'I've been working with them for years. They're decent people, open-minded compared with people in other countries I've worked in.' The grumbler objected: 'I worked in Bahrain and the people there don't make us feel they're better than us.' The man in the cap laughed and winked at his friend. 'And you can buy a drink there too,' he said. The grumbler got upset and waved his hand dismissively. 'They're useless,' he said.

Listening to them, I felt torn between Kuwait and the Philippines. I hardly knew myself. Ibrahim didn't think of Kuwaitis in this way. He had never told me all this. 'All they have is money,' said the grumbler. The man with the camera pointed at him and said, 'What makes you angry is that Kuwaitis are really lucky to be born Kuwaiti, and you resent their good fortune.' 'Bullshit,' the grumbler replied angrily. The bald man, the oldest person present, intervened. 'That's enough. Happy New Year, Happy New Year,' he said. The man with the camera ignored the interruption and continued his conversation with the grumbler, who poured more drink into his glass. 'I have lots of friends here and they're not the way you portray them,' he said. The effeminate man agreed and made an obscene gesture. 'I have lots of friends too,' he added.

I downed the rest of my drink and asked for more. Their criticism of Kuwaitis rang in my ears. I thought of my father, Khawla, Hind and Grandmother. The group went on talking a long time. Others joined them and some moved away. I turned to the grumbler and said, 'Go back to the Philippines if you don't like it here.' He looked at me disapprovingly and said, 'Are you happy to stay here?' Since I couldn't work out how to answer, I had to leave the party. I thanked the host and left, rather the worse for wear, thinking about what the man with the camera had said about Kuwaitis being lucky to be born Kuwaiti.

Outside the flat, three young men were waiting for the lift. The landing rang with their laughter. Apparently they had just finished their own party. '*As-salam aleekum*,' I said as I walked past them.

Making fun of my accent, the man in the middle answered me like Grandmother's parrot: '*Salamuuu alekooom*.' With his index fingers, he stretched his eyes into slits, mocking my Filipino features. They burst out laughing. He then made fun of me by greeting me in Filipino: '*Kumusta ka.*' I don't know why, but I felt insulted. They started talking to each other in Arabic and roaring with laughter.

I opened the door of my flat. I now felt an urge to insult these people, though I had been angry when the Filipinos at the party next door had maligned them. I glowered at the one who had made fun of my greeting. '*Sira ulo,*' I said without thinking – Filipino for 'crazy head' or 'idiot'. They looked at each other in puzzlement. Damn! Even my insult took me back to my mother's country.

I remembered another word. I said it to myself first to make sure I had it straight. Then I pointed at the man in the middle and let it out. '*Himara!*' I said.

I slammed the door behind me, grateful to Grandmother's parrot.

5

Kuwait, one year on.

I started playing with the idea of going back to the Philippines and visiting the family house. Although she missed me, my mother was against the idea and implored me to stay in Kuwait longer. I didn't know whether she was asking me to stay for my own sake or for the sake of the family, which was better off because of the money I was sending them. I gave up the idea of making the journey, not in deference to my mother's wishes, but because I was sure that if I went home before I had established roots in Kuwait, I would never come back.

Ibrahim promised to help me get a job. I had declined to join him and his friends in their missionary activities because I didn't know enough about it and I wasn't ready for things like that. I had only just begun to explore my relationship with God and how comfortable I was with that relationship.

Ibrahim was a nice guy but very simple. He proved to be a loyal friend. Whenever I asked him for anything he was quick to help me. He called me brother and when I asked him why, he said, 'A Muslim is brother to all other Muslims.' I was grateful for the way he felt towards me. I never told him I wasn't yet sure that I was Muslim because I was still feeling my way, but if I did become a Muslim he would definitely have been one of the reasons for my decision. There were three things that I discovered through Ibrahim and that made me sympathetic to Islam and taught me more about it: the film *The Message*, a book called *The Sealed Nectar*, a biography of the Prophet, and the fact that Ibrahim treated me well and took an interest in me.

Although the cars are one of the most striking aspects of Kuwait and I could have bought a modest one, I made do with a bicycle, which I bought with Ibrahim's help. I used to ride it around the neighbourhood and nearby areas. It was a smart black bike. I attached a Kuwaiti flag to the back of it. Although I had seen the flag everywhere – on my first day in Kuwait, when I saw it at half mast near the airport, in people's hands at the National Day celebrations in February, and flying in various sizes from people's cars – it didn't mean anything to me until I saw it covering the remains of that Kuwaiti poet and Ghassan told me that my father's remains had been covered with the Kuwaiti flag in the same way. After that the Kuwaiti flag had special meaning for me and stirred something inside me.

After I bought the bike I could say goodbye to taxis and their extortionate fares. I could cruise the streets at will and sometimes I couldn't believe how far I had ridden on my bike. It was extremely hard work but any effort I made to ride my bike was better than sitting in a bus seat, scanning the streets through the window, and leaning forward and putting my head between my knees whenever I caught sight of boys standing on the pavement, braced for the fragments of glass that might land on the terrified passengers if a stone hit a window.

On my first outing on my bike I went to Qortuba, crossing the bridge that connects Jabriya to al-Surra, and then crossing Damascus Street. I rode my bike parallel to the pedestrian street in Qortuba. I was horrified at what I saw near my favourite spot in the narrow lane near the main street, the spot where I used to sit that was full of trees. In the dusty area behind I saw an enormous truck in a chain-link enclosure with barbed wire at the top. It was a flatbed truck with many wheels and it was carrying a large container with a long metal pole sticking out through the roof. Without much thought and without needing to guess I realised that what was going up before my eyes was a mobile phone relay tower. The similarity between this tower and the one that took up a corner of Mendoza's land left no room for doubt. Strange that the two of them should have gone up in places that I loved.

From that day on I never went near the pedestrian street.

★ ★ ★

Apart from its basic function, food was a way of passing the time. If I felt bored, as I often did, I would amuse myself by working in the kitchen.

Life was simple compared with the life of my family in the Philippines. I had a kitchen that was fully equipped with the latest appliances and gadgets without me having to borrow a cent from the greedy Indian moneylenders as my family had done when they were poor, when they had to wait years before buying their next appliance. When I opened the fridge I remembered the story about the time when a fridge first arrived in our house in the Philippines. When I turned on the stove I didn't calculate the time as Mama Aida did. I watched the small blue and yellow tongues of fire around the metal ring. Sometimes I lit the stove when I didn't need it. I just enjoyed watching the gas burn. A large cylinder of gas didn't cost more than three quarters of a dinar. If it ran out, I didn't have to cook the food by burning wood in the courtyard like Mama Aida. She did that because a cylinder of gas cost more than six dinars in the Philippines, and that was a cylinder half the size of a cylinder in Kuwait. I enjoyed lighting the stove because I felt I was getting revenge on behalf of Aida.

One evening I called a taxi to go to the gas depot near the central market to change an empty cylinder. One of the streets in Jabriya was severely congested. Jabriya is always crowded. But congestion like this, with cars hardly able to move, only happened if there was an accident or a checkpoint. As I expected, at the end of the street there were police cars with lights flashing blue and red. The police were standing by the side of the road checking driving licences and car papers. The taxi driver opened his window and handed his papers to the policeman. The policeman examined them and before handing them back to the driver he asked me for my identity card. I stuck my hand in my trouser pocket but my wallet wasn't there. I panicked. I pointed back down the street and said, 'It's in the flat.'

He didn't understand me. *'Iqama, iqama,'* he demanded in Arabic, meaning he wanted proof that I was a legal resident in Kuwait.

Because I'm Kuwaiti and don't need a residence permit, I said, 'No *iqama*.'. Apparently I failed to explain myself. He told me to get out of the taxi. I tried to explain to him but he was shouting at me so rudely that I couldn't say anything. I took out my mobile phone to call my Aunt Hind. I don't know why her in particular, but she didn't answer my call anyway. I sent a text message to Khawla, saying, *The police are detaining me*. The policeman pushed me from behind and suddenly I found myself in a van parked on the kerb, packed with migrants who didn't have identity papers or valid visas. There were Arabs, Indians, Filipinos and Bangladeshis, and me – a Kuwaiti who didn't look like other Kuwaitis.

The van set off. Some people look frightened and others indifferent. 'The worst that can happen is we'll be deported,' someone said. I told the policeman standing by the van door that I was Kuwaiti. I don't think he heard what I said. He pointed to the seats at the back and spat out some words I didn't understand. Terrified, I went back to my seat.

A stunningly beautiful young Filipina who was sitting close by turned to me and said, 'The weekend starts today so we'll have to stay in the cells at the police station till the officer comes after the weekend.'

I opened my eyes wide. 'But I'm Kuwaiti. I don't need a visa,' I said.

She smiled. 'You'll have to prove that, after you've spent some time in detention,' she said. An older Filipina woman was crying and the young Filipina turned to her.

'I've been working in Kuwait without a valid residence for months after running away from my employer's house. I have a family that will die if I'm deported,' said the older woman.

'If it's that serious . . .' said the younger woman. She paused a moment. '. . . then you'll have to make some concessions.'

The woman gasped in shock at the possible implications of what the girl had said, then laid into her with the foulest insults, such as 'filthy whore' and so on.

The young woman turned to me and said, 'But it doesn't look as if you have anything to offer.' She gave a vulgar laugh. 'I have an old mother and three younger brothers. I've sacrificed everything for their sake,' she added.

The woman had experience. This wasn't her first time. She said she didn't usually stay in jail long. If the policeman in charge on the morning shift was incorruptible, his colleague on the late shift probably wouldn't be. If the first day went by without someone trying to seduce her in exchange for setting her free, then that certainly wouldn't continue through the second day. 'I've often paid for my residence permit by illegal means. Sometimes it happens in an empty room at the police station, or in their car or in an apartment where things like that take place,' she said.

'Do you know how many policemen I have on the contacts list in my phone?' she concluded defiantly.

Our mobile phones were confiscated. Before anyone questioned us, we were moved from the van straight to a foul holding cell. I thought to myself it would have been much better if I'd run into a fake policeman like the one who had taken ten dinars from my wallet a year earlier. That way losing the money would have been the end of it, rather than meeting a real policeman and ending up detained in the police station.

I spent two nights behind bars in the cell, at least by my watch. But it felt like many nights more. It was a small room, as dirty as the ten inmates. The smell of the place and of the people was unbearable. The dry January cold numbed my fingers and toes and went right to the bone. People looked calm. Except for me, they all knew what was in store for them. I didn't know how long I would be held there. We could hear women's voices nearby and I later found out that the cell for women was at the end of the corridor. The older Filipina woman had been crying since we were in the van but now it was louder. She kept complaining, sometimes in English and sometimes in Arabic, in the hope that someone would understand and give her a chance to get out. 'They'll die of hunger if I'm deported. I beg you, I beg you,' she said. My fellow prisoners fell asleep one after another. The woman's wailing grew even louder. From behind the bars I saw a policeman with a black stick hurrying towards the women's cell.

I cowered where I sat, imagining what might be in store for the woman. '*Allahu akbar, Allahu akbar,*' I murmured. 'Don't let him do her any harm.' The policeman shouted something unintelligible. My heart raced. The woman shouted back. I pulled my knees up against my chest and mumbled, 'Please don't provoke him.' They shouted louder. 'Please don't hurt her,' I said to myself. A loud crack interrupted their conversation. The prisoners woke up around me. The policeman was hitting the bars of the cell with his stick. Then the place fell silent. The policeman went back where he came from and my pulse reverted to normal. The men went back to sleep, but I couldn't even close my eyelids. I gave a long sigh. '*Allahu akbar,* God is the mightiest, thank you,' I said.

At least once every ten minutes someone would wake up, call for the warder and ask to go to the bathroom. I don't know how the others managed to sleep, what with the cold, the loud snoring and the wailing of the Filipina woman in the cell nearby.

I had my knees pressed up against my chest and my back against the wall. The later it was at night, the more desperate I felt about the prospects of getting out of the place. When I sent the text message to

Khawla, I never imagined I would have to stay long in detention, but nothing of what I had hoped came about. Had Khawla abandoned me?

Late at night, when everyone else was asleep, I heard the sound of footsteps coming down the corridor. Steady footsteps. I looked up at the metal bars and saw a policeman walking past our cell without looking aside and then continuing down the corridor. The sound of his footsteps stopped. I heard the jangling of keys and hushed whispers. Someone opened the metal door. The Filipina woman had apparently been sleeping but now she woke up. She resumed her crying and pleading. Someone closed the door. The sound of footsteps returned, coming closer. I was still looking through the bars. The men around me were still snoring in their sleep, oblivious to the woman's crying. The policeman walked past in the other direction, his body erect, his face fixed firmly forward. This time the pretty Filipina girl walked confidently behind him. She looked towards the cell I was in. We made eye contact for a moment as she passed. She raised her eyebrows and gave me a smile that reminded me of what she had said in the van. They disappeared. I stayed awake till morning thinking about the girl. Somewhere she was making illicit payment for her residence permit before being released.

I wondered whether my Aunt Hind, who was interested in human rights, knew what was happening here. Should I tell her what I had heard and seen? And most importantly, would she be able to do anything if I told her what was going on in the cells?

On the first day after the weekend my name was called. I stood to attention in front of the policeman, with the iron bars between us. He asked me for the keys to my flat. I gave them to him and he went off without saying a word. About an hour later I was taken to the room of the officer in charge before I could be released. I found Ghassan waiting for me there: he had brought my papers to the police station and he spoke to the officer, who was polite with us. He gave me my mobile phone back and apologised. 'Don't forget your wallet next time,' he advised me.

I left with Ghassan. In his beloved Lancer on the way home, he said, 'Khawla told me on the first day and I did everything I could.'

'Thank you,' I said, interrupting him. He didn't say anything more. His silence irritated me on the way. I wanted him to talk, to defend himself against Grandmother's allegation that he was taking revenge on the Tarouf family through me. I wanted him to make excuses or show regret for what he had done if he couldn't justify it. But he stayed silent, adding to my anger with him. I looked towards him when he was busy driving. I examined his face. *Damn you,*

Ghassan, your face isn't the real you. Some of the sadness on his face touched me deep inside. I looked away, out of the window, to escape his sadness and my own uncertainty. Like Grandmother, I wondered what Ghassan wanted to gain by helping me this time.

6

In one of our webcam chats I asked my mother about Merla. 'We haven't had news of her for some time,' she said. 'When we asked Maria, she said she didn't know anything about her. Your Aunt Aida is going almost crazy. Hasn't she been in touch with you?'

I said I hadn't logged into my email account for a while. I logged in straight away. I found it was full of adverts, along with one message from Merla that she had sent nine days earlier. She had left the subject line empty.

'José! Can you see me?' Mother asked me, waving her hand at the camera.

I was busy with my email. 'Yes, Mother, but I'm busy. Let's talk later,' I said. I turned the webcam off and went back to my email. I deleted the adverts and kept Merla's message without opening it straight away. Something told me the message contained unwelcome news. She had signed off her previous message with a quote from Rizal: *The victim must be pure and spotless if the sacrifice is to be acceptable.* What was this crazy woman referring to?

Just as she had ended her previous message with a Rizal quote, so she started her next message:

José,

'Death has always been the first sign of European civilisation when introduced in the Pacific Ocean.' Do you remember that saying of José Rizal's? Anyway, I'm reminding you of it. You may wonder what this has to do with my message. I don't know myself, but it's been on my mind for days. Is it a prediction that comes true for everyone who goes near Europeans? I'm not talking about death during the occupation, which is what Rizal meant, but another death. When that unknown European man invaded Aida's body, he left me like a seed in her womb and disappeared. A few days before I was born death showed up and snatched away my grandmother, who I've only seen in photographs. Ever since then death has lodged in our house without us noticing, disrupting our lives, even if our hearts have kept beating. Aida, who you love and call Mama, has been dead a long time, ever since the massacre of the cocks that we – you and I – heard about when we were growing up. I was born dead, in a living body. Aida nursed me on death from her breasts, which I hate because they were readily available to the hands and mouths of disgusting men, one of whom – I don't know which – was my father. The death that Aida nursed me on is now feeding on my feelings year after year. I grow up and my feelings die towards macho men and submissive women and whatever hatches from their eggs.

José, do you remember something I said years ago in Biak-no-Bato? You may not remember, but I remember. You told me that only cowards who can't face up to life try to commit suicide. Do you remember now?

I was annoyed when you unintentionally described me as a coward. I didn't want to be a coward. But today I feel differently. Yes, I'm a coward and I haven't been able to go on living complacently. In what you said to me in Biak-no-Bato, you told me half the truth and left out the other half. Those who try to commit suicide are either cowards who can't face up to life or brave people who are able to face up to death.

Do you think that European man gave me life by invading Aida's body? I won't let him change what Rizal said: 'Death has always been the first sign of European civilisation when introduced in the Pacific Ocean.'

MM

★　★　★

Some families in the Philippines with Chinese Buddhist roots hire people to mourn for their dead. These rites are usually performed in temples. The idea is that the mourning helps the soul move on to the other life and find acceptance there.

After reading Merla's letter, I needed to perform such a ritual. I needed to have loud weeping and wailing in my flat, simply because I was so shocked that I couldn't shed a tear. Was it the surprise? Or was it because I dismissed it in disbelief? *No, Merla isn't dead. Merla's still alive*, I said to myself. *One day we'll meet again. She's no longer Catholic and nor am I, and I'm the only man she doesn't feel hostile towards, she said. My old dream will now be easy to achieve.* I was sitting at the laptop ranting to myself, unable to believe that Merla . . .

★ ★ ★

With their compassion, women are more than human. All I needed was the embrace of a woman, a mother, a female friend or a sister. I called Khawla and said, 'I want to see you.' She didn't object. In fact she was very pleased. I rode over to Qortuba on my bike. I didn't plan to tell her about Merla. I just wanted not to have to think about Merla's message. I could have spoken to my mother again on the webcam but I was worried about telling her about the message because, if I did, I would kill Mama Aida.

Because Merla stood for what I found most beautiful in the Philippines, I escaped the Philippines on my bike and went to Khawla, who represented for me the best aspect of Kuwait.

Khawla opened the door for me. I leaned my bike against the wall in the inner courtyard and looked around. There was no one. I wrapped my arms around Khawla and she laughed at what I was doing. I held her in my arms a long time. She tried to break free and said, 'Isa, are you all right?'

I tightened my grip. 'Yes, please stay as you are,' I said. I let go of her a few seconds later.

She looked right into my eyes. 'What's the matter?' she said.

I shook my head. 'Nothing,' I said. 'I just missed you.' I would have burst into tears if I had told her about Merla's message.

'Grandmother's upstairs,' she said. 'Go and visit her as soon as she's finished her physiotherapy session.' She saw I was surprised, so she explained: 'As soon as you left Grandmother hired a masseuse for her legs.'

I bowed my head. 'I didn't leave because I wanted to. She was the one who wanted it,' I said.

Khawla pretended she hadn't heard my last remark. She took me by the hand and led me to Father's study. 'This is the third masseuse to come and see Grandmother. After every session, she says, "She's not as good as Isa",' she said. I pretended not to hear.

She had me sit in the chair at Father's desk and she sat down on the other side, with her elbows on the desk and her head on her hands, looking into my face. 'So? How's Kuwait?' she said.

I smiled at her. 'The search continues. I haven't found it yet,' I said.

'I'm worried you might have found it without recognising it,' she answered sadly.

I was horrified by the idea that Kuwait was the Kuwait I had experienced every day since I arrived. 'I'm ready to take the trouble to look for it, as long as there's more to it than what I've seen so far,' I said.

'And how does it look to you so far?' she asked.

'Lots of images, all different.'

She looked into my face and said, 'Tell me about Kuwait, Isa.'

Kuwait, an old dream that would never come true for me, even when I went there and walked on its soil. Kuwait for me was a sham reality, or a real sham. I don't know, but Kuwait has many faces: my father, who I love, my family, towards whom I have contradictory feelings, my homesickness, which I hate, my sense of belonging, which I feel – as a Kuwaiti – whenever someone insults Kuwaitis. Kuwait is the fact that Kuwaitis have failed me by looking down at me. It's my room in the annex of the Taroufs' house. It's a lot of money but little love, not enough to build a real relationship. Kuwait is a luxurious flat in Jabriya full of emptiness. Kuwait is a dark cell where I spent two days through no fault of my own. And sometimes it's more beautiful – I see it as a big family whose members greet each other in the market, in the street or in the mosque. '*As-salam aleekum*' . . .

'*Wa aleekum as-salam.*' Or I see it in the guise of a kind old man who lives in a large house opposite the building where I live. I often see him from my little balcony. He stands at his front door after dawn prayers every day surrounded by men in yellow uniforms carrying brooms and black plastic bags. He gives them money and food. Kuwait is Nouriya, who hates me and refuses to recognise me, and Awatif, to whom it's all the same whether I exist or not. Kuwait gives and doesn't give, just like Hind. Kuwait is a society that's like the Taroufs' house. However close you go, however long you stay in one of the rooms, you'll still be at a distance from the others who live there. Kuwait, Kuwait, I don't know what Kuwait is.

'Look for a job, Isa,' Khawla said. 'Only by working can you assimilate with the people here.'

I told her I was serious about working and that Ibrahim Salam had offered me a job and had taken me to various places to show me what the work was like, but working without speaking Arabic properly was impossible. She advised me to look in the private sector, where many companies depended on English in their business dealings and where the salaries were higher and they gave bonuses to employees who worked hard. The government also subsidised private-sector Kuwaiti workers by supplementing their income as part of a project called the National

Workforce Subsidy, designed to encourage young Kuwaitis to find work outside the public sector. I couldn't help laughing when Khawla finished giving me advice. She looked at me doubtfully. Before she had time to ask, I said, 'Kuwait's very generous when it comes to money.'

Khawla scowled. 'Is that praise or . . .?'

'I have enough money,' I cut in, 'but I needed something that's more important.'

To change the subject, I asked her about all the papers piled up on the desk. 'What's all that?' I asked.

I was surprised to hear that she was still reading the novel that Father couldn't finish because he was captured. 'As soon as I finish the last line, I can't help going back to the first page and reading it all over again. I correct some spelling mistakes and try to understand the things I couldn't understand the first time,' she said. She stopped a moment and looked at the sheets of paper on the desk. 'It's a difficult novel,' she continued. 'He says what he thinks about some things very openly, and sometimes he just hints. He speaks about certain things when he means different things.' She stood up from the desk and went to one of the shelves full of books. 'In order to understand Father more, I'm reading more of the books that he read,' she said. 'I'm still young. I'm getting older and

I have a growing dream of finishing off what Father set out to write, to make his dream come true and publish his first, and last, novel.'

She suddenly shivered as if she had had an electric shock.

'I have an idea!' she said.

I looked into her face quizzically.

'When you asked me one day,' she explained, 'I told you that in his novel Father portrayed Kuwait as he saw it, with tough love. He wanted to change reality with a novel that was candid and harsh, but his only motive was love.'

I nodded in agreement.

'You . . .' She paused a moment. 'You can see many aspects of Kuwait. Why don't you write about Kuwait as you see it?'

'Me?' I said, taken aback. 'What do I know about Kuwait that I could write?'

'That's exactly what you would write,' she said with a broad smile, 'what you don't know about it.'

I thought before replying. 'What I might write would be painful for the Tarouf family,' I said.

'Rashid al-Tarouf didn't care about the Taroufs when he had you,' she said with indifference. 'So why should you?

'Haven't you inherited anything from Father other than your voice?' she added with a smile.

I didn't think seriously about what Khawla said about writing. I'm not a writer and I'm not good at Arabic and I don't think I could write at length in English for people who mostly don't read that language. So am I going to tell Kuwaitis my story in Filipino? Besides, Khawla had already told me that Kuwaitis don't read. Whenever I criticised anything in Kuwait, she'd say, 'Because we Kuwaitis don't read.'

When I told her that writing a book wouldn't work, she gave me a pleasant surprise by saying, 'If José Rizal had thought like you, the Spanish would never have been driven out of the Philippines.'

I smiled. 'After an occupation that lasted more than three centuries,' I said with pride.

She looked at me with no less pride than I felt. 'And for eight centuries Spain was under the control of us Muslims, many years before they occupied you,' she said.

The part of my patriotism that belonged to the Philippines was in full sway, running strong. 'We threw them out in the end,' I said.

Khawla was about to say something but she stopped and seemed to be thinking.

'Why have you stopped talking?' I asked.

She bowed her head and acted shy. 'We threw them out in the end!' she said.

7

A feeling like an electric shock hit me whenever I remembered Merla. When Mama Aida pressed Maria for news of her, Maria said, 'She's fine but she doesn't want to talk to anyone.' Mama Aida was reassured but I was sure Maria was hiding the truth. Merla didn't answer my emails. I had sent dozens of messages, but it was no use. My last message went:

Merla, you are reading this message from me. You must be. The idea that you never open your email inbox terrifies me. Please answer me, if only with an empty message.

I was unusually frank with Merla, perhaps because I fully believed she had carried out what she had hinted at and couldn't read what I was writing, or maybe because I believed she was somewhere reading my messages. I ended up saying things I had never said before, such as the feelings I had had towards her since early adolescence. I revealed to my cousin everything I used to conceal out of embarrassment. It was just an attempt to confess:

Merla, you may not know how I feel about you deep down. Or maybe you think that your admission to me one day that you weren't attracted to the opposite sex might deter me from coming too close. Mama Aida tried but failed to make me stop thinking about you when she told me, when I was young, that the Church wouldn't allow us to have a relationship. When you made your admission in one of the caves at Biak-no-Bato, you too failed to make me forget you. You are still the dream that visits me in my sleep and when I'm awake. Many of the girls I walk past every day here move something inside me but they fall short as soon as, unintentionally, I compare them to you.

I stopped writing to read what I had written on the screen. I didn't know what to think. She wouldn't read my confession, so I might as well say more.

Merla, did you know I felt jealous of José Rizal because he had such a strong influence on you? Although I admire him, I get upset when I read references to him in your messages. But in one of your messages you said something that stopped me feeling jealous. I felt very self-confident when you wrote, 'You're the only man I don't feel hostile towards.' When I read that I wanted to hug the laptop screen.

I had an overwhelming desire to hug her. I remembered her face in our last conversation by webcam. She looked tired but she was still Merla, the woman who came to me in my dreams to make me feel like a man. I would confess everything to her. She would read my confession. I had to say more.

Merla, I don't know whether dead people read emails. But you're not dead, are you? If you're reading what I'm writing, please come back so that I can tell you something I've long wanted to say. I love you.

  José Mendoza

★   ★   ★

Absence is a form of presence. Some people may be absent but they are present in our thoughts more often than when they are present in our lives. Merla's absence was a constant presence. She visited me in my dreams to tell me things and for me to tell her things. When I woke up, I would continue our conversations awake. When I went back to sleep, in my dreams we would do rather more than just talk.

Death is powerless against the desire to meet, even if the meeting is of a different kind, in another world. We are loyal to the dead only because we hope to meet them again and believe that somewhere they are watching us and waiting.

I never lost hope of seeing Merla again. If I had lost that hope, I would have given up living shortly after she disappeared, just as Inang Choleng died after the death of the hope for which she had lived such a long life – my grandfather, Mendoza.

I didn't reread what I had written in the last part of my message. I clicked on the 'send' button. I closed the email page and folded the laptop screen on to the keyboard. Behind the laptop there was the bottle with soil from my father's grave. A question came to my mind: if I had to choose which one of them to bring back to life, my father or Merla, who would I choose?

I would choose my father.

Because Merla, a voice in the back of my head told me, was still alive.

★ ★ ★

For many days I didn't open my email. I was confident, almost certain, that one message among the dozens of adverts would be from Merla.

I no longer thought about her being dead, as long as the hope inside me was still alive and kicking. I set about looking for a job. I would live in Kuwait like any other Filipino expatriate struggling to fulfil his dreams. In the Philippines I expected to fulfil my dream in Kuwait; in Kuwait a new dream started to take shape in my mind, a distant dream.

The fact that I hadn't finished secondary school made it impossible to find a job in a private-sector company, as Khawla had hoped. After a gruelling search, with help from someone from the flat next door, I got a job in a well-known fast-food restaurant close to where I lived in Jabriya. My Filipino neighbour was working in the same restaurant. Khawla was disappointed when I told her about the job. 'You don't know what you're worth, Isa. You're Isa al-Tarouf! Grandmother will be shocked if she finds out that Rashid's son is working in—'

I interrupted her. 'But I was going to serve the guests at Umm Jabir's place, with her blessing. Have you forgotten?'

'But,' said Khawla. She had nothing to add.

8

My work was in the kitchen, which was just behind the counter where they took the orders, and I was paid 170 dinars a month plus the National Workforce Subsidy that the government paid to Kuwaitis working in the private sector. I wore special clothes, like all the other staff. We kitchen staff were different from the others in that we had to wear hairnets and plastic gloves. On ordinary days the work wasn't hard, but at the weekends it was. I worked like a robot, dipping chips in oil, cutting up lettuce leaves and onions and tomatoes, and taking the thin sheets of plastic off the slices of cheese while the pieces of meat were cooking, neatly arranged on the grill.

All the workers in the restaurant were from the Philippines except for two or three from India. The atmosphere at work was cheerful. One day when I was really busy, my colleague, who was also my neighbour, asked me why I had agreed to work there. 'Kuwaitis don't do this!' he said.

'You're right. They don't need to do this kind of work,' I replied. 'But they're missing a great pleasure,' I added in a mumble. I'm not sure I was being serious when I said this.

Some of the customers, many of them in fact, had really bad manners. I didn't like the way they behaved at all, but at the same time I didn't like what the restaurant staff did in response to the bad treatment they received from some people. Some people make themselves look bad by the way they treat others. I often heard someone shouting and swearing over something trivial, for example if the server had given them the wrong size of soft drink, or forgotten to add a slice of cheese to their burger. The server would apologise for making a mistake and replace the order, but unfortunately the angry customers had no idea they were about to devour something they never imagined. We kitchen staff would often hear people insulting and shouting at the staff who took the orders. The staff would quickly apologise, wheel around to face the kitchen and, red-faced in anger, shout, 'One chicken burger with cheese special,' for example. The word 'special' meant something quite different from what the customer imagined. 'Special?' the kitchen staff would repeat before starting on the order. The server would nod, wink and say 'special' again. There's no need to go into the details of how the special burgers differed from the usual burgers the restaurant served. When the mistake was corrected by removing a slice of tomato or adding slices of cheese, other ingredients might be added to the meal.

On the first days there I felt sick, but as time passed and the process was repeated – the shouting, the apologising, the making special meals, I got used to the situation. 'Bastards taking revenge on bastards,' I said to myself in justification.

★   ★   ★

My work helped me get over my loneliness. I was in contact with Kuwaitis every day, even if it was limited to observing them from a distance. Although I was busy in the kitchen, I had a chance to observe the Kuwaiti customers, especially the young ones. They seemed friendly towards each other. They were always smiling, provided the smiles stayed within their own circle. Another thing about Kuwaitis in general caught my attention. Staring at other people seemed to be part of the culture of their society. People stared at each other in a strange way. They would look away into the distance if they made eye contact, then quickly go back to examining each other. I had thought that staring into someone's face sent a message of some kind: a sign of admiration, or disapproval, or curiosity. But here it was none of that. I rarely came across someone who didn't stare into people's faces. I'm not claiming that I didn't do it when I was in the Philippines, but I was discreet. Perhaps I inherited this habit in my genes and it found expression after I came back to Kuwait.

When I told Khawla I had noticed this habit, she smiled. 'No one does this more than us, and no one is more critical of the habit either,' she replied. People are not unaware that it's wrong. They know, just as they know what's right. But they have no scruples about practising their vices knowingly. 'Do you realise why the women here use so much more make-up than women in other parts of the world?' Khawla asked me one day. I looked to her for the answer. 'It's not that women in other places are more confident about their appearance. It's just that no one stares at their faces and counts the number of spots they have, like many people here do,' she said. 'It's not just staring at other people's faces,' she added with a laugh. 'If people moved their ears when they were eavesdropping, then you'd see ears flapping like wings when it's crowded.' I laughed out loud at the idea.

I started staring insensitively into people's faces when I noticed that everyone else was doing it. I was looking for something I didn't know. But I gave up the habit after it led to an incident I'll never forget. I saw a man in his mid or late forties who looked rather odd. His white headdress was tattered and his long hair showed underneath. He had a bushy moustache and dark yellow teeth. His beard wasn't fully shaved and there were some grey hairs in it. Despite his strange appearance he was staring at the people around him. I was also staring at people. As soon as our eyes met he winked at me and gave me a knowing smile. I looked away and pretended to be busy working. I didn't look towards the counter, where the customers were lined up to order. I didn't foresee what would happen at the end of the day. When my shift ended I left work and there was the man waiting in his car in the small car park outside the restaurant. I pretended not to notice him. I walked towards my flat, as I did every day.

The car came up alongside me and the man rolled down the window. 'Would you like a lift?' he said.

I shook my head and said, 'Thank you, sir, I live close by.' I kept walking, without looking towards him. I was so frightened of the man that I walked along the main road instead of taking a short cut through the minor streets and lanes, which were quieter. The man drove off and I breathed a sigh of relief. Reassured, I walked on, but my peace of mind disappeared when I saw the man's car at the turn at the end of the street. He was driving back along the street that ran parallel to the road I was on. He drove past me, going in the opposite direction. He looked back. My heart sank when I saw the car making another turn and coming back towards me. I gave up the idea of going back to my flat in case this suspicious character worked out where it was. He slowed down, leaving some distance between himself and me. I decided to go to Ibrahim's place in the hope he might know how I could shake the man off. I called him on the phone but he was far away in some desert part of Kuwait with some Kuwaiti friends, organising a camp for new converts to Islam. When I hung up, my only concern was to get somewhere other than my own flat. The man was still lying in wait for me. My heart was racing. Why was the man following me? I didn't look like one of those effeminate types, though many of my compatriots were. I thought of heading for Grandmother's house in Qortuba. I'd have to cover quite a distance, from Jabriya to al-Surra across the flyover that connects the two areas and then on to Qortuba. I wasn't going to risk going all that way when I wasn't sure what was going on in the head of the man who was following me. I crossed the street by standing on the central reservation and waiting for a gap between the speeding cars so that I could cross to the other side where there were some houses. I turned towards the man's car. It was speeding towards the turn again to

'To give you an Arabic lesson,' he said with an evil smile.

I turned the key in the lock and swung the door open. Before I could close it, the man was pushing from the other side. With all the strength I could muster I managed to close it and lock it with the key. The man started pounding on the door with his fists. From the sitting room I heard the sound of Ghassan's voice. 'Who is it?' he said, rushing into the little corridor. He had a cigarette in his hand and looked surprised. 'Isa!' he said. 'Why are you wearing those clothes?' he asked, before I had time to explain.

I pointed to the door, postponing any answer to his question. 'There's a madman following me,' I said.

He patted me on the shoulder. 'OK, OK, calm down,' he said. He handed me his cigarette. 'Hold this,' he said. From the expression on his face, I had a better idea of what a sorry sight I must have been. He pulled the door wide open and faced up to the man. The man was taken aback. They had a conversation and voices were raised. The man laughed. Ghassan shouted at him and gave him a push. The man withdrew to the lift with his headdress on his shoulder and clutching his black head ring in his hand. Ghassan closed the door. He put out his hand, two fingers splayed like a pair of scissors. 'My cigarette,' he said. I gave him what was left of it. He took it between his fingers disapprovingly. Blowing smoke out of his nostrils, he looked at me and burst out laughing.

He went back to the sitting room, saying that the man was a drunk. 'Why were you laughing?' I asked.

He shook his head and said, 'The man was saying I had good taste.' I followed him into the room. He sat behind his desk and I sat on the sofa opposite.

'What did you say to him before you pushed him?' I asked. Ghassan looked right into my eyes. 'I said . . .' He paused a moment and looked away. 'I said "You've been following my son, you . . . ."' He used a word that was apparently a Kuwaiti insult that I didn't understand. He then pretended to be busy with the papers on his desk.

What about me? I too needed something I could pretend to be doing, to distract me from what he had said. As he tidied up his papers, he asked me what I'd like to drink. I ignored his question, although I was thirsty and my throat was dry.

'Ghassan?' I said, to call his attention. He looked up at me. I hesitated before continuing. 'Did you bring me to Kuwait to get revenge on my family?'

He smiled. 'I see you've become Kuwaiti sooner than I expected,' he said. I knitted my eyebrows in puzzlement. Ghassan continued: 'Suspicion, mistrusting others. In Kuwait the trust that used to exist is no longer there.' He didn't elaborate. He said no more.

'I misjudged you,' I said. He still said nothing. 'Why didn't you explain, defend yourself, complain?'

He pulled another cigarette from the packet on his desk. When Ghassan lit the cigarette I prepared to hear something interesting. He took a long drag. Then the words came out from deep inside him, along with the smoke. 'Over many years I've suffered various injustices and I haven't complained.' My eyes filled with tears. 'So why should I hold it against you when you misjudge me in this way?' I didn't say a word. 'I don't have time for that, my friend,' he said with a smile.

'Your friend?' I said, irritated by the word. He was puzzled by my question. 'I was your son just now, at the door,' I explained.

How could a smile and tears appear on one face at the same time in this way? He was smiling broadly and his eyes were red and glistening with tears. He had to struggle to get the words out. 'OK, my son,' he said.

I was happy, and deeply moved. Now that I had gained Ghassan as a father, after missing him all those months in his role as my father's friend, I prepared to leave.

9

In April 2009 Kuwait was transformed into a vast advertising display. There were thousands of posters of various sizes in all the streets. The numbers grew day by day and in the end there was a poster wherever you turned your head – along the sides of the streets, on the roundabouts, on the back windows of cars and on the roofs of buildings.

As I was riding my bike to Ibrahim's place one day, I suddenly had a feeling I was being watched by all the faces looking out from the posters. Some of the faces were smiling, others were grim. There were sharp, intelligent faces, expressionless faces and stupid faces. Most of the men on the posters were wearing traditional Kuwaiti dress, but some appeared in suits and ties. Very few of the advertisements had pictures of women. I later found out that this bonanza of posters in the streets was part of the preparations for their parliamentary elections.

Their? Why *their* and nor *our*? I was about to delete the word or change it, but it would jar if I changed it to *our*. I'll leave it as it is. *Their*.

I got to Ibrahim's place and found him in a bad mood, despite the welcome he gave me. I wasn't used to seeing his face without his calm smile that made it distinctive, or that he made distinctive. He brought me a cup of tea. He asked me how I was and how work was going. I ignored his questions and said, 'You don't seem your normal self.'

He apologised and said, 'You're right.' He handed me two newspapers and pointed to stories he had circled in pen. He had underlined some of the words and drawn arrows pointing to comments he had written in the small blank spaces on the page. I looked from one report to the other. One of them had a picture of a young woman hanging from a ceiling fan by a rope.

I handed them back to him. 'They're in Arabic,' I said, puzzled.

Ibrahim tapped his forehead and said, 'How stupid of me! I'm sorry.' He went to the corner of the room, where there was a computer. He tapped on the keyboard until the printer churned out two pages. He handed them to me and said, 'That's my translation of what was in the Kuwaiti papers this week. I'm going to send it by email to the newspapers in the Philippines. I've started to hate this work,' he mumbled.

I picked up the pieces of paper to read. *Filipina Maid Slits Baby's Throat in Revenge on Employer*, said the first headline. I didn't read any further. *Filipina Maid Hangs Herself,* read the second. The report sent a shiver down my spine. I read it carefully. In her late teens, in her room in her employer's house, suicide by hanging, a rope, the ceiling fan.

I read the report word by word and I could hear my heartbeat in my ears. In my repeated readings of the report all I was doing was looking for the name of the woman. Any young woman who committed suicide, anywhere in the world, might as well have been Merla.

I felt depressed and I was about to leave. 'Where are you going?' Ibrahim asked me.

'I just remembered something important,' I said, heading for the door.

*　　*　　*

I rested the laptop on my legs. The email sign-in page was on the screen waiting for me to put in the password that would take me to my inbox. I wrote the first numbers, then waited a little. I looked at them, then deleted them. I started again but I didn't complete the number. The idea that there might be a message from Merla drove me to put in the rest of the number and press 'enter'. But I was so frightened that the message I expected might not be there that I folded down the screen, cursing my weakness and helplessness and Merla's strength and craziness. Why was all this happening to me?

I picked up the phone, my hand shaking. I scrolled through the numbers. I called the number and waited for the other side to answer. There was no reply. It was 9.30 p.m. where I was, 2.30 a.m. in the Philippines.

I called again, and again, many times.

I got angrier and angrier. I swore I wouldn't stop trying until I received an answer or my phone battery went flat.

At last! 'Hello,' I said.

'Yes, who's calling?'

Apparently I had woken her up, but her voice still sounded sleepy.

'It's Isa.'

'Who?'

'It's José,' I said, correcting myself.

She didn't say anything.

'Maria!' I said. 'Tell me, where's Merla?'

As soon as I uttered my cousin's name, her sleepy voice woke up and she started to cry. I repeated my question, terrified. She fought back her tears and said, 'She doesn't want to talk to anyone.'

I lost my nerve and shouted at her. 'Enough!' I said. 'You can save lies like that for Mama Aida.'

Her voice suddenly disappeared. 'Hello, hello?' I said.

I could still hear rapid breathing, so she was still on the line. I didn't say anything more, in case I heard bad news. When the other person is silent, it can sometimes be more frightening than when they tell us a truth we'd rather not hear. That kind of silence opens the door to terrifying possibilities that may be worse than what we are frightened of. What might she be hiding? Why is the world spinning around me? I hoped she would keep crying so that she wouldn't say what I didn't want to hear. *Go on, go on, cry, Maria. Mind you don't say anything. It's better that you cry at my question than that I cry at your answer.* She was still breathing fast. Words and phrases from the story that Ibrahim had translated floated in my head. 'In her late teens', 'hanging', 'rope', 'ceiling fan'. Terrifying images flashed before my eyes. The story in the newspaper. The picture. The lines that Ibrahim had drawn under the words swirled around me, surrounded me, pulled at me. The circle he had drawn around the story was wrapped around my neck like a noose, getting tighter, strangling me.

'Listen,' said Maria. I shut my eyes and pricked up my ears. She went on angrily: 'I don't know anything about her.'

'Maria, please.'

She didn't say anything for a while. I didn't ask her again. I waited for her to calm down. Then she continued: 'She changed a lot before she disappeared. She started to hate being with me.'

10

One weekend night I was on my way home in my work uniform after a tiring day. I stank of food for which I no longer had any appetite. My stomach turned whenever I saw an advert for the meals I prepared robotically every day. I would go back to the kitchen in my flat dying of hunger and enjoy some food that I had made with my own hands, as if the stuff I prepared all day long wasn't really food.

In the lobby of my building that night I pressed the lift button and leaned back against the wall, waiting for it to arrive. My eyes were glued to the panel that showed which floor the lift was on. It started at 8, then 7, 5, 3, 2 and finally G. The lift stopped. Other things stopped too – my brain, my heartbeat and time itself.

It wasn't just the lift door that opened. It was a door to Kuwait that opened, a door I had glimpsed in the Philippines when I was impatient to visit my father's country. Suddenly it was wide open.

Through the door came a young man who didn't even notice I was there. He probably wasn't interested in the Asian standing in front of him in the uniform of a restaurant worker. My back was still against the wall. I was so surprised I couldn't speak. The man ambled towards the main door.

'Hi,' I shouted after him, 'a moment, please.'

The man wheeled round and looked blankly into my face. He looked around him, then pointed a finger at his own chest and asked, 'Me?'

I nodded. '*Shloonak*?' I asked him in delight.

The man grimaced. I went up to him and put out my hand to shake his. He raised his hand out of the way and recoiled in disgust. 'Keep your distance. Don't touch me. I'm not the type you're looking for,' he said.

I was taken aback. I was about to say, 'Yes, you are one of them. Where are the others?' but I was worried this might confirm his misunderstanding, especially as he didn't seem to be completely sober. He turned away to leave, muttering angrily.

'I'm Isa!' I shouted after him. He walked on, paying no attention. 'Hey!' I said. 'Boracay Island! Red Horse beer!'

The man suddenly stopped in his tracks and turned towards me. He pointed at me and took a close look at my face. 'You?' he said. I smiled in confirmation. He came back into the lobby. 'The Kuwaiti Made in Philippines?'

'Yes, yes,' I replied with a laugh.

Still pointing at me, he continued, 'You're the one who . . .' He leaned forward and shook his shoulders as if dancing.

'Yes, yes,' I said, nodding again. We both burst out laughing. The doorman, disturbed by the noise we were making by the lift, came out of his room.

'You're the one who . . .' the man said again. He put his hand on his head and bent his legs. He jumped up and as soon as his feet landed back on the ground, he turned and walked slowly, shaking his shoulders.

I couldn't control myself. It was the dance I loved and that I'd danced with him two years ago in the Philippines. I went up to him and stood face to face. I began copying the way he was dancing. 'Yes, yes. It's me,' I said. I stretched my arms out and he did the same. We began to pull on that invisible rope. Both of us were shaking, partly from the dance itself and partly because we were laughing so much.

The doorman didn't come beyond the door to his room. He shook his head disapprovingly, clapped his hands and disappeared back into his room without saying a word.

Could I say it was the first time I'd had a proper laugh in Kuwait?

Yes, I could.

We exchanged phone numbers, Mishaal and I. Mishaal, who I called Michel because I couldn't pronounce the difficult *'ain'* sound in the middle of his name, was one of the crazy young Kuwaitis I had met in Boracay when I was working there. He was the guy with the glass of beer who danced with me on the beach. By strange coincidence I danced with him again in Kuwait, close to two years after we first met. Some coincidences are wonderful: they suddenly appear like a bend in a road that leads to the unknown. Mishaal's reappearance in this manner gave me an opportunity to get close to my Kuwaitiness, which I had hardly been aware of.

Mishaal usually spent the weekend in his flat on the eighth floor of the building I lived in, doing what he couldn't do anywhere else, as he put it. When he noticed I was intrigued, he showed me what he meant. He put out his hands, took hold of an imaginary glass in one hand and began to pour air into it from an imaginary bottle in his other hand. Then he pretended to drink. 'You all claim that alcohol's forbidden,' I said with a laugh, 'but it's as plentiful as water.'

He nodded and said, 'As plentiful as water, and as expensive as gold.'

I asked him about the rest of the gang. He said they were well. Although they lived in different parts of Kuwait they got together almost every day in the *diwaniya* of one of them in an area nearby. 'Why don't you meet here on the eighth floor?' I asked, pointing upstairs.

'As you know,' he replied, 'no one else in the gang drinks alcohol. Besides, places like this arouse suspicion.'

I thought that remark was odd. 'But I live here!' I said. 'Do I arouse suspicion?'

He patted me on the shoulder and laughed. 'Don't worry,' he said. 'It only arouses suspicion in the case of Kuwaitis.' I let it pass. Perhaps he didn't mean it, or he'd forgotten I was Kuwaiti.

'Does that mean they're frightened of the police?' I asked.

'The police don't frighten anyone,' he said. 'They're frightened of what people will say.' He held out his hand as if holding an apple. 'Kuwait's a small place. Everyone knows almost everyone else,' he said.

*　*　*

I took off my work clothes and threw myself down on the sofa in the living room, elated by the encounter, which had added a touch of happiness to my evening. But too much happiness is rather like sadness. It's irritating if you can't share it with someone. I called Ibrahim. My words couldn't keep up with my feelings: 'Ibrahim! Would you believe it? Two years ago. By chance. Kuwaitis. Young guys. Boracay. Crazy people. We're going to meet again. My friends. Kuwaitis. Kuwaitis. Kuwaitis.'

After a long silence in response to the news I brought, Ibrahim said, 'All this excitement because you met some drunk guy?'

427

I tried to explain: 'In fact he wasn't completely drunk.'

'Brother,' Ibrahim broke in, 'choose your friends very carefully. You don't need people of that kind.' I didn't respond. 'I know you're looking for Kuwaiti friends, brother Isa,' Ibrahim continued. 'Join our group and not only will you have lots of friends, but you'll have Kuwaiti brothers, as you wanted, to guide you to the right path and to give you assistance.' I thanked him and the conversation ended. If Ibrahim had known what my Aunt Hind had to say about his group he wouldn't have blamed me for being reluctant to accept his repeated offers. Why do things have to be so complicated? Ibrahim was warning me about the Boracay gang, while Hind was warning me about Ibrahim and his group. Didn't I have the right to choose what I wanted? I wanted them all. Hind, Ibrahim and the gang of crazies. I ignored what I heard from him and from Hind.

I called Khawla to share my happiness at meeting Mishaal, after the disappointing response I'd had from Ibrahim. 'As-salam aleekum, shloonik?' I said.

'Ana zein, inta shloonak?' she replied with a laugh.

'I'm fine,' I said.

'Isa!' she said. 'Grandmother was just asking about you,'

'I guess her knees must be hurting,' I answered mischievously. I regretted my horrible joke.

'Or perhaps she misses Rashid's voice,' she said earnestly.

'I'm sorry, I didn't mean it,' I cut in.

'Never mind, but don't be too hard on Grandmother. She loves you, Isa,' Khawla said. My heart raced. 'Would you believe it?' Khawla continued. 'I wish we belonged to some other family.'

Khawla sounded upset, and unusually sad. She immediately took the conversation in a different direction, nothing to do with why I had called. She wanted to talk about the family name and she came out with things I didn't understand. 'All the advantages the family name brings to family members are in fact no more than restrictions and a long list of taboos,' she said.

Puzzled, I asked, 'And what does this have to do with now?'

'Because you still have something against Grandmother, but she's not that bad,' she said. I didn't deny the charge. I just said nothing. 'People envy us for no reason,' Khawla continued. 'In fact they're freer than us.' I was still puzzled. 'Do you mind if I share my thoughts with you this evening?' she said after a pause.

I had planned to share my excitement at meeting Mishaal but it doesn't make any difference whether you share your happiness or your sadness with someone else. What matters is the sharing. 'Yes, yes, with great pleasure,' I said.

'If we belonged to one of those families we like to describe as . . .' She hesitated. Perhaps she was about to describe them as lower-class but she checked herself. 'Ordinary families,' she said, 'then Hind would have been Ghassan's wife long ago and no one would dare speak badly about us or make fun of our family name. The Taroufs marry their daughter to a bidoon man! Even if that bidoon man is descended from the same tribe as the Tarouf family! If only we belonged to some other family, an ordinary family. Then you would be living with us now, instead of Grandmother trembling all over whenever someone visits the house, in case they find out about you. Isa, I know how badly you've been treated but there are things you have to understand. Grandmother and the aunts don't bear full responsibility. The people around us are full of envy. They're trying to catch us out, waiting impatiently for any opportunity to do us down. We're constantly being monitored. Some people may think a man can marry a Filipina woman, but if the man comes from a family of high social status, then it would be a crime condemned even by those who come from . . .' She hesitated again, but this time she spelt it out: 'humble origins.' She continued to air her frustrations. 'Dozens of young Kuwaitis die from drugs and no one cares, but it's a big deal and a great shame if it happens to someone of good family. He may rest in peace but his family inherits the shame when he's gone. If some businessman goes bankrupt all his problems come to an end as soon as he's declared bankrupt, but if someone from an old family goes bankrupt, then they'll never hear the end of it. People's tongues will lash him like whips for the rest of his life, and his descendants after him. If someone succeeds at work and makes a fortune then he's a self-made man, but if Faisal al-Adil, Nouriya's husband, succeeds, then he's a thief. Hello, hello, Isa, can you hear me?'

She rambled on. To be the victim of a tyrant is normal, but to be the victim of another victim! My sister tried to explain. And did I understand? Even if I did understand, was I convinced? And even if I was convinced, what did it matter?

'Yes, carry on, Khawla. I can hear you.'

She continued: 'You know you're from the Tarouf family, but do you know what the word *tarouf* means? I don't expect you to answer this question because it's a purely Kuwaiti word and many people here hardly know what it means. A *tarouf* is a net that

Kuwaitis use for fishing. It's set up in the sea like a volleyball net and big fish get caught in it as they pass by. And we, the members of the family, get caught in this *tarouf*, caught in our family name, and we can't escape it. We can move only as much as the net allows. But you're a small fish, Isa, the only one, and you can slip through the mesh of the *tarouf* without getting caught. Isa! You're lucky! You're free. Do what you want.' At last Khawla was done with her speech.

Ignoring everything she had said, I replied, 'So I'm a small fish, a rotten one that spoils the rest of the fish, as Grandmother says.'

'You're not like that, Isa, you're not like that,' Khawla said gently.

I gave a long sigh, then said, 'I wish I were beside you in Father's study, listening to you. I miss you, Khawla.' Should I tell her I saw her smile through the telephone? 'Soon I'll invite you to a special session in the study, but after we've dealt with the question of Aunt Hind,' she replied.

'The question of Aunt Hind?' I asked.

'I'll tell you later. It's something excellent for the family in general, and especially for Hind,' she said.

Without thinking I found myself making that 'colololooosh' sound. 'So Hind's going to get married?'

432

Khawla burst out laughing. I pressed the question. She put down the phone or moved it away from her ear. Her laugh sounded distant. Sometimes she was laughing and sometimes coughing. I waited for her to end her laughing fit. 'You made me laugh, you crazy,' she said when she came back. 'No, no, she's not getting married. I'll tell you later. Good night.'

'Good night. Sweet dreams.'

I was about to hang up but she called me back: 'Isa!'

'Yes.'

'I love you a lot.'

I smiled. I didn't add to what she'd said. Words are too limiting for some feelings, which prefer silence.

'Goodbye,' Khawla concluded.

I held the phone in both hands, tapped out a message with my thumbs: *And I love you more*, and sent it to her.

I leaned my head back and remembered why I had called Khawla in the first place. I had forgotten to tell her that I'd met Mishaal and that he would soon arrange for me to meet the other Kuwaitis from Boracay.

I knelt on the ground and bent down to look under the sofa. Nothing. The other sofa. Nothing. Under the television table. There she was! I picked up Inang

11

A few days after meeting Mishaal, I finally went to a *diwaniya*, one of those places my mother had told me so much about. There's hardly a house in Kuwaiti that doesn't have one – an outer room where friends meet. The image that the name evokes is the one my mother planted in my imagination when I was young. It was where my father, Walid and Ghassan got their fishing tackle ready, where they discussed books or important political events, where they gathered round the television to watch big matches. I wasn't planning to do any of that. Just going into a *diwaniya* was enough for me.

A little after sunset my telephone rang and it was Mishaal at the other end. 'Are you ready?' he said. 'I'll meet you in five minutes in the car park under the building.' What could he mean by 'ready'? I'd been ready for a day like this for years, ever since my mother had talked about my father and his friends when I was on Mendoza's land, when I wanted to have friends like my father's friends.

I waited for him in the car park. He arrived in a yellow sports car. I cursed my bicycle and taxis and buses. He shook my hand and said, 'It'll be a surprise for the other guys.'

'I wonder if they'll remember me,' I said.

★ ★ ★

'One, two, three.'

I counted the pairs of shoes at the *diwaniya* door before we went in. Taking your shoes off isn't just for people who go to mosques. I turned to Mishaal and pointed to the shoes by the door: 'There are three people inside and you're the fourth. Where's the fifth?' 'This is Turki's *diwaniya*, and he comes in from the other door from the inner courtyard,' he said with a laugh. So there was an inside door and an outside door.

Mishaal pushed the door open and waved me in. The floor was spread with carpets. There were no sofas, just mattresses on the ground for sitting on, with hand rests between them and cushions against the walls to lean back on. One of the men was playing with his mobile phone, another was lying in the corner under an open window blowing cigarette smoke into the air. I recognised him immediately: he was the one with the oud. Two of them were glued to the television screen. I thought they were watching a football match, but then I noticed they were holding controllers and playing with the buttons. They were busy playing football on PlayStation. No one paid us

436

any attention except for the guy with the cigarette. He looked from me to Mishaal in surprise. '*As-salam aleekum*,' Mishaal said. I quickly added my own '*As-salaam aleekum*.'

Everyone turned to us. '*Wa aleekum as-salam*,' they said. Mishaal spoke to them in Arabic, referring to me as 'our Kuwaiti friend'. Their reactions varied from smiles to surprise. Some of them laughed. They all gathered around me in disbelief, saying things like 'It's you?' or 'I didn't believe you were Kuwaiti' or 'We forgot all about you as soon as we left that place'.

I put out my hand to the guy with the cigarette and Mishaal introduced us. 'This is Turki,' he said. I shook his hand. I leaned over and brushed cheeks with him the way Kuwaitis greet each other. Mishaal pointed to the man who'd been playing with his mobile phone and introduced me. 'That's Jabir,' he said. Then he pointed towards the two who were sitting in front of the television, 'Abdullah and Mahdi,' he said. I shook hands and brushed cheeks with all of them in turn.

★ ★ ★

They were amazing. So cheerful and friendly – that's what I can say about the Boracay gang. I was happy to meet them and enter their world.

How could a country have so many faces? Which of these many faces was Kuwait's real face? I wondered.

I dropped in on the *diwaniya* every day, or almost very day, depending on Turki, who called me up whenever the gang was meeting at his place. Fortunately Turki's house was in Adailiya, which wasn't far from Jabriya. The others lived nearby too, except for Abdullah, who lived in some remote area. But that didn't mean Abdullah needed a plane to get to Turki's place, as he might in some remote parts of the Philippines, because it only takes about half an hour, give or take a little, to reach the most remote residential area in Kuwait.

Sometimes I went to the *diwaniya* alone after work on my bike. Sometimes the Kuwaitis would take turns coming to my place to give me a lift. Everything would have turned out as in my dreams, if it hadn't been for the language barrier, which I couldn't overcome, though I could pick out some words when they spoke to each other in Arabic. I felt really sorry for my friends when they felt they had to abandon their own language just to bring me into their world. Mishaal spoke English fluently, Turki and Jabir less so, while Abdullah and Mahdi spoke to me the way Grandmother spoke to Babu, Raju, Lakshmi and Luzviminda. I think it's wonderful when people stretch language to the limit, peppering their own language with words from other languages, or supplementing it with gestures, just so that they can tell you how they feel towards you: 'I am happy *katheeran li-anni* see you after long time', for example. Kind words don't need translating. You only have to look at the face of the person speaking to understand how they feel, even if they're speaking a language you don't understand. Abdullah didn't realise this when he told me how happy he was to meet me again.

Despite their differences their craziness united them. They lived in separate neighbourhoods and belonged to different families. Turki and Jabir were of high social rank, maybe level with the Taroufs. Mishaal didn't recognise such things. He thought that family wealth was enough to break down all these class distinctions. And he, by the way, was very rich. As for Abdullah and Mahdi, I don't know much about them, perhaps because their English was poor. All I know about Abdullah is that he was more committed to his religious observances than his friends and more modest in the way he dressed. He seldom wore anything other than the traditional thobe. Mahdi didn't speak much. I hardly heard his voice except when he screamed in delight or anger at the result of a football match between him and Abdullah.

I did provide one service to the crazies, perhaps the most important thing I had done for them since we had met. Only when I was with them in the *diwaniya* could they play their favourite card game, *koutbo sitta*, which requires six players. It may seem trivial but for the first time in Kuwait I felt that my presence mattered, even if it was only to make up the number needed for a game of cards.

We spent our time in the *diwaniya* playing cards or watching football matches, either real ones or virtual on-screen games between Abdullah and Mahdi. Sometimes Turki would strum his oud, and if we were bored, they would start talking about their love affairs. Abdullah was very meticulous about performing his prayers on time five times a day. Could I do that? Five times a day? When I asked him how he could keep it up like that, he answered confidently, 'It makes me happy to have you with us in the *diwaniya* day after day. Wouldn't you like to have God with you (he raised his hand and spread his fingers) five times a day?'

We used to pray together, led by Abdullah. I don't know why I prayed. Did I honestly want to, or did Abdullah make me feel embarrassed? Why didn't Mishaal feel at all embarrassed?

Although I didn't know the real reason why I prayed with them, that doesn't mean that I wasn't sincere when I prayed, even if I didn't know how to pray properly. I went through the motions of praying like them, but I said the prayers in a way that no else did. Perhaps the only word that we all spoke aloud and in unison was 'Amen'.

Mishaal didn't budge when Abdullah called us to prayer by shouting '*Allahu akbar, Allahu akbar*'. The others quickly formed a line behind Abdullah. We went through the motions of the ritual by following what Abdullah did, and said '*Allahu akbar*' between each stage and the next.

Mahdi was also meticulous about praying but he prayed in a slightly different way. I was probably the only one who noticed this because I sometimes lost concentration and absent-mindedly watched the others. When we were kneeling with our hands on our knees, I examined their feet. Turki's toes were very small and close together. Mahdi's feet were big and white and his toes were covered in thick hair. Turki and Jabir pressed their hands to their chests when they were standing upright during prayer, but Mahdi didn't do that. We prostrated ourselves, bending down till our foreheads touched the carpet. Mahdi put a paper handkerchief on the carpet and touched that with his forehead. After prayers once, I stupidly asked Mahdi if he had an obsession with hygiene. He smiled and shook his head. Seeing I was confused, Abdullah stepped in to clarify some things about Islam I didn't understand. 'Islam . . . sect . . . Sunni . . .

Shi'a.' It all seemed complicated to me, or perhaps Abdullah's language – Arabic interspersed with broken English and mysterious hand gestures – didn't work for him this time. I shook my head to show I didn't understand. Mishaal intervened. 'We're Catholic Muslims, and they're Protestant Muslims,' he said. Everyone roared with laughter, but nonetheless I understood from Mishaal what Abdullah had failed to explain.

Abdullah and Mahdi sat cross-legged in front of the television and fought it out at their favourite game. Turki started tuning his musical instrument. Jabir lay on one of the mattresses, busy sending and receiving text messages. Mishaal pestered Jabir by blowing kisses at him as he fiddled with his phone. Then he picked up his own mobile phone and started jabbing at the keys like Jabir. He whispered words of love in Arabic, and also in English to include me in their circle: 'Darling . . . I love you.'

My heart suddenly missed a beat and I felt the same electric shock I knew from the past. It was Turki on the oud, filling the *diwaniya* with magic. He ran the plectrum across the strings in the middle of the oud while the fingers of his other hand slid up and down the strings on the neck. He only had one instrument but it sounded to me like the notes were coming from several instruments at the same time. Mahdi shouted in jubilation when he won the football match. Mishaal was still pestering Jabir by blowing kisses and saying, 'I love you.' Abdullah invited Mahdi to play again to get his revenge.

As for me, I was in the *diwaniya*, but my heart was in the Philippines with Merla.

12

I rested the laptop on my knees. The email homepage appeared on the screen. How long before I plucked up courage? How long could I keep clinging to a hope that was tinged with doubt? Without thinking I wrote the password in the box. There was just one step left: clicking on the 'sign in' button.

I left the page as it was, with all my data inserted, without moving on to the next step. I moved the laptop aside, off my legs. I stood in the middle of the sitting room of my flat and looked around at the walls. 'Which direction would it be in?' I wondered. I spread the prayer rug, a gift from Awatif I had never used. There were many possible directions. I chose the direction that took my fancy. How many times did I have to bend forward? How many times did I have to touch my forehead to the ground? Should I put my hands together on my chest or leave them hanging by my sides? I didn't know, but I did pray.

I stood on the prayer rug. '*Allahu akbar*, God is the mightiest, You have been kind to me. You sent me the crazies that I dreamt of meeting. I'm grateful to you, my God.' I leaned forward and put my hands on my knees. '*Allahu akbar*. God is the mightiest. I've been waiting for a message for some time. Isn't it time the message arrived?' I stood up straight again. 'Make my dream come true. Don't ruin my life by allowing the person I love to die.' I lay down on the floor and touched it with my forehead. 'I have plenty of money, I have wonderful friends.' I sat up. '*Allahu akbar*, God is the mightiest. I pray to You as a believer, in the hope that You will accept my prayer. Amen.' I looked to the right and then to the left to finish off my prayer.

Someone rang the doorbell. It was my Filipino neighbour inviting me to someone's birthday party. I stood facing him at the door. I looked towards the laptop screen, then at my neighbour. I began to interpret things Grandmother's way. Perhaps Fate had sent him to spare me the torment of not yet receiving the message. I accepted his invitation with a nod, with complete faith in Grandmother's view of the world.

★ ★ ★

Filipinos, at home or abroad, are always the same: they attach an almost reverential importance to some occasions. Birthdays are very important. They celebrate them every year with the same enthusiasm, as if it were the first time. They give each other presents, even if they are modest, and the recipients are happy with them, however inexpensive they might look.

445

The person whose birthday it is looks delighted, even before he or she knows what the present is. Sometimes the present is important but the most important thing is that the giver hasn't forgotten the occasion and has taken the trouble to look for a present to make the person happy. It doesn't matter if it's just a pair of socks, a key ring, a picture frame or a leather wallet pretending to be a well-known brand. The only thing that matters is that it's a present. Filipinos aren't only interested in birthdays. Holidays also have a special meaning for them. Why *for them* instead of *for us*? Am I choosing my words properly? What a muddle I'm in!

At Christmas celebrations in Manila, you can feel the occasion as much as if you were in the Vatican. Am I exaggerating? I've never been to the Vatican to know, but anyway, it's nothing like in Kuwait. In the Philippines, the occasion has a special warmth and you can almost see the effect on the faces of those around you. There's an atmosphere of faith. Prayers. More people going to churches and cathedrals. That might be easy to explain, given that ninety percent of the population is Christian – eighty percent of them are Roman Catholics and the other ten percent of various other Christian denominations. But what is odd is our interest in other celebrations, such as the way Filipinos mark Chinese New Year. People come out on the streets to celebrate and some streets are decorated with

Chinese lanterns and coloured streamers. People beat drums and some of them wear traditional Chinese costume and dance with brightly coloured dragons. We're people who love to celebrate like no one else. We'll never miss an opportunity to party.

As usual my neighbours had decorated their sitting room with streamers. On one wall there was a sign reading *HAPPY BIRTHDAY TO YOU*. The place was full of singing and dancing and all kinds of food and drink, including home-brewed alcohol – what the guests most wanted to find, however foul it might taste. I drank a lot that night. Everyone stopped dancing and the lights were turned off, leaving the place romantically lit by candles. It was time for videoke, the Filipino version of karaoke. The microphone was ready and the television was playing famous songs, with the words on screen. Being in Kuwait had helped me see Filipinos more clearly. We Filipinos love to sing.

We?

Yes, *we*.

The microphone was passed around. People sang solo or in groups. Helped by the words on the screen, they sang to the music song after song. I couldn't help joining in when the music started up for *Parting Time* by the Filipino singer Erik Santos. I grabbed the microphone and I didn't need the words on the screen. I listened to the piano intro and waited for my cue to start. I shut my eyes to sing and thought only of my memories of Merla.

Everyone listened to my song in silence. I sang louder as the end of the song drew near and the rhythm picked up. I gave a bow with the microphone still in my hand. As the piano music faded out towards the end, I whispered the last line: 'I remember the days when you're here with me.'

The sitting room broke into whistles and clapping. People toasted me with their drinks. I bowed theatrically and blew kisses around in the air. The music began again. People gathered round the microphone to sing together and I withdrew quietly to my own flat.

I put the laptop on my knees. The browser was still on the email sign-in page. The fact that I was only half sober made it easier to press the 'enter' button. The inbox had many messages. Adverts, messages from my mother, pictures of her with Alberto and Adrian. The pictures reeled drunkenly in front of my eyes. I smiled at my brother's big smile in the picture, and the stream of drool from his mouth. I missed my chubby little brother. There were pictures of my mother's house and of our house. The money I had sent them had changed many things. But my sense of happiness with the messages and the pictures didn't last long.

Merla, why?

13

The atmosphere in the *diwaniya* was no longer what it had been and the crazies weren't the crazies I had known. They had given up everything to devote themselves to the parliamentary elections. Their conversations had become more intense. They were no longer interested in including me in the conversation so Arabic dominated their discussions.

One evening Turki asked me to go somewhere with him, along with Mishaal and Abdullah. 'Where?' I asked him.

'It's not far,' he said. The four of us went off, leaving Jabir and Mahdi in the *diwaniya* organising files that contained lots of phone numbers. I later found out that Jabir and Mahdi were working for the election campaigns of several candidates. Since they weren't yet old enough to vote they had decided to serve their country in another way, they said.

Turki had a small pick-up he'd borrowed from a friend. He stopped in a street in the nearby district of al-Surra, in front of a school. We got out of the car. He asked me to help him carry a large cloth banner that was in the back, while Mishaal and Abdullah were busy unloading some metal stands and bags full of sand.

We put the banner on the pavement and Turki spread it out. It was black with Arabic writing in yellow. Mishaal and Abdullah set up the stands and held them in place with the sandbags. 'Isa, hold the cloth from the end here,' said Turki.

I stood where I was and said, 'Not before I find out what the words in yellow mean,' I told him.

He put his hands on his hips and said, 'Not now, Isa.'

I shook my head and insisted: 'Yes, now!'.

He gave in to my obstinacy. He pointed to the words in turn, translating as he went: *Sorry, al-Surra is not for sale. Kuwait is more precious.* Mishaal and Abdullah had finished setting up the metal stands. They each took a corner of the big piece of cloth and helped Turki carry it. Soon the banner was up, facing the street. We looked back at it as we drove off in the pick-up for another site to put up more banners. The other ones said, *Sorry, we won't be ruled by the dinar. Kuwait is more precious.* In the Kaifan area we met some other young men trying to attach banners to the wall of a mosque. *Sorry, the consciences of those who resisted the Iraqi occupation are not for sale,* they read.

I gathered that what we were doing was voluntary work and that the Boracay gang were not the only people doing it. In fact many young people in various parts of Kuwait were putting up similar banners against bribery, condemning the practice of vote-buying by some parliamentary candidates. 'In some areas, the price of a vote has reached 2,000 dinars,' Turki told me in disgust. 'They're not selling their votes. They're selling Kuwait,' he added sadly. I don't know whether Kuwaitis needed that amount of money, given that the poorest of them seemed rich to me. All I knew was that my friends had shown me an aspect of themselves that I hadn't seen in the days we had been together in the *diwaniya*: their persistence, their enthusiasm for their candidate in the parliamentary elections, their willigness to volunteer to work in the campaigns, distribute leaflets and put up banners in the streets warning people against selling their country.

Their commitment reduced me to silence. I didn't ask many questions when they were talking in Arabic. I just observed their faces and enjoyed their enthusiasm, which was so infectious that I forgot about my Asian features when I was carrying leaflets and putting them under the windscreen wipers of cars, repeating to myself the words I hadn't been able to read: 'Kuwait is not for sale.' In those days I was more Kuwaiti than I had ever been before. My sense of belonging to the country – the country in whose four-coloured flag my father's remains had been wrapped – was at its peak. I recalled what Merla had said in one of her emails: *Don't bother about the way you look. I don't bother about the way I look. Prove to yourself who you are before you prove it to others. Believe in yourself and those around you will believe in you, and if they don't believe that's their problem, not yours.*

Merla was right in what she said. I needed her more than ever, and I needed her to tell me more.

★   ★   ★

When we had completed our mission, Turki took us back to the *diwaniya*. Jabir and Mahdi were still doing their paperwork, happy with the number of calls they had made, to ask voters to come to election meetings and to promote their candidates. I leafed through their papers. There were leaflets and pictures of candidates surrounded by Kuwaiti flags and a map of Kuwait. The map was small and easy to draw, rather like a bird's head. I thought of the map of the Philippines, with its hundreds of islands and many irregularities.

My friends were supporting four candidates. I saw pictures of three of them on the leaflets that Jabir and Mahdi had, but the fourth leaflet didn't have a picture. I asked Mahdi why not. 'That candidate's a woman,' he said. 'Maybe she prefers not to put her picture and just to make do with her name – Hind al-Tarouf.'

14

I was stunned to hear the name. For a moment I was oblivious of everything around me. So that was why Khawla was so happy that time when I went 'colololooosh' down the phone. It had never occurred to me that this might be why my sister was so pleased. Mahdi was hoping that Hind would win the elections and said this would be good for Kuwait. But Khawla had said, 'It would be good for the family in general.' If it was good for Kuwait, it would be good for me as a Kuwaiti. If it was good for the family I doubted it would matter to me.

When I heard Mahdi mention my aunt, he noticed how surprised I looked. 'What's wrong?' he asked me.

I was reluctant to tell him, but he was so enthusiastic about her winning and I was so proud to be related to her that I had to reveal it. 'Hind al-Tarouf is my aunt,' I said. Everyone was tongue-tied. The crazies stopped their work and exchanged glances with each other, then looked towards me, staring at me with curiosity. 'You're joking!' said Turki.

I shook my head and said, 'Hind Isa al-Tarouf is the sister of Rashid Isa al-Tarouf, my father.'

Jabir sat up straight. 'You're lying!' he said. I didn't say a word. Their surprise made me regret that I had spoken out so hastily. If only I had held my tongue. What was odd about Hind being my aunt, I wondered, though my mind was gnawed by doubts. Jabir continued, 'Ever since I was young the Taroufs' house has been like a second home to me. I know them as well as I know myself. But I've never heard of you!'

I replied with cautious confidence: 'So you know Mama Ghanima, Awatif, Nouriya and Khawla.' His eyes opened wide when he heard the names. I continued: 'Maybe even Raju and Babu and Lakshmi and Luzviminda. But even if you've never heard of me, that doesn't mean I'm not Isa Rashid Isa al-Tarouf.' He was speechless. My answer, supported with names, struck him dumb. 'What's wrong?' I asked him. 'Will my aunt lose the elections because of me too?'

Embarrassed, he shook his head. 'No, I don't mean that, but,' he said. He put one hand on his head, not the way he would if he was dancing one of those Kuwaiti dances, but from the impact of the surprise. I gave him time to take it in, but this time it was me who would be taken by surprise. 'About a year ago,' he said, 'I don't remember exactly when, but Rashid's mother got a new Filipino servant.' I nodded. He put his other hand on his head and said, 'His name was

Isa.' The other guys were listening to our conversation in silence.

'I'm Isa,' I said.

He put out his hand to shake mine in an ironic, theatrical gesture. 'And I'm Jabir, the son of your neighbour, Umm Jabir.'

Mishaal was sitting cross-legged in the far corner. He clapped. We all gathered around him. He looked straight at me and held out his hand as if holding an apple. 'Didn't I tell you? Kuwait's a small place,' he said.

★   ★   ★

It wasn't wrong of me to tell my friend I was related to Hind al-Tarouf. But I did make a mistake when I didn't ask him to keep it a secret, as my family wanted. If only this little country were bigger! If it were, would I have had to do all that? It's almost impossible to live when you have to be so careful about what you do, what you say and where you go. How could I bring shame on my family when I was nowhere near them? What is this power that people have over one another? Why is the tongue the thing that people in Kuwait fear more than anything else? It's just a small muscle wet with saliva, but it can do plenty of damage.

What Jabir had heard reached his mother, and from his mother it spread to the houses nearby and then to other people, and because Kuwait is a small place where almost everyone knows everyone else, and because words have wings, the news flew through the realms of gossip, especially places where women gathered. The news landed comfortably on the tongue of one woman only to fly off once again.

Khawla didn't have an opinion on the matter. She took the middle ground, between me, her only brother, and the rest of the family. I couldn't make out her attitude when she called me. I needed someone to stand by me. I hadn't done anything wrong. I had left the Tarouf house voluntarily because I didn't want to impose my curse on anyone. When I was driven out of the house with my father many years ago, the house started to enjoy good luck. Why didn't good luck descend on it when I left it voluntarily this time? Which of us was jinxing the other? Grandmother said I was a curse on the Taroufs but the way I saw it the Taroufs were a curse on me.

I still remember some of what Khawla said in that conversation. 'Umm Jabir is despicable. Grandmother is ill. Nouriya is making threats. People we're related to have found out about it and are saying Rashid had a son by a Filipina maid and so on.' She suddenly stopped.

'And what next?' I asked her.

'Some of the relatives have made it clear they feel sorry for me,' she answered hesitantly. 'They say it will reduce my chances of finding a decent husband.' Grandmother had said the same thing to my father in the kitchen years earlier. It seems she was right. Awatif and Nouriya had escaped the curse of Josephine, but now it was about to strike my sister.

When I didn't respond, Khawla continued, 'I'm sorry, I don't mean. . .'

I interrupted her: 'Not at all, I'm the one who should apologise.'

Kuwait really was a wonderland, but very different from the wonderland I had imagined all the time I was in the Philippines. This wonderland wasn't the one in my dreams. The only thing that the country in my old imagination had in common with the new reality was that they were both wonderlands.

★ ★ ★

Rashid, Josephine, where did you stand on the mess I was in? Did you have the right to bring me into the world and then abandon me like this? If you had the right, you certainly didn't live up to your responsibilities. We come into life involuntarily. We arrive either by chance, unplanned by our fathers and mothers, or because they planned us and decided when we should arrive. If we are conjured out of nothingness, if we really exist before our souls are breathed into our foetuses in the womb, then prospective parents should line up in front of us, for us to choose our fathers and mothers from among them. If we can't find anyone who deserves to have us as their child, then we should revert to nothingness.

When I shared these thoughts with Abdullah in the *diwaniya*, he replied with a paraphrase of a Qur'anic verse that says that the soul is a secret known only to God, because we humans have only a little knowledge. When he'd finishing explaining the verse, he added, 'But who knows? Maybe we did in fact choose our parents before our memories were allowed to start another life in new bodies.'

'Do you believe in Buddhism?' I asked immediately.

He shuddered defensively. 'I'm a Muslim,' he said.

'But you're talking about something that's similar to reincarnation,' I explained.

'"*They will ask you about the soul. Say: The soul is by command of my Lord, and of knowledge you have been granted but little,*"' he said, reciting the Qur'anic verse in question as if atoning for a thought crime he had committed.

Ibrahim Salam had a different opinion. He was upset that the idea had even been brought up. His answer was another Qur'anic verse: '"*Every soul will*

15

I had three options: to hate myself for what I had brought upon my family, to hate my family for what they had done to me or to hate both them and myself because I was one of them.

My doorbell rang and then kept ringing until I opened the door. A shark with its jaws ready to strike, accompanied by a pitiful dolphin, broke into my flat, dragging behind them a net, a *tarouf*, from which they hadn't been able to break free. I, the little fish, tried to escape by slipping through the mesh of the net.

'Nouriya?' I said in surprise. I was stepping backwards for fear she would grab the collar of my shirt, as she had done the first time. On that occasion she had been at pains to control herself in case anyone in Grandmother's house noticed. But in my flat, in the tank of the little fish, as Khawla had called me, there was no escape from the shark.

Awatif looked more conciliatory and I hoped she might do something but she didn't. I pointed towards the sitting room and said, 'Please come in.'

They didn't budge. Everything in Nouriya's face signalled contempt for me: her raised eyebrows, her thin upturned nose, her poisonous tongue.

'Listen,' she said. 'I'm not Hind. I'm not Khawla. You're to leave Kuwait immediately. Understood?'

Her arrogance outraged me. I don't know how I dared but I blew up in her face. 'I left the Taroufs' house long ago. You have no authority over me,' I said.

Her eyes opened wide as if she'd been slapped on the face. 'You're to leave Kuwait immediately,' she shouted.

'Kuwait isn't the Tarouf household,' I said.

Her eyes opened so wide it was frightening. She turned to Awatif in disbelief at my quick retort. 'Are you defying me?' she asked.

'I'm not defying anyone.'

'My mother has decided to cut off your monthly allowance. Hind is going to stop helping you. Don't you understand?'

'I have a job and a fair amount of money, enough to live for the rest of my life here.'

I looked down defiantly. 'In Kuwait,' I added.

Her lips trembled. She looked back and forth between me and Awatif in amazement. I don't blame her. When a little mouse roars, it has more impact than when a lion roars. Her eyes glistened with tears. A flood of tears, streaked with kohl, rolled down her cheeks. She looked awful. Between sobs, she said something to Awatif, then turned to me. 'I'll pay you whatever you want,' she said.

'I don't want anything,' I snapped back.

She exchanged glances with her sister but I couldn't work out what it meant. 'May we come in?' asked Awatif.

I waved them into the sitting room.

They sat next to each other opposite me. Nouriya sought Awatif's help after her own approach had failed to persuade me to leave. Awatif spoke in something resembling English, helped by her sister. 'Do you pray?' she asked.

'Yes,' I replied tentatively.

She smiled approvingly and said, 'That's good. I was confident you were a sincere believer.' I looked from one to the other, trying to work out where this was leading. 'Be a strong believer. Accept your fate. Be content with what God has decreed for you,' she continued.

'God?' I asked.

She nodded with a calm smile. From the confidence on Nouriya's face I knew how confused I must look. 'Almighty God didn't create you to be here,' she said, as calm as ever.

I must have looked like a wax sculpture, expressionless and immobile except for my eyes, which looked from one to the other in scorn. My God, they were trying to corner me into doing what suited them.

463

'The right place for you is there, in the Philippines.'

I stood up. They looked up at me as I made a move to leave the sitting room.

'Where are you going?' Nouriya asked.

'Just a minute,' I said. I came back carrying my briefcase of photographs and documents. I sat down opposite them. I took out my blue passport and my black certificate of nationality from the briefcase. I waved them in the air. 'I'm Kuwaiti,' I said.

With irritating composure they shook their heads. Nouriya looked right through me and said, 'You're illegitimate.'

An electric shock ran up my spine like lightning, all the way to my head.

'You are a believer,' Awatif said.

I put my hand in the briefcase and pulled out a picture of my father. My arm shaking with anger, I waved it in front of them. 'I'm the son of this man,' I said.

Their confidence threw me off balance. Nouriya was trying to disarm me with her look. Awatif shook her head and smiled sadly.

'I'm Isa Rashid al–Tarouf,' I said.

'Rashid isn't your father,' Awatif said with the same smile. 'You've no right to claim him as your father or use his name.' Her self-confidence seemed to be slipping. 'You're a believer,' she added, reminding me. 'Illegitimate children take their mother's name.'

Nouriya cut in. 'Yes, on that basis, you're Isa Josephine.'

What a lot of names I have! It's time to settle on just one of them. I put my hand in my briefcase looking for the papers. My right hand took hold of a folded piece of paper. I opened it out. I knew it from the signatures of Walid and Ghassan.

Nouriya took the initiative. 'I expect you're going to show me the marriage certificate of Rashid and Josephine. Don't bother. Even if you are Rashid's son under Kuwaiti law, you're not his son by Islamic law,' she said.

Awatif joined in. 'You are a believer,' she said.

I ignored her remark and looked defiantly into Nouriya's eyes. I let her finish off what she wanted to say. 'I think you know that your mother,' she stopped and rephrased it, 'that our maid Josephine was pregnant with you before this piece of paper was written, that is before the marriage.' I let her continue as I looked through the papers. 'Listen, Josephine's son, you don't have the right to use our name. You don't have any inheritance rights. Under Islamic law that wouldn't be allowed. And yet you insist on staying. Don't you have any dignity?' Nouriya said.

'Or faith?' added Awatif.

I found the document I wanted. The marriage certificate was still in my right hand. 'You're right, Aunt Nouriya,' I said. I emphasised the word 'aunt' to stress the relationship that existed whether she liked it or not. 'My mother did get pregnant several months before this document was written,' I said, waving the marriage certificate signed by Walid and Ghassan. 'But a few hours after *this* document was written,' I added, waving another piece of paper in my left hand.

They looked at each other sceptically. With a confidence that she was trying her hardest to sustain, Nouriya said, 'What is that document?'

'This is a certificate of what they call common-law marriage,' I said, with the same composed smile as Awatif.

Nouriya exploded. She threatened, she menaced, she cursed, she snarled, she issued warnings in Arabic, in English and with hand gestures. Awatif took refuge in silence with a face that fluctuated between shock and sadness.

Nouriya left my flat a defeated shark. Awatif covered her head with her black abaya. At the front door, before I closed it, she turned to me in tears. 'Oh God,' she said. 'Oh God, I'm sorry.' She wiped her face with part of her abaya and said, 'You are Kuwaiti. You're my nephew, Rashid's son.'

From the open lift Nouriya called her impatiently: 'Awatif!'

'Forgive me. God forgive me,' Awatif added, before joining her sister.

I faked a smile and said, 'You are a believer' and closed the door.

16

I didn't tell Jabir what trouble he had caused me by telling his mother about me. I was angry with him but I suppressed my anger and didn't tell him anything. I wasn't so crazy as to lose one of the crazies.

One evening Jabir and I were in the *diwaniya* while the others were out at an election meeting for Hind al-Tarouf, my aunt. The crazies were keen she should win, except for Abdullah, who didn't want a woman to represent him in parliament. 'Doesn't Kuwait have any men left?' was his view. He didn't say that in front of me but Jabir told me about his attitude. 'Abdullah thinks women can serve society in positions other than in parliament,' he said.

Jabir, who knew my aunt closely, spoke to me about her, her election programme, her vision for the future of Kuwait and her reputation for always standing on the side of human rights. 'Do you expect her to win?' I asked.

He pursed his lips and said, 'It's not that easy. Women have only had political rights for three years. It's still something new. She may win in the years to come.' His mobile phone beeped to say a text message had arrived. He picked up his phone and read it. 'It's

Turki saying *You missed quite a scene. Massive turnout for the Tarouf meeting.'* He picked up his car keys. 'Come on then, up you get,' he said. I shook my head. He grabbed my arm. 'Don't be a coward. We'll stay in the car, man,' he said.

★   ★   ★

Hind's election headquarters was in Qortuba, close to the front of the religious institute on Damascus Street, not far from the relay tower on my favourite spot. I couldn't see inside the building. There were lots of cars in the car park of the religious institute, and other cars parked on or parallel to the pavement. My aunt's voice was coming out of loudspeakers set up in various places. She was speaking in the same tone as when I heard her in television discussions. Turki, Mishaal and Mahdi were standing at the main entrance to the hall, giving out leaflets to people as they arrived. The children of Awatif and Nouriya were also at the door with badges hanging from their necks. All I could make out on the badge was a large number 3. 'That's the number of the constituency,' said Jabir.

Among the crowd outside I caught sight of Khawla wearing the same badge. I took out my mobile and called her. 'Hello, what are you doing outside? Go into the hall,' I said. I could see her from my place in the car.

She looked around in the crowd. 'Where are you, you crazy? Aunt Nouriya is here!' she said.

I put my arm out of the car window and waved to her. 'I'm here,' I said. She was still looking around. 'Here, here, turn towards the street, to the right, to the right,' I said. Jabir helped me by honking his horn three times. 'Beep, beep, beeeeep.'

Khawla waved her hand and ran towards the car with that smile that I loved. '*As-salam aleekum*, How are you, Isa?' She bent down to look through the car window and looked at Jabir behind the wheel. She gave an even bigger smile. 'How are you, Jabir?' she asked. The tent behind her broke into applause. I had goosebumps and my heart began to pound. Involuntarily Khawla began to clap too.

'How are things going?' I asked her. She laced her fingers together over her chest and said, 'If only Father were here, Isa, in the audience. He always called for women to be included in social development. I wish he could see his sister today.' She stopped and bent down lower till her head was almost coming through the car window. She looked back and forth between me and Jabir with one eyebrow raised. 'Our neighbour, a childhood friend, and my brother, both in the same car! How fate . . .'

'Kuwait's a small place,' I broke in, putting out my hand and making the same gesture as Mishaal – as if holding an invisible ball.

★ ★ ★

Jabir and I went back to the *diwaniya* and found Abdullah waiting for us there. Turki, Mishaal and Mahdi soon came back too, after the election meeting was over, looking glum. They spoke to Jabir in Arabic and Jabir's face soon changed too.

'So, how did it go?' I asked Turki. He didn't answer. Mahdi stepped in: 'It began perfectly.'

'And then?' I asked.

'It ended really badly,' replied Mishaal. They went back to talking in Arabic and I understood some words but not others.

For the first time I found myself interrupting them. 'Could you let me in on the conversation? Please,' I said.

They turned towards me. Turki nodded and said, 'Your aunt is crazy.'

'She's lost the election,' added Mahdi.

'But the results haven't come out yet. Today isn't even voting day,' I said in surprise. 'We read the results on the faces of the people who walked out of the meeting,' said Turki.

'You shouldn't say everything you know, even if it's true. Your aunt is reckless,' Mishaal concluded. Abdullah, who had been silent so far, spoke in English that I could hardly understand. His theme was that women are governed by their emotions, but I couldn't work out if this was criticism or praise.

★　★　★

After Hind made her speech she had started to take questions from the audience. Everything was fine. She was confident, quick-witted, with an answer to every question. The last question, or what turned out to be the last question, came from an elderly woman who seemed eager to put Hind on the spot. 'In the past we only heard about you in the context of what you call the rights of the bidoon. Their cause was one of your priorities,' the woman said.

'And it still is,' Hind responded immediately.

'Do all the bidoons deserve Kuwaiti nationality?' the woman asked.

'Yes, of course, in just the same way as other Kuwaitis,' Hind replied, or blurted out, as they put it.

The woman picked up her handbag and stood up. She shook her head in protest as she began to leave the hall. 'God have mercy on Isa al-Tarouf,' she said. The hall rang with applause as soon as the old woman mentioned my grandfather's name. She walked out and many other members of the audience followed her out. The meeting broke up before my aunt had a chance to explain what she meant.

I called Khawla to console her. She was shocked and sad. 'People don't want to listen. They didn't give her a chance,' she said bitterly. I asked how Hind was. 'She's fine, but Grandmother is very upset,' she said, fighting back tears. 'Grandmother's in her room, with Awatif and Nouriya trying to calm her down.'

'And you? How are you, Khawla?' I said, speaking gently in response to her sadness.

She gave a long sigh. 'Me? I don't know. I almost believe what Grandmother believes,' she said. She started breathing rapidly. 'Everything that happens to us is because of him. Ghassan is a curse,' she added.

17

The elections took place on 17 May 2008. It was no surprise that Hind lost, especially after some newspapers reported what she had said at the meeting. One well-known newspaper had a banner headline reading: *Casting Doubt on the Patriotism of Citizens: Hind al-Tarouf says Kuwaitis Don't Deserve to Have Kuwaiti Citizenship.*

There was a mournful atmosphere in the *diwaniya*, given the reaction in the newspapers that attacked my aunt. The Boracay gang knew the result before it was declared. Hind's defeat was no surprise to me: the real surprise was that Nouriya had carried out the threat she made when she came to visit. She had been telling the truth when she warned me and now she had done it. It wasn't unexpected that Grandmother would stop paying me my allowance, but for Aunt Hind to do so too!

I suddenly found that all I had was what I earned from working in the restaurant and the allowance from the government, and the two amounts would hardly cover the rent. I started spending from my savings, month after month. I worked out how much money I would need in the future and found that, if things continued as they were, I would be broke within a few months.

The gang offered to help me financially. Jabir was the most enthusiastic, maybe because he felt guilty. Mishaal invited me to move into his flat on the eighth floor of my building. 'I only need it at weekends,' he said.

'You can live temporarily in the *diwaniya*, until you find a place to live that suits you,' offered Turki.

Ibrahim Salam, although his place was small, didn't hesitate to help. 'My little room has made space for you before and it won't hesitate to take you in again, my brother,' he said. After much discussion back and forth, he reluctantly agreed to rent me space to sleep in his room for thirty dinars a month.

★ ★ ★

Only one week after I moved into Ibrahim's room, the shift leader in the restaurant called me aside. 'You'd better make some plans for the future. This is your last week working here.' And the reason? No reason.

I made up a reason of my own – Kuwait was spitting me out.

Khawla called me a few days later. 'Have you really been fired from your job?' she asked. 'Damn! Nouriya did that,' she said.

Disputes broke out in the Tarouf household. Hind and Awatif had a serious disagreement with Nouriya, who was behind me losing my job. 'Leave the kid alone,' they told her.

Nouriya was furious with Hind because of what she had said in the election campaign and because she had lost. 'If Isa al-Tarouf were still alive, you would have been the death of him,' she said.

Grandmother was in a bad way because of what was happening in the house. The sisters were at odds. Khawla left to live in her other grandmother's house, saying the situation in Grandmother's house was unbearable. 'Grandmother slaps her thighs all day long in grief, and asks God to have mercy on her husband and on Rashid. She lifts her arms to heaven and says, "May God avenge you, Ghassan."'

'Khawla, I want to understand. Please. These are complicated things,' I said.

There was silence from the other end of the line. 'Please, answer me,' I said. Still silence. 'Who's the reason for all these problems?' She still didn't utter a word. I spoke louder. 'Ghassan?' I asked.

'No,' she said faintly.

I lowered my voice too, afraid of the most likely answer: 'Me?'

'No,' she said, louder this time.

I let out a sigh of relief – relief that I had been cleared of blame.

'There's no one else,' she continued. I didn't say anything. 'It's the Taroufs,' she concluded.

18

I left a lettuce leaf in the middle of Ibrahim's room while I waited for Inang Choleng. I'd forgotten to feed her for some time. She wasn't in the habit of going without food for long. I was really anxious. I found her under the computer table, dried up inside her broken shell.

Inang Choleng had died – that silent, patient creature that was so good at listening and never complained. That morning was so sad. *O God, you alone know how much I wept.* Who could console me? Who would understand why I was crying over her? When Ibrahim came back from work he saw the sadness on my face. I didn't tell him about the tortoise when he asked me. What was the use of talking about something he wouldn't understand? I left him in the main room and escaped to the bathroom. I turned on all the taps in the basin and the shower and burst out crying, unable to hold it back. Ibrahim knocked on the door when he heard me sobbing. 'Brother! Are you all right?' he said.

I tried as hard as I could to make my voice sound normal. 'Yes, I'm fine, but the water's cold, brother,' I said.

How could a dead tortoise leave such a gap? She didn't have a voice for me to miss, and wasn't even a permanent presence since she spent much of her time under sofas, cut off from everything, hidden in her shell and oblivious to the world. By her death all I lost was my own presence and my voice, which I only heard when I spoke to her, and the lettuce leaves in the fridge.

No one was better than Inang Choleng at putting up with my fickle moods – my sadness, my anger, my complaining – and now she was dead. My companion had died in Ibrahim's room after sharing my wanderings – in the annex of Grandmother's house and in my large flat in Jabriya.

What loneliness! Kuwait was closing its last doors on me, just when I thought I was part of it. I suddenly felt that it wasn't my place, that I must have been wrong when I thought that a bamboo stalk could take root anywhere.

'He who does not know how to look back at where he came from will never get to his destination,' Rizal once said. But apparently I had misread his remark. I believed in it as if it were a prophecy. I saw Kuwait as the place I had come from, since I was born there, and it was the place I had decided to return to after an absence, but when I looked behind me all I saw was the Philippines – Manila, Valenzuela, Mendoza's land.

Suddenly Kuwait felt claustrophobic, no bigger than Ibrahim Salam's room. It felt even smaller, the size of a box of matches, and I was just one of the matches.

I remembered that phrase they often used: 'Kuwait's a small place.'

★   ★   ★

It was a boring day, like all the other days. I balanced the laptop on my knees to check if there was a message from Merla, but there was nothing but messages from my mother and annoying adverts.

Had Merla read my emails, I wondered. If only I knew.

But I could find out.

Suddenly I remembered something that hit me like a thunderbolt. Why hadn't I thought of it all this time? Wasn't it me who set up Merla's email account in the first place? I had chosen the password. What if she had never changed it? In that case I could check myself.

I opened the email page in the browser and put in Merla's details – her username and the password I had chosen. Amazingly it took me straight to her inbox. My heart raced. Dozens of messages appeared on the list: my emails with the subject lines I had chosen, emails from Maria and many other messages. But the important thing was that the subject line for my emails and Maria's emails were not in bold, which showed that someone had opened them to read them, unlike the other messages, which were still in bold. That meant Merla was still around.

I felt a throbbing in my temples. With trembling fingers, pressing the keys hard down on the keyboard, I wrote her a message. I waited and then checked what happened to it. Within a few hours the subject line on the message had switched from bold to plain.

I hadn't cried when I thought that Merla had gone missing, but I cried buckets for joy when she reappeared. The tears poured out whenever the subject line changed, showing that Merla was there.

Now it was fun. I would send a message, saying everything I wanted to say to my dear cousin, day after day. I could see someone was reading them. I felt more and more confident that she was somewhere, reading my confessions.

19

Ibrahim was busy going through the week's newspapers looking for stories about the Philippines to translate and send to the Philippine newspapers. It was summer. The Boracay crazies were going round the world spreading their craziness. Maybe that summer they were operating in Spain, or London, France, Thailand or Malaysia. Maybe they would come across some half-Kuwaiti on the beach in one of those countries, God alone knows.

I found myself more alone than I had ever been. I had no work and no place of my own. The temperature was in the fifties, enough to melt me and my bicycle if I thought of going outside. My tortoise had died. My friends were abroad. It was impossible to meet my sister now that she had moved to her other grandmother's house. My father, as always, only existed in pictures. My mother and Mama Aida were in another part of the planet, and Merla, although I believed she was around, wasn't close by. I was avoiding Ghassan because I didn't want to add to his troubles.

I had no incentive to stay in Kuwait much longer but I didn't have enough money to buy a ticket to the Philippines. I was at a loss.

During her summer break Khawla read Father's unfinished novel, for the millionth time perhaps. She was sad. 'It'll take me many years to finish it off,' she said. She translated some passages of the book for me. As a dedication he had written: 'To the two of you, Kuwait and you.' The Arabic made it clear he was referring to a woman. Khawla said that for the years she had been reading the novel she thought Father was referring to her mother, Iman. But with repeated readings, she realised that he really meant the girl he had been in love with as a student, the one that Grandmother had rejected.

'The one that, if he had married her, he wouldn't have got involved with Josephine,' I joked.

From what Khawla read to me I realised that my father also felt alienated in some way in his own country. After our conversation I asked Ibrahim for some paper and a pen and I began to write in English:

Although I'm different from you, and perhaps also backward compared with you in many ways, although I look like a stranger among you, despite my accent and the way I pronounce words, despite all these things I have the same documents as you have, I have exactly the same rights and the same duties as you have, and despite everything, I have had only love for this place, but you, for some reason I'm not aware of, prevented me from loving the place where I was born and for which my father died. You prevented me from carrying out my duties and you deprived me of my most basic rights.

When I was still young in the Philippines, your country was the dream. I say 'your country' and not 'my country' because in spite of my documents, it is not my country. In years past Kuwait was the paradise that I would one day win and that people in the Philippines predicted for me.

I was a stranger, and I still am. I have tried by various means to fit in with everything, although it has been hard, everything.

I have tried to break through the barriers and the walls that stood between us, but every time I managed to cross the barrier I was driven back. You disagree on many things but you agree on one thing — rejecting me. I'm like a grain of pollen or a speck of dust that comes to you on the wind after a long odyssey. As soon as you breathe it in, it irritates your nose and you sneeze it out. It goes back to wandering again and you whisper 'Thank God' and others reply 'Bless you'. 'God guide us and God guide you,' they say. So it's Praise the Lord, and May He Grant You Mercy and Guidance, while my fate is curses and ruin.

I tried my hardest to be one of you, but you didn't make any effort. I forgive you, because it doesn't matter to you. Do you mind if I continue with my story about something that doesn't matter to you?

I will go on. I might feel somewhat relieved when I've let out all the words bottled up inside me. When I go back to the Philippines I want to have lost any desire to talk about you, or about myself when I was in your country.

Damn Darwin and his stupid theory. How can humans be descended from apes when I stopped being human when I was with you? I retrogressed and turned into a lower creature whose descendants might one day produce apes. That proves Darwin's theory, but the wrong way round!

Understand why I am being so frank, so bold, or so insolent. I liked you because I thought I was one of you. That's how I came to hate you and to hate myself.

And because I don't want to take my feelings about you back to the Philippines, I'm writing them down here now, so that I can leave them here.

You might read my words and what some people think of you. I might have a child in the Philippines one day and tell him about the land of dreams and point my finger towards paradise. Then he might pack his bags to go there and find that the paradise he has heard of really is a paradise.

I apologise for being so harsh. It may not be your fault but the fault of my father, who brought me to your land after I had spent many years in the Philippines. He wanted to replant me, forgetting that tropical plants don't grow in the desert.

Take these pages and give me back my humanity, or take what humanity I still have left.

Take my humanity, which you didn't recognise, and let me live like an ant, like a bee, like a cockroach, but without those antennae that insects have.

★   ★   ★

She was crying as I read to her over the phone.

'Shall I stop?' I asked her.

She laughed despite her crying. 'Go on, go on reading, you crazy,' she said. I went on reading what I had written. She gave a long sigh after I finished reading, while I said nothing. 'You made me happy, as much as you made me cry,' she said. 'Isa,' she finally pleaded, 'I asked you to write before, and now I beg you – write, for yourself, for me, for Father, for Aunt Hind and Ghassan and everyone here.'

'What I might write will be painful to everyone, Khawla,' I replied.

'There's no need to remind me,' she said confidently. 'Father never cared about anyone in what he said or wrote or did. Why shouldn't you be like him?' She paused, and then continued, 'If I wasn't caught up in this family net nothing would stop me writing honestly. Have you forgotten? You're the only person who can slip through the holes in the net without getting caught in the mesh.' She hung up and I found myself asking Ibrahim, who was busy working, for more pieces of paper.

I picked up my pen and resumed writing, in English – *My name is José*. I stopped and thought of that José Rizal saying: 'He who cannot love his mother tongue is worse than a beast and smells fouler than dead rotten fish.' I don't want to smell worse than a rotten fish and if I was a rotten fish it would spoil all the fresh fish around it, as Grandmother says when she's worried about me coming into contact with her other grandchildren.

I decided to write in Filipino, even if the script is the same as the script used in English. I turned to Ibrahim, who was lying on his mattress getting ready to fall asleep. 'Ibrahim,' I said. He turned towards me with sleepy eyes. 'Would you translate a text for me?' I asked.

'That's my job,' he said with a smile.

I sat up straight. 'It'll be a long text,' I explained.

He looked at me sceptically. 'It depends what's in it,' he said.

I explained my idea to him. He was hesitant at first, but he agreed after setting some conditions. 'You'll be free to translate it however you like, given your experience here, but mind you don't write my name in a way other than it's written in the Philippines – José.' He fell asleep but there was no way I was going to sleep. I picked up the pen again and wrote in Filipino:

My name is José. In the Philippines it's pronounced as in English, with an h sound at the start. In Arabic, rather like in Spanish, it begins with a kh sound. In Portuguese, though it's written the same way, it opens with a j, as in Joseph. All these versions are completely different from my name here in Kuwait, where I'm known as Isa.

THE FINAL PART

Isa . . . Looks Back

'If the land rejects our bodies, the hearts of friends
will provide a home for our spirits.'
José Mendoza

The Last Chapter

I finished writing the first chapter of this story on my last day in Kuwait. I handed it to Ibrahim in hard copy on the day Ghassan took me to the airport in his beloved car, and we agreed that I'd send him each chapter from the Philippines by email as soon as I finished it.

The airport was sad, though not in the way it was on the day I arrived. The flags were not at half mast and the chairs in the café were not upside down on the tables. But Khawla's face and the faces of my crazy friends were all like Ghassan's face.

At the departures gate, as I stood with my blue passport in my hand, the Boracay gang gathered around me, along with Ghassan and Ibrahim Salam. Some hugged me, others shook my hand and others slipped envelopes full of money into my hand. 'This is the last call for passengers on Kuwait Airways flight 411 to Manila. Please proceed to the departure gate immediately.'

The circle of friends broke up to make way for Khawla to come through. She came forward slowly and then hugged me tight. The hug went on a long time. 'That's enough, Khawla,' Ghassan said. 'The plane's about to take off.'

'Good,' she said, her head buried in my shoulder. My friends moved apart around me. The circle widened to let through Hind, who took me by surprise by turning up. Ghassan withdrew and left, and my other friends stepped back. Hind took hold of my sister by the shoulders and tugged at her gently. Khawla hugged me tight and insisted on staying with me. She squeezed me in her arms. Hind slipped her arms between me and Khawla and pulled her back. Khawla held on to me. She was still crying and Hind patted her on the back. Hind looked at me with a face as sad as all the other faces. 'Forgive me, Isa,' she said.

With a big smile, and plenty of tears, I nodded without speaking. I turned away from everyone and went through the departure gate, and only then did I turn back and look through the glass. Everyone was watching me leave except for Khawla, who was in Hind's arms, and Ghassan, who had disappeared as soon as Hind appeared.

I left Kuwait in August 2008, about three years ago, abandoning everything except the bottle with soil from my father's grave, the small Kuwaiti flag that had been attached to the back of my bicycle, a copy of the Qur'an in English, a prayer rug (I don't know whether I'll use it regularly), and the empty, cracked shell of my dead tortoise, Inang Choleng.

Today is Thursday, 28 July 2011, and it's half past eight in the evening. In half an hour a football match between the Philippines and Kuwait will kick off – a qualifying match for the World Cup in Brazil in 2014.

A few days ago the Kuwaiti players arrived to train at the University of Makati stadium in preparation for today's match, but shortly after they arrived Manila was hit by an earthquake that measured six on the Richter scale. I made a link between their arrival in Manila and the occurrence of the earthquake. Who is jinxing who? I drove the idea out of my head.

The Boracay crazies aren't far away. They're now sitting in the Rizal Memorial Stadium to support their team. I met them at Nino Aquino airport yesterday and tomorrow I'll be seeing them off. If they decide to stay longer, we could go visit Boracay again.

I'm going to submit this chapter of my book to Ibrahim Salam in hard copy, as I did with the first chapter. The crazies will take it to him and when he's translated it he'll give it to Khawla. Maybe, once she's seen the last part written by hand, even in a language she doesn't know, she'll be encouraged to finish off Father's novel.

★   ★   ★

I'm now sitting in the sitting room in front of the television in our house in Mendoza's land, with my last piece of paper in my hand. Everyone is here and they are all watching excitedly as the players come out on to the pitch, except for Adrian, who's off in his own world. On the carpet in the middle of the room my little baby boy is crawling, oblivious of everything around him.

When the Kuwaiti players started to sing their national anthem a shiver ran through me, from deep inside me to my hands and feet. 'Kuwait, my country, may you be safe and glorious! May you always enjoy good fortune!' I found myself singing along as the camera moved down the line of players. The players finished singing and I stopped too. Then the cameras switched to the line of Filipino players and the people around me started singing: 'Country Dear, Pearl of the Orient, The blazing of the heart, In thy chest is alive.'

The feeling was indescribable. As much as I could, I tried to concentrate on the piece of paper I was holding but it was no use. I looked from my son to the television screen. I had expected my son to have blue eyes and fair skin but he turned out quite different – a swarthy Arab complexion and large eyes like those of his Aunt Khawla.

My mother wanted to call him Juan. I almost agreed but then I remembered that in Filipino we pronounce it the English way, with an *h* sound, while in Portuguese it starts with a *j* sound like John and in Arabic it's like in Spanish, with a *kh* sound. I told her I preferred not to inflict so many names on the boy and, besides, by tradition he should take his grandfather's name – Rashid.

Little Rashid burst out crying in alarm at all the shouting that suddenly erupted in the sitting room when Filipino midfielder Stephan Schröck kicked the ball into the back of the Kuwaiti net in added time at the end of the first half. There was cheering and whistling on the screen and in the sitting room, and smiles on the faces of those around me. Everyone clapped for joy, except for me, who felt like I'd scored an own goal.

The second half began. Everyone was disappointed in the sixty-first minute when Yousef Nasser scored for the Kuwaitis.

Here I am, scoring again in my other goal.

The result so far is satisfactory, as far as I'm concerned. There's still another half an hour to go but I don't want to watch it. I don't want to take sides. I don't want one of my teams to defeat my other team. With the result like this, I'm neutral.

A Note on the Author

Saud Alsanousi is a Kuwaiti novelist and journalist, born in 1981. His work has appeared in a number of Kuwaiti publications, including *Al-Watan* newspaper and *Al-Arabi* and he currently writes for *Al-Qabas* newspaper. He lives in Kuwait, and *The Bamboo Stalk* is his first book to be published in English. He is currently working on his next novel.

A Note on the Translator

Jonathan Wright has translated a dozen novels and other major works from Arabic to English, starting in 2008 after thirty years as a journalist, mostly in the Middle East. He won the 2013 Banipal Prize for Arabic Literary Translation for Youssef Ziedan's *Azazeel* and the Independent Foreign Fiction Prize in 2014 for his translation of Hassan Blasim's *The Iraqi Christ*.

A Note on the Type

The text of this book is set in Bembo. This type was first used in 1495 by the Venetian painter Aldus Manutius for Cardinal Bembo's *De Aetna*, and was cut for Manutius by Francesco Griffo. It was one of the types used by Claude Garamond (1480–1561) as a model for his Romaine de L'Université, and so it was the forerunner of what became standard European type for the following two centuries. Its modern form follows the original types and was designed for Monotype in 1929.